Treeborne

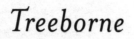

Treeborne

CALEB JOHNSON

PICADOR

NEW YORK

TREEBORNE. Copyright © 2018 by Caleb Johnson. All rights reserved. Printed in the United States of America. For information, address Picador, 175 Fifth Avenue, New York, N.Y. 10010.

picadorusa.com • instagram.com/picador
twitter.com/picadorusa • facebook.com/picadorusa

Picador® is a U.S. registered trademark and is used by Macmillan Publishing Group, LLC, under license from Pan Books Limited.

For book club information, please visit facebook.com/picadorbookclub or email marketing@picadorusa.com.

Designed by Steven Seighman

Library of Congress Cataloging-in-Publication Data

Names: Johnson, Caleb (Caleb Rich), author.
Title: Treeborne : a novel / Caleb Johnson.
Description: First edition. | New York : Picador, 2018.
Identifiers: LCCN 2017060104 | ISBN 9781250169082 (hardcover) | ISBN 9781250169099 (ebook)
Subjects: LCSH: Women—Southern States—Fiction. | Small cities—Fiction. | Southern states—Social life and customs—Fiction. | Change—Fiction. | Home—Fiction. | Alabama—Fiction.
Classification: LCC PS3610.O32375 | DDC 813'.6—dc23
LC record available at https://lccn.loc.gov/2017060104

Our books may be purchased in bulk for promotional, educational, or business use. Please contact your local bookseller or the Macmillan Corporate and Premium Sales Department at 1-800-221-7945, extension 5442, or by email at MacmillanSpecialMarkets@macmillan.com.

First Edition: June 2018

10 9 8 7 6 5 4 3 2 1

For the women who raised me up in stories—
Debra Johnson and Celia Sampley

What the self is tangles itself knottily with what his people were, and what they came out of.

—JOHN GRAVES, GOODBYE TO A RIVER

Behold, that which I have built I will break down, and that which I have planted will I pluck up, even this whole land.

—JEREMIAH 45:4

Treeborne

Stories We Tell

TODAY

The water was coming, but Janie Treeborne would not leave. She'd lived alone in this house perched on the edge of a roadside peach orchard in Elberta, Alabama, ever since Lee Malone sold it to her. *Sold* maybe not the right word for the price she paid, the price he would take. But it was hers and she would not leave. Rather the water take her too.

She'd been telling her visitor exactly how she came to own the house, which once was Lee's office and, before that, his boyhood home. A complicated matter. To tell how this house and the surrounding property became hers she needed to tell how it became Lee's, and to do that she needed to first tell about a man named Mr. Prince.

"See, back then folks thought Mr. Prince wasn't but a rumor and a last name," she continued. "But he was real. Lived in one of them mansions down on the river. Anyhow, Lee started working at The Peach Pit not long after the storm.

"Worked here for years. Then one day Mr. Prince carried him to lunch out at Woodrow's. The Hills would of been about the only place they could eat together. They ordered and sat down and Mr. Prince said he was selling the orchard, the old cannery, and a little cottage he owned in town for whatever was in Lee's billfold right that moment. Can you imagine? Mr. Prince died not too long after. Most of my growing up, folks still thought Lee wasn't nothing but the orchard manager. Would of got to a certain kind of person. Not him, not to Lee Malone."

Janie Treeborne'd come to own the peach orchard—and the other properties once belonging to Mr. Prince—the same way as Lee Malone. She sat at a greasy tabletop inside Woodrow's Pit Cook Bar-B-Q where, years before, Lee'd counted out of his billfold two-dollar-five-cent and a receipt for a bag of dog food, and she searched for what money she had in the depths of a purse she felt foolish toting around. Lee's heart was weak by then. He had considered turning the land over to Janie for a long long time.

She thought she would of handed everything down to her visitor, this young man sitting with a tape recorder on his lap and a long microphone gripped in his hand. So why'd she not? Janie couldn't remember. Did it matter? He was here, he was home. Had her same big forehead and freckled nose, her granddaddy Hugh's thick black hair and high-cut cheeks. A Treeborne, she thought, through and through, right down to the bone.

"Do you remember how much it was you paid?" he asked.

"Foot yes, I do," she said. "You reckon your grandmomma'd up and forget something like that? It was sixteen dollar and a pack of chewing gum."

"Did you ever regret not paying him more?"

"Regret, foot," she said. No amount would of been sufficient. This place was priceless. But how to explain that? "Lee's body might of blunted," she went on, "but his mind stayed sharp till the end. I always tell that if mine ain't then somebody please shove a gun right here and fire that sucker twice. There's one right yonder in the dresser drawer. I don't give a rip if it sounds morbid! Life's morbid! Love sure enough is.

"Lee Malone taught me everything about the peach-growing business. Everything. Even helped run the fruit stand through his last good summer on earth. Could still sing his head off too. Them trees yonder, we planted them together. Look out thataway you'll see where the house he died in once stood. Wasn't much to the place itself, but it was in Elberta and belonged to him, and there was a time that meant something. See?

Other side the road there, just below the water tower Ricky Birdsong fell off of."

"Are there any pictures of Mr. Malone?" the young man asked.

Janie got up from her recliner chair and took one of the dozens of photo albums shelved in the living room and stacked in cardboard boxes pushed against the wall. She opened to a picture of the old Elberta water tower. Pointed, turned the page. Black-and-whites of folks standing by water, with dogs, by log houses and woodpiles, next to pickup trucks and wagons, at school, at church, in decorated cemeteries, along fencelines and unidentifiable roadsides and hedgerows. Somehow not one picture of Lee Malone.

She turned the page again and pointed at a girl with straight black hair touching bony shoulders. "There's me," she said, squinting as if to be sure. "Would of been the year before MawMaw May died—if I'm right."

"Do you still think about it?" the young man asked.

She closed the album. "I try to keep a routine for the sake of my mind, but there's only so much you can do now."

Janie Treeborne first received a notice from The Authority, say, three years ago. Plenty warning. The Hernando de Soto Dam had served its purpose for nearly eighty years. Her granddaddy, Hugh Treeborne, helped build it. Her daddy, Ren Treeborne, an engineer. Janie understood that if The Authority didn't implode the dam then its concrete would give to time and further neglect. A disaster would sure enough occur. The notice claimed there'd be payment for her property, relocation services, the works. Miss Treeborne, the letter called her, just needed to fill out the accompanying forms and mail them back. Janie knew how this story went. She took the notice and she deposited it right in the trash.

"The Fencepost sure does miss its big-talkers and bullshitters," she said. "I still hear their voices rattling around and around . . . Air here's always been full of voices to my mind. Pedro agrees and he abets with a daily dose of radio. Lets them dogs that's always running around sleep

inside the station if it's cold or raining. When one comes up lame. He
feeds them scraps. But, hellfire, I do too when they roam up here. Jon D.
used to say one was going to give me rabies. Foot. I told you Pedro
started reading out our names on the air. A roll call, I reckon. Lucky
that us fourteen remaining can dial him in another day yet. For that
much we're blessed. Pedro and me share a sense of humor. Laugh to keep
from tears."

The young man wanted to know how Janie spent her days. What it
was like living in Elberta now and what all she did.

"Sometimes after breakfast I'll drive out at The Seven and prowl
around them woods for a spell—same way me and Crusoe did. You'll
have to go by there. A Treeborne ain't lived on them seven hundred acres
since Aunt Tammy moved here with me. Used to though, the highway'd
be backed up nearly all the way into town with folks come to see what
all Granddaddy Hugh—be your great-great—what all he painted and
assemblied and left out yonder in them woods. I still call it The Seven
instead of whatever the hell they named it. Some of them folks who
ran the place treated me like I ought to be put on display alongside all
them things he made. Art, not things. That word's always got away from
me. Time, they wanted me to give a series of talks on it. On him. This
was back in The Seven's heyday—eighties-early-nineties—when some
loud awful band put Granddaddy Hugh's art on their record cover. Sold
a million copies, they tell. Told them I was too busy to give talks, which
was no more than part-truth."

Janie eased back down in her recliner. She fixed the hem of her gown
over her liver-spotted legs then patted the arm of the chair two times.

"I'll tell you," she went on, "it's fools who claim the ones you're expecting to go ain't so bad as those you don't. Treebornes never have been
long-lived though. Aunt Tammy lasted longest of her siblings. Daddy
was the oldest, Uncle Luther, then her. I can't speak for the long-livedness
of Malones, but Lee dying was bad on me, buddy. And me in my twenties when it happened. Not bad like MawMaw May, but bad. I was just
a fool girl when she died. Like to of ruined us all."

Janie turned her head to better see the young man, gazing as if she'd only then recalled he was in the room. Blinded on one side most of her life, the damaged eye looked like the inside of a grape. The young man was growing used to it, though when Janie leaned forward and clasped his hand he startled.

"There ain't a thing I'd trade," she said. "They tried and they tried and they tried to get me to. Some of our own kin, the government, Authority, different buddies over the years—Jon D. Crews among them. Says he's through begging me. Ain't heard from him in, I reckon, more than a month. Wouldn't trade calling this land home not even to get my eye back. Shit fire, you could say, Janie, we come up with a way to stop all that lakewater from spilling down into the valley, The Peach Pit can stay open for all eternity, but you got to move off from here. No sir. Me and this place—and I don't just mean what you can look out yonder and lay eyes upon—me and this place is just too tangled up. But I reckon you know that, don't you, coming up here with a tape recorder to get a old buzzard's stories."

Days Her Missing

1958

Wooten Ragsdale had always been afraid she'd leave—not just him but this entire place. Tammy'd threatened to since the night she saw her first movie, at the Elberta Rampatorium. Fourteen, sitting on a grassy terrace next to a senior named Bobby Davis.

"Oh my lord," she said after the closing credits.

"What is it?" Bobby had dozed off when he realized she wasn't game to fool around.

"I got to go to Hollywood," Tammy said.

"Hell, right now?"

"No you fool. But one day, you watch, I'll be gone."

This realization occurred before Wooten knew Tammy, before the Ragsdales moved to the valley and he ruined his right hand at work. Tammy was, he thought after they met, more than pretty enough to be on the big screen. A face he could cup in his one good hand, bright-green eyes, thick black hair, and a good-size chest. If a Treeborne ever went for Miss Elberta Peach, though none ever did, Wooten liked to brag that it would of been Tammy.

After she graduated school she'd moved down to the Gulf of Mexico. Not quite Hollywood, but still. Wooten was two years behind Tammy at Elberta County High. He remembered hearing she'd moved away, but they ran with different crowds, and it didn't much register with him busy playing football for the Conquistadors and working at his daddy Leland's chickenhouses. About a year later Tammy moved back and started work for the county water department. Everybody figured her adventure to the Gulf Coast would of satisfied her Hollywood dreams. But Tammy kept making threats, even after she and Wooten began dating. It was cute, he thought—at first. But as she aged, and their relationship did too, the threats wore on him. The way Tammy acted was kin to being a grown woman who still pops and plays with her chewing gum. I'll leave this goddamn place tomorrow! she'd say. Wooten didn't know how to handle her outbursts. He was nervous by nature. Sometimes he wanted to just yell back, Well go on then!

One night a few years into their marriage, Tammy ranting and raving about going to Hollywood and becoming a movie star, Wooten dragged a hard blue-plastic suitcase out from the closet and began frantically stuffing it with clothes from their shared chest of drawers.

"What on earth do you think you're doing?" she asked.

"If leaving's what you want, then come on! Let's go." He was a man without much past anyhow. Why not up and leave?

She stood there watching him for a moment, wondering could they actually leave together, then said, "No. Stop it Woot. If I'm going it's got to be by myself."

Despite Tammy saying this, and the next four years of regular threats, Wooten Ragsdale did not decide till the second night of her missing that Tammy'd finally made good on her promise and gone.

He was sitting in a recliner chair eating fried pork skins from a brown paperbag while the new television bled blue light throughout the living room of their singlewide trailer. The embarrassing realization landed on Wooten from above, like bird droppings. His wife had gone to Hollywood, California, and left him here all by hisself. He finished the bag of pork skins then, knowing not what else to do, got in the new used pickup truck he'd bought from Big Connie Ward and drove out into the county.

The pickup was a beautiful thing with wood running boards and white capital lettering across the tailgate. Wooten drove and he drove, trying to believe he'd catch up to his wife if he just kept on. Pull over and she'd hop in. Drive back into town and eat a hamburger all-the-way, large fry, split a chocolate milk shake with whipped cream. The summer air all thick and buggy, they'd get in bed and talk about the house they were building on Tammy's folks' land till one fell asleep in the other's arms. Be like one of those damn movies she was always dragging him to see at the Grand Two ever since the Rampatorium shut down. Tammy had been furious when this happened. She believed there was no better way to see a movie than outdoors underneath the stars. She'd watch anything—westerns, love stories, murder mysteries, even kiddie cartoons if that's all that was playing. She said it felt like her innards were being squeezed by the moving pictures and the light. Something important happening. She told Wooten how, when she was a girl, she used to take frames that the projectionist threw out and bring them home, where she held them to lamplight and made up stories for the people and places she saw. Wooten and Tammy did not fool around during movies, way other couples did. This embarrassed him too. Folks sometimes called the Rampatorium a passion pit. He just knew everybody noticed his and Tammy's public display of celibacy. On occasion he tried to kiss her, tried to unbutton her britches and slip his bad hand underneath her bloomers. "Quit it Woot," she'd hiss, removing his hand like one might a pesky insect. "I don't want to miss what happens next."

When Wooten got back home later that night he tripped over a bowl of dog food on the porch. Dry pellets dropped down between the gapped boards. He cussed then hollered, "Martin, Martin, come on now!" The dog did not come. Odd, he thought, going inside and turning on the television. He tried to find wrestling. Martin was his little buddy. A chubby brown-and-white beagle mix. Wooten thought he might let the dog sleep inside since Tammy wasn't around to fuss about the shedding and the stinking. He grew tired of flipping channels. Onscreen a comedian introduced a band that he didn't recognize. The picture dimmed. Wooten got up and smacked the side of the wood console with his bad hand. Still good for clubbing. The screen brightened. He readjusted one of the little ceramic figurines he gave Tammy on birthdays and holidays—this one Hernando de Soto astraddle a horse—then sat down and fell asleep.

Next morning he woke up and drove over at The Seven. He primed his chain saw while waiting for the Crews boy to show up. This alone seemed fishy, folks said when they found out Tammy was missing. But work had always soothed Wooten Ragsdale—even after his hand was mangled by a band saw when he was halving warm chicken carcasses for his daddy. Wooten couldn't say the same for Lyle Crews though. The boy was plumb lazy. All summer Wooten had been waiting for Lyle to quit. Looked like, he thought, tearing open the packaging of a snack cake with his teeth, today was going to be the day.

He checked the foundation that'd been poured the other week. With good weather the concrete would cure and he could start building soon. He grew tired of waiting and began work without Lyle Crews, downing several hardwoods, chaining them to the dozer then dragging them into the pasture alongside the others. He logged through lunch, not noticing Sister and Crusoe missing from atop Tammy's daddy's old artist studio, where his niece and the dirt boy doll she toted had been keeping watch on him every single damn day since he'd started.

Come evening Wooten drove over at Freedom Hills and bought a sack of tamales from Dyar's. The tamales, made of corn and filled with juicy pulled pork and diced red chili peppers and onions, were wrapped in steamed husks that scalded his fingertips as he peeled them. He finished the entire sack before he got home. The dog food remained where he'd spilled it the night before, minus what raccoons had eaten. He hollered, "Here now dog!" Didn't figure Tammy'd take Martin with her. What if something was wrong? Dogs are apt to wander though, he told hisself as he carried a dozen cold beers onto the porch—and Tammy could be spiteful, just like her momma. He sat on the metal glider and drank. The beers tasted all the crisper in the early August heat that would not break, even after the mean orange sun fell beyond the black hills. He drank all twelve beers then started feeling real good and sorry for hisself. Tammy never had qualms letting Wooten know she despised this in him. He despised the inclination too, though he couldn't help it any more than a stone could its stillness.

Later that night he drove to the limits of Elberta County, following pitiful dirt roads without names that snaked in and out of the wooded hillfolds. Spotted nothing but whitetail deer in briar-choked fields, fat possums that sneered as they ran in front of his tires, millions upon millions of papery moths and mosquitoes and gnats that gathered momentarily in his headlights before being smashed to smithereens against the warm grille. Buying this new used pickup had been Tammy's idea. The thought of Wooten driving it aroused in her some affection toward him that'd long been absent. But this affection had dulled just like the free wax job Big Connie Ward threw in with the purchase. If Wooten had married any other woman in Elberta, Alabama, he knew, they would of silently figured out a way to live out their predicament. Unhappy marriages common as clay. But he hadn't married just any woman. He'd married a Treeborne and, goddamn it, he was paying for it.

He pulled up near the water tower and drank six more cold beers while watching the other vehicles strategically parked in moon-cut shadow. He got hisself riled up thinking Tammy might be in the backseat of one with an even younger man than he—maybe a member of the Conquistadors varsity squad. He got out and listened at a high school couple rut and moan. Nearly yanked them through the cracked window, then he caught hisself. Young love. The dial tuned to The Peach. It was late enough that Pedro Hannah could get away with playing rock-and-roll music. Nobody awake to hear but kids like these and the men who worked owl-shift at the coal mines down in Bankhead and, tonight anyway, Wooten Ragsdale. Between songs Pedro said there was nothing new to report about last week's Peach Days incident. Wooten was so drunk he did not register what incident the boy meant nor his wife's involvement in it.

The sun was up, slowly turning the valley blue as if it'd sunk underwater, time Wooten arrived at the Hernando de Soto Dam. He knocked on a metal door. When it opened there stood his brother-in-law, Ren

Treeborne, wearing nothing but a pair of red-and-white-checkered drawers and a gold chain around his hairy neck.

"Hell is it Woot?"

"She's gone."

"Who?"

"Tammy," he said. "She ain't been home the last three nights."

They took Ren's pickup, the floorboards littered with lakeshore sand and pinched cigarettes. Empty coke-cola bottles rolled out from underneath the seat then back again. Ren cranked down the driver's-side window with a pair of pliers then handed them to Wooten. Hot air stirred up the sparkling floorboard grit as Ren turned right onto 31. From there it wasn't far to Wooten and Tammy's trailer.

They walked around inside then throughout the yard, hunting for signs among the weeds and the construction materials and the aboveground swimming pool. Found nothing that could be interpreted as such. Near the edge of the woods Ren believed he caught a whiff of rot, though he couldn't be sure. Wooten said the dog was missing too. Ren knew Tammy wouldn't of taken that damn mutt if she'd run off.

"We ought to call Aaron," he said.

"Let's wait just a day or two."

"Woot."

"I can't stand admitting she's left me Ren."

"She's my sister Woot."

"I know it."

"What if she's somewhere hurt and needing help?"

"I know it," Wooten said. "Don't you reckon I know?"

Ren hated seeing a grown man so ashamed. He knew his baby sister could be flighty. They'd all worried about her marrying Wooten. Tammy had sworn she'd found pure-dee love this time. Who was Ren to doubt? Wooten had invited Ren, Luther, Hugh and Maybelle to witness the proposal outside the Ragsdale chickenhouses and slaughtering facility. One of Elberta's biggest employers since Prince's Peach Cannery shut down in the twenties. Tammy had just got on at the water department.

Wooten owned some land on which he'd parked a trailer. This trailer. Tammy was, she told her family, a year older and much wiser than she was after high school when she left for the Gulf Coast.

"Alright," Ren said. "Let's see if she don't turn up tomorrow."

"Thank you," Wooten said. "Thank you Ren."

Folks remembered seeing Wooten Ragsdale down at The Fencepost Cafe at lunch that day. Said he ordered a bloody steak and a baked potato big as a newborn baby. He ate alone, Ren gone back to the De Soto Dam. Wooten's check, the money him and Tammy were making logging the land she'd inherited after her momma died earlier that summer, the house they were building there, these were the subject of hours of big talk and bullshitting at the little restaurant. Folks paid special attention whenever the couple came in to eat. Strange, they thought that day, Tammy not meeting Wooten for lunch. The county water department office was, after all, just down Madrid and other side of the square.

After lunch Wooten took a peek at the blind tiger in back of the restaurant. No longer a need for pretending there was an exotic animal on view, but the speakeasy's name had stuck. He took another peek and then another one till he was so drunk he had to cover one eye to see the road straight. He managed to arrive at The Seven unharmed, though he wasn't able to do much work. The chain saw missed each time he tried to lay into a tree. He took a nap in the cab of his pickup truck then drove over at Livingstown to see about that Crews boy.

Wooten found the boy's daddy Van in the shop building where he kept three llamas he'd bought off a traveling sideshow run by a spectacular midget. Van Crews swung a pistol onto Wooten when he barged in demanding to see Lyle.

"I don't keep up with him."

"Lie!"

"I ain't arguing with you about it," Van said, jostling the pistol. He lowered it when he realized how drunk Wooten was then turned his attention back to the llama's milk soap he had on to boil. Forever chasing fortune, Van Crews had noticed Elberta women becoming more concerned about their upkeep. He was working on a llama's milk shampoo too—made with real llama butter for extra shine.

"You ain't got any of that dope do you?"

"Not for you I ain't," Van said, pointing the snubbish pistol again. "I'll tell Lyle you was hunting him. Now go on home Woot. You look like twice run-over shit."

Wooten could piece together nothing between leaving Livingstown and showing up at football practice later that afternoon, though, when asked, he'd tell Sheriff Aaron Guthrie that he'd gone swimming. It was blamed hot enough for this to make sense—problem was, grown men in Elberta didn't just go swimming by themselves.

Wooten started out on the concrete bleachers with all the other used-to-bes who had nothing better to do than watch a bunch of high school boys running into each other time and again. The Elberta County High School Conquistadors jamboree game was a few weeks off and practice tempo had adjusted accordingly. Wooten gradually drifted down onto the sideline for a better look. He'd been a fair ball player on a couple good teams in the forties. He followed Coach Williams up and down the field. Coach carried hisself like a war hero, wore short gray cotton shorts and looked like a turtle from the neck up. Every Conquistador who'd ever played for him adored him to death. He gave these boys and the men they became scant approval in return, which only made them adore him more.

During one play a Conquistador—folks later told it was the Snell kid—came running toward the sideline on a passing route too fast to pull up. Coach Williams dodged, but Wooten Ragsdale held his ground. The Conquistador fell flat on his back. All the used-to-bes laughed and spat and clapped. Coach Williams even smiled around his polished silver whistle. Wooten helped up the Conquistador and slapped him on the rear end. When the Conquistador jogged back onto the field for the next play, Wooten followed. The Conquistadors didn't know what to do when he leaned into the huddle. The grown man smelled like booze and tree-bark. Realizing Coach Williams meant to let it ride, the quarterback lined everybody up and snapped the ball on two. He shoved it into the Snell kid's gut going up the middle on a dive. Wooten had plowed a path so clear the kid ran half the field before getting tackled from behind. Coach Williams blew his whistle and hollered for him to come on off the field.

But Wooten would not.

He called another play, another and another, leading the offense to the goal line in the same sweat-soaked clothes he'd worn the last four days his wife was missing. All the used-to-bes stopped laughing and clapping. During the touchdown play Wooten drove a boy named Winchell hard into the ground. The boy's cleat caught in the grass and his leg bent backward at an unnatural angle. The break, the used-to-bes later claimed, could be heard from the bleachers. Boys who saw the injury up close puked on themselves.

Coach Williams sprinted up to Wooten. "Get your sorry goddamn ass off my field right this second before I kick it all the way to goddamn fucking Bankhead and back."

But still Wooten would not.

The fight was over time Ren got there. The used-to-bes had gathered around their vehicles to rehash what'd occurred. Sometimes old Conquistadors got in on practice, but it was usually ones no more than a year or two removed from school. Wooten had been out coming up on a decade. He sat alone on the bleachers, the boys he'd whipped pacing the trampled sidelines with tiny paper cups of water. Ren waved to his brother-in-law then went to apologize to Coach Williams, who had a good-size welt on his right cheek. Bertrand English, an assistant, boasted a missing tooth and busted lower lip. Ren apologized to him too and asked about the Winchell boy. He'd been carried to Doc Barfield's. Ren promised to stop by and look in on him. He knew this story would hit The Fencepost before the dinner rush. Liable to make the next day's *Elberta Times-Journal* too. Coach Williams said not to worry about it, and he was sorry for bothering Ren at work.

"I tried over at the water department, but Tam wasn't in. Everything alright?"

"She ain't been feeling too good lately," Ren said.

"Well, it ain't easy what y'all been through this summer."

Ren grimaced as he shook his coach's hand.

He kept Wooten at the dam that night. Only had the one cot in his office, which he helped his brother-in-law onto after feeding him dry toast and as much water as he could stomach. Ren ate the last of some okra and butter beans then made hisself a pallet on the cold concrete floor. If he turned on his side he could hear the turbines working in the gallery fifty feet down below. He slept little that night, wondering if Tammy really had fled Elberta. If she had at least she'd waited till their momma wasn't around anymore.

Next morning Ren felt like he was the one who'd taken on the Conquistadors varsity squad, the coaches and the used-to-bes. Wooten was smiling and drinking black coffee in the break room with Willy Ramsey, one of two engineers at the De Soto Dam. Ren grabbed the *Times-Journal* off the table and carried it to the bathroom. His stomach complained to be emptied as he unzipped his blue jeans. His morning ritual was reading the *Times-Journal* all the way through while squatted on the toilet. Later in the afternoon he'd go back and hunt for any unread morsels. He read the paper to be up on things. There always seemed plenty in Elberta to be up on too. Other day one of the Farleys had a heart attack on his tractor. Unguided, the machine crashed into a haybarn and spun its tires so long that before anybody realized Junior Farley was missing all the gas ran out and the engine died same as the man. There was nothing about Wooten's fight in the paper. Thank God. Ren flushed then washed his hands.

Willy Ramsey was eating a baloney sandwich. Through a mouthful he said, "Woot here tells that Tammy's run off to be some kind of movie star."

"Ah," Ren said, setting the newspaper back down.

"Well I hope it ain't got nothing to do with that Peach Days mess," Willy said. "Not that I'm blaming her. This used to be a nice little town. Now I just don't know."

Ren called Sheriff Aaron Guthrie and asked to meet at the trailer.

Then he called the library to let Nita know what was going on. She boo-hooed into the phone. Ren didn't know how to comfort her. In this respect he was not the best husband.

When they got to the trailer, biscuit crumbs yet clung to the sheriff's navy-blue shirt. He was built like many Elberta men: a gut, twig-legs and thinning hair. He and Wooten searched inside the trailer. Meanwhile, Ren walked down at the mailbox.

Among the usual grocery store flyers set a peach pit. Couldn't of been but a handful of days removed from a fruit's flesh. Ren carried the pit inside. The sheriff held it up to his face like a jeweler would a diamond. "How long you say she's missing for?"

"Five days," Ren said.

The sheriff grunted. He had plenty of questions, namely how come they'd waited so long before telling him. Aaron Guthrie was good at his job without going so overboard he didn't have time to fish De Soto Lake, or sit around The Fencepost and bullshit two meals a day.

"I was ashamed for anybody to know."

"But you told your brother here?"

"Brother-in-law," Ren said, wishing he'd just bit his tongue.

The sheriff held up the peach pit again. "And this was in the mailbox?"

"She's gone off to Hollywood," Wooten said. He sat down in the recliner chair and the frame groaned. "That's what she's done to me."

"You ought to of said something right off the bat," the sheriff said. "Now what else ain't you told?"

Wooten began crying, his good hand cupping his forehead and the bad one pressed against his bearded jaw.

"The dog," Ren said.

"I don't know where Martin is neither!"

"I'll call Connie," the sheriff said. "Get his hound over here."

The three men smoked cigarettes while waiting for Big Connie Ward and his black-and-tan Troop to arrive. A crayon-green lizard crawled across the porch then up the heat-cracked banister. The lizard gazed at the men in unrepentant fashion before disappearing behind the trailer's aluminum siding as if it was no more real than magic.

"I'll have to carry you in and get this all on the record," the sheriff said.

"Fuck you Aaron."

"This right here ain't good enough?" Ren asked.

"There's appearances I got to keep."

"Fuck you straight to hell," Wooten said.

"Heard you was down at ball practice yesterday."

Wooten sniffled and blew smoke.

"Broke that Winchell boy's leg clean in two."

Wooten sat on the porch steps. "I just want my wife back home with me."

"Then you best start helping me goddamn it."

Wooten tried to recall the last time he'd seen Tammy. His memory skirted away though, not wanting to be caught and dissected. He realized how little he marked what seemed like, in the present, ordinary days. They hadn't fought more than usual, he said. Sure, they fought, who didn't, but he never laid a hand on her. Not once. He thought he remembered her tanning her legs by the pool. That white swimsuit. She wasn't acting particularly odd, not that he could tell. Didn't Treebornes always act somewhat odd? Sorry. He looked at Ren. None intended. The keys to her pickup truck right yonder on the counter. That's right, smooched her cheek then left to fill up the gas cans so I wouldn't have to do it come morning. Call and ask Dennis down at the Pump-N-Save! Dennis would remember. Would of filled up the cans earlier but I had to drop off the Crews boy down at Livingstown on the way home then—

"What about him?" Ren said. "Talk to Lyle and see what he remembers."

The sheriff ignored this suggestion. "Reckon it could be to do with her momma?" he asked. "You know how women get whenever somebody passes."

The heat was rolling waves off the gravel and dirt driveway time Big Connie Ward pulled up in a red pickup truck. When Troop stepped down from the cab Wooten held out one of Tammy's silk nightgowns for him to sniff. The hound found no signs of her but soon discovered Martin's remains in the woods just beyond the yard. Troop grabbed the poor dog's body and shook. Plump maggots and shiny black beetles tumbled out of Martin's innards like candy from a piñata till Big Connie wopped Troop upside the skull and said quit it. The hound tucked tail then and sat, holding high his flat head and panting.

"Just sick," Big Connie said, leaning over to inspect Martin's decapitated body.

"You don't reckon a cult did this do you?" Ren asked.

"Not no cult," Big Connie said. "Just pure-dee sickness is all it is."

"But what about that clay man Woot?" Ren said.

"What clay man?" the sheriff asked.

"It ain't anything Aaron," Wooten said. "Found him strung up on the porch other week ago. I don't know, big dummy-looking thing made of dirt and leaves and shit-what-all else. Probably just some kids messing around."

"And you ain't even going to talk to Lyle Crews?" Ren said.

Big Connie cut a look that made the sheriff frown.

"I'll talk to Van," the sheriff said. "See what we can't find out."

They got together a search party at Woodrow's Pit Cook Bar-B-Q. Men who'd soon die as look a black person in the face would yet go over at The Hills for Woodrow's pulled pork and ribs. Never ate inside the low block building though—their usual compromise was to carry out. Come lunch you'd see pickups parked all along Jaybird Ridge, which divided Elberta from Freedom Hills, and men eating from foam containers balanced on the hoods. This day they made an exception and did not carry out. Woodrow's ribs were ringed with a beautiful pink halo just inside the hard black bark, and required a gentle tug of the teeth for the meat to come loose from the bone. Perfect. The pulled pork came by the pound and dressed with a vinegary tomato-based sauce that had peaches in it for sweetness. Woodrow'd learned to smoke hogs from his great-granddaddy, who was a Louisiana slave, and he kept what he claimed were a real set of iron shackles in a glass case built into the counter.

Aaron Guthrie went over the search plan while the men sopped puddles of dark-red sauce with pieces of white loafbread. They'd start out down below Wooten and Tammy's trailer along the Elberta River, he said. The bank was karsty, all run-through with sinkholes and caves where Tammy might of, the sheriff gently put it, got lost. Others would search The Seven and its dense woods. A crew was on its way from Poarch County to drag De Soto Lake. After the sheriff finished talking he asked Wooten if there was anything he wanted to add.

Wooten stood up, ducking a ceiling fan coated in one hundred years of dust and grease, and thanked everybody. But, he said, it didn't matter one lick where in the valley they looked for Tammy. "She's five hundred miles away by now," he said. "And if there's one thing I know it's she ain't ever coming back to Elberta, Alabama, so long as she lives."

There were a few halfhearted attempts to encourage Wooten otherwise. Then the men finished their barbecue and set out in a line of pickup trucks. Hound dogs on toolboxes, pink tongues dangling like flags in the wind.

"Why don't you come with me," the sheriff said to Wooten. He popped a little white heart pill in his mouth and crunched it with his molars. "Down at the office."

"Go ahead and arrest me Aaron. Only way you'll keep me from being out yonder with every other damn fool you done gathered up for this."

The sheriff relented, and Ren and Wooten headed out to catch up with the rest of the search party. Other side of The Peach Pit they met Lee Malone in his truck and stopped in the road to speak. He was carrying Ricky Birdsong home. After Ren told what'd happened, Lee wouldn't have it any other way but to come search for Tammy too. Bad idea, Ren knew, especially since the Peach Days incident and everything prior to Maybelle's death.

"Ricky didn't look good," Ren said after they'd pulled away.

Wooten grunted and scratched his beard. Sawdust sprinkled onto his britches. He brushed it off and readjusted how he sat.

Ren fooled with the radio. Sometimes The Peach faded out the closer you got to the Prince Building, as if all the voices and music were being shot out at too steep an angle to be heard in town. Ren wanted to know if Pedro Hannah had broken the news about Tammy being missing yet.

Pedro was midcommercial though, rambling on about an upcoming bean supper at Elberta Second Baptist Church, then about Big Connie Ward extending his Peach Days sale for one more weekend and one more weekend only.

"Everybody had it hard," Wooten said.

"I reckon so." Ren shook out a cigarette from a smushed pack then lit it. "You'll have to answer the sheriff about these last several days, you know it?"

"You might have to answer for some things too," Wooten said. "It ain't no secret you and Tam's been at odds over this mess with your momma."

Ren inhaled then blew out and coughed. "Well," he said.

"You really don't reckon I'd hurt your sister do you?"

"I sure hope not," Ren said. "I sure sure hope not."

At the river landing the men plugged tobacco into their mouths and pretended to look away while Wooten held the nightgown for the hounds to sniff. The sight of the gown gripped in his bad hand, which looked like a skint dove the way it shined with barbecue grease, sickened them. It was obscene too the way the hounds buried their wet noses into the silky fabric. The men were jealous—not only of the hounds, but also of each other, wondering which confederate among them had made it with Tammy Treeborne Ragsdale way back when. Of this they felt sure: Wooten had done something to his wife because she'd betrayed him. Killed her, chopped her up into a million pieces and sunk them in the lake, buried them somewhere off in the deep woods where they'd never be found. Still they had a duty to fulfill. They traced calloused fingers across a map, then set out in a loose line for the river.

The current picked up speed as limestone bluffs pinched toward each other. The men poked the ground with sticks and hoe handles, with the butt-end of rifles and handed-down shotguns. They swapped off hollering her name, and shared drink and cigarettes. Near downtown they spotted Deputy Polk at a landing other side the river. Big Connie bellowed directions while the deputy acted like he understood. After Polk drove out of sight the search party headed on.

Farther downriver they came to the Hernando de Soto Bridge. A pickup truck was parked beyond the guardrail. Lee Malone leaned against its side. Big Connie made a joke about a gorilla escaped from the zoo and Ren shot him a look. Big Connie said, "Come on and join us Brother Lee! And bring that mutt too!"

Lee and Buckshot ambled down the slope. Lee's clothes were sopping wet and he had, for him, a near frantic expression about his face. Buckshot hiked a leg and pissed on a sapling while staring up at Big Connie Ward.

"Everything alright?" Ren asked.

"Uh-huh," Lee said. "Yeah."

Ren trusted Lee's word, but he also understood how this appeared to the rest of the men. Folks knew about Lee's relationship with Maybelle Treeborne. Many predicted it would end in just the kind of tragedy that'd befallen her. The circumstances too perfect, Lee Malone squirrel hunting the exact part of The Seven where Maybelle'd been found dead. Some folks suspected Lee was involved with Tammy's disappearance too. Ren's word would carry only so much weight. Treebornes just a step above white trash to begin with. The further time distanced the town from the days of Mr. Prince, who, in many folks' minds, had crowned Lee Malone by bringing him out of Freedom Hills and letting him run the peach orchard, the less likely folks were to bend toward, what they saw as, the eccentricities of a dead man and the few folks, like Ren Treeborne, who dared defend them as just.

"Y'all hear they found a peach pit at the scene of the crime?" Big Connie Ward said. The men mumbled. "Seems to me like somebody who knows about peaches might could reckon why a pit'd be left behind thataway."

"Fuck you Connie," Lee Malone said.

"Not in this life nigger," Big Connie said back.

The men laughed and jeered.

"Let's keep walking," Ren said.

Sinkholes and gaps opened like mouths in the earth. Weak-rooted trees laid downhill, their tops baptized in the Elberta River. Limestone

white as milk showed through thousands of years of dead leaves covering the unreliable ground. The men checked each hole best they could,
letting the hounds nose the blackness till they just about slipped and
hung themselves by the neck. Daylight was bleeding out, playing shadows
everywhere they looked. Gnats circled the men's sweating heads, and
mosquitoes lit onto their flesh and sucked and sucked. They slapped themselves and each other. To an onlooker, the men would've appeared insane.
Nobody wanted to be the one to say it: They ought to just quit, come
back and try again tomorrow. Ren picked up on this feeling and spoke for
the group.

"Might ought to head in before it gets too dark."

"Just a little farther," Wooten said.

He led them through a poison-ivy patch. The hounds sneezed and
pawed their snouts. Some men threatened to turn back, but Big Connie
Ward threatened them if they did. They traversed a hillside strewn with
trash: drum rings, blown-out tires, a washing machine and a dryer. They
weren't far from a road. Tammy, they hollered in echo of each other.
A breeze carried woodsmoke upriver from Livingstown. Somebody
mentioned Van Crews being absent from the search—and him distant
Treeborne kin.

"Van's delivering a vehicle for me," Big Connie said.

The men knew what that meant, and they said no more of it.

They wandered into a maze of mountain laurel and let the hounds
off chain rather than stop to untangle them every few feet. Wooten kept
out in front of the group. Ren and Lee tried keeping up with him, but
it was no use. All sudden, the unloosed hounds bayed and sprinted, and
Wooten took off after them at a run.

They'd already sniffed his niece and backed off time Wooten got there.
Her dress was torn at the neckline. She was dirty, pinestraw caught in
her black hair, and she held on her hip the dirt boy doll her granddaddy'd
made. Crusoe, they called him. Fear caused the girl to appear younger
than her thirteen years.

"Where's your other boot at?" Wooten asked.

The girl did not answer.

"Sister," Ren said. He touched his daughter's head, still not used to the eye patch on her face. "Is that gasoline I smell? Listen to me, your aunt Tammy's gone missing."

The girl seemed stunned stupid.

"Give them some room," Big Connie said.

The men chained their hounds. Wrong scent idjit, they muttered. While Ren and Wooten tended to the girl, the men pulled ticks and smashed them against bootheels. Dusk came full. Dry-flies screeched in the treetops. The men grew more agitated till Big Connie Ward pulled a small blue-green bottle out of his shirtpocket. Then they held back their heads in turn and dripped dope underneath their curled red tongues till the bottle was emptied. They thought little of the Treeborne girl being out in the woods thisaway. She had plenty of her grandparents in her. That sort of blood, the men figured, which had them traipsing out here to begin with, was reason enough for her appearance.

The Peach Pit

1958

Lee Malone stood at the high end of the peach orchard watching the pickers down below. Six this time of year. Julio, Tony, Pee-Po, Bear, Fred and Raul. The number would shrink further in fall, winter, swell again in spring before the branches budded. Most of this fruit would be made into jelly or pickled and sold on the shelves at The Peach Pit's roadside stand. The orchardfield looked alive with the bees and yellow jackets and red wasps drunkenly tumbling across fallen peaches turning to mush where they lay. Lee swatted a stray insect.

From this part of the orchard he could see all the property he owned. More than any other black man in Elberta County. The tip-top of the last crumbling smokestack at the old cannery and other side of the road, the two-bedroom house where he lived with his dog Buckshot. The first nigger to come out of The Hills, he liked to say. If Lee squinted he could see the cottage in town he'd rented to Maybelle Treeborne after her husband died. She couldn't tolerate living on The Seven without Hugh. Lee understood. Town never suited her though, he thought.

He whistled for Buckshot. When the dog came running Lee was struck with a young man's urge to take off too. Fifty-six and could feel five-hundred-and-six. His back was still stove-up from spending the night on that jail cot during Peach Days. But today neither a bad back nor being practically deaf in one ear from the blast of a pistol could get him down. He was still getting used to wearing a bulb jammed inside his earhole. He fiddled with it as he watched Buckshot snapping at grasshoppers this big around flinging themselves into the air.

The dog got distracted and trailed off another direction. This orchard was Buckshot's kingdom, and he did as he pleased. Lee loved the dog to death. He'd found him living out at the abandoned Rampatorium, a crusted-black shotgun wound on his side. He nursed the dog to health with lukewarm chicken broth, raw bacon and pure-dee love. Lee saw in this four-legged creature's salt-and-peppered face what he imagined folks meant when they uttered the word *God*. What Momma Pat and Mr. Robin, the white folks who raised him, thought Lee the boy saw as he stood at the altar whupping a homemade guitar, legs jostling inside too-big church-britches, and singing songs so old they'd never even been written down, as if pencil markings would vanish from paper if somebody dare tried. Mr. Prince, Lee now thought, knew better though. He'd confessed he came to the church out in the county for the music itself—not what the music represented. Lee whistled for the dog to come on.

While he waited he picked a peach and bit into its tender flesh. What makes an Elberta peach so sweet, Lee Malone knew, is how long it's allowed to trouble the tree. That and, he believed, something in the dirt here and nowhere else on earth. May'd believed it too. Died in the month of her name. It was early August now. Most times Lee fought the fool's urge to plot his past, as if doing so might yet change how things'd wound up, but lately, he'd struggled.

He checked a few trees for blight. Worried one on this row would need to be pulled up. The stems were ashy and black. He'd replace it with another from a nursery in Poarch County, though. Spending money didn't bother him. Never been much in peach growing anyhow. Lee knew that even before he came into this business with a handshake and a couple dollars. Growers didn't make out like bankers did. He needed to find someone who understood this—and other essentials—to leave The Peach Pit to one day. He had no family. The place had to belong to somebody who understood that peach trees were miracles. Marvel at how roots found moisture, how leaves gathered sunlight into food so buds begat plump fruit. Foot, Lee weren't no scientist. Neither had Mr. Prince been. Lee Malone cherished mystery as much as knowledge. Maybelle'd thought the same exact way. He could confess such foolish feelings to her and to nobody else he ever knew. He loved Maybelle Treeborne, and now she was gone. Among the black treebranches there was a still-green peach though. He pinched off some leaves so the hard fruit would get better sunlight and have a chance to ripen yet.

When Buckshot caught up he flopped and rolled on his back. Lee watched the dog revel. He glanced downhill and saw somebody coming thataway. Lee held up a hand and squinted—whoever it was was moving at a good clip. It didn't take much longer to put a name to this particular gait: dip, the leg swinging out wide. Ricky Birdsong's hip was bad to come out of socket, a torment since he made his living mowing yards and cleaning the hallways and bathrooms at the Hernando de Soto Dam. The sight of him walking would break your heart if you remembered the old galloping motion: compact and deer-sprung as the boy dodged the outstretched arms trying in vain to bring him down before he scored for the Conquistadors yet again.

Ricky was talking to hisself, which wasn't unusual. The boy often saw Jesus. The shirt he wore was filthy and half-buttoned wrong though, and the thin brown hair at his widow's peak cowlicked. He usually kept up a handsome appearance. The women whose yards he mowed couldn't help remarking about it at The Fencepost on Saturday or in the pews of Second Baptist on Sunday. Some men noticed too, chiding the women in the same breath for fawning over somebody who was, you know, thataway.

"What say Ricky?"

Ricky did not answer. Hands balled tight except for the first finger on each fist, which moved like they were following the path of a blowfly.

"Mower tear up on you again?"

If the boy registered Lee's words he did not let on. Buckshot sniffed Ricky's britches then huffed. Maybe he's got sunstroked, Lee thought. Way the boy worked he came near being so at least once a summer. It

had been hot and dry lately. Most folks in town worried not what more
the sun could do to Ricky, but Lee and a few others did their best to
care for him. The Conquistadors booster club gave him a small check
for helping tote the marching band's equipment on and off the field
during halftime performances. It was, after all, partly the club's blame
Ricky Birdsong'd wound up thisaway.

He tried walking past and Lee caught him by the shirtsleeve. The
boy's one eye widened while the other yet drooped. Some folks referred
to this one as his pussy eye. Lee held on tight, knowing the violence that
once made Ricky Birdsong so beloved yet lurked inside his body. Looking at him, it was easy to forget he was still a young man. As if the injury had changed the shape of his skeleton, the makeup of the bones
underneath his tanned skin, as if the injury had become him.

"Let's go get us something to drink," Lee said.

Ricky eased up and Lee let go. He picked a ripe peach and handed
it over, noticing something gummed-up around the boy's fingernails and
in the hair on the back of his hands. Too flaky, he thought, for engine
grease or motor oil. Maybe paint? Lee heard his white momma, Momma
Pat, say idle hands were the devil's best tools. Foot, he thought, after a
lifetime spent working with his own two. He made sure Ricky had ahold
of the peach before letting go, wondering might the boy rear back and
let the sucker fly, way he used to a baseball, the peach sailing across the
road and splattering on the roof underneath which Lee and Buckshot
slept. Baseball nothing but a distraction in Elberta, Alabama, till the next
coming of fall, when the Conquistadors returned to action. Lee enjoyed
the sport though, its leisurely pace, the long moments of silence punc-
tuated by the pop of leather, the crack of wood, mild hollering from a
handful of folks sitting on lopsided wooden bleachers. The youngest
Crews boy, Jon D., looked like one hell of a baseball player. Lee'd given
him his first bat seven-eight years ago. Now the boy was playing two
years above his age group. Ricky Birdsong could of made out at baseball too. But in Elberta it'd always be football first.

Buckshot crawled underneath the cabin Lee used as his office and
flopped down on the cool packed dirt. Lee could hear the dog panting

when, inside, he opened two coke-colas then dragged over a chair for
Ricky to sit. A cypress cabin propped on four riverrock columns rubbed
smooth as eggs by the Elberta's waters. Lee'd moved the structure onto
the orchard shortly after Mr. Prince sold to him then died. By then
Momma Pat and Mr. Robin had no use for it. Two rooms all the cabin
was, and Lee the boy had once slept on the wide-spaced floorboards, laid
by the white couple who raised him, where now he kept a big oak desk
with nothing much in its drawers but for a pack of spearmint chewing
gum, a bottle of watered-down whiskey he sometimes aimlessly lipped,
a notebook stuffed with various business receipts he'd never need, weather
observations and half-reminders to hisself about one thing or another.
Lee had little use for a desk other than as a form of decoration, something to fill an otherwise empty space. It was, Momma Pat would of
said had she been alive to see it, plumb gaudy of him.

The desk's primary purpose was to display one of Hugh Treeborne's
assemblies. Lee caught Ricky looking at the thing. You couldn't help but
look at Hugh's stuff. Art, Lee thought, correcting hisself. The making
of which being one of two things both men loved but never spoke the
truth about. And now it too late. Hugh dead how many years? Maybe
one day in heaven, Lee sometimes tried to believe. But heaven, foot.

The assemblie was made of wound guitar strings, filed-down pennies
and hunks of colored glass melted onto wooden backing. What they
called abstract. Lee moved the assemblie over just a hair then resituated
how he sat, bumping a suitcase record player on the floor. On it set the
only recording Lee Malone ever made. It was awful-sounding, guitar
down in a hole and breathy vocals up front, the acetate mixed with
Wisconsin dirt.

> I don't go to church on Sunday if
> I'm hungover from Saturday night.
> A girl from Mississippi and a bottle of whiskey,
> just trying to feel alright. But soon enough
> they both run out, and I am left without a doubt
> that there ain't no substitute for you.

Lee shook these words out of his mind. "Reckon how the Conquistadors'll do this year?"

Ricky said nothing. Hands resting on thighs, finger yet pointing, clutching the peach so tight, Lee knew, he'd bruised the delicate red and orange innards.

Lee rubbed at a coffee-cup stain on the desk he didn't need in the office he didn't need in the cabin where he'd been raised after his momma momma stepped on a nail poking out from a rotten board in the yard and, later, after her foot swoll like a water-filled carnival balloon, died. No government folks around to carry off an orphaned nigger those days, but a white couple calling themselves missionaries, who prayed straight to a crucified Jesus hanging on their wall, brought Lee the boy out of Freedom Hills and into the far western reaches of Elberta County. Momma Pat and Mr. Robin were against plenty kinds of fun, but not against singing and guitar-playing—so long as it was for God's glory. Lee hisself never came around to this way of believing, to becoming what the church folks called a True Believer. Neither did Mr. Prince. Once, after Lee'd started working at The Peach Pit, he asked Mr. Prince if he ever felt guilty for faking in church. "The joy I get is real," Mr. Prince said. Same with Lee and music, with Mr. Robin teaching Lee the boy how to hunt the woods, with Momma Pat teaching him how to grow a big giving garden, how to cook what you grew in any season so it tasted better than just something you could simply stomach. The joy was real. For this, and for a gapped roof over his head all those years and now, Lee Malone was grateful—even if hunting wasn't the same anymore, and he had nobody to cook for but hisself and the fool dog panting ninety-to-nothing underneath the cabin, and he hadn't picked up his guitar Rosette since Maybelle died almost three months ago. The only place other than church where a black man was welcome to play and sing anyhow was a decommissioned riverbarge turned beer joint called Roger's Lounge.

"That Snell kid'll be running it this year," Lee said. "Big-old boy. I remember his daddy too." Conquistadors football could always draw Ricky Birdsong out of his moods. The sport had ruined but also made him—and here you were nothing if not what you came from. "Well, maybe they'll be alright," Lee said then took a long drink of coke-cola.

Out the window he could see a picker hacking at briar and beggar-weed. The orchardfield could grow over fast. Another picker toting baskets down at the fruit stand, where a box truck was backed up to the loading bay. Lee had worked up an agreement to deliver fresh peaches to a grocery store down in Bankhead next season. The box truck an investment on this deal, which he hoped would yet hold up. Feared it would not after his recent stint in the Elberta County Jail. Don't ever give them a reason, his momma momma used to say. And look here what Lee Malone had done. Whole town talking. There was no changing what he'd done. Like Lee told the sheriff, he wasn't fixing to just leave Maybelle's body out there in them woods.

Down by the road stood a giant fiberglass peach Lee had put in before last season. Folks loved making pictures with the peach, hugging the big-old sucker best they could reach around it, especially during the Hernando de Soto Peach Days Festival, when a parade brought oodles and oodles of folks out to the orchard and fruit stand. Beach traffic had been good this year too. None of those folks knew Lee Malone's personal business. They bought baskets upon baskets of ripe Elberta peaches to eat on the sugar-white sand rimming the Gulf of Mexico. There'd be one more rush of tourists come Labor Day. Maybe his last.

Lee was surprised how many folks came to The Peach Pit after what happened during this year's Peach Days parade. Or so Ren Treeborne told it when he came by the jail with a sack of banana-and-mayonnaise sandwiches. They ate and listened to Pedro Hannah. His report didn't mention Tammy, what she'd done, only Lee Malone's arrest on suspicion of foul play in the death of Maybelle Chambliss Treeborne. Doc Barfield had been by to tend Lee's ear, which felt like somebody had gobbed it up with honey. The gunshots so loud. Time Pedro was ready to go off-air for the night, Ren nearly had Aaron Guthrie convinced to let Lee leave under house arrest. Seemed like the sheriff didn't truly believe Lee would hurt Maybelle either. But he worried what the *Times-Journal* would say. Outside a reporter lurked. Ren hung around till morning light, Lee telling him to get on and rest. But go where, rest what for? Ren had troubles of his own. Lee hated seeing a young man thisaway, especially one as good as Ren Treeborne.

"Well," he said to Ricky, and took another drink. The coke-cola made him thirstier. He wanted to splash whiskey into it, but he wouldn't drink that stuff in front of the boy. It wasn't right to think of Ricky Birdsong as a boy. But Lee did. A dirt dauber landed on Ricky's hand, hunting the peach in his fist. Lee reached into his shirtpocket and adjusted a dial on the little box till he could hear the dauber's shiny buzzing wings. "Hotter than Hades," he said, a little too loud. Then quieter: "I don't reckon it was so hot this time last year, was it?"

Ricky said nothing. Like talking to a wall, Lee thought, remembering his momma momma saying the same exact thing about his daddy. That and, he knew I couldn't stay mad no more if he banged on the piano, the sorry-ass devil. The instrument was still in the house when Lee's momma momma died from the rusty nail, when Momma Pat and Mr. Robin came for Lee the boy. In good condition too for an instrument from before the war. Lee had no memory of how the piano came to be. Far as he knew it had always been—just like the bald bluff that gave Freedom Hills its name. The piano stood tall and upright against the newspapered wall. Lee the boy begged Momma Pat and Mr. Robin to bring it. Instead Mr. Robin carved the boy a guitar and strung it with dried animal guts. Lee the boy had never touched a guitar, but his hands knew where to go, like a piglet knows how to find a sow's hard plum-colored teat. One Sunday service the True Believers got so touched by the Lord they fell upon Lee the boy playing his homemade guitar at the altar and broke the instrument into a hundred pieces while hollering hallelujah-glory-be-hallelujah-to-the-Lamb. When the service ended Mr. Robin glued the pieces back together, prayed the instrument dry, then restrung it.

A few years after he'd been taken by the white couple Lee the boy returned to the four warped walls between which he'd been born. The house had been plundered and smelled like old piss. A small black turd lay curled on the floor where Lee the boy used to play with the cornhusk dolls his momma momma tied—way she did for herself and her siblings as a slavegirl in Marion. The piano, Lee discovered, had been busted and burnt as kindling. Its ivory keys and steel strings toted off. He found a fake jade comb melted in the cold fireash. Knocked the comb against his britches a few times. His momma momma used to brush his hair with it in quick short yanks that made him shiver all over. Momma Pat now kept Lee's hair shaved down to the itchy scalp, and Mr. Robin would play at using the boy's head to clean mud off his boots.

Lee watched as Ricky Birdsong slowly raised his sticky fist and bit into the peach it held. Juice trickled down his chin as he chewed like a bored steer, considering whatever it was that he couldn't, for the life of him, seem to speak.

"Just tell me," Lee said. He fiddled with the wire connecting the little box in his shirtpocket to the bulb inside his earhole. "I can't do nothing son if you won't tell me."

Maybelle would know what to do. The thought drove into Lee again and again. He wished he could just ask her. He didn't believe in prayer, in talking to God or to the dead by shutting your eyes tight and mumbling under your breath. He believed that doing what you loved to do was near as you'd get to communicating with anybody on this earth or beyond. And look what Lee'd done. Look what he was doing. Hadn't sang since her funeral, didn't play Rosette. Forget trying to come up with a new song. He hadn't written a new song in years.

Buckshot came inside and lapped water from a cereal bowl, tongue flashing against the yellowed ceramic. He trotted over and nosed Ricky, then sat down and thumped the underside of his chin four times.

"Let me give you a ride over at the house then," Lee said.

Buckshot sat between them on the bench seat. Lee waved at Raul and Pee-Po sharing a jug of water in some shade as he steered the pickup onto the road. They'd just passed the Quik-Stop when a line of pickup trucks came flying from the opposite direction. Buckshot barked at the hounds standing atop toolboxes and leaning over the sides of the truck-beds. Lee recognized most every vehicle in this line and the white faces behind the dirty windshields. Ren Treeborne brought up the tail end,

Wooten Ragsdale sitting passenger. Lee stopped in the middle of the road and spoke to them.

"Where's the fire at?" he said. Buckshot leaned over, panting for attention, and Lee shoved the dog back with his elbow. "What say Woot?"

Ren stuck his head out the window. "Tammy's gone missing. Ain't been home for several days. Hey now Ricky."

Ricky didn't acknowledge Ren. He'd eaten the peach and now held its wrinkled brown pit in his hand. He popped the pit in his mouth and sucked like it was candy.

"Let me drop him off and I'll meet you," Lee said.

"You don't got to."

"I'm coming," Lee said.

"Well, we appreciate it."

Wooten leaned forward and placed his bad hand on the dashboard. Gave a grim nod. Lee nodded back then pulled away.

He patted Ricky's leg and turned up the radio. He recognized the song being played but couldn't remember its name. So memory sometimes went. Tammy'd gone missing. The bulb in his ear whistled and Lee adjusted the dial on the box. Words wormed up from out of his head, words of his own making, and he began to sing: *Bleary-eyed and lonesome, out in Freedom Hills, wondering when they'll carry me to The Elberta County Jail* . . . Filtered through whatever machinery was hidden within the glass bulb, his voice disagreed with the tune. Sounded less him. Time he got to a chorus, Lee couldn't stand hearing himself thisaway and hushed.

He parked among a herd of lawn mowers. Some broken down for parts, others rusted orange brown and forever seized up. Elberta County High School let Ricky Birdsong keep his best mowers in its shop building in exchange for mowing the ballfields. The kids in shop class did all sorts of meanness to Ricky when he came to retrieve or deposit one. As punishment they wrote winding sentences assigned by a teacher who couldn't pronounce his *r*s when he got angry. Getting the teacher riled up was part of the kids' fun too. They loved asking the teacher about turkey hunting, turning red-faced as he recounted waiting in the woods for a gobbler to walk out in front of him and show its fat breast.

The Birdsong house was cinder block and built underneath a towering black walnut tree. The air smelled bitter with rotting nuts. Time, the house was also Mrs. Birdsong's flower shop. Silk remains and busted green foam blocks yet scattered the property bordering a never-named creek. Ricky opened the front door and Buckshot ran inside. Lee remembered when cemetery flowers were made of delicate crepe paper and dipped in wax to protect them from rain. Roses, peonies, gladiolas, dahlias. Pretty enough to eat. Mrs. Birdsong's shop was called Flowers Para Los Muertos. She claimed Spanish bloodlines, way many in the valley do. But Elbertans shortened the name to Debra's Place rather than trip over their tongues. Around Decoration there'd be a line down the road. Ronnie Birdsong would make slabs of peanut brittle to share with those waiting for something to put on their loved ones' graves.

Ricky went to the bathroom and shut the door. Lee stepped over sports magazines and old copies of the *Times-Journal* on his way to the refrigerator he'd given Ricky when Dyar's Tamale Shop got a new one. An open pack of pink baloney meat, loafbread, half-used jar of mustard, jug of spoiled milk. Lee'd let bringing over groceries slip amid all else that'd happened this summer. And now Tammy was missing. Seemed it did rain and pour. Lee knew the sheriff, knew everybody, would be asking him about this before long. One reason why he'd volunteered to join the search party. The other reason being Maybelle herself.

He walked out back to the patio and opened a deep freezer. Running low too, he saw, moving around packets of freezerburnt meat from animals he'd shot and cleaned, other cuts he'd bought at Beachy's Butcher Shop. Lee worried Ricky would burn down the house one day while trying to cook for hisself. The boy was forgetful even before the injury and the volunteer fire station was on the other side of town. But what could Lee do? He kept up a constant negotiation about protecting Ricky and letting him live on his own terms. Lee started counting the packets, doing math in his head. He was nearly through when he noticed something down at the bottom of the freezer. He grabbed ahold and pulled till it came loose.

He unballed an ice-crusted longsleeved black shirt and draped it on a folding chair then leaned back down in the freezer. Something else. He grabbed and pulled. His hand slipped and his elbow banged the side. He hunted for something to chip the ice. Nothing he could find but silk flowers and fishing poles. He grabbed ahold again and pulled. This time the fabric ripped. He unballed a piece of camouflage britches, laid it out by the shirt he'd freed then tried to imagine what would make Ricky Birdsong stuff his clothes down inside a deep freezer. When was the last time he'd even seen the boy? Before Peach Days, was it not? And that, what, a week or more? Maybelle's funeral for sure. He remembered Ricky Birdsong being there. Hell, Ricky dug her grave. But that was months ago.

What worried Lee Malone was the idea that there was no root cause to Ricky Birdsong's behavior. This just another sign of something they'd known to be coming since the boy was knocking heads on the football field while they all roared as if there'd be no tomorrow. Something confirmed when Ricky was sent back home from college in Mississippi on a big silver bus after falling out during one of the first practices. Ten years they'd pretended otherwise. Given him work, food, carried him home when he turned up somewhere lost. Ten seasons the Conquistadors presented him with a peach home jersey that said BIRDSONG on back above the number 42. Everybody in the bleachers chanted, Fly, Ricky, Fly! Fly, Ricky, Fly! and clapped and hollered even louder when Coach Williams gave a speech that was, truth, a eulogy, like all this aftermath was beauty to behold.

The ice had melted. The clothes hung limp on the chairback, little pool of water beneath them. Lee resituated the meatpackets then shut the deep freezer. He picked up the clothes to head inside and ask Ricky about them. Doing so, he stepped in the icemelt. It was, he noticed then, tinted pink. He squeezed the clothes and pink water ran down his wrists. He searched the fabric till he found one vein of yet unmelted ice colored dark red, almost black. He picked with his thumbnail, rubbed till the ice melted, and blood smeared on his skin.

He could hear water running, pipes buzzing inside hollow walls, as he made his way through the dark house. Buckshot was pawing at the bathroom door. The hall carpet soggy-wet. Lee jiggled the doorhandle. "Ricky, Ricky," he said. "Open this up!" No answer came but for running water. He hunted for something heavy. At the side of the house he found a garden hoe. He hacked around the doorhandle till the door gave.

The water in the tub looked like weak tea. Ricky hisself had turned a light purple underneath his eyelids and around his mouth. Lee pulled the boy out and began pumping his chest. He pushed back Ricky's lips. Something was blocking the airway. He pried apart Ricky's teeth and ran his hand down the boy's fishy throat. Something lodged there. Buckshot pawed Ricky and whimpered and shivered. Lee counted to three then shoved his fingers in the boy's mouth, deep as they'd go. Ricky convulsed as if touched by a live-wire. Lee plunged deeper yet. Buckshot barked, a high-pitched aarf aarf! Lee was in up to his knuckles when he got ahold of the thing and pulled it out. The goddamn peach pit. He dropped it in the sink and let it rattle down the drain.

After Ricky stopped puking Lee blew fresh air into his lungs. He turned off the bathtub faucet and unstoppered the drain. The pipes gurgled, bringing Lee back to handling Maybelle's body the day she died. He thought about how little Janie Treeborne'd helped wash her grandmomma. First that, now her aunt. Lord lord lord.

Lee stripped off Ricky's wet clothes then toted him to bed. He wrapped the boy in a quilt. Buckshot jumped up onto the bed and licked Ricky's forehead till Lee made the dog quit. He wondered if he should let Ricky sleep. The dog settled down with a grunt then began washing his own big paws. Ricky fought loose from the quilt. "This summer," Lee said, tucking Ricky back in, "it just ain't going to let up is it."

Every so often Lee placed his hand on the boy's chest and felt it rise and fall, rise, fall, rise. Ricky kept struggling loose from the quilt. Once when the boy had, Lee noticed a red mark in the shape of teeth on his arm. Looked no more than a few days old. "Good Lord have mercy," he said, petting the boy's still-wet head. "What have you done?"

Peach Days

1958

Folks put out chairs and buckets the night before to save spots from which they could watch the Hernando de Soto Peach Days Festival parade putter past. But Ren Treeborne was buddies with Gene Kilgore, who roped off the sidewalk in front of his pawnshop, iced down beer and grilled hamburgers and hot dogs, meaning Ren could avoid the rush to save spots.

Before heading to the parade he needed to make one final pass through the cottage Maybelle had rented from Lee Malone after Hugh died. The place was sorry with memory. Squirrels nested in the attic and the crumbling plaster walls. Ren had saved for last his momma's clothes, which yet smelled like the coconut lotion Luther bought her from a mail-order catalog. Time, Maybelle cared about the way she dressed. Her more recent outfits could be confused with something used to cover windows or a tabletop though.

Ren taped a box shut then toted it to the living room where Sister sat fooling with the dirt boy Crusoe. A vehicle pulled up out front. Tammy was all done up for the holiday, wearing a linen dress with sequined peaches strung along the neckline.

"Lord at this place," she said.

"Grab a drawer," Ren said, emptying the contents of one onto the bed. "Just about through."

Instead Tammy wandered into the kitchen. She turned on the faucet and brown water petered out. When they were kids she complained without end about living way out on The Seven. Begged to move into town. Civilization, she called it. Tammy was a Treeborne to the bone though. She needed wilderness, space, even as she denied it. The proof was in her and Wooten's decision to now build on the land she once tried to refuse.

"Ever remember her wearing this one?" Ren asked, holding up a pale blue dress. "I can't tell the difference no more."

"It nearly looks good in here with all the mess cleaned out," Tammy said.

"You hear from Luth?"

"I went by the veterans' hall yesterday."

"I wish he'd just come stay with me," Ren said.

"Where at? The dam?"

"Or he could stay here. Lee wouldn't care."

Tammy adjusted her bra strap. "Maybe Luther'll learn something from this," she said. "Bad as it seems, a cleansing can be good." She fooled with her hair and smacked her lips at a window reflection. "Oh, you won't believe what happened the other day."

"What?"

"Woot come out the front door and there was something like a mannequin on the porch."

"A what?"

"Tumped over and like to knocked him down." Tammy pointed at Janie where she sat with the dirt boy Crusoe. "Looked kindly like a bigger one of them."

"I'll be," Ren said. "How you reckon it got there?"

"Don't know."

"Kids probably," he said. "You know how wound up they get come Peach Days. Remember that time in school when you and them Bryant girls—"

"Ren, back then's ancient history to me."

Janie toted Crusoe outside before she betrayed herself. Did her aunt
Tammy know? So what if she did? The girl was mad at herself for caring. She longed to be reckless as she felt this summer. She'd tried so hard
to stop her aunt and uncle from logging The Seven to build that stupid
new house. At first Jon D. Crews even helped. They poured water into
the gas cans and the bulldozer her uncle Wooten had borrowed from
Orville Knight. Jon D. assured her the engines wouldn't run afterward.
Lie, Janie thought the next day as she watched the chain saw roar. Did
smoke a little more than usual, quit two-three times, but that was all.
Next they set loose a bunch of snakes in the clear-cut early one morning.
None of them were poisonous—Jon D.'s condition. The snakes either
slithered right back into the woods or just lay there till Wooten came
along and lopped off their heads. Janie heard her uncle making fun of
Lyle Crews, ignorant to why the boy would not help kill the snakes.

Crusoe had begged Janie to quit this mess—told her what they
needed to be doing was toting the art down at the spring.

Janie ignored the dirt boy's plea. Toting art? She was one-tracked,
believing she could stop this change to The Seven her way yet. "Besides,"
she told him, "we ain't supposed to move them assemblies from where
Granddaddy Hugh put them." This had always been her grandmomma's
one rule about playing in what she called the junk garden. Janie wasn't
fixing to break it now that her grandmomma wasn't around.

Summer'd wound on. Janie wasted afternoons with Jon D. at the
baseball field—a cracked table of orange clay on the westside of town.
For bleachers the town'd set up hard boards on upright cinder blocks,
and built two chickenwire dugouts with tin roofs along either crook-
edly chalked baseline. Feedsacks filled with riversand passed for bases
on an infield littered with sharp rocks washed down from a knob rising
just beyond third. Jon D. and the other boys didn't give a rip about the
field's condition. They'd of played on broken glass. In sports the line between winning and losing was clearly marked. Bunch of Elberta County
boys had a say in how things turned out. For the rest of their lives they'd
carry the puckered scars and swoll joints and offset bones to remind
themselves it had, for a glorious time, been thisaway.

Only time Janie could get her mind away from what was happening to The Seven was when she and Jon D. rode his motorcycle down at The Washout—a deep slough hemmed between sandstone bluffs where older kids partied and sometimes camped. Janie and Jon D. would strip down to their drawers. She'd paddle out while he climbed the bluffs, took off running then jumped—arms and legs windmilling till he splashed into water warm as piss. She counted Mississippi how long it took him to come back up. Owls roosting in some pines kept time with her and, come dark, the birds swooped out to hunt. Most nights Janie and Jon D. stayed long after stars had spilled across the sky like sugar on a counter. They'd float on their backs, lakewater lapping up against their heads and blurring the edges of their sight.

It was down at The Washout in early July when Jon D. told Janie that a dope shipment had gone missing. Lyle had swapped vehicles with Big Connie Ward's mechanic, same as usual, and drove down to Livingstown. Nothing was packed inside though. Not up underneath the engine, not in the door panels, not between the cab and the bed. Way Jon D. told it, Van and Lyle tore the entire vehicle apart hunting for the missing dope. So far they'd kept this secret from Big Connie Ward by giving him some money Van had saved. But Elberta's dope supply was drying up, and Big Connie's patience with it.

"Lyle says him and Goodnight might just run off."

"Where to?" Janie asked.

"Somewhere that ain't here. He asked me to borrow money."

"You going to let him?"

"Ain't got none," Jon D. said. "I bought me a new glove."

"Uncle Woot's paying him."

"Ain't enough," Jon D. said.

It occurred to Janie then that she might could pay Lyle Crews to sabotage her aunt and uncle. At least buy some time. She didn't get much further than that though. Next she went over at The Seven, Wooten had plowed Hugh's assemblies into the edge of the woods so he could level ground for the new house's foundation.

After discovering what her uncle had done, Janie toted Crusoe into the studio and they sprawled out on the ground. That's it, she thought. Her granddaddy's incomplete history loomed overhead. Looking up at it was like looking down at the valley from some great height. *History* an insufficient word, but the one the Treebornes used. Time had been brought together at once in this enormous assemblie. One unfinished area of paint-spackled clay and glass, Janie thought, looked like a face if you stared long enough. As she did a new idea began percolating. Time she got up off the ground the girl knew what she had to do.

She finished most of the work in a four-day spurt down by the spring while Crusoe stood watch. Never set out for the thing to look like her grandmomma, but as Janie Treeborne drank from the cold spring where tadpoles shivered next to the bank, as she squatted behind bushes and scratched dirt overtop her hard black leavings, as mosquitoes sucked her blood and she did not squash them, she began to feel a particular wildness that manifested itself in the thing she made and called Her.

"Gives me the creeps," Jon D. said when she showed him.

"You going to help me move Her or not?" Her weighed, Janie bet, close to a hundred pounds.

"Where's the lady parts at? God them teeth Janie."

"Jon D.," she said.

"Okay, but we ought to wait for dark."

Her was good and hard; Janie'd made sure. Yet the girl worried the thing'd come apart during the move. Clouds had spread across the sky like jelly under a knife. Heat lightning pulsed on occasion. Rain could ruin Her—and, in turn, Janie's last-ditch plan.

She and Jon D. could see light from the television through a window in the singlewide trailer. Wooten probably watching Thursday night wrestling. Another yellow light illuminated the scummy surface of the aboveground swimming pool where her aunt Tammy liked to lay on the deck and tan her legs. Janie had offended her aunt no telling how many times by turning down offers to come over and swim. The girl didn't understand why you'd choose a pool over De Soto Lake or the Elberta River.

They lifted Her and started toward the trailer, staggering under the weight as if they were a couple sots from Hernando's Hideaway. Martin ran up, but he didn't bark. They somehow mounted the porchsteps without alerting Wooten to their presence. Jon D. was for laying Her out like a dead body, but Janie convinced him to get some rope instead. They rigged Her upright against the door then hustled back down to the road, the hard-packed dirt now covered with toadfrogs hoping for rain. In their despair some were eating others, legs kicking out of mouths. Martin grabbed one fat toadfrog and toted it back to his hiding spot under the porch. Beyond the hills thunder rumbled a yet dry promise. Jon D. and Janie got on his motorcycle. She braced Crusoe between them. On they roared, Jon D. Crews laughing his head off. This night all in fun for him. But for Janie Treeborne it wasn't a far leap to much more serious behavior.

When Janie came back inside the cottage, her aunt Tammy had stopped folding clothes and was eating boiled peanuts from a bag. "Sister, that thing's got you filthy," she said. "And it Peach Days. Come on let me clean you up."

She followed her aunt into the bathroom. Tammy took Crusoe and set him in the tub. A spider hurried down the drain. Janie caught sight of the pistol in Tammy's purse when she took a handkerchief out. Sheriff Guthrie must of given the pistol back since taking it the day they found Maybelle's body on The Seven.

"Feels like me and you ain't seen each other in forever," Tammy said, dabbing her niece's cheek with spit.

"Yeah."

"Woot sees you poking around The Seven all time though."

"Uh-huh," Janie said.

"I worry over you Sister. I know it's hard having your daddy at the dam so much. He's a good man though." Tammy licked her thumb then rubbed a spot on her niece's orange dress. She glanced at Crusoe, who'd slumped down in the bathtub as if he might follow the spider's path. "Folks'll get the wrong idea about you toting that thing around," Tammy said. "And I can tell you too, the hardest thing to change is a mind once it's been set."

They loaded the last boxes of Maybelle's belongings into Ren's pickup truck. What wouldn't fit went in back of Tammy's, alongside her water-meter-checking equipment. A square shovel, six rolls of orange flagging, a few gummed-up wrenches. Ren took out his billfold and a pack of Blue Mountain cigarettes from the glove box. He lit one then put the pack back where it'd been—right on top of a copy of Maybelle's will. Janie'd found the document while prowling one day while her daddy went in the Quik-Stop:

> *I, Maybelle Treeborne, being of sound mind and memory, do this twelfth day of March, 1957, declare this document to be My Final Will and Testament.*
>
> *I give all my possessions and property to my only daughter, Tammy Treeborne Ragsdale. If she is deceased at the time of this document's execution, I give all my possessions and property to her husband, my son-in-law, Wooten Ragsdale. To my sons, Ren and Luther Treeborne, I leave five dollars each—and any of their daddy's old junk they may want and can find.*

Tammy offered Janie the boiled peanuts. The girl shook her head no. She loved boiled peanuts but would of rather eaten rat poison that moment. She knew her aunt had put her grandmomma up to writing the will. MawMaw May would never be so hateful. The Seven was supposed to be split equal among the kids. Everybody in the family knew that. Janie's daddy had promised part of The Seven would one day belong to her. Now she doubted it would.

The Elberta County High School marching band came past the cottage, tuning their instruments for the parade. It was time to go.

"You want to stand with us Tam?" Ren asked.

"I'm meeting Woot. Y'all have fun though. This ought to be one for the books."

On the way to the parade Janie and her daddy passed by The Fencepost Cafe. The front door was propped open with a brick, letting escape the smell of frying bacon and butter biscuits. Somebody had The Peach turned up loud, and every stool facing the window was taken up by bleary-eyed big-talkers and bullshitters and used-to-bes who were trying to defeat hangovers of this magnitude or that. They all greeted Ren when he ducked inside for a coffee and a biscuit to-go, leaving Janie and Crusoe on the sidewalk.

Folks funneling toward the square gave strange looks to the girl and the dirt boy she held in her arms. Janie watched her daddy pass beneath framed peach-and-white jerseys, and pictures of old Conquistadors hung on the restaurant's walls. Pictures of hisself, Big Connie Ward, Van Crews, Ricky Birdsong, Uncle Luther, other Conquistadors the girl knew and some she did not. Willy Ramsey was trying to get Ren to sit. He shrugged Willy off though, came back out and put his arm around Janie, and they kept on toward the square.

The crowd bottlenecked at the corner of Madrid and De Soto. Ren blew into the wax paper cup. He held an egg-and-cheese biscuit toward Janie. She shook her head no. Day before the parade the floats lined up at the old riverdocks. They paraded up through downtown, pausing at the square for the announcement of Miss Elberta Peach before going on out to The Peach Pit. Around midnight everybody would head over at the ballfield to watch the first Elberta County High School Conquistadors practice of the season in buggy light cast by vehicles parked around the sidelines and behind each end zone.

Ren and Janie squeezed through the crowd toward the pawnshop. Gene Kilgore shook Ren's hand and said hello to the girl. A stage had been built underneath the statue of Hernando de Soto. Gene's Pawn & Gun was a prime viewing position. Standing on the stage was Mayor Karl Hearn and the five high school girls vying to be the next Miss Elberta Peach. The girls wore crushed dresses of different light colors, and their hair and faces were done up to a tee. Smiling like loony birds at the crowd gathered below them in the grass and on the sidewalks. Behind the girls stood the ECHS marching band. When the lead parade vehicle turned the corner, the uniformed kids struck up "Fight, Fight, Fight On You Conquistadors!" and everybody whooped and clapped and sang along.

"There it comes," Ren said, squeezing Janie's shoulder.

She tried to act excited for her daddy's sake as Lee Malone waved from behind the wheel of an orchard truck and tossed handfuls of hard candy into the crowd. This was tradition, The Peach Pit orchard truck leading the parade, established by Mr. Prince before he died. Even the girl noticed Lee was the only black person who participated in the parade. All the faces in the crowd white too. In back of the orchard truck waited Miss Elberta Peach's throne—stacked haybales under a threaded arbor of peach tree branches.

The first floats followed the orchard truck. Washed-and-shined show vehicles followed them. Then folks steering tractors and riding lawn mowers, motorcycles, antique wagons, anything that rolled, really, followed by folks walking prize heifers and hogs, a strange herd of yellow-eyed billy goats with brass bells a-clanging, Boy Scouts and social clubs toting banners and flags, various church groups, and on till the end.

When the parade halted, Mayor Hearn stepped up to the microphone. He tapped it and a screech shot out through the square. The mayor apologized then began reading from a stack of index cards slid out from his coat pocket:

"Welcome to our annual Hernando de Soto Peach Days Festival. Sure is good seeing so many of y'all here with us. I know it's hot. We thank you for coming out.

"Now the time's come to crown our new Miss Elberta Peach! We'd like to thank each and every one of these beautiful young ladies up here. Give them a hand folks!"

The mayor went on. Janie tuned him out. The girl'd never given a rip about Miss Elberta Peach. She and MawMaw May used to make fun of these girls. Wouldn't know a snake if one raised up and bit them, Maybelle would say. And Janie would laugh while her momma, Nita—who'd vied for Miss Elberta Peach her senior year—glared. Her momma was skipping out on the parade this year. The girl wasn't sure why. She'd heard her aunt say to her daddy that Nita seemed awfully depressed.

Janie scanned the crowd for folks she knew. There stood boys from Jon D.'s baseball team selling raffle tickets for an Italian-made shotgun.

Jon D. hisself wasn't with them. Janie hadn't seen him since the night
they left Her on Tammy and Wooten's porch. The Wards stood in some
shade next to the post office. Big Connie dressed in full De Soto outfit
and Pud, his son, digging in his nostril like he might strike oil. Janie
spotted her uncle Luther and some other veterans sitting on a bench.
Looked like they'd been drinking watery beers all morning down at the
hall, where Luther was living since his house burnt down, while they
watched old war movies till the film melted and the reels had to be
thrown out. She spotted her aunt Tammy and uncle Wooten near where
Lee Malone had stopped the truck. A man trying to get a better view of
the stage spilled booze on Janie's boots. Crusoe let his mouth fall open
and the man backed off. "You devil," Janie whispered in the dirt boy's
snail-shell ear.

"This year's Miss Elberta Peach," the mayor continued. "This year's
Miss Elberta Peach is June Renee Bishop!"

The marching band struck up the fight song once again while June
Renee made a real show, Janie thought, of winning. June Renee was a
tall girl and so stooped when the mayor placed the crown on her blond
head. Somebody from the *Times-Journal* took pictures. The marching
band parted so the mayor could lead June Renee offstage. Lee Malone
let down the tailgate then set up a stepladder so Miss Elberta Peach could
climb up onto her throne. June Renee waved and waved and waved as
she mounted those steps. Meanwhile Lee slid behind the wheel to whisk
her off to The Peach Pit, where she'd pose for more pictures with little
girls who aimed to grow up and be just like her one day. Made Janie
want to puke. Before Lee could put the truck in gear though, Sheriff
Guthrie grabbed him by the elbow. After a brief exchange the sheriff
gestured for Lee to get out of the truck.

"Son of a bitch," Ren said, stepping off the sidewalk and into the crowd.

Janie pushed toward De Soto then used a bench to climb up onto
the statue's base. From there she could see that Deputy Polk had got
behind the wheel of the orchard truck. He was trying to pull away,
but folks pressed in to congratulate June Renee Bishop till the deputy
had nowhere to go. Meantime the sheriff was leading Lee Malone to his

cruiser parked at the corner of Water Avenue. Their path had been blocked by the marching band though. Janie spotted her daddy, who stood a head taller than most everybody, moving toward the sheriff and Lee. She spotted her aunt headed the same direction. Tammy had her right hand shoved down inside the purse slung on her left shoulder and moved with a purpose that Janie understood in her gut before her mind.

Tammy pushed through the marching band, hand still hidden in that purse, till she could of almost touched Lee Malone's back, then she pulled out the pistol and aimed at his head. There was such wild cheering, such crashing of cymbals and tooting of horns, that nobody heard the first deafening shot. Two more quickly followed. The sheriff wrestled the pistol away from Tammy as the marching band cascaded to a halt. Folks who could do so dropped flat on their faces. Others tried running, but there was nowhere to go in the crowded square. The statue Janie held to tightly rang a long clear note.

After a brief delay the Hernando de Soto Peach Days Festival parade went on as planned. Accounts of what had happened varied. Somehow nobody made flesh was hit. The next day's *Times-Journal* would run a picture of the dimple in De Soto's bronzed back though, right next to the picture of June Renee Bishop's crowning. A bullet was found lodged in the wall of Gene's Pawn & Gun as well. Gene would not fill the hole with putty for weeks so folks could gawk, maybe buy something while they were there. Nothing could be said for sure, everyone there agreed. But not a soul claimed he'd seen Tammy Treeborne Ragsdale pull a pistol out of her purse, and fire it at Lee Malone's head.

Not a soul except Janie Treeborne herself.

※

After the parade Ren sent Janie on to The Peach Pit with her aunt and uncle while he went down at the jail with Lee Malone. The girl got loose from Tammy and Wooten soon as she could though. Wasn't hard to do among the Peach Days crowd. She toted Crusoe across the road to Lee's house, hoping to find evidence that proved he had nothing to do with her grandmomma's death. Janie knew what folks thought. But she didn't know what she was looking for, which led her to give up and listen to Lee's recording instead. She mashed a button on the player then set down the needle, just like Lee'd taught her to do.

I don't go to church on Sunday if I'm hungover from Saturday night . . . The needle hit a scratch and jumped ahead in the song. *Ain't no substitute for you, no there ain't no substitute for you.*

Even his voice would not soothe her. She wanted to scream. Buckshot could sense this too. The dog licked the back of Janie's hand. First her aunt'd logged The Seven, started building that new house, and now she'd tried to shoot Lee Malone in front of the whole damn town. And nobody'd done a thing about it! Put Lee in jail. For what? The only way to prove what happened in those woods, Janie thought, was by being there.

She turned to Crusoe. "Were you not?" she said. "Tell me, tell me did you not see!"

The dirt boy wouldn't answer.

None of us were there, she thought. Died alone. Scared and, for some reason, trying to haul a big metal box out of the woods.

When the recording ended Janie told Buckshot to come on. She could see a fire burning up near the water tower. Voices announcing themselves in the night. She was dying to tell Jon D. what she'd seen during the parade, but he was stocking the fruit stand. Meantime, she'd find somebody else to tell about what her aunt had done.

Buckshot trotted in front with his tail held confident. Passing clouds played moonlight shadows across the tall grass. Janie recognized some of the voices around the fire. But not in time to stop the dog from wandering right up to Lyle Crews.

"What you doing out here dog?" Lyle said.

"Ain't it that nigger Lee Malone's?" Pud Ward asked.

Lyle grabbed a stick out of the fire. He knocked off the ashy end, exposing a glowing tip, then took Buckshot by the tail. "Y'all ever seen a scalded dog before?"

Pud and some of the other kids laughed. Lyle pulled Buckshot closer and moved in with the hot stick. Janie hollered and stepped into the firelight.

"Look at baby with her doll," Goodnight said.

Janie shot the older girl a bird and told Lyle to let go.

"Don't get yourself in a damn tizzy," he said but let go of the dog's tail. Buckshot slunk up to Janie then trotted back down to the house. Lyle poked the stick back in the fire. "You want a beer?"

"Yeah," Janie said.

The beer tasted like soap. She plugged the opening with her tongue whenever she sipped. She listened at the older kids talk, watched them get drunk. A few climbed partway up the water tower. Afraid to go all the way to the top. There were several cars parked along the ridge. Every so often a head or two feet appeared in silhouette through fogged rear windows.

Pud Ward lurched up from the ground. "Who wants to go riding?"

Most of the kids weren't interested. But those who were piled into Pud's red pickup truck, the fat boy hisself behind the wheel. Janie and Crusoe sat up front next to an acne-scarred kid she did not know, Lyle and Goodnight and a few others rode in back and chucked empties at road signs.

Pud wanted to talk about the Peach Days shooting. He was slurring his words. "Reckon it was somebody after Miss Elberta Peach?"

"No," Janie said.

The other kid in the cab wondered aloud what a kid like Janie would know anyhow.

"I ain't a kid," she said.

This kid and Pud both laughed.

Lyle slapped the roof as they approached De Soto Bridge. Pud stopped and everybody jumped out. The county was repainting the guardrails. Lyle picked up an orange safety barrel and chucked it over the side. The barrel sounded like a cannon going off when it hit the Elberta River. Goodnight got Janie to help with the next one. Then she showed the girl how to take a paint can and explode it against the pavement. Truth, it was satisfying. Sky-blue paint splattered up onto Janie's dress, her legs,

her black rubber boots. Another vehicle came over the hill. They all
jumped back into the truck and Pud peeled out.

When Lyle next slapped the roof Pud pulled off into a ditch. They
all piled out and headed across a yard toward what was left of Janie's
Uncle Luther's cabin. A heater for his tropical flowers, the fire department had decided, must of tumped over in the night and caught fire to
a rug. An accident. Had Luther not passed out at the veterans' hall that
night he would of burnt up along with everything else he owned.

"Damn at all them plants," Pud Ward said, stepping over busted pots
that Janie and her daddy had already sifted through to see if any roots
survived. Big-old plants with inappropriate blooms Luther'd brought
home from the Pacific, or bought from the mail-order catalogs he kept
piled on the floor next to the commode.

Lyle kicked the ashes till he found a melted hunk of the surfboard
Luther had brought back from the service—he'd threatened to surf the
Elberta River itself. Never did. Lyle whacked a charred wall, and ash
sprinkled onto Goodnight's curly hair. She smeared some onto Lyle's face.
He grabbed her waist and smeared ash onto her throat and her chest.
They played around like this for a few minutes then started kissing. Lyle
pulled Goodnight into the woods, and most of the other kids started
walking back toward town.

Pud and Janie sat on the rock steps and waited for the couple to return. The fat boy cleared his throat till he'd done so enough times to
come up with something to say. "Heard they took Lee Malone to jail
over what happened to your grandmomma."

Janie didn't respond.

"Daddy says she wasn't in her right mind no more."

"Your daddy don't know shit," Janie said.

Lyle and Goodnight eventually emerged from the darkness like
wounded soldiers. He sat on the steps and she fell onto his lap.

"How many days now baby?" she asked.

"Daddy'll come after y'all," Pud said. "I'm telling you."

"Fuck your daddy, fat boy," Lyle said. "We'll go so far off till he can't."

"You ain't got the money to," Pud said.

"I got some money," Janie said.

Lyle made a sound like he didn't believe her.

"That right?" Goodnight asked.

Janie spilled her guts—and an idea with them.

When she'd finished telling, Lyle still wasn't sure. Said he had a man in Bankhead who'd buy all the rattlesnakes he could catch. This was his plan for escaping Elberta. Selling snakes. But Goodnight, it appeared, now possessed other intentions.

"We'll do it," she said.

They discussed a plan on the way back to The Peach Pit. Time they got there, everybody had left for the Conquistadors practice, except for a lone figure stumbling through the fruit stand. Pud shined headlights on Luther Treeborne, who was feeling all over stacks of gold-and-pink-streaked peaches, despite a handpainted sign that plainly said PLEASE DON'T SQUEEZE US!

"You want a ride?" Pud asked.

"I can walk," Janie told him, stepping out of the truck to take her uncle by the hand.

Thicker than Blood

1958

Janie didn't know how Lyle, Pud and Goodnight could stand wearing long-sleeved black shirts, camouflage britches and plastic Halloween masks in such heat. She herself wore but a cotton dress and black rubber boots that neared her kneecaps. Playclothes, her grandmomma used to call them. This was the tail end of July, and they were hidden in the woods watching the singlewide trailer where Janie's aunt and uncle lived. The girl'd stopped by The Peach Pit on her way, but Jon D. wouldn't speak. He'd already said he'd have no part in this. When Jon D. Crews said something, he meant it.

"Now what about that money?" Lyle said.

"I'll give it to you after," Janie told him.

"Maybe they ain't no money," Pud Ward said.

Janie set down Crusoe and pulled a wrinkled paperbag out from her boot. She unrolled the top and held it where Lyle could see. She'd fattened the stack with *Times-Journal* clippings so it'd look like enough. Lyle eyed the contents through the slits in his mask—a bone man. Pud's a gorilla. They'd won the masks last week during Peach Days. Goodnight kept off to the side, smoking a cigarette, her mask—a red devil—pulled up on her high forehead. She'd uttered barely a word, which made

Janie—a natural-born talker—even more nervous about what they were fixing to do.

"Alright," Lyle said. "Ain't like we don't know where you sleep at."

He told Pud to go on down at the truck and wait for the signal. The fat boy lumbered off a cutbank to an old logging road where one of his daddy's pickup trucks was hidden. The pickup was a candy-colored red rarely seen in Elberta and had a brand-new radio in the dashboard. Dial never moved from 1570AM-The Peach, which it was told picked up on the Mexican border, though no Elbertan ever went so far to confirm this. Riding over, Pud had tried impressing Janie with the speakers. Like she gave a rip.

"What's that?" Lyle said, pointing at the trailer, which was white with green shutters and a matching skirt. A single vehicle was parked out front: old gray pickup belonging to the County of Elberta. They'd watched Janie's uncle Wooten put plastic gas cans in back of the other truck and drive off maybe twenty minutes ago. That was the moment when what they were doing felt real to the girl—when her aunt was home all by herself.

"I don't see nothing," she said, propping Crusoe between her knees. Dead leaves were stuck to the dirt boy's caved-in face. She could feel wire poking out from his shoulder. He was in rough rough shape. If I can just be done with all this, she thought, then I'll spend time working on him. I'll get him back right.

"Maybe it wasn't," Lyle said.

He sat down by Goodnight, took the cigarette from her and started humming church music. Lyle Crews wasn't religious, but he'd latched on to the music after nearly getting killed by a wild hog the year he turned fifteen. Two before this. The hog had been turned out or busted loose from its pen. The *Times-Journal* wrote up its victims: a prized bird dog, a trio of unsuspecting sows, a riding lawn mower, a volunteer watermelon patch. When some farmers put a reward on the hog's head, Lyle went after the creature with nothing better than a dull kitchen knife. He was found lying in the paddy fields and holding his guts inside hisself

with his fingers. The hog beside him—dead as a doornail. Doc Barfield
sewed Lyle shut for no charge. The puckered scar starting just below his
waist and running up past his ribs was still oozing when Lyle, drawn by
the voices of the choir, first walked into Elberta Second Baptist
Church. He joined the choir that day yet did not sing then or ever. Just
stood up there rocking on his heels, happy to be awash in glorious sound.
Nobody knew what Lyle's singing voice sounded like—not even his
Goodnight.

There was no denying that Goodnight looked just like Big Connie
Ward. Her momma was the youngest of the last family of Elberta Indians in the valley. They'd kept apart from town till time came when they
could no longer get by without a vehicle. One day all eight Goodnights
walked to Big Connie's used-car lot and bought a poorly aligned station
wagon, leaving the car dealer with their savings and a lovesick heart. He
knew something would go wrong with the wagon. When the youngest
Goodnight girl walked back to the lot and told him it had, Big Connie
explained just how she could get some free transmission work—unaware
that a daughter would result from this new deal.

Janie stomped her feet to get the blood flowing. She watched Martin
tote rocks from the driveway and hide them underneath the porch. He
was a good dog, if dumb. Nothing like Buckshot, who Janie loved as
her own. Martin sniffed a stack of lumber. A foundation had been poured
for Wooten and Tammy's new house. Soon they'd start hauling this
lumber and other materials across town to The Seven. Hunkered there
in the woods, Janie reminded herself why she was doing this. Somebody
had to protect The Seven now that her grandmomma was gone. She'd
tried other ways. Maybe this would open their eyes. Still the girl was
scared shitless and troubled by doubt.

"What if I changed my mind?"

"Too late babygirl," Lyle said.

"You can have the money," she told him. "And I swear not to talk."

"Too late."

As if to prove this Goodnight stood up and pulled down the red devil
mask. She wasn't much taller than Janie, but she had five years and the

full bodyshape of a woman on the girl. Janie had spent enough time around Goodnight that summer to notice certain things. The monumental nose carved out of her face, the way she smelled like corn chips when she sweated, the hickeys like gobs of strawberry jam along her collarbone and up her neck where Lyle Crews placed his lips and sucked and sucked. This, Janie thought, was what being a woman meant. She felt a tinge of jealousy. Goodnight unzipped a bag and pulled out a rust-splotched machete. She brushed her thumb across the blade, checking it was sharp.

"You said you wasn't going to hurt her."

"We ain't," Lyle said. "Scare her's all it's for."

Goodnight swung the machete back and forth. "Quit being such a pussy." She headed off, making her way through the woods toward the trailer's backside.

Lyle settled on his heels. Janie grabbed Crusoe and squatted beside the older boy. He hummed, drank from a bottle. The stuff inside smelled like kerosene, but Janie took a drink anyway when offered. Her innards caught fire.

After some time passed Lyle got up and prowled the bag till he found a snack cake. He ripped the plastic then took a bite. "How come you tote that nigger dummy all over?"

Janie gave him a look and put her arm around Crusoe. Sand spilled out the dirt boy's side and made a rattling sound in the dry leaves.

"You gonna have to quit that mess," Lyle went on. "I tell Jon D. the same damn thing. Always toting that ballbat everywhere with him. Too old for toys and dolls, shit like that. Don't you want you a boyfriend?"

"If I did," Janie said, "it wouldn't be one lowdown as you."

Lyle laughed so hard a fart squeaked out. He finished the snack cake, licking white frosting off the cradle of his palm. "I don't usually go for kin anyhow," he said. "But remember babygirl, you're the one come to me about this."

"Me and you's barely even kin." Janie's granddaddy's uncle Frank was cousin to Lyle and Jon D.'s momma Ouita, who'd died when the boys were young.

"Don't go denying blood," Lyle said. "Might wind up all you got left."

Shadows continued spreading throughout the woods as Janie hunted for Goodnight across the way. Lyle kept glancing over his shoulder till Janie worried he'd set her up. Was Sheriff Guthrie coming? No, surely not. She wondered how long they'd been out there, feared her uncle Wooten would return from wherever he'd gone. This evening had to be it. The Seven depended on them pulling this off tonight.

Lyle finished what wet the bottle then chucked it into the brush. There came a quiet as dusk lent itself to early dark. In this lull Janie heard somebody walking thataway. She stood up, holding Crusoe on her hip. She figured it to be Pud, hoped it'd be Jon D. after all. It wound up, she saw, being neither of them.

Ricky Birdsong wore the same long-sleeved black shirt and camou-flage britches as Lyle and the rest. He held in his hand a mask made to favor an Egyptian mummy.

"You're late," Lyle said, loud, like Ricky was hard of hearing.

"I had to—"

"It don't matter."

"Hey Janie," Ricky said.

"Hey Ricky, what you—"

"You ready?" Lyle said.

Ricky nodded.

"Didn't I tell you there ain't no need for that?" Lyle snatched the mask from Ricky and threw it on the ground. "And how come you to dress thisaway? Goddamn the ever-loving shit Ricky, I said just come as your own damn self."

Ricky Birdsong wiped his face and blinked. He glanced around the woods as if they might speak for him.

"Hell, just go on," Lyle said. "You remember what to do don't you?"

Ricky said he did. Then he stepped into the yard and started walk-ing toward the trailer.

"What's he doing here?" Janie asked.

"Got to get her out the door." Lyle fished a snake rattle hanging by a string around his neck out from underneath his shirt then rolled it between finger and thumb. "She'll be too skittish if it ain't somebody she knows."

"Call him back."

"You going in his place?"

Martin had spotted Ricky. When the chubby little dog came at him, Ricky stopped and kneeled and let him sniff. Martin's tail wound like an off-kilter propeller. Ricky talked slowly as he picked up a rock. Martin bowed, wiggled. When Ricky reared back and chucked, the dog took off toward where the rock landed other side of the driveway.

"She'll see it's him!"

Lyle clamped ahold of the girl's jaw, shook, and said, "You had plenty chances to change that mind."

"He'll tell."

"Now listen to me," Lyle said, "Ricky Birdsong don't know his ass from a hole in the ground to tell what or how, if they even try asking him."

It didn't matter. Ricky was already knocking on the door.

Seemed like forever, that door opening. Then there Tammy stood, backlit by milky television glow, wearing high-waisted pink shorts and a see-through blouse overtop a white swimsuit. Ricky grabbed her. She fought, but it didn't matter one lick. Lyle bolted into the yard, whooping for Pud to come on. Goodnight emerged too, running with the machete held upward, as if to battle. As Ricky was dragging Tammy down the steps she managed to bite a plug out of his arm. He hollered and let go. Tammy began sprinting right toward where Janie hid. The girl didn't know what to do. She scrambled for something, a weapon, tried to remember why she hated her aunt so much. It was easier to hate her, something real. Just before Tammy reached the woods Goodnight tackled her. Martin, a slobbery rock in his mouth, took off running toward them right when Pud Ward wheeled into the driveway.

"I run him over," Pud bellered, nearly falling out of the pickup truck.

Martin was yelping, pinned underneath the tire.

"Put on your goddamn mask," Lyle said.

Pud did. Sobbing, he went to let down the tailgate. It was stuck. The dog still yelping. Pud yanked and yanked. The tailgate wouldn't come down. Ricky took back ahold of Tammy and held her like they were slowdancing partners. He patted the back of her head and shoulders, Martin still yelping where he was smashed between the tire and the ground.

"Move," Goodnight said. "Move before the whole damn valley hears." She rolled the pickup backward then got down and dragged the dog out from underneath. Pink guts dangled from his crushed rear end. Goodnight lined up the machete. Martin hushed after the first blow. She swung again, the blade sparking gravel. She wiped the dog's blood off her hands and said, "Just put her in over the damn side."

Ricky lifted Tammy into the truckbed. Lyle tied her wrists and ankles. Pud tried stuffing a sock in her mouth. She bit at him too till Goodnight pressed the machete to her cheek. Then Tammy accepted the sock. They covered her with a tarp. Lyle ran down to the mailbox and placed a peach pit inside. Raised the flag as a final touch. Goodnight got in back, Pud driving and Lyle shotgun. Just like that, they were gone, except for Ricky Birdsong.

And Janie.

Janie didn't move. The dry-flies were blowing like organ pipes. Or was it in her head? She watched Ricky Birdsong pick up Martin in two ragged pieces and tote him to the opposite treeline. Once the shadows swallowed them both, she grabbed Crusoe and took off toward the river fast as she could run.

Treebranches switched her face and neck and arms. Briar picked holes in her dress. She ran and she ran. Tried keeping one arm up to protect her face, but Crusoe was heavy and awkward to tote at such a clip. Where she was running to she had no idea. Just needed to run. The plan had been to meet at Jimmie Nell Duncan's old houseplace, where Lyle and Goodnight had been living throughout the summer. Janie knew she wasn't going there though. Not now. It'd been so easy to imagine before the horror of what they'd done had revealed itself and the truth of what now lay ahead. Not now, the girl thought. No more.

She could catch an occasional glimpse of the river through the brush and the treebranches that yet lashed her. On she ran. All it took was one branch growing at just the right height, pointed just the right direction. Her eye accepted it. She staggered, but didn't quit running till she'd made it underneath De Soto Bridge.

She set down Crusoe, stripped off her boots, and flung herself into the Elberta River. The paperbag had spilled when she shed her boots, money and the newspaper clippings fluttering down the bank. Let it, she thought. Her eye stung. She touched the lid, already swoll and matted up with gunk. She splashed with water then wiped with the tail of her dress. God it hurt. She held a hand over the eye that hadn't been poked. The world turned foggy and she jerked back like she'd been bit. Crusoe stumbled down the bank. "Don't," she told him. "No." He waded in up to his bloated belly and grease tailed off from him on the gentle current. A vehicle passed overhead. The underside of the bridge rang long after the vehicle had gone. Janie covered her good eye again, keeping her hand there long enough to be sure of this new truth.

She sat down in the sand and Crusoe crawled onto her lap. He was slick and he stained her dress a blue-gray. He smelled like coming rain. She petted his knotty head and cried a little. He made bird sounds back to her, trying to speak.

"I can't see a thing," she told him. "I can't see nothing."

What Mine Eye Hath Seen

1958

It'd been five days.

Janie bypassed downtown. She'd read that criminals tended to return to the scene of a crime. She was surprised to see Lee Malone's pickup truck parked on the shoulder by De Soto Bridge. She eased down the slope. No bucket, no poles, no Lee or Buckshot. There were bootprints and pawprints all in the sand though. The girl didn't know, but she'd just missed her aunt's search party. Most of the money and newspaper clippings she had come to get rid of had already blown away. Good. She climbed back up the bank and headed to The Seven. She just knew that the first time all summer she came down onto the family property and didn't hear a chain saw would thrill her to the bone. Foot if it did. The absence like to struck her down as she cut across the weedy yard toward her grandparents' house.

Though nobody had lived in the house for years, Maybelle kept the place in shape enough that a person could. Janie opened the door to what'd been her grandmomma's bedroom and laid down on the mattress, trying to smell her there. Geronimo yowled from another room. Janie now the cat's one-eye kin; an owl had snatched Geronimo's eyeball when he was still a kitten.

Doc Barfield had been kind and spoke softly to Janie while examining her. His hands were cold and butter-smooth. He hadn't flinched at Crusoe when the girl toted him into the room like he was a plain doll. Doc Barfield saw oddness all time, Janie suspected. His family was old Elberta and he lived in one of the mansions by the river, a few doors down from where Mr. Prince had lived. They tell Doc's granddaddy killed and boiled the bones of a black man so he could study putting a skeleton back together—and that's how the Barfields got into medicine. A nearby national forest was named after his kin: N. W. Monroe Barfield, a lawmaker who got subsidies for peach growers, and made the Hernando de Soto Peach Days Festival an official state holiday. Not the kind that gets you off work or out of school, but still, folks were proud of this distinction. Doc gave Janie a bottle of eyedrops and a patch. She would not regain the vision in her injured eye, he said. Janie's momma, Nita, was far more distraught over this injury and what it meant than the girl was herself. Nita'd hoped her daughter might one day go for Miss Elberta Peach. Janie Treeborne was a pretty thing. Hair black as Bankhead coal, eyes and nose and mouth just a little too big for her soft round face. Tall like a Treeborne. Nita herself was short, but she'd been a pretty thing too. In yearbook pictures she's slim and petite, perky set of tits and a thousand-dollar smile. She was a Dautrive and had a dark mole right there on the chin. Janie's blindness tore up Nita more than it ever did the girl herself, who always kindly liked the strangeness of it.

Janie checked Geronimo's food and water. At least her aunt and uncle were feeding the yellow cat. On her way out to the studio, she cracked the door so Geronimo could come and go as he pleased.

Together she and Crusoe stared up at her granddaddy's history. The assemblie sagged at its most paint-heavy parts. Over the years some of the nails securing it to the rafters had popped loose. The pulley long paralyzed. Her granddaddy, Janie knew, had started work on this assemblie sometime after the storm of 1929. Twenty-six people died, and Hugh was badly injured. She could pick out certain things among the assemblie's incompleteness: the true wilderness, a tribe of Elberta Indians, De Soto and his caravan marching through the valley, clearing and cutting and planting done by early peach growers, downtown Elberta rising in wood then in stone along the river it was named for, the war, the dam, the wide-eyed dead and a manicured football field grown over them, radio towers, more war, so on and on forth. There were people portrayed amidst all this. Janie did not know who they were in truth, but she liked imagining these figures as her family and others she knew around town. Her granddaddy died in 1947. The girl often wondered what the history would of become had he lived to keep working on it. Maybe taken up the whole studio, grown so expansive it had to be hung in the pole barn. Dirt daubers and wasps had added mud and paper parts, spiders their gauzy webs, and dry-flies their shed skins, same as the insects had on all the shelves yet filled with cardboard boxes and wooden crates Hugh Treeborne had left unsorted but to his own mind. These filled with bolts and washers, motors, strange gears and teeth, animal bones, radio parts, dishes, jars of blood and paint, bent and rusted metal plucked from Prince's Peach Cannery. If something was loose or could be pried so Hugh Treeborne would tote it to The Seven.

She took down her granddaddy's toolbag and arranged his instruments on the hard-packed ground. She recited names MawMaw May'd taught her: chisel, scuth, file, rasp, gouge, fishtail. With her grandmomma gone the girl felt responsible for remembering these names and many others. Maybelle had been the girl's connection to Hugh, making her death twofold. Janie had learned the story of Crusoe's creation from her grandmomma. The dirt boy loved hearing it told. Sometimes tee-ninesee salt crystals would form ecstatic all over his blue-black body while he listened. As they sat there he asked for it and Janie obliged.

After she told the story they climbed up on the roof. The hot tin bent and popped. This had been their perch all summer. They could see across the untended pasture to her uncle's clear-cut, where splintered stumps were left half-burnt in the broken ground, and trees too small to fool with had been scraped barkless and now bowed in shame. Other trees had been pushed over, so an underside of pale fibrous roots showed like a woman who'd bent over and raised up her skirt. In the holes beneath, what little rain had fallen collected in muddy red puddles, where tadpoles awaited a leggy transformation beneath bobbing gold clouds of gnats. The biggest hardwoods were stacked along the edge of the pasture. The timber company had paid Wooten part up front. Among this wreckage was a foundation for the new house. Janie saw Geronimo rolling on his back on the sun-warmed concrete.

The cat would often follow, like a dog, Janie and Maybelle on their walks. It was these walks that Janie could not reckon with losing. Her grandmomma naming plants and trees, showing what could be eaten and not. In her thirteen years Janie had tasted nearly every root, berry, leaf, shoot, fruit and bark in this valley. Maybelle showed animal signs and told stories about the creatures that made them. Maybelle didn't go to church, said she praised God by loving his creations. On these walks they hunted for lost pieces of Hugh's art too, and took turns toting Crusoe. Maybelle'd seemed no different last spring than any other time Janie could remember her. But she must of been. What else could explain her dying like that? Janie needed to figure it out. Maybe if she retraced enough of their walks, she thought. The logging, her aunt and uncle's new house, was a threat to this. A threat the girl could not abide.

A motorcycle in the distance. Janie climbed down and waited. Jon D. Crews slid to a stop but kept the engine running. Thunder, the old wooden ballbat given him by Lee Malone, was propped across the handlebars. The barrel had cracked and Jon D. had long outgrown being able to use the bat in games.

"Look," Janie said, lifting the patch covering her eye.

"Get on."

"Don't you want to—"

"Get on," Jon D. said. The engine choked. He played the throttle till it leveled out. "Leave that," he said, meaning Crusoe.

"I ain't doing it."

Jon D. waited to call her bluff, but Janie meant what she'd said. She hadn't been without the dirt boy since her grandmomma died. "Just get on then," he said.

They roared down 67 past Big Connie Ward's used-car lot. A couple burnt-out vehicles by the road. When Big Connie couldn't sell something he found ways to collect on the insurance. The motorcycle bounced across De Soto Bridge, the fresh paint job already peeling. The Elberta River ran clear and slow beneath. Janie could see the safety barrels she and the older kids had chucked off Peach Days night. Seemed of another time. Jon D. slowed down then turned right onto a cut. He swerved in and out of ruts and washes. The air got cooler the deeper they rode. The cut funneling down till briars and branches scratched from both sides. Janie tucked in behind Crusoe and Jon D. till the way opened up again. They came out in an overgrown clearing where a house stood and, across from it, an old chickenhouse.

She got down after Jon D. shut off the engine. Her legs felt wobbly and her face vibrated from the ride. She yanked at her bloomers where they'd crawled up her crack. Jon D. handed Crusoe to her then he grabbed Thunder. They headed for the house. It'd lost most of its paint and a pine tree grew up through the collapsed front porch.

"Daddy told me about your eye," Jon D. said. "Does it hurt?"

"Not really?"

"Let me see then."

She stopped and lifted the patch.

"Sickening," he said.

They walked on, stopping at the foot of the remaining steps.

Lyle appeared in the doorway. "Am I seeing a ghost?" he said, coming down into the yard. "I wonder could my eyes be playing games on me."

"I brung her," Jon D. said, nudging Janie with Thunder. She turned around and slugged him on the arm, and he quit.

"How many days it been?" Lyle asked. He wore a pair of sky-blue coveralls that stunk to high heaven. "What happened to meeting up babygirl?"

"Can I not go?" Jon D. said.

"Yeah, go on," Lyle said.

But Jon D. didn't leave right away. His betrayal, maybe, dawning on him.

"You retarded or something?" Lyle said.

"My glove."

Lyle went inside then came back with a baseball glove. A fat rubber band kept it folded tightly shut. Though it was new, the glove had been dipped in motor oil, rubbed with gritty riversand, then baked so many times it looked softer than a calf's ear.

After Lyle handed over the glove, Jon D. shot his big brother a bird and jogged back to the motorcycle. Straddled, stomped, the engine sputtered to life. The treeline devoured him except for white exhaust left in his wake.

Lyle led Janie into the kitchen. Nobody had lived here since Jimmie Nell Duncan, the house a one-story square box that still smelled like snake. Jimmie Nell Duncan had owned hundreds of snakes. Most she kept penned in the old chickenhouse, but her favorites she let crawl and nest among her wherever they pleased.

She put on a show every year at the elementary and the high school. Beautiful violet fangmarks dotted the inside of her arms when she held up writhing snakes for the kids to see. End of every show Jimmie Nell picked several to hold a python named Samson. Somebody from the *Times-Journal* would take a picture of this that teachers later cut out and tacked on bulletin boards. This tradition went on till the year Jimmie Nell broke from her usual snake stories and started talking about evolution. Janie remembered it well. She'd ran to the gym ahead of her class so she could sit on the first row of bleachers, hoping to hold Samson.

"Do you honestly reckon God made all this then just stopped?" Jimmie Nell asked.

The kids had never considered what God did after creation. The scalps of the few that did that day might as well of been peeled open and their brains scrambled with a fork.

In the kitchen Lyle Crews opened a cooler and sloshed around for a tub of ice cream.

"Where's Goodnight at?" Janie asked.

"Town." He took a mixing spoon from the sink. The ice cream was vanilla and it dripped down his chin as he slurped. "They pick up Ricky yet?"

"I don't know."

"Probably will before long," he said. "Happened to your face?"

"Where's she at Lyle?"

"Where's my money at?"

"I ain't got it with me right now," Janie said. "Is she okay?"

Lyle finished the ice cream then dropped the empty container in the sink. Janie followed him outside and across the yard. He slid open a noisy door. The floor inside the old chickenhouse was silty and quartered off by warped boards and chickenwire. Snakes thumped against wood and sunlight filtered through plastic tarp tacked over holes in the walls and the roof. It was hard to breathe. Lyle reached into a box and grabbed a handful of white mice. They wrapped pink tails around his fingers and clung to him by their claws. He walked over to a pen then shook them loose. They fell onto the floor next to five rattlesnakes—one bigger around than Lyle's forearm. The rattlers weren't immediately interested in the confused mice though. They flicked their tongues to taste the air then halfheartedly coiled up.

"Are they some of hers?" Janie asked.

"Goodnight and me caught these," Lyle said.

"Where from?"

He grinned. "Come on." Lyle grabbed a gas canister that had a spraywand attached to it. "You might want to leave that," he said, pointing at Crusoe.

"Nuh uh."

"I ain't asking."

Janie propped Crusoe up against the wall. Lyle handed her a forked pole and he grabbed a bunch of burlap sacks. They crossed the yard then tromped through a pitiful orange stream trickling into the woods, and they headed up a steep hillside covered in pine needles and the scraggly trees that'd shed them. Janie kept slipping. She used the pole for balance. At the top of the hill Lyle stopped near a cluster of rocks. He jabbed the spraywand into a hole then pumped the canister several times. The smell of gasoline wafted throughout the air. Janie covered her nose and mouth with the neckline of her dress.

"Now some'll come out looking drunker than a nigger over at Roger's place," Lyle said. "Be ready. There's some fire out fast as greased lightning."

The first hole wound up a dud. Lyle moved on to another one. He pumped, clicked the trigger, waited. All sudden a rattler slithered out into the pinestraw. Janie stabbed with the forked-end of the pole, but missed.

"We'll add that one to your tab," Lyle said.

They gassed, maybe, a dozen more holes, catching just two stubby rattlers with scales that reminded Janie of the dried pinecones scattered across the ridge. After Lyle had knotted the tops of the burlap sacks he sat down and unbuttoned the top of his coveralls. He idly scratched the tip of the purple scar on his chest then unscrewed the spraywand and huffed at the opening of the canister.

"Thousand miles away before long," he said, taking another good deep breath. "You best be too when the shit all hits the fan."

He was right, Janie knew. She had but one option now. She wasn't sure she had the guts to go through with even it. She sat down beside him. "Is she okay Lyle?"

"Last I saw," he said, and started humming. Hummed so loudly Janie thought his lips would come apart and his voice sing. But they did not. He stopped and turned toward her. "Well," he said, "am I going to have to take it?"

After enough time had passed that Janie should of answered, Lyle lunged on top of her. She hollered while he felt all over for the money, yanking off her boots and shaking them. When he found nothing he chucked one boot off into the woods. Janie grabbed the spraywand and swung. Lyle caught it in his palm and slammed her head against the ground. Bursts of light appeared on the underside of the black patch covering her blind eye. Lyle cussed then got up, grabbed the burlap sacks and headed back down the ridge. Janie lay there for a moment before getting up too.

He was staring into the pens when she got there. She worried if she could stand seeing the rattlers feed. The girl had, her grandmomma used to say, her uncle Luther's tender heart. The mice were fine though, climbing all over each other in one corner of the pen while there in the middle the biggest rattler had its jaws clamped on Crusoe's head.

Janie tried to go over the side. "Hold the fuck on," Lyle said, pushing her back. She looked down. Another rattler ready to strike. Lyle nudged the snake that had Crusoe with the forked pole. It would not release the dirt boy. Panic moved in waves up Janie's chest, around the back of her neck and her skull. Lyle tapped the rattler again. Still wouldn't unhinge its jaws. He pressed down and dragged the snake, and Crusoe, across the pen.

"Can't hurt that thing no way," he said.

"Please."

"Please what?" But Lyle knew. He grabbed a hoe. "You'll have to," he told her.

When she brought the blade down behind the rattler's head, its body spun across the pen as if propelled. The jaw still clung to Crusoe's face. While they waited for it to let go, Lyle took the body and quickly skinned it. He rinsed the blood and meat off the underside then laid the velvety skin out to dry. "Sometimes they'll bite for hours after they're dead." He reached for the lacquered rattle hanging around his neck. When he rolled the rattle between his fingers it sounded like rice being sprinkled into a bowl. "She could get them to do nearly anything just by talking to them. Never have seen anything like it."

When word spread that the school'd canceled Jimmie Nell Duncan's snake show, Lyle Crews thought she might no longer need her snakes. He had Samson, the python, partway out the chickenhouse when Jimmie Nell came on him with a shotgun. She didn't call Sheriff Guthrie, way he figured. Instead she fixed a pot of coffee on the stove and served him vanilla ice cream with crushed candied nuts on top. Time he'd finished the first bowl Lyle had agreed to help tend the snakes. It was more work than Jimmie Nell could handle herself. Lyle loved the work—and soon her. They were in bed the first time somebody chucked a flaming beer bottle at the house. Together they beat out the burning curtains and swept up the broken glass. There were more flaming bottles, chunks of concrete the size of cantaloupes. What she'd told the school kids could not be unsaid. She had to leave. Lyle wanted to go with her, wherever she wound up. But one day she was just gone.

He found a note and the snake rattle. This was, she wrote, where he was meant to be—and Lyle Crews had despised Elberta for it ever since.

When the rattler's head let go of Crusoe, Lyle raked the dirt boy to the edge of the pen then lifted him out. Janie fingered the sticky puncture marks on his face.

"What's your deal with that thing?" he asked.

"My granddaddy made him."

"Well it's too bad he ain't worth nothing."

As they waited for Goodnight to arrive, the odor of gasoline, the blurred afternoon light, the rattlesnake drone tired Janie. Lyle paced the pens, stopping twice to pull out a shed skin and hang it on wire. Janie held Crusoe tight. The dirt boy mixed with her sweat and streaked black down the insides of her legs. She shut her eyes for what she meant to be a moment. Somewhere in the depthless dark she heard singing: *Love lifted me, even me. Love lifted me.* She wanted to open her eyes, but it felt like fishing weights had been tied to the lids. *When nothing else could help, love lifted me.* The singing seemed to hurt whoever was doing it. She wanted the singing to stop and to keep going too. Her eyes were still closed and she was rubbing against the hard floor—felt like somebody else doing this; not her in control of her own body. She moaned and her eyes jumped open.

There sat Lyle Crews on a tumped-over barrel, coveralls now rolled down to his waist, singing, *Love lifted me. Love lifted me. When nothing else could help, love lifted me.* As he rocked, the snake rattle swayed on the string tied around his neck. Janie dared not move from where she was prone and let Lyle know she was awake. She licked her lips and tasted dirt. She admired how hard singing was for him. Truth, she knew, only hard things were worth doing. The Seven had to be preserved, her aunt kidnapped. Hard. Life ain't easy Sister. She began to see a confederate in Lyle Crews as she watched him repeat those lines over and over.

When Goodnight pulled up outside, Lyle stopped. Janie still pretended to be asleep when he shook her shoulder, told her to come on, get up.

Goodnight stood next to a pickup truck far too nice, Janie thought, for anybody in Elberta who was their age and not named Pud Ward to be driving. Goodnight kissed Lyle on the neck and said, "Thought I'd surprise you."

"Well," he said, scratching the back of his head. He wouldn't look at Goodnight. At either of them. He sulked into the house.

Janie and Goodnight faced each other. Goodnight looked the girl up then down. Her dress had been stretched and torn in the fight with Lyle, stained from sweating against Crusoe and the ground in her sleep. She was old enough to understand how this looked and she was, Janie remembered then, nervously wiggling her toes, also missing one boot.

"What was y'all doing in there?" Goodnight asked.

"Lyle was just showing me them snakes y'all caught."

"That right?"

Guilt showed on the girl's neck like day-old sunburn. But guilt for what? She didn't take time to reckon with it at this moment. Off she ran, Goodnight hollering for her to stop, hollering for Lyle to get after that sorry little bitch.

Janie made the woods, breaking branches to throw off Lyle and Goodnight. She stumbled down to the river then followed it up toward town. The bank petered out. She cut farther up into the woods, pausing every little bit and listening for Lyle and Goodnight. After a while she found a mountain laurel grove and hid there.

Around dusk she heard voices. The hounds surprised themselves coming up on her like that. They stood this tall to her chest, pressed cold noses to her skin and sniffed as if to consume her. Janie shut her eyes. A hound nipped her thigh. Another tried grabbing Crusoe, and Janie popped it on the head. She felt sorry as the hound backed off. She looked up. There was Buckshot! Then she saw her uncle Wooten coming down the hillside ahead of a dozen or so other men—her daddy, Lee Malone and Big Connie Ward among them.

"Lord, you got dirt all over you Sister," her daddy said as he touched her face. "Does your momma know where you're at?"

"What you doing running around without no shoes on?" her uncle Wooten asked.

Janie couldn't answer them. If she opened her mouth and spoke she would of betrayed herself, her home, everything.

"Your aunt Tammy's gone missing," her daddy said. He touched her face again and winced like it hurt him to do so. "I'll see if Lee can't carry you home."

She propped Crusoe on the seat next to Buckshot, who sat next to Lee Malone. The sun had dipped below the treeline and lightning bugs splattered the woods with dull green-yellow blotches. Janie caught sight of herself in the side mirror. It was like seeing kin who you don't know yet—but deep down do. Lee turned on the radio. Pedro Hannah reminded everybody to watch for Tammy Ragsdale, missing five long-awful days, and any suspicious behavior. We're all praying for a safe and swooft return, the radio announcer said, pushing a fiddle overtop his voice. This song goes out to her, wherever she may be.

In the Beginning

1929

Everything stopped for the crane. You couldn't get a wagon through the streets for gawkers watching the machine being unloaded off a barge. It was named Goliath and, The Authority said, ran on steam. If you owned a camera you could make two-three bucks some weekends off folks wanting a keepsake. Goliath was followed by a whole mess of equipment and by men dressed in new wool suits making a price on folks' land, threatening jail time and court fees if you said no. Many houses were pulled apart nail-by-nail and hauled out of the county. It was those folks who stayed put that came and watched Goliath roar to life. A marching band played. The wild game fled to places unknown or forgotten. Change had come to Elberta, Alabama. From there on out the racket continued day and night, rumbling and explosions, and a concrete wall rose up where once had been but treetops and unbroken sky.

The Hernando de Soto Dam was little more than two enormous concrete boxes built in the edge of the river the summer Hugh Treeborne took a job with The Authority. The morning of his first day he'd found what he thought was an inquiry tacked to his house. He'd heard they were through buying and his land, which was called The Seven, was nowhere near the dam or where the lake would soon back up, filling hollers and topping hills. A man with a red-brown birthmark on his face was deciding which crew Hugh would join.

"You work building ever?"

"Little bit," Hugh lied, watching workers climb shaking scaffolding erected against the concrete face.

The birthmarked man picked his nose. He had a pistol jabbed in his belt. "Well you can learn it," he said. "Meantime we'll put you to digging."

The Authority gave Hugh Treeborne a shovel and a lunch of greasy sardine sandwiches wrapped in butcher's paper. The fish smelled slightly rotten and tasted salty, the bread stale. Hugh ate anyway. After lunch he wet his shirt in the Elberta River then tied it around his forehead. The other men on the crew nicknamed him Chief for this.

Nearly one thousand men were working on the Hernando de Soto Dam, pouring three million cubic yards of concrete that would reach four hundred feet at its highest point, flooding more than ten thousand acres of deep woods and pastureland and homesteads that'd belonged to generations of local families. Most of these men did not consider such numbers or loss, nor did they have time to worry over what it meant for the valley. Hugh recognized but a few of the workers on his shift. They did not acknowledge each other. A job with The Authority meant a chance to start over from hard lives turned harder for reasons they weren't sure of, reasons the paper said had to do with places faraway as New York and Chicago. These men had seen war, felt hunger. But this? This was something else. Foot, they joked, if nothing else the dam'll make a good spot to leap from—way old Chief Coosa did.

At the end of the day the birthmarked man fired his pistol. As the shot pealed down the river Authority men started home like ants fleeing a kerosene-soaked hill. Along the washed-out path to town Hugh walked past cut timber, much of it rotten and growed-up with jewel briar and goldenrod and blackberry. Off in the distance fingers of black smoke curled up from a collection of burnpiles. Hugh counted one two three four five. . . . Ash from these fires and others since burnt out mounted in the streets, compromised rooftops, drifted inside stables, where sag-backed horses and mules grunted and stomped for feed that was no longer available. The Elberta Valley like another world from the one Hugh the boy had known. He was glad his daddy, Caz, wasn't around to see.

He came upon a snapper lying in the weeds, its thick shell busted and all the innards pulled out but for a handful of brown and green organs. A group of kids appeared on the path. Bones pressed sharp against the underside of their dirty skin, ash dusting their hair, grime blackening their eyelids, and fingernails telling of sooty fields and inky creeks where they yet played. When Hugh looked thataway, the kids laughed, took off. Folks in Livingstown worried what the ash would do to the rice crop. It was smothering gardens. Fortunate the ash did not reach The Seven, he thought. Before long the only thing left to eat would be whatever canned food The Authority doled out.

As he passed through town he saw several drunks sitting in front of the charred remains of Tupelo's Hardware and Tack. The store had caught fire some weeks ago, flames spreading to six other buildings before being put out with riverwater and sand. One of the drunks grabbed Hugh by the britchesleg. He kicked loose and made like to strike the man. This—all of it, he thought—progress. That's what the paper said. Heard it bandied in the streets too, by men The Authority paid or promised to pay. He watched one of The Authority's photographers taking pictures of the drunks, who leered and drooled and cackled when the bulb flashed. The photographer was young, looked like a yankee. More and more outsiders coming into the valley. A skinny woman walked her kids across the street, covering young eyes from this lurid scene. From a new reality, Hugh thought, The Authority's promise of a new South: electricity, jobs, warm and sturdy rental houses, and the time to enjoy a healthy family who bought all its food from The Authority store rather than raising it on your own free land. Look around and see all this progress. Explosions day and night, hundred-year-old trees toppled, fires burning and burning and burning, like hell risen up onto earth, and the valley itself rumbling as if the ground might come apart and swallow them whole. And now him part of it. Hugh Treeborne, an Authority man.

He bought a piece of vinegar taffy at Gus's Buy-All and chewed, trying to forget his latest sin, as he passed the square where Hernando de Soto stood tall on a limestone pedestal. The Authority aimed to name the dam and the new lake after the conquistador. What might the old Spaniard think? Ash had piled on his brow and shoulders. This particular statue a gift from Elberta, Texas, the town's sister city. Folks told that De Soto came down off his pedestal and walked the valley some moonless nights. Casabianca, Hugh's daddy, used to scare Hugh the boy with such stories and threats. Not too long ago a string of stolen horses had been blamed on the conquistador. The real culprit, Hugh figured, climbing up onto the pedestal, more likely a hungry Elbertan who needed to feed his family. He dusted off what ash he could reach. He'd always admired the statue—De Soto was an outsider too. Though the conquistador had somehow, over time, become them. The statue was the first piece of art Hugh'd ever seen. He still felt envious of what bronze could do that the clay he dug up from creekbanks could not.

Other side of the square stood the post office, where a tall woman from out of town had recently been made postmaster. Hugh sat down and watched folks hurry in the cut-block building before close. The *Times* had written against the new postmaster's hiring. She was maybe the first woman in the state to hold such a position and folks did not appreciate that distinction being associated with Elberta. Sometimes Hugh saw her walking Sampley's route, Sampley the mail carrier dependable as a gnat on a good day. She took long and determined strides, and toted the heavy leather bag on her shoulder as if it was nothing. Hugh never spoke when he passed the postmaster on his uncle Frank's wagon, though he did wonder if she noticed him too.

When he got home another inquiry was tacked to the doorframe. He did not read it. He chucked the paper in the woodstove. "Let them try," he said, starting a fire there. He went to the springhouse and grabbed a fistful of sauerkraut. With the other hand he picked up Crusoe from where he'd left him on the bank. An earthworm wriggled out of the dirt boy's head. Hugh pitched the worm into the water then walked back up at the house.

When the flames died down and the coals turned hot-white, he fried pork belly in a cast-iron pan then warmed a slice of cornbread in the rendered fat. He liked his pork crispy, his cornbread buttered. He had no cows for the latter. The pork had been a gift. The sauerkraut was cold and bright on his tongue and a big broad smile crossed his face as he chewed, jaw muscles stretched that hadn't been in some long time. Work would do that for a man. Hugh Treeborne maybe hadn't smiled so hard since he was a boy working at Prince's Peach Cannery, which was now shuttered and starting to give itself over to weed and to vine and to what-ever animals nested inside its machinery and walls. Now those were good times. Days yet Hugh hunted doves in the tall grass grown around the cannery. Bricks beginning to fall off like dried scabs, large rooms once filled with the beautiful noise of local work otherwise gone silent. Even Mr. Prince wasn't immune to what was happening with the world.

When Hugh was through eating he propped Crusoe up on his lap. Looked like the dirt boy had been walking around on his own. Missing a toe, and the bottoms of his feet were cracked. He toted Crusoe out at the studio and searched the shelves for the right clay, yawning as he ran fingers across buckets and jars. When was the last time he'd set foot here? Days he didn't make art carried little meaning and were often hard to recall. Lived too many artless days period, he thought, since Caz died eleven years ago.

For some of those years, once the cannery closed, Hugh'd picked peaches and done other piecemeal work, like in the paddy fields of Liv-ingstown, during summer. In winter he spent many idle nights at Lee Malone's place for the company and the warmth. Lee hisself now worked as a dipper at a mill out in the county. Dangerous—the trip there for Lee and the work he did. He came home with arms stained blue up past the elbows. It was good reliable work though and the foreman let Lee cut firewood off company land. Let him, but wouldn't of said so had Lee been caught. Lee gave what he couldn't burn to Woodrow, who used it to smoke whole hogs that'd been splayed open down the gut and wrapped in chickenwire so the meat held together as they slow-cooked. Hugh Treeborne and Lee Malone met in the church where Lee the boy slapped guitar and sang. Hugh wasn't holy; his daddy had wandered in during service and, crazed, started prying up the floorboards. Had a splintered stack four-five feet tall time Hugh caught up to him. The True Believers were speaking in tongues and laying hands on Caz, which did not a lick of good in the long run. Hugh never would forget the way Lee sounded that day—raw as the floorboards his daddy had pried loose searching for gold that did not exist.

Some winter nights Lee would sit up late late, and play and sing songs from his boyhood, others he'd picked up traveling the chitlin' circuit in Florida and South Alabama and Georgia, while Hugh contentedly listened. Lee'd seen and played with the best guitar players of that time and place. Men named Papa, Blind-this-or-that, Sonny, Skip. Some with no name at all. Time, he figured to play the circuit till he could make a recording. Blacks up north with money would spend it on a decent recording, he'd heard.

Then one off night in Mobile Lee saw a hillbilly star pack out the civic arena. The big room smelled of cow shit from a rodeo held the night before. Lee and the rest of the black folks in attendance sat high up near the rafters, under watch of several fat policemen. The hillbilly star was gaunt. Looked like a string bean down there onstage. Lee knew his songs from the white folks who'd raised him. He began singing along under his breath, out of fear that the policemen would deem him a disturbance. Before long his neighbors in the balcony were cutting him looks. At first he did not care. He loved the songs and was taking what he could learn from the hillbilly star's pitch to use in some of his own music. This is what he did; sponged. Then somebody kneed Lee in back of the head. He turned around, thinking it might of been an accident, and was confronted with rows upon rows of indignant faces. He did not wait for the show to end before leaving his seat and exiting out the side of the arena into the humid night.

He needed to get drunk to tell this story to Hugh for the first time.

Between that night in Mobile and the night he told of it, he'd been asked to make a recording. Given a train ticket to go do so in Wisconsin. But Lee Malone had not gone yet. Instead he'd given up playing the circuit and taken the job at the mill. And for what? Hugh wasn't sure, and he didn't fully understand what'd happened in the civic arena that night.

When day began breaking Hugh got up and stumbled to the back porch. Waking up early felt like getting away with something. He pissed a gallon while listening to a mockingbird test its voice. Crusoe was waiting in the old chicken coop Hugh used as his studio. The dirt boy had laid out his tools and uncovered an assemblie set on tin they'd found at an abandoned houseplace near Livingstown. The assemblie had to do with De Soto's boyhood home. Horses. Wouldn't Spain have some kind of a desert? Hugh found his materials strewn all over the Elberta Valley. Felt like the land was offering up things, urging him to make art. Not even make, but frame, assemble. That's how he'd come up with the word for the things he made. Crusoe came along on these walks and worked kindly like a magnet sometimes. The Elberta River too carried objects up onto its banks and into the woods when it flooded in early spring. The wind blew things down, rearranged what was already there. Pounding rain could unbury something lost. Most folks never noticed. You had to look. So much was thrown out, even during these tough times. Hugh gathered and assembled these objects to resemble the images filling his head, and when he was finished, he toted his assemblies off in the woods and left them there.

It was this last part that drove Lee Malone up the wall. Scared, he'd say, trying to taunt Hugh so he'd quit leaving his work to ruin. Hiding it like cat shit. Lee wanted him to share his art with the world. What world? Pot calling the kettle black, Hugh'd say. Then Lee'd turn the argument toward skin color, so he wouldn't have to answer for why he'd quit the chitlin' circuit and still hadn't gone to make that recording. This argument went on till, often, Hugh'd let slip the word *nigger*, or something close enough to it, and the men came to blows.

Hugh lit a pine knot and burnt some of the paint already gobbed onto the assemblie. He covered his nose against the smoke. Crusoe stood on his toes and watched.

"Tell," the dirt boy said.

Hugh waved him off, unwound a spring then began pounding it flat. Crusoe kept on begging. Stories were Hugh's daddy's thing; assemblie-ing his.

"Tell," the dirt boy said. "Come on, tell." He showed his animal teeth and pumped his hands like he was squeezing something.

Hugh finally gave in and told the story of Chief Coosa losing his soul to an owl, chasing the creature right off a bluff and breaking his body on the jagged rocks down below. While he told he mixed clay and began layering it onto the assemblie. Crusoe begged for a dab or two on his curved back. The dirt boy purred when Hugh obliged. Soon it was time to leave for work. Hugh toted Crusoe down at the spring and left him till evening.

Life went thisaway for weeks. Hugh stole from the day, working on assemblies while Crusoe watched. Didn't drink much; didn't see Lee at all. The work with The Authority allowed Hugh something near to peace. His long-sunk mind bobbed up. Crusoe noticed the signs in Hugh's hands, which moved like a heron spearing toadfrogs from clear water. He finished the De Soto assemblie then three smaller ones that had to do with animals that'd disappeared from the valley since his boyhood. Panthers, bears. Native predators now gone. During these bliss-ful weeks Hugh Treeborne often had a dream in which he uncovered a pit of bones in the channel the Authority men were digging to divert the river from the dam site. Digging was in his blood. Jarred awake, he'd return to the studio and assemblie till his eyes ached and his hands wouldn't do right. This penance also pleasure. He never remembered going back inside, just woke next to Crusoe come morning, and a late owl hooting in a split oak out back.

※

He'd learned to read and write from pamphlets Caz would bring home from trips into town. The pamphlets would have titles like *Our Caribbean Allies* or *How to Get Out from Under Debt*. Rarely in life was reading and writing useful for Hugh Treeborne. In fact he hadn't written more than his name in who knew when. So, the day he sat down to write something he could mail, it took effort to recall the shapes of letters and the order in which they went. He had no idea where the letter he was writing would wind up going once he turned it over to her. He wrote, *If you some how git this I am sorree.* He folded the paper twice then sealed it with wax. On the outside he wrote, *To Frank Treeborne.* When the wax'd dried he stuck the letter in his britchespocket then headed into town on his raggedy-ass mule named Byron.

Hugh stood next to the De Soto statue for several minutes before getting the guts to cross the street. A little bell chimed when he opened the door. To the right was a wall of brass boxes with ornate glass doors which folks rented out to receive mail. To the left was the service counter. The new postmaster stood behind it. She wore a blue wool dress with big gold buttons and had her hair styled up and pinned to her temples.

"How can I help you?"

Hugh set his letter on the counter. "I want to send this."

She picked up the letter and looked at it. "You don't have an address?"

"Right there," Hugh said, pointing to his dead uncle's name.

The postmaster kindly frowned. "This isn't the address," she said. "Do you know where Mr. Treeborne lives?"

"No," Hugh said.

"You don't know where he lives, but you're trying to send him a letter?"

He didn't know what to say. He'd assumed she'd just stick on a stamp and that'd be it. The letter was nothing but an excuse to talk to her anyhow. His uncle Frank had been dead longer than his daddy. "Well, thank you," he muttered, then turned to leave.

"Now hold on," the postmaster called out.

But it was too late. Hugh had rushed out the door.

Embarrassed as he felt, Hugh didn't let this foolish attempt at courtship curtail the routine he'd established since starting with The Authority. Each morning he took a couple hours from the day by working on his assemblies. One such morning, hands crusted with blood from the gill plate off a carp he'd pulled out the fishpond, he heard a vehicle coming down a nearby path. He set down his tools but for a scraper and watched as a tar-black car came speeding down the hill. A thing so rare in this valley it might of been an airplane. Most folks in Elberta couldn't afford to keep up a vehicle, let alone put gas in one. Not anybody who'd come down at The Seven anyhow.

A stranger climbed out of the driver's seat. Hugh let him get all the way up onto the porch before sneaking up from behind and pressing the scraper to his neck. "I ain't selling," he said, "so you can go on."

"I was passing by and noticed—"

"I ain't selling my land," Hugh said, pressing down harder. The scraper was so dull he'd need to saw if he meant to break skin. "I work for The Authority now too."

"I believe you have me confused." The stranger spoke in a clipped accent. If he'd of said Mississippi he'd of pronounced every last letter. Hugh let go and backed up. The stranger's dark hair had been poorly slicked down against his squat skull. He was, in fact, plain slouchy-looking all over, and when he opened his mouth to speak again he revealed unseemly red gums. "Do you intend on using that?"

Hugh lowered the scraper. "I seen them notices y'all left."

The stranger laughed a laugh too big and healthy-sounding for his appearance. He fixed his tie, which had a little yellow bird painted on it. His shirt collar was smashed and sweat-browned. He raised his eyebrows then walked back to the vehicle and took a fruit jar out from underneath the front seat. He sloshed around the pissy-looking liquid inside then drank from the jar and held it out toward Hugh.

"I can do without."

The stranger drank. "Like I was saying before you held a knife to my throat, I was—"

"This ain't no knife."

"Does it happen to be for sale?"

Hugh looked at the scraper in his hand. "Does what?"

"Listen," the stranger went on, "I purchase art. I'd like to purchase that odd little piece by the road if it's in fair enough condition. I assume it's yours?"

Hugh had forgotten about this assemblie—as he did all of them over time. It'd been growed-up in a honeysuckle vine since one drunk night Lee Malone decided to take it home rather than let Hugh tote it off into the woods and leave it. Lee got no farther than the path before deciding the assemblie too big and left it there.

"Mister, look—"

"How much?" It was a question impossible to answer, making a fool of Hugh in the most terrible way. "Here," the stranger said, "let me show you something."

He retrieved from the vehicle a stack of pictures wrapped in tissue paper and bound with twine. On back of each one a year had been scrawled: '27, '18, '23, so on. Some of the art in these pictures looked kin to Hugh's own. Up to now, whenever he saw art mentioned in the paper or a stray pamphlet, it'd been made long ago by a person now dead, and usually in some far-off land. Art itself being, he thought, a dead practice. But here was something made only a few years ago by people, according to the hard-to-read scrawl, from Memphis, Mobile, New Orleans and on over to Tallahassee. This angered and thrilled him. The stranger took some flyers out of a briefcase, making sure Hugh saw the prices printed on them in red.

"I believe you get what you pay for," he said. "And I pay only for the best."

"That right?"

"It sure is, Mister . . ."

"Treeborne," Hugh said. "Jesse Absalom Treeborne. But folks call me Hugh."

"Christ!" the stranger shouted, taking another swig from the jar. He gasped as he swallowed the firewater and fanned hisself with the flyers clutched in his hand. "People will love this. Name's Loudermilk. Let me ask you a question Hugh. How long have you been one?"

"Been one what?"

"An artist," Loudermilk said.

Hugh felt ignorant considering an answer. "I always been thisaway," he said.

"Perfect!" Loudermilk shuffled through the pictures as if he'd forgotten why he was there. "That's just perfect. People are going to love this!"

Loudermilk wanted to see more assemblies. As they walked The Seven, Hugh had a hard time getting a word in—and him born into a family of talkers. Loudermilk said he'd just come from the Gulf, but was originally from up north. He wanted to hear all about Hugh Treeborne, he said. But Hugh could not tell about growing up on these seven hundred wooded acres of old-growth cool and dim as a cave, of how some afternoons a flock of passenger pigeons blacked out the sky for seven Mississippi seconds, how bright yellow mushrooms like to walk on as steps grew up the trunks of those trees, or how Indians once lived here, and not the worn-out kind, but those whose descendants fought De Soto when the Spanish traipsed through hunting for gold not there, and how, centuries later, Hugh the boy picked up discarded birdpoints and broken pottery in the field his daddy plowed for a garden and a cotton patch, and how he picked up bird bones and tore those mushrooms loose from the trees and assemblied these objects, and others, according to what the land offered and what he saw in his head. Nor could he tell how the sweet smell of syrup and sugar and mashed fresh fruit used to drift down from Prince's Peach Cannery so you could breathe cotton candy if you had a good strong set of lungs, how him and Lee Malone used to catch bats underneath the Hernando de Soto Bridge and tie string to the poor creatures' feet, then let them swoop and soar after bugs while taking turns holding on to the shaking end, let alone did Hugh get to tell anything about his daddy's sickness and the years after Caz died, about making Crusoe—now that would be a story, but Hugh couldn't tell it yet—or how he was beginning to feel like he'd betrayed all the things he loved by joining The Authority, which was changing the valley in a way no one could yet grasp, because Loudermilk cut him off every chance he had, just like a damn yankee would.

Hugh remained wary. He slept with a rifle the first night Loudermilk camped on The Seven. He had a hard time believing anybody would pay for something he'd made. Doubted anybody cared what he did on these seven hundred acres—or if he even lived. A way of thinking rooted in his family's past.

But as the week wore on and Loudermilk pulled more assemblies from the woods, his enthusiasm birthed in Hugh some fragile belief that maybe this wasn't a con. Maybe he was telling the truth and folks up north would pay good money for his assemblies. He wanted to believe. He also reasoned that if there was money to be made from his art then Loudermilk would return for more. If not, Hugh figured, he'd be no worse for a few less assemblies sinking into the ground from which they'd come. The gamble seemed worth it.

Hugh waited for Loudermilk to make his pitch. He had lined up several assemblies he thought were interesting, he called it, alongside the studio. "It's not often I come across something like this," Loudermilk said, stepping back to take them all in at once. "There's enough here to put on an entire exhibition of Hugh Treeborne."

Hugh let his silence speak. He noticed Crusoe in the shadows of an azalea bush and toted the dirt boy to a bucket of filmy water and began wetting him down. As he worked, Crusoe's coloring bled onto his hands and ran down his arms onto his shirtsleeves. Reshaping the dirt boy sounded like kneading too-wet biscuit dough.

"Let me talk to my people," Loudermilk said. "I can return in a month—maybe less. Of course I'll need proof. My camera, it's busted and—"

"Go ahead, take them."

Loudermilk seemed surprised. He wrote out a contract on butcher's paper Hugh found wadded up in his shirtpocket. "Keep collecting," he said after he'd filled the backseat. They both signed the contract, then Hugh watched the vehicle depart, wondering despite hisself if he would ever see the yankee, or the art he'd given over, in this valley again.

Stories We Tell

TODY

TODAY

❦

"You still taping?"

The young man said he was.

Outside the sun blazed late noonday heat, so it seemed like the world was made of old-timey glass. Same as the kind stuck in the window-frames of this three-room house on the side of a hill. Inside the house smelled like the occasionally smoked cigarette, like body odor, spent coffee grounds, scented pinecones and baby powder. Janie Treeborne was trying to remember who exactly came up with the name Hugh Tree-borne's Seven Hundred Acre Junk Garden. Maybe it was one of the dozens of art collectors who visited The Seven in those early days of re-discovery, she said. Could of been, on second thought, some magazine writer. She was sifting through a cardboard box filled with articles upon articles about her granddaddy Hugh and the art he made and the seven hundred acres he littered with it.

"Nobody expected there to be money in such a thing," she went on. "Wasn't ever much. Not even once it got wrote up all over the place. Beat all to me, seeing Aunt Tammy talking to folks from New York and California."

What began as a local oddity turned into a not-for profit with one year-round paid employee and a few volunteers. Soon it became too much for Tammy Treeborne Ragsdale to manage on her own. An executive director was hired, a board of directors assembled. Janie steered clear of the whole enterprise. A young woman yet, she had her orchard and her fruit stand. Summers busy back when Elberta was on the main route to the Gulf Coast. She'd direct folks out to The Seven to walk paths past her granddaddy's art if she thought they seemed like the kind who'd be interested. Otherwise she kept apart.

"Them days passed," she said, "till all the place run off of was donations and pitiful government grants. I remember the first day it opened though. Jon D. and his boy Henry was there. Spitting image of his daddy, I mean. Henry is. Got some Lyle in him too. Jon D. likes you saying that. Handsome might of skipped Jon De Soto Crews, but not his boy. I got a picture somewhere. Boy, foot—I reckon Henry's grown now. About your age. ECHS marching band played the day it opened and Aunt Tammy led the first tour group."

Janie couldn't find the article she was looking for, but she did find a newspaper clipping she hadn't seen in years:

Maybelle Chambliss Treeborne, 58, of Elberta, died shortly after dawn on Saturday the twenty-fourth of May. She is survived by three children and one grandchild. Maybelle was preceded in death by her husband, Jesse Absalom "Hugh" Treeborne.

Maybelle was born in Bankhead, Ala., a nearby coal town, where she graduated in a class of four students from the Bankhead School in 1916. A photograph from this time shows a smiling young girl with thick hair pulled back and styled into a type of pompadour then popular. Through fate, she often said, Maybelle wound up in Elberta, where she served many years as our local postmaster, including during and after The Storm of 1929, until retiring two years ago.

Maybelle married Hugh Treeborne, who is remembered by family and friends for the unique art he made. Together, the couple raised three children—Renton, Tammy and Luther—on a large tract of land to the north and west of town. This untamed acreage stirred much jealousy in the hearts of local children—enough that some ventured onto it from time to time and imagined their own tiny kingdoms there. Trespassing is not an act this writer advocates, but, on the occasion of Mrs. Treeborne's passing, will confess to having committed on the acreage at least once.

Maybelle Chambliss Treeborne will be remembered for having been one of the first female postmasters in the state of Alabama. She seemed to know the entire history of our lovely river valley and of all who reside here. If she didn't know something, Maybelle simply made it up—like any storyteller worth her salt—and our lives became all the more wondrous for it. Maybelle prized her family, especially her granddaughter, Janie "Sister" Treeborne, who is surely the spitting image of her grandmother, or this writer is not sitting here, looking out onto Water Avenue and the beautiful river which gives our town its name.

Janie hung her grandmomma's obituary on the fridge, securing it with a magnet shaped like Alabama.

"The day it happened Daddy and me was fishing over at the dam," she said. "Not a lick of college to his name. The Authority would still train you thataway back then. Anyhow, I remember poor Ricky Birdsong hollering, 'Telephone! Telephone!'

"We was fishing this finger of deepwater where summer before the lake'd dropped so low it turned up a rusted-out car with a dead body in the driver's seat. Woman behind the wheel was from Arkansas, the paper said. Well we'd done caught us a good mess of bream, aiming for Momma to fry them up that night, when Ricky Birdsong hollered that that telephone was ringing for Daddy.

"I watched the lines while he went to answer. Fishing was our thing, same as it'd been with him and his daddy. If you was to ask my first memory though, it wouldn't be fishing. Be Granddaddy Hugh's big ugly foot poking out from underneath a sheet the day they slid him in back of that hearse bound for Blessed Assurance Funeral Home. Nails this thick and second toe longer than the first. That's it. See here though: mine too."

Janie kicked off a pink slipper and held up her wide flat foot, laughed as she wiggled five long toes at the young man.

"Then I heard a door open and Daddy was just-a-hustling toward his truck. Never had seen him move so fast. It thrilled me to the bone. Cigarettes flew out the pocket of his shirt and hair blew back from his forehead. Seeing him run thataway made it easier imagining him playing for the Conquistadors, easier imagining who he was before I came along. Anyhow, I dropped my pole and took off too. The engine was running, passenger door slung open for me. You want to talk regret? Let's talk how much I wish I'd kept Daddy's pickup after he died. Shit, I can't even remember how I spent the money I got from selling it."

Seven Hundred Acres

1958

As they drove away from the dam Janie imagined the valley a map in her head. She pinpointed their place on it and, by direction, figured they were headed to The Seven. It'd been a few days since she'd last seen her grandmomma. Her daddy drove fast and with the radio off. Empty bottles clinked on the floorboard. Janie liked riding in her daddy's pickup truck better than nearly anything in the world. It was big and steered like she imagined a ship would. A spotted hawk's feather hung from the rearview mirror, twirling at every bump in the road. She loved the stink of cigarette upon smoked cigarette and burnt motor oil wafting into the cab. She tried getting by without washing it out of her hair, especially since her daddy'd started sleeping at the dam so much. Her momma usually caught her and stood in the bathroom door while Janie got back in the tub. Wash good, Nita'd say. And Janie half would. Some Saturdays she and her daddy rode for hours on end with no true destination in mind. Stopped when they pleased, pissed in the edge of the woods, bought coke-colas and egg-salad sandwiches and salty potato chips from whichever country store they came upon, and listened to 1570AM-The Peach loud as they could stand it. The whole valley felt like theirs. These rides an appraisal. But today was different. Today the smells were making her nauseated. Something's wrong, she thought, picking at the little round brown burns in the seat fabric.

She was surprised when her daddy flew past the house and out into the bumpy pasture. He jarred to a stop next to the pole barn, left the engine running and jumped out, and disappeared into the woods behind Granddaddy Hugh's gravesite before Janie could get out herself. She chased, ducking branches and briars. Two of her steps made up one of her daddy's. She was breathing hard time she caught up with him at the edge of a holler.

He grabbed at a sapling, then began sliding down the bluffline. Janie tried telling him she knew a better way. It was like he didn't hear. She could make out a yellow splotch in the hollerbottom. The month of May, practically summer, the woods already an unnatural green. Dirt and leaves avalanched ahead of them. The yellow splotch moved. It was, Janie realized, Lee Malone. He was standing over something covered up with his tan hunting jacket.

"Lord, I'm so sorry," he said when they reached him. He hugged both their necks. He smelled like gun oil and squirrel and spearmint chewing gum—way he always did to Janie, even after he no longer hunted, which began this day. "I don't know what on earth she could of been doing fooling with this big-old thing by herself."

It was like Ren didn't hear Lee Malone, nor pay mind to the big-old thing he'd mentioned. The rusted metal box favored a generator. There was a round opening at one end. In all her wandering around The Seven Janie had never seen this thing, though she figured it had something to do with her granddaddy, like everything did.

She watched her daddy pull back the hunting jacket covering Maybelle's body. Ren held his momma to his chest, picking groundtrash out of her white hair. There was a deep blue cut on her leg and her lips were parted where you could see the coffee-stained backs of her teeth. A rubber band pinched her wrist—reminder of something, a leftover habit from her post office days. He held her hand and picked at dirt—or rust one—caked underneath her nails. She was barefoot—missing both shoes. Ren was crying now. He kept saying, "Momma, oh, my momma. Momma, Momma, Momma."

Lee put a hand on Ren's back. When he found her he'd ran over at Varnado Price's place to use the phone. His yellow collared shirt was soaked through and stuck to his chest. "Ren, I told her she ought not be out in these woods by herself anymore," Lee said. "But Maybelle was going to do what she was going to do."

Buckshot came galloping up the holler. The dog sat on Janie's boot and leaned hard into her leg. She scratched his neck down his side where the pellets that gave him his name were yet lodged up underneath the skin. He looked like a bird dog you'd see in a sporting magazine, but lacked any such talent. Buckshot licked Janie's hand and grinned stupidly at her. When she stopped scratching, the dog trotted over and flopped down on a stringer of shot squirrels. He rolled and he rolled.

Lee's rifle lay there as well. Janie picked up the rifle and checked was it loaded. It was not. The weight of the thing in her hands felt comforting somehow. She sighted down the holler, where the underside of oak leaves flashed dull silver. She scanned a grove of laurel blooming wild-pink, spotting a piece of storm-blown tin among the tangled bush. She squeezed the trigger and made a firing sound in her head. Buckshot was sniffing the groundcover for something else worth rolling in. He snorted and shook his head. Thinking nobody looking, he picked up one of the shot squirrels and began slinking off.

"Quit that," Lee said.

Janie nearly dropped the rifle. But Buckshot knew who Lee meant. He spat out the squirrel as if it had climbed into his mouth, then sat down and casually thumped his ear a few times with his hind foot.

"Careful Sister," Lee said.

He'd taught her how to use this very rifle. Her daddy never was much for hunting. Had no problem with it, or with guns, or with his only daughter using them to kill wild game. Lee just knew more. He'd told her you held a gun tenderly, way you do a woman. Then, realizing his mistake, cleared his throat and said, Well. Lee'd learned to hunt from the white man and woman who raised him after his momma momma died. Janie had been obsessed with this time in Lee Malone's life, but getting stories out of him could be like drawing water from a hidden leak in the roof. Nothing like her grandmomma. Like her grandmomma was, she thought. The first past tense. This is life now. Stories had gushed out of Maybelle Treeborne as if her mouth was a wellspring. Janie propped the rifle against a poplar tree then told Buckshot to come on. The dog tilted his head, cocked his ears then followed the girl.

They walked alongside a mossy-banked stream broken up in turn by orange sandstone as big as a person's skull. Her grandmomma's shoes being missing irritated Janie to no end. This was something she could do. She aimed to find them or else. Maybelle always wore the same white canvas shoes when she went walking. When the shoes wore out she went down at Holly's Fine Dress and bought another pair same as the last. Janie imagined herself wearing shoes like them when she became an old woman. She wanted to be just like her grandmomma—from her short and high haircut to being without a husband. Janie already felt old, wanted it to be so. She lay in bed at night and strained to age the way some kids strain to grow taller.

She watched the groundcover and sandy mud for footprints. She wondered if her grandmomma had taken off her shoes to wade this stream. Maybe stuck them under a bush and forgot. Maybelle, Janie knew, loved water even though she couldn't swim herself. Janie hollered if Buckshot wandered too far off. She didn't want to be alone. The girl and the dog rested on the streambank for a little bit. Cedars curved upward through the hardwood canopy. Janie saw a salamander that looked like a coal escaped from a fire on bottom of the green streambed. She didn't feel like catching the creature though. Not right now. She didn't feel like anything at all. She got up, called Buckshot, and headed back the way they'd come.

Her daddy and Lee Malone had picked up the body and were toting it out of the holler. Maybelle's head hung to the side. Janie could see her grandmomma's cotton bloomers sagging where she'd messed herself. These details didn't register so much in the moment, but came to the girl in memory, time over, growing smoother as she aged and handled it through the years. She noticed Lee's rifle and the stringer of shot squirrels had been left behind. She picked them up. The squirrels stiff as a board and bottleflies crawling through their fur. She ran, Buckshot beside her nibbling at a squirrel when he could. Lee usually cut off the tails and gave them to the dog to chew on, to hide somewhere he eventually forgot. Janie could see Lee and her daddy were struggling to carry her grandmomma's body up the steep slope. Maybelle's dress kept getting hung up on brush. Lee tripped on a treeroot, and they dropped her. Way the body landed and rolled, it looked to Janie like her grandmomma had come back to life.

They sat down and rested. Buckshot walked past licking each man and Janie in turn. Nobody spoke. Janie watched a black piss ant crawl up her grandmomma's freckled arm. She wanted to brush it away, but she was afraid to go near the body. She felt more ashamed of this than she ever had felt about anything in her young life, treating MawMaw May like a curse she might catch. The girl knew better. Death was all around. She'd killed animals herself. But this was different. This was a person. This was her grandmomma. This had been her grandmomma. This was no longer her grandmomma. She didn't have a grandmomma anymore. What was was through and what would be had now commenced. A slow-blooming understanding that tormented the girl.

As they continued around the bluffline and up the slope, Janie pretended to pick birds out of the treebranches with Lee Malone's rifle. She kept lookout for Crusoe too. First chance, she thought, I'll find him and tell him what's happened. Without realizing she began making firing sounds out loud instead of inside her head. She worked the bolt, squeezed the trigger. Schklikt, klikt, poomb. Schklikt, klikt, poomb. Buckshot bounded up and sniffed Maybelle's bare foot. Lee gently kicked the dog away. Janie fake-fired and fake-fired. Schklikt, klikt, poomb. Kept her from thinking. But her daddy, he didn't understand it thataway.

"I told you!" Ren bellered, dropping his momma and grabbing his daughter by the arm. He yanked off his belt in one motion then began whipping her.

Janie dropped the rifle and highstepped to dodge her daddy's belt. The stringer of shot squirrels flopped everwhichaway as she danced around him. He wrenched her arm and landed a few across her back. She screamed, her shrill voice rolling throughout the woods, and swatted at his swinging hand as he whipped her ass.

Ren finally let go and quit. "Hush," he said. "You ain't killed." He shakily looped his belt back around his waist then picked up his momma's body again.

The pickup truck was still running. They put Maybelle in back and Lee got in with her. Janie slid the rifle behind the seat then climbed up onto the passenger side. "Move over," Ren said, motioning toward the steering wheel.

She could barely toe the pedals. Ren told her he'd shift if she just mashed the clutch and steered. She'd never driven a vehicle by herself. It wasn't but a couple hundred yards of open land between the barn and the house though, the only obstacle a towering pecan tree. She stalled a few times. A rainshower had blown up while they were in the woods. Elongated drops pinged the hood and streaked the windshield. Buckshot gave chase, barking, hopping sideways like a bronco. The pickup lurched, stalled again. Ren switched on the wipers and they beat time while Lee started to sing. Janie had never heard a voice prettier than his—and she'd heard many voices on the radio and on the console Lee kept on his screened backporch with the recordings he collected. His voice was deep by nature, but he could move it around where he desired. Janie wasn't the first Treeborne woman to admire it. She'd noticed the way MawMaw May acted whenever Lee Malone took out his guitar and let his voice put flesh to bone.

Lee sang while they unloaded and toted Maybelle's body into the house she had not lived in for years. He sang through the kitchen, the coffee fixed before her walk now gone cold, and down the hallway to the bathroom, where they set her in the tub then filled it with water. Geronimo jumped up and watched the running faucet till Lee ran the cat off. Ren left to use the phone at Varnado Price's place. Lee kept singing. Janie didn't know the names of these songs—if they even had names. Songs he'd sung no telling how many times, never imagining he would like this. But maybe that's not giving Lee Malone due credit. Song, he knew, could not be called on only in good times, or else it'd be no more useful than a blown-out wall socket. So he sang as he rinsed his love's lifeless body, her granddaughter watching from the hall.

"Come on help," he said. "You're big enough to I reckon."

Janie got down on her knees and leaned over the tub. Lee handed her a washrag and she wet it then touched the ball of her grandmomma's shoulder, where plum-colored freckles favored drops of paint. Suds raced down Maybelle's arms and wrinkled tits. She felt like jelly to Janie, who still half-expected her grandmomma's eyes to flash open when she touched the rag to her forehead. Of course they didn't. Death would not give second thought. Maybelle Treeborne was gone, and nothing Janie could do would change that.

When they'd finished Lee unstoppered the drain. Maybelle's body slouched down as the water ran out. They dried her off, skin warm from the water, then Lee picked her up. He stumbled getting her in bed and fell on top of her. Some of Hugh's arrowheads glued to a framed square of green velvet and wall-mounted shook as Lee pushed off the bed. The rainshower had passed. Outside the sun shined all over. Steam rose up from black fallen leaves and burnt off midair. Lee put Maybelle in a clean cotton dress, and Janie cracked the window to let out her grandmomma's ghost and let in what breeze, if any, might come.

❧

Janie could hear Sheriff Aaron Guthrie, her daddy and Lee Malone in the kitchen, drinking fresh coffee and waiting on Millard Andrews to show up with his hearse. *Squirrel hunting. Say you went and called Ren after you found her? Up at Varny's? Uh-huh. Your rifle too? How many bullets left? Well count them motherfuckers then. I wish y'all would of just let her be. I wasn't leaving my momma off in the woods Aaron. Bugs'd already got at her. I know it, but be a whole lot easier had y'all just let her be.*

Janie put on her boots and went outside. Buckshot had chased Geronimo up a stunted peach tree. The dog circled and the cat slicked back its ears, that one eye narrowed to but a bright blue slit. Janie plucked a peach from the tree. Hard as a hickory nut and too sour to eat. She chucked it off in the weeds and let the animals alone. She needed to find Crusoe.

Halfway across the pasture she heard a vehicle coming down the driveway. The pickup she recognized right off the bat, and she could make out through its bug-splattered windshield a bright-colored Hawaiian shirt—her uncle Luther. Seated next to him, her aunt Tammy. The pickup slid to a stop and the siblings hustled inside the house.

Janie followed the old path of the storm toward her granddaddy's junk garden. Her grandmomma had given this clearing that name. Lovingly, the girl reckoned. Anyhow it was apt. Looked like the junk grew up from the ground. But truth, the ground was eating it. Janie and her grandmomma had walked this path umpteen-thousand times. Summer, Maybelle toted a garden hoe for killing snakes. She despised these creatures, which seemed to relish making the junk garden their home, nesting all up in and underneath the assemblies Hugh'd toted out there and left. Janie and her grandmomma walked together all over The Seven. Scanned the treetops for stuck assemblies, poked at the groundcover for buried ones, turning up leaves that showed spiderwebs like cotton bolls, and earthworms squirming in dirt black as coffee brewed at night. They toted whatever they found out at the junk garden and laid it there among the rest. Some days they found not a piece. That was alright. Maybelle just told Elberta stories then. Some of the stories she'd learned from Hugh—the rest she made up.

When it was warm weather their walks ended down at the spring. Day her grandmomma died, Janie stripped off her boots and waded in. She hollered for Crusoe. The spring his main haunt, the place Hugh had taken him from by the bucketload. She checked the old springhouse. Empty, Crusoe wasn't there. A few comb-headed jays and redbirds looking like they wore makeup were streaking colors among the hickories and oaks as if nothing out of the ordinary had happened that day. To them, Janie thought, it ain't. There wasn't a breeze, but Janie noticed treebranches bobbing as if there was. The hair on her arms stood up at the thought that her grandmomma's ghost might of blown past—might blow here forever.

She tucked her dress into her bloomers and waded out till water came up past her scabby knees. Squirrels barked and chucked acorns her way. Janie cussed them and waded farther out. The spring was kindly shaped like a lima bean and bubbled from underneath a warty limestone ledge. Sometimes she would stick her arm into the spring's dark mouth and scoop out handfuls of sand and sticks and leaves to increase its natural flow. It drained down a holler into Dismal Creek, which ran into the Elberta River, which ran on and on, out of the county if you followed it far enough. Janie often imagined doing so. She stepped out of the spring then sat down where coon and deer and birds had tracked the mud. Hollered for Crusoe again and watched water droplets sliding down her legs through newly come blond hair.

When he, a creature of her granddaddy's creation, showed up, Crusoe was dragging a crumpled sheet of tin that'd been shot through with pinky-size holes. Janie picked up one end and they toted it over at a flat-bottom boat her uncle Luther and daddy had abandoned as boys. Their second boat. The first a baby's coffin the boys mistakenly purchased from Gus's Buy-All. Chicken-legged Luther and dark-headed Ren aimed to sail clear to the Gulf of Mexico yet got not even out of hollering distance from the pasture before giving up. Elbertans a people of great ambition sometimes lacking see-through, but Lord at the glory that comes from a spark.

Janie and Crusoe flipped over the boat. Underneath its spidery bottom was more of her granddaddy's art: angels spiraling down from out of a stormcloud painted on wavy windowglass, a crusty black man playing guitar with his big long blue-roped toes. They flattened out the sheet of tin and on it was painted an alligator garfish. Inside the fish's belly you could see all the things it'd swallowed across time, including a house where a family stood waving from a cluttered porch. Crusoe slid this piece in next to the rest of the art he'd toted there.

"I was hunting you," Janie said.

Crusoe shucked his cutoffs and waded in. The water turned oily on top and flowed away in a rainbow slick from the dirt boy's distended belly. When he bent forward rusted metal innards poked out of his blue-black skin. He splashed hisself a few times and sappy droplets rolled down his little body like mercury from a busted tube. He sank down underneath the surface. A mushroom cloud rose all around him then tailed off like wet smoke.

He climbed out and sat down next to Janie. Crusoe stunk in that agreeable way old things stink. He smiled borrowed teeth then cupped his softened face and mashed down hard, shaping his head back the way it ought to of looked—or closer to it. Way Crusoe truly ought to look lost forever the day Hugh Treeborne died on the screened porch while the dirt boy, his masterpiece, sat there on his lap.

"Help," Crusoe said.

"Help what?"

"Tote."

Before Janie could ask tote what she heard hollering up toward the house. She could make out her aunt Tammy's voice above the rest. No true surprise. When she heard Lee Malone though she knew to take off and see what was going on.

She found them in the front yard. Her daddy and the sheriff on the ground while the others—Tammy, Lee and Luther—watched. Ren had an arm locked around the sheriff's throat, squeezing. It wasn't out of place in Elberta to see grown men fight, but this fight, Janie immediately understood, was different. The tighter Ren squeezed the more the sheriff's eyes bulged. Before long they favored two peeled eggs. His leg kicked and kicked like Janie'd seen rabbits' do when they'd been shot. Ren might of choked the sheriff to death had Tammy not pulled a pistol out of her purse.

"Quit it now," she said, bright red nails clicking against the underside of the barrel as she struggled to get a grip. "Quit this bullshit right this minute!"

Ren let go and got on his knees. The sheriff sat up too and rubbed his throat. Ren held out his hand toward her and said, "Tammy—"

"You want to take up for this, this . . ."

"That ain't what this is about Tam," Ren said.

"Ain't what this is about? Then you tell me what it's about Ren Tree-borne. Tell me, because it looks to me just like what this is about."

"Tammy," he said.

She stepped toward him.

"Put that thing up," Lee Malone said.

She wheeled around and shook the pistol way you do something sticky from your hand. "Don't you say a word," she said. "Don't you say one single goddamn word to me. I'd just as soon shoot you as ever lay eyes on your sorry face again."

"Tammy," the sheriff said. He had his gun drawn now and partway raised. "Let's put that thing up now before somebody gets hurt."

She ignored him. She was staring at Lee Malone in a way which Janie had never seen anybody stare at another person.

The sheriff said her name again.

Luther giggled at something mysterious to everybody else.

Tammy ignored all of it, focused on the bloodspot she saw pulsing out of a dime-size hole in Lee Malone's chest. Ren stepped between them and this image was no more. Tammy shook the pistol and wailed as if something deep inside her had torn loose. The need to piss just over-came Janie right then. She pinched together, but it didn't matter. Warm yellow ran down her legs and collected in the bottom of her boots.

"You ought to live with all you done," Tammy said to Lee. She dropped the pistol and the sheriff hurried to pick it up.

Tammy grabbed Geronimo from where he lay in a clump of mon-key grass. The cat meowed. Tammy banged through the screendoor. All the windows stood open, so she could be heard going back to the bed-room where her momma's body lay in waiting. A door slammed shut then it was quiet, like the whole scene had been dreamed up.

Janie snuck off before anybody saw her. She set Crusoe down and peeled off her wet bloomers. The dirt boy staggered toward the woods. Janie slid aside a piece of plywood covering a gap in the house's founda-tion, balled up her bloomers and chucked them far up underneath the house, where they're liable to remain this day yet.

The Artist at Work

1929

Beyond town the lane became little more than a mossy path littered with slick patches of black fallen leaves. A man on horseback who Maybelle Chambliss didn't recognize galloped past and tipped his brown hat. She hurried on as morning settled. Summertime flat-out oppressive in this valley. A few gaunt cows munched goldenrod and thistle in an otherwise untended field. At least there was no ash and soot this far out, she thought, passing the rock Dee Sargent had mentioned looked like a ship run aground. Getting close now. A redtail hawk pealed into the sky. Maybelle came to the last turn on the map Dee'd drawn for her. She climbed underneath a fence, hid in a honeysuckle clump and waited.

Before long Hugh Treeborne came walking up the path from his property. Shirt and britches stained red and stiff with mud and clay. The Authority's *A* was stitched high on the right sleeve. He was taller than Maybelle remembered him being the day he came into the post office trying to mail a letter without an address. Uglier too, she thought, fighting back a laugh. He walked right by the honeysuckle, then turned down the lane toward town.

She was bursting to tell what she'd done time Dee showed up again needing to mail four fighting roosters to Sapmore, Louisiana. Since becoming Elberta's postmaster one year ago, Maybelle had sent the

Sargents' fighting roosters faraway as Mexico. While Dee handled the shipping, her husband, Tucker, waited at a coffee stand where mule traders and drunks lingered and ate boiled green peanuts, so a great fart-cloud hung around well into the afternoon. Maybelle loved seeing who mailed what where. She'd make up stories about how come they might be doing so. She loved walking the delivery routes whenever Sampley, the lone letter carrier, got drunk at Hernando's Hideaway. Maybelle just loved talking to folks—well the ones who'd talk back to her. She could of filled a book with the stories they told. Taking on the past of this place sure as shit beat turning over the nagging parts of her own.

She toted the caged roosters out back and set them in some shade till the postal truck came and carried off all the mail that wasn't local. Kids would chase the truck, falling back and picking up at unspoken locations, like a relay team, to the town limits. She popped a rubber band around her wrist so she'd remember to water the roosters till then. It was a smoky day. The roosters scratched for bugs among the ash blown in their cages.

Dee rolled two cigarettes and handed one to Maybelle. "I remember us little girls thinking his daddy was handsome, bless his heart," she said, grinning what teeth remained in her small head. "Treebornes always have been strange."

"How come you to say that?"

Dee shrugged, inhaled, then blew smoke right in Maybelle's face. Maybelle slapped her on the arm, and Dee giggled and coughed.

"Well'd you just gawk or what?"

"I hid in a bush!" Maybelle said, going into a giggling-coughing fit of her own.

"Lord, you two'd about deserve each other," Dee said. She puffed five quick times then ground out the cigarette against the wall. "Well, I got to get Tuck."

"Love you," Maybelle said.

"Love you back."

Dee Sargent was the closest thing to a friend Maybelle had in Elberta, Alabama. Thirty years old, never married, Maybelle heard folks

talk from day one in town and felt the looks shot in her direction like
arrows. It would of bothered the younger Maybelle, a girl whupped by
her upbringing till nearly all she cared about was what folks thought of
her. Preacher's daughter, his sole precious blessing. Dee Sargent was all
the time on Maybelle about finding a man. Maybelle wasn't opposed to
men, though, time, the idea made her squirmy—same as anybody with
good sense. This too she blamed on her folks, who'd hammered beliefs
into their child as if she was a piece of lumber meant for a million nails.
She used to keep a pencil drawing of them that had been done during
revival at the church where her father preached to the coal miners who
went down into tunnels burrowed beneath Bankhead. I send God with
them, Jim Chambliss said, and what else is there? Maybelle had been
with men—two in all. Hurt less than she'd expected, not nearly as fun
as she'd hoped.

Later that night, in the little apartment she rented above Beachy's
Butcher Shop, Maybelle fixed baby turnips in chicken fat. Sweated out
the greens and ate them too with hot pickled peppers, half a raw onion
and a piece of cornbread. The onion stung her tongue and made her
eyes water in a pleasurable way. She washed down the meal with a jar
of buttermilk then sat on the windowsill, watching distant burnpiles
thrust flame into the darkening sky. Beside her were four uprooted but-
tercup bulbs wrapped in damp newspaper. She'd dug them from a little
graveyard she passed one day when she got turned around walking Sampley's route. Maybelle aimed to find a new place to live soon, somewhere with a yard, and plant these bulbs. Perennials, they'd return each
spring. She could pick the flowers then, remembering them as bulbs
and this time in her life. She liked marking memory thataway. But nobody would rent a houseplace to a single woman. Not even with so many
now abandoned. The apartment was fine if you didn't mind the sounds
and smells of the butcher shop, the river of blood running down the back
alley every evening when Beachy rinsed his knives and saws and thick
cutting boards. Dozens of stray cats gathered at twilight to lick up bits
of flesh and fat spinning down this red river. Beachy cussed the foul crea-

tures and the eternal racket coming from where The Authority was building that hydropower dam. The racket was omnipresent, The Authority's progress inescapable. Maybelle knew exactly what her father would say about it—world's headed straight for hell in a handbasket.

The shift had just begun when a piece of the spillway's support wall broke loose and nearly killed two men digging in the channel down below. Hugh Treeborne helped drag them out. Velston, the foreman, a wild-man from the far northern reaches of Alabama, toed the men till they came to. They'd lost their shovels, so would use buckets the rest of the day. Hugh was a strong swimmer, but he respected the river. He thought it foolheaded to move it. To plug it seemed impossible. His daddy used to say a big fat woman lived in the Elberta and made its waters sing so. Hugh doubted this, but never the river's power.

During lunch everybody swallowed sugar pills this big around, pills The Authority told their men would protect against mosquito bites. Hugh swallowed, but he had little faith in anything The Authority said. He was using It, and It using him. Taking part in such work felt like a negotiation with hisself that Hugh was not yet ready to enter into.

He watched Velston sitting in the shade with a roasted chicken on his lap. The foreman handed the birthmarked man a drumstick, way one might a dog, and the birthmarked man gnawed off the meat then snapped in two the bone and sucked what marrow could be found there. Some of the workers thought Velston wasn't a wild-man from the far north of the state at all, but instead De Soto hisself, come down off his pedestal in town and made flesh. Just look, spitting image of Him. Balding head, hair long on the sides and in the back, and dark eyes. They speculated on the subject while eating sardine sandwiches, washing the food down with handfuls of the river. Hush, they said when Velston got up to throw the chicken caracass into the river, he's coming thisaway.

After lunch they stacked sandbags to staunch the river where it swoll near a buried sandstone knob. Some of the builders hollered from the scaffolding at the diggers toiling on the ground. In reply Hugh led his crew in baring their backsides, bending over and spreading wide their hairy asscheeks, which they wiggled back and forth. Down in the channel again, they dug deeper into a hard layer of clay and bailed buckets of bloodred water up where Velston and the birthmarked men paced. The sun beat down without repentance while Hugh tried not to wonder about Loudermilk, who'd left a couple weeks ago. Hugh wasn't sure how long it took to drive up north and back. He tried not to think about it, but his mind raced that direction like a spooked rabbit toward its hunter. Before Hugh realized it, the birthmarked man had raised his pistol and fired, signaling the day was done.

Rather than leave directly Hugh sat on the riverbank. As he did daily, the birthmarked man waded ankle-deep and shot at fish. Hugh watched a few stragglers hustling down the wobbly ladders. Most of the builders came from up north too, where they'd raised skyscrapers and laid track and built oceangoing ships. Steelworkers, they looked down upon Elberta and its structures of wood and tin and hand-cut stone. There'd been trouble, especially at places like Hernando's Hideaway. Killings and cons. Hugh wanted to believe this Loudermilk fellow was different. But hope, he knew, was a dangerous thing. The birthmarked man fired two more times, interrupting Hugh's thoughts. Hugh looked at the turbines where they waited sealed in crates big as cabins, the riverbank washing out from underneath them. The Authority had hired men from Freedom Hills to guard this machinery, as if anybody had the means to run off with something so enormous. The paper said the Hernando de Soto Dam would be completed in four years. The second hydropower dam built by The Authority in what was now being called the Alabama Watershed. Folks had started picnicking some days on a grassy rise to watch the slow build of progress. History made before their eyes. Everybody wanted a piece. Why not Hugh Treeborne too? The pistol clicked in the birthmarked man's hand. A shot-dead garfish floated near the bank, half-open mouth showing hundreds of little sharp teeth. The birthmarked man stuck the pistol in his britches then walked into a stretch of woods.

Even after what was fixing to happen, Hugh Treeborne could not put a name to the thing that compelled him to follow the birthmarked man. He should of gone straight to The Seven and hunted more assemblies. But he did not. Another crew was cutting the woods that lay ahead of the diggers. Gone for the day, the slashed woods silent except for sticks snapping underneath Hugh's heavy workboots. The Authority wasn't supposed to fool with timber however-many feet below the lake's designated shoreline. Let the water cover it all. But these trees, when cut and skinned, were free money.

As Hugh followed the birthmarked man, he thought back to a day Caz'd caught him down at Dismal Creek shaping little mud horses and setting them on rocks to dry. Hugh couldn't of been five or six at the time. Caz called it a curse and whipped the boy with a rope till his legs bled. This whipping and the ones that followed were not some key to understanding the man Hugh'd become. He didn't know much, but he knew the past could not be organized in such a nice neat manner. The word *curse* terrified and shamed Hugh the boy though. He tried to stop making art and couldn't, compelled then as now by forces unknown toward acts deemed unacceptable. Cursed. In secret he began sculpting other forms and figures from materials he could find or take from the world around him. These assemblies became bigger as he did, and harder to hide—like the uncontrollable bulge he sometimes got in his pants when he saw a girl in town. Over the years he'd stashed assemblies all across The Seven, which made tracking them down for Loudermilk a difficult task.

Up ahead in the woods Hugh heard a shovel singing against dirt and rock. He continued toward this sound till he came to a cemetery quartered off by a low stone wall. Velston and the birthmarked man stood among the listing headmarkers. Hugh'd heard that The Authority would relocate every grave the lake might cover. Judging by its look this cemetery likely had no name remembered by anybody not resting in its patch of earth though. Hugh hunkered down before he could be spotted and he watched Velston climb into a dug-up grave. Before long the foreman struck a coffin then heaved out a corpse, which the birthmarked man checked for anything of value. There was nothing.

"Pretty out here ain't it?" the birthmarked man said, squatting on his heels.

Velston ignored this ponderance. But the birthmarked man's words had prodded Hugh Treeborne. He crawled nearer and could make out the dates on some markers, which belonged to folks born before Alabama was a state. Folks long forgotten and soon to be forever lost, he realized, picturing the river's impending path. The names were weatherworn fragments, indecipherables. Alone they meant nothing, but as a collection they told the story of a people, a place, a history, a time, which suddenly bared down on Hugh Treeborne with irreconcilable weight. People's memories, he believed, were worth preserving. Memory the only thing keeping us from being nobodies from nowhere.

Deep panic stirred inside him. He had to do something. He grabbed the wall and a stone came loose in his hand. The stone about this big, double the size of a ripe peach. He gripped it tight as he watched the foreman move through the soft ground into another grave. Soon Velston struck wood again and dragged out another corpse. A woman, long red hair still connected to her tobacco-colored skull. She had not been buried with anything valuable either. Velston kicked the corpse and a hole opened up as if she was made from newspaper. The birthmarked man fingered this opening, then hurriedly unhitched his britches and fished hisself out. "Little dry," he said, poking his dick in and out of the corpse. Velston watched for a moment then began digging up another grave. The birthmarked man laughed and kept on, pumping faster faster . . . Hugh Treeborne rose to his feet, realizing with terrible certainty what he was fixing to do.

One blow in back of the head and down Velston fell. Hugh kicked the shovel out of arm's reach. The birthmarked man looked up from his filthy business and grasped for his pistol. Too late. Hugh smashed the stone into his face. He swung again and again, till it looked like the birthmark had grown to cover all that was left hanging on the man's skull.

Maybelle caught him from behind this time. Rather than walking he drove a wagon hitched to an ancient-looking mule. She followed at a distance, dodging mounds of mule shit. It was early morning. She wondered where he'd been all night. The wagon creaked under a heavy load. Something lumpy, maybe melons. Did this wagon trip have something to do with him being an artist? The story she'd seen in the newspaper the other day told how Hugh Treeborne's art had been taken by a collector named Loudermilk all way to Philadelphia, Pennsylvania.

She hid in the same honeysuckle clump and waited. Took him a long while to return in his Authority clothes this time. He appeared dazed, troubled. She let him get a good distance down the path toward town before crawling out of the vine. She looked both ways then headed down onto his property at something like a run.

The house had been set up on smooth stones above a black dirt and moss-covered clearing. It had a stone chimney and a cluttered porch. Not just any clutter though; this was, Maybelle realized as she approached, his art. She'd never seen anything like it. Never seen art period, her father's church not even ornamented with colored-glass windows. It was too much for the human eye to take in. She blinked and she blinked as if her vision might adjust. This, she thought, was what her father meant when he spoke about God-with-a-capital-G. It'd taken thirty years for Maybelle Chambliss to understand.

Inside an old chicken coop behind the house she found more. She wondered what to call it. Not paintings, not sculptures. A mix. She had no word. The art was stacked on top of itself and propped against walls. Looked like this coop was where he fashioned it. She wondered where he found all the objects he used as she pilfered boxes and crates and jars and buckets and sacks filled with—to her, detached from order— meaningless junk.

Something fell.

She spun around, expecting to be caught by him, and saw a little burnt boy lying on the floor. No, just some strange doll. Crooked animal teeth smiled and hard cloudy eyes shined where they were set in a misshapen blue-black face. Maybelle noticed a tuft of pinestraw sticking out of the doll's side and poked it back in. Did the thing move? Foot, she thought. No, it surely did not. The doll was heavy and it smelled old. Maybelle took big breaths of this pleasant odor as she toted the doll around the property, time getting away from her.

When she arrived back in town, folks were waiting to be let inside the post office. She apologized for being late, dabbing sweat off the back of her neck where her thick blond hair fell. The customers said they'd worried something terrible had happened to her. One woman in particular seemed disappointed they'd been wrong. Where had she been this morning, and what on earth were those greasy stains all over her pretty dress?

After work that evening Maybelle sat on the fire escape and ate a peach. Wasn't her first Elberta peach, but this one better than any she'd eaten before. She could taste things in its flesh she could not name.

The sky had slabbed over. Faraway heat lightning flashed, burning the scene in the alley below onto her eyes for a moment. Beachy and the stray cats, the butcher banging a long curved knife against the brick building. Rather than scare off the cats the sound served to call more. Yowled and paced and hissed. Maybelle waved to the butcher, who wiped his forehead bloody and waved back, then doused the cats with a pail of soapy pink water, sending them fleeing down the alley to lick themselves dry.

She tried reading a book. Pages turned as if they were made of cement. Her father would of told her to pray about it. Pray May. Pray. Pray, foot. Prayer his answer to everything. Maybelle the girl used to pretend she heard God just to satisfy him. She put down the book. Tomorrow would be Saturday. She'd finish work by lunch—then what? From her window she could see the partly built dam by light of the moon and the ever-burning fires. The Authority paid men from Freedom Hills to patrol the area, toting riverstone-sharpened blades and tending coalfires. There'd been threats to dynamite the thing, she'd read in the paper. And the recent disappearance of that foreman and his simple assistant. Awful. Sometimes Maybelle toted mail to an Authority address out near the dam, meeting along the way those bone-tired watchmen headed back to Freedom Hills, which had been founded after freed slaves tried leaving the valley and were turned back by armed riders. Even children killed, little heads jammed onto pointed limbs planted along the road like a fence. If Freedom Hills received mail it came through a system unknown to her. She'd written a letter to her supervisors about fixing this, but so far had heard nothing back.

She opened a jug of muscadine wine. After a few sips her tongue felt doubled in size. She'd never been good at waiting. According to her father patience was a virtue. Drinking a sin. She finished the jug of sweet wine, then she went out walking—too damn stubborn to admit to herself where she was headed till she'd arrived there.

The mule surprised her in the path. Good way to get yourself killed, she thought. Surely Hugh Treeborne owned a rifle. She wondered how getting shot felt. Time, she'd wanted to be an actress. Left Bankhead for Birmingham to audition for a role. Some actress you would of been, she thought, can't even imagine getting shot. She clucked at the mule, which swished its tail and threw back its head. She patted the creature's rump and it stepped aside so she could pass.

The air settled into something beyond stillness. She knew this feeling, this calm, and she took it as a sign, though for what she wasn't sure yet. Her folks had nailed the notion of signs into her so crooked and deep it could never be pried out. She'd tried to remove it ever since leaving Bankhead. Her father lived by signs, hisself an interpreter of them. Brother Jim saw signs everywhere, and preached to his congregation their joys and dangers, mysteries, the obviousness of some, how others could appear—just like that—or be teased out slowly over the course of a lifetime. Following signs required faith. You got to keep ever-diligent watch, he'd shout from the pulpit as he slammed a veiny fist, and be faithful-true! The coal miners and dirt farmers of Bankhead, Alabama, listened with pure-dee awe as Brother Jim preached on signs twice a week. They'd continue to do so till the day he missed a sign telling him that a woman's boils were beyond his power of healing. The sores soon covered the preacher's body and he died too.

Maybelle could see a light burning inside the old chicken coop. All sudden there was the clanging of metal striking metal. She waited for it to quit. When she snuck closer she saw Hugh Treeborne hunched over a big metal box, faded red with white lettering that said BRGS-STR. He finished attaching a chute to an opening on the side, then he removed a panel and poured in a glug or two of gasoline. He yanked a cord and an engine rattled, but did not catch. He yanked again. This time the engine caught. He held his hand up to the chute, turning it back and forth, waiting, feeling for something unseen.

"What is that thing?" Maybelle said.

Hugh grabbed a wrench. "This is private property!"

"Hold on," she said. "My name's Mayb—"

"You need to go on. I know exactly who you are."

This thrilled her to the bone. He remembered her. She ducked inside the coop. "What's that thing for?"

After a moment Hugh put down the wrench. "Keep things cool," he said.

She held her hand near the chute and felt chill air blowing out. "It ain't art?"

"What you know about that?"

"Just what I seen in the paper," she said, grinning. "What's it keeping cool?"

Hugh turned off the engine and the box rattled then stilled. "I don't care much for strangers and their questions."

"Well you best start getting to know me so I ain't one then."

Hugh did not ask her to leave as he piddled around the coop, though he also gave no indication that he cared whether she did. Maybelle was surprised when he invited her onto the porch for coffee. It was late, but she drank anyhow. She could taste chicory mixed in to make the beans go further.

"This'll keep me up all night," she said.

"You want some more?"

"I'm fine," she told him.

"Well, reckon I will."

While Hugh went to fix more coffee, she peeked inside. Maybelle hadn't set foot in a country house since leaving Bankhead. She'd forgotten how primitive one could be when compared to the apartment she lived in now, or where she'd lived in Birmingham when she began working for the postal service, or even the steel-mill workers' shotguns in the company towns surrounding the Magic City. The inside of Hugh's house brought forth memories Maybelle would of just as soon denied. She noticed a quilting rack hanging from the ceiling in the front room and wondered if he had a woman after all. He was coming back. She returned to the porch.

"Did you ever get that letter sent?"

"Oh, no," he said, sipping from his jar.

He appeared embarrassed by her question, so she decided to change the subject. "How'd you find this yankee to buy your art?"

"He didn't buy it," Hugh said. "And he found me."

She was confused by this answer. Hugh Treeborne wasn't easy to talk to. After he'd finished his coffee he offered to take her back into town. She rubbed the mule's ears while he loaded a shovel, a pick and some burlap in back of the wagon.

"What's that for?"

"Something I got to do," he said.

He didn't speak again all way into town. Maybelle thanked him for the ride then climbed down off the driver's seat.

"It was my uncle," he said.

"What was your uncle?"

"I was mailing that letter to."

"Well how come you not just tell me that? We could of looked him up in the regist—"

"My uncle, he passed away."

Maybelle was even more confused now. Folks came to the post office trying to mail all sorts of things, but never a letter to the dead.

"I shouldn't of said nothing."

"No," she said. "It's alright. All of us grieve—"

Hugh chuckled, trying to hide a smile.

"What on earth is it?" she asked.

"My uncle's been dead years," he said, full-on laughing now. Tears streaked his face. "I wanted to talk to you and couldn't think of nobody else's name to put down."

Dee was right—Treebornes were strange. But Maybelle liked it. After this night she visited The Seven, what Hugh called his property, every day that summer after close. Sometimes he wasn't there when she arrived. She'd track down the dirt doll, which Hugh called Crusoe, and walk the property herself. The Seven more gorgeous than any piece of land she'd ever traipsed. Walking it felt like stepping out of time and seeing what Earth might look like had man not come along with ideas and aspirations.

That cooling machine had disappeared since the night they met. She didn't ask where to, or where Hugh went with the mule-drawn wagon each dark of night, or what he was hauling onto The Seven. He didn't care for questions, especially when he was working on an assemblie, he called his art. Not asking questions went against Maybelle Chambliss's nature. She pieced together that he was gathering assemblies for when that yankee returned. It just about killed her to not ask how come he'd toted all of them off into the woods in the first place. The trade-off for not asking was she got to watch Hugh work. To her it was an impenetrable mystery how he could take cast-off junk and paint and burn and twist and sculpt and nail and shape it into such beautiful objects. Assemble it. Asking how would be a cruelty, she thought. Something plain as understanding could only ruin it.

She tried describing this feeling to Dee next time she came by the post office to mail fighting roosters. Dee seemed less interested in what Hugh did with his art than what he did with Maybelle and didn't delay asking whether they'd made love yet.

"You witch!" Maybelle answered, puffing a cigarette. "Of course we ain't."

Dee patted her arm. "Sure, sugar, course y'all ain't." She paused and grinned. "And I'm the Queen of England."

Maybelle was not a prude. She wanted these moments for herself. Hugh rolling up her dress, her legs wrapped around his waist, feeling overcome by panic and pleasure when he finished. They'd lie there after—in the house, in the yard, once in his studio with the dirt boy almost watching—and hold hands. Oftentimes Hugh would talk. He told of his daddy Casabianca, or Caz, and the tragedy of how he died. He told of creating Crusoe from clay dug up by the spring they'd made love beside on a moon-runny night. He told of his best friend Lee Malone, who, after weeks visiting The Seven, Maybelle still had not met. He told stories about Hernando de Soto and about Chief Coosa, the leader of the Elberta Indians. Remarkable stories that deserved to be heard by others, she thought, just like his assemblies deserved to be seen. One day she asked where in the world he came up with all this.

"My head," he said.

"Did you ever write any of it down?"

He told her no.

"What do you reckon'll happen when you're dead then?"

Hugh seemed to consider this question more closely than most. "It'll go with me," he answered.

To Dirt She Returneth

1958

❧

Ricky Birdsong dug a grave two days after Lee Malone found Maybelle Treeborne's body in the woods. She would be buried in the pasture next to Hugh. You could still do things thataway back then. Tammy'd asked Ricky to dig the grave because she knew he would for free. She, both brothers and her niece stood underneath the pole barn watching Ricky use an excavator to scoop clods of grass and dirt into a big steel-toothed bucket and make a pile by the gravesite. Ricky waved as he dumped another load.

"Reckon he could work any slower?"

Ren said, "He's doing alright Tam."

"I'm getting my hair done this afternoon."

"He'll be through before long," Ren said. "If not, me and Luth can handle it. You go on to your appointment."

Luther raised his eyebrows at mention of his name. He pinched the front of his Hawaiian shirt and fanned his herniated gut.

"I should of known not to ask Ricky Birdsong to do anything," Tammy said. "Never have been able to be nice to that boy."

Ricky had a crush on Tammy-then-just-Treeborne back in high school. Him the Conquistadors star running back, her a curly-headed virgin who smoked cigarettes behind the marching band building during lunch. Tammy watched her figure and wore gaudy earrings. Her year-book pictures made everybody else on the page look uglier than ham-mered shit. High cheekbones, green eyes set inside lids like halved nutshells. She was tan and tall, like her momma and daddy, and made average grades. There was no acting club or drama class at Elberta County High School, so Tammy prepared for the day she'd become an actress by watching movies at the Rampatorium every chance she got. Ricky Birdsong often saw her there. Him and the other Conquistadors sat on the far back terrace, drinking and cutting up. It wasn't just Tam-my's looks that got to Ricky. Like everybody within earshot, he knew her plans to leave Elberta, Alabama, and admired her ambition. Would of done anything for her, and Tammy couldn't of cared less. Ricky, she always said, was provincial. Tammy had ideas and she clung to them. No telling how many weekends she conned boys to carry her out yon-der at the Ramp so she could envision herself up on that screen.

Ricky Birdsong never was one of these boys though. She didn't date Conquistadors, and Ricky was the greatest of them all. The used-to-bes tell it took six boys to bring him down, legs yet pumping long after the referee blew his whistle. Never would step out of bounds, which helped get that scholarship from Mississippi—and also wound up doing him in. Ricky made it partway through the second summer practice then fell out while running sprints. He woke up in a hospital room with a win-dow looking out over a cotton field bordered by pines. He felt no differ-ent, but the doctors assured Ricky that his life had changed entirely. His brain, they said, could not endure another blow to the head. Just the sloshing around caused by all those sprints had been enough to put the boy in a shallow coma. He had to be careful now, protect hisself, yet even so, the doctors said, his brain would over time degenerate.

News of this condition beat Ricky Birdsong home. When he stepped off that silver bus, the whole town was waiting with streamers and signs. The ECHS marching band, dressed out full and splendid, played the fight song again and again and again. Folks filled up the Birdsong house with casserole dishes and somebody'd strung a painted banner on the water tower: FLY, RICKY, FLY! It was like a death had occurred.

"I just want to move on from all this ugliness," Tammy said to her brothers over the excavator's roar. "Ren, I hope you ain't still upset over that will."

"Now ain't the time Tam." He fished a cigarette pack from his shirt-pocket and smashed it twice against the heel of his hand. "If that's how Momma wanted it, then that's how it is."

"She always had a mind of her own," Tammy said. "Momma was going to do what Momma was going to do. Just ask Daddy."

This was the second time that day Tammy'd brought up Maybelle's will. She'd met Ren and Janie at The Fencepost for breakfast. Still tried to watch her figure, but Tammy loved a biscuit with just a dab of peach jelly and an egg so runny you'd dare not call it cooked. Truth, the will had been her doing. She'd played on her momma's guilt and her feeble mind. Tammy felt bad that her brothers would wind up with none of The Seven. Oh, she could give them some land on down the road, but it wouldn't be the same as if their momma did.

Ricky jammed a lever and the excavator heaved forward. The bucket came swinging down almost to the ground.

Tammy continued fussing about how long it was taking Ricky to do the job. She had on a bathing suit underneath her see-through blouse and high-waisted shorts. Summer days now long enough she might yet get to tan her legs before dark. She needed to look her best for her momma's funeral. They were expecting a big turnout for the burial. Peach Days was just about two months away too. Tammy couldn't afford to let herself go this time of year.

Ren said, "I'm going to see Millard down at Blessed Assurance this evening and set up a installment plan."

"Luther told me you asked a nigger to sing the funeral."

"I asked Lee."

"Well I can't believe Aaron just let him out thataway," Tammy said. "A murder and only kept him in jail one night? That don't seem right."

"Nobody's calling it murder Tam."

"Well, nobody ain't either," she said. "And what about Daddy? Does he not matter?"

"Daddy's been dead ten years."

"Eleven," she said.

"Lee's always been good to this family."

"Good, hell. He's liable to've led her off in them woods and—"

"Don't Tam."

She glanced at her niece, who, looked like, was squatted down peering at the dirt. The girl was odd. Always had been and now her with that bizarre doll Hugh'd made. Ren'd said Janie hadn't let the thing out of her sight these last two days. Even slept with it. "Sister," Tammy said, "what're you doing toting that filthy thing around?"

"I like him," the girl said.

"She ain't hurting nothing," Ren said.

Janie stood up and wandered down the other end of the barn where her uncle Luther had laid back in an old claw-foot tub. His arms and legs dangled over the sides. She set Crusoe on his lap then stepped over a tangled roll of barbed wire and began picking through water-damaged boxes filled with foggy green jars meant for canning vegetables. Sometimes the girl could find a pearly snakeskin down in bottom of one, maybe a dry-fly shell clutched ahold the rim. She collected things like this and kept them on a windowsill in her bedroom.

She heard her uncle Luther talking to the dirt boy. In the corner of her vision she watched her uncle pull a blue-green bottle out from the pocket of his Hawaiian shirt then drip two clear droplets underneath his bulbous tongue. He offered the dropper to Crusoe, chuckled, then slouched back down, staring up at the underside of the roof, where swallows slung a universe of mud and straw nests. Before long Luther'd dozed off. Janie stood over him and watched the hula dancers on his shirt sway with his wheezy exhalations. She picked up Crusoe and rejoined her daddy and her aunt.

"Momma wasn't always in her right mind," Tammy was saying. Ren lit another cigarette and jammed it between his pursed lips. He'd smoked probably an entire box of Blue Mountains over the last forty-eight hours. "None of us wanted to face it," Tammy went on. "We believe whatever's easiest to believe, you know."

"I reckon so," he said. "She just always told me the land'd be split up between the all of us. I don't know. I reckon it don't matter."

"I'll give you your piece of the land Bubba," Tammy said. She rubbed his shoulder, causing the ash-end of the cigarette to break off. "Right after we take care of this funeral mess. Then you ought to clear it like Woot and me are fixing to do. Timber's high right now. You could take Nita somewhere with the money. Y'all ain't took a trip since your honeymoon have you?"

"It ain't about money Tam."

"That's nearly always what it's about Bubba," she said.

Their conversation was interrupted when, all sudden, the excavator revved then groaned like it might come apart. The arm folded and the bucket crashed into the partially dug grave. Ricky Birdsong helplessly jammed every lever he could as the machine violently shook beneath him. Tammy ran thataway and Ricky nearly took her out when he managed to get the bucket raised again. Mixed with dirt and grass clods was splintered wood. Tammy hollered, waved her arms. When Ricky saw her he shut off the engine, stuck a half-chewed cigar behind his ear, and asked what was the matter.

She didn't bother answering as she peered down into the grave. Through a hole smashed in a coffin she saw her daddy's face. Lips stitched into a grin and big-old ears shrunken like fruit left out on the countertop. She could see the lapel of his navy-blue suit and the knot of a red tie she'd bought for the occasion of his death.

The racket had woken up Luther, who strolled over and stood graveside with his sister and brother. "Looks like he didn't die but yesterday."

"I sure wasn't expecting to see him again so soon," Ren said.

The brothers snickered and Tammy gave them a look. When Ricky Birdsong saw what he'd done he hollered, "Lord Jesus forgive me!" Ren told the boy it was alright, an accident, but this did little to soothe him. "Lord Jesus forgive me!" Ricky bellered again and again while the others just stood there looking down at Hugh Treeborne as if he was going to rise on up and say, How y'all been? Of course he did not. But there rose up in his place a muffled sound, kindly like a boot being pulled loose from deep mud, and a terrible terrible stench.

"Shew," Janie said, covering her nose and mouth, "something's rotten."

This just destroyed Ren and Luther Treeborne. They laughed till they cried. Janie stepped back from the grave. She'd never seen her daddy and uncle laugh so hard. Their faces looked like busted tomatoes. It was a little frightening to witness.

"Bunch of damn fools," Tammy said. "All of you lost your everloving minds!"

After the brothers calmed down, they found a piece of tin and fit it over the hole in the coffin. Ren screwed the tin on tight. Tammy had gone on to her hair appointment. With some encouragement, Ricky Birdsong climbed back on the excavator. Dug a little more to the side this time, talking to somebody who the others could not see while he finished the job.

After Ricky left, Ren and Luther went to the house. Prepared food was coming by the carload, the kitchen given life again. But the brothers had decided to fix peach and mayonnaise sandwiches, like when they were boys, and have coffee before heading over at Blessed Assurance, where Maybelle's body was being kept.

"Hungry Sister?" Luther asked.

"Nah," the girl said. She grabbed Crusoe. "We're going to play."

Big yellow grasshoppers clung to weedstalks shooting up between Hugh's assemblies. This was the first time Janie'd been on The Seven since the day they found her grandmomma. It felt the same, looked the same. This bothered the girl deeply. Nothing stopped, nothing changed, except it had—MawMaw May was gone. The grasshoppers buzzed in flight ahead of Janie and Crusoe. The girl took off running till the whole entire junk garden hummed as if it'd been rigged with electricity and a brown mass of insects swarmed above her head.

"Seen this?" Crusoe asked, holding up an assemblie done on a round lid. It showed a bridge and, underneath the bridge, stacked peaches. A man was smashing the fruit and painting handprints on the pillars with innards and juices.

"Nuh uh," Janie said.

He set aside the assemblie then fished out another one.

"You can't move that."

The dirt boy ignored her and continued his work.

An hour passed. Crusoe had moved the assemblies he'd chosen into the edge of the woods above the spring when a chain saw started up across the clearing. Janie ran thataway and found her uncle Wooten. The chain squealed as he pushed the saw through a sweetgum tree with his good hand. The top of the tree got caught on the way down and Wooten had to section the trunk where it hung. The chain saw spewed white smoke into his face. He kicked uneven pieces out of the way then started into another tree. Birds lifted up from branches and sweetgum balls rattled loose. Wooten used his elbow to brace the chain saw up against his leg. The second tree he let lay whole where it fell. The one after that gave him trouble. Sawblade got bound up, and when he let go the motor died.

Maybe that's it, Janie thought. Maybe he'll quit.

She knew better.

Wooten wouldn't quit.

He worked the saw loose, fixed the chain, then laid into the tree from the other side. When it crashed down, Janie felt the earth beneath her shake.

❧

Two men from Blessed Assurance Funeral Home had pitched a canvas tent next to the gravesite and lined up folding chairs in its shade. Lee Malone stood in the sun though, next to Hugh and Maybelle's headstone, the guitar he called Rosette slung on his shoulder and Buckshot by his side. The dog panted, tags on his collar jangled. Lee'd considered not showing. He'd packed a bag, thinking to light out for the Gulf of Mexico then work his way down Florida like he did back when he played the chitlin' circuit. Sheriff Guthrie had warned him against leaving town till the exact cause of Maybelle's death could be determined. Foot, he wasn't worried about no fucking Aaron Guthrie. Wasn't the threat of jail—or worse—that made staying in Elberta, Alabama, unimaginable, but the thought of Maybelle Treeborne no longer in it. Besides, Lee thought, Ren would of hunted him down. He could hear the boy where he sat in the tentshade saying, over and over, Monday's a good day for a funeral ain't it? And Nita, his wife, squeezing Ren's big fingers and telling him, Uh-huh sugar, it sure is.

Ren and Nita were good together. They'd grown up on the same end of town. The Dautrives worked for The Authority, and for the telephone company over in Poarch County. Ren played for the Conquistadors in school and Nita, while she didn't have the guts to go out for cheering, never missed a ball game. What else would you do Friday night in Elberta? Fall chill beating down from the hills, whole town dark but for multitudes of headlights trained on a hundred-some leveled yards of rich green grass. Ren would pick Nita out of the crowd before kickoff and give a secret wave. They married at sixteen and honeymooned in a cabin Nita's cousin Bennie owned in the Smoky Mountains, brought back boxes of saltwater taffy and postcards with black bears and such foolishness on them. Janie too, birthed nine months later, a wet-lunged eight-pound pink thing with a smear of black hair going down the backside of her pretty head. They were good together, Ren and Nita—till they weren't. It was impossible to point where this began. Spring before his momma died, Ren had started sleeping at the dam. At first he blamed it on work. To cope, Nita ate and she ate. Time of Maybelle's funeral, the blame could no longer be mislaid. Ren wanted to fix things. He simply lacked strength. Now, with his momma dead, he was surely sapped.

The mourners spread across the pasture. Some gathered underneath the pole barn to keep out of the summer sun. Brother Goforth joined Lee Malone at the grave, a Bible held in his tattooed hands. His sermon would not save a soul that day, but Brother Goforth preached as if this would be the crowd's final chance at salvation. As if Death would not return to Elberta, Alabama, and they would not reconvene to remember this truth.

When the sermon ended the men from Blessed Assurance moved the flower arrangement onto the headstone then began lowering the coffin into the grave. Lee stepped forward and sang, *Oh, Lord, my God, when I in awesome wonder* . . . drawing out the words toward a chorus that, when he got there, *Then sings my soul, my Savior God to thee* . . . sounded like all he could do to keep his voice from busting up. Everybody else could stand to cry though—and did. At one point Ren lunged out of his chair and knocked on the coffin four times, like he wanted to be let in there with his momma. The crowd did not gasp at this final good-bye. The son's gesture, it was later said by many, was sweet. Nita calmly led Ren back to his seat, where he sang along to the hymn at the top of his lungs.

When the coffin hit bottom the men from Blessed Assurance yanked out the ropes from underneath it and wound them around their arms. Lee hushed singing and picked guitar quieter. "Close your eyes now," Brother Goforth said. An occasional sob rose up from the mourners as Brother Goforth thanked The Good Lord then thanked everybody for being here today. "There'll be food for the family at the house," he said. Nobody ate so well as they did come a death in Elberta. Red velvet cake, butter beans with smoked ham, chicken dressing, butter biscuits, purple-eyed peas, collards, fried chicken. "Amen."

Folks milled around the pasture. Janie hunted for Jon D. Crews among them. She saw Pud Ward leaning against the black hearse his daddy'd loaned for the funeral. A nicer one than what Millard Andrews owned. The fat boy Pud had made baloney and cheese sandwiches on the hood, letting them rest there till the orange cheese melted. As Janie made her way through the crowd she hugged necks and accepted smooches to the cheek and forehead from mourners. The men from Blessed Assurance began shoveling dirt into the grave. Janie saw her daddy excuse hisself and take a turn with the shovel. The clods landed with a hollow thud. It was just so unexpected, so surprising, the mourners repeated, exactly the way they were supposed to. Janie couldn't find Jon D. anywhere. She was stopped again and again by folks saying they remembered her in diapers. Even the most distant Treebornes had come to see Maybelle buried: Idis, who kept pictures of his bird dogs in his billfold; Savannah, who wasn't a Treeborne by blood but had married enough to count; Dan, who rented an apartment with somebody all the adults called "that boy." Janie'd had enough and returned to her seat.

She watched her aunt stroking her uncle's bad hand the way you do an anxious dog. Though the girl didn't know this at the time, Tammy had been married once before to a sailor she met when she waited tables down at the Gulf of Mexico. It wasn't Hollywood, but no woman in Elberta acted thataway back then. Single, off to live alone on the beach. The marriage ended when the sailor left town. Tammy soon left too, coming home to Elberta, where she met Wooten Ragsdale one day while checking the water meter in front of his daddy's chickenhouses and slaughter facility. This job for the county how come Tammy toted a pistol in her purse—in case a snake was curled up around a meter when she opened the lid. She had buried a bullet into many scaled heads and draped yet-twisting bodies on the nearest fenceline, way her daddy'd shown her, to bring on the blessing of rain. Wooten was tall and substantial, favoring men in her family, and covered in downy black feathers from the chickens he'd killed that morning. He stopped her as she was leaving, said he had a question about the water payment.

"Then you'll have to call billing," she said.

"Wait, don't I know you? Went to school with Celia and them?"

"Class of forty-six," Tammy said. "You was two years below us."

"Hey, you hungry?"

"No," she said. "But I could stand to watch a movie after work."

It was nearly a year after their wedding when, one day, Wooten was sending warm chicken carcasses through a band saw and the blade warped and sliced off most of the fingers on his right hand. Ruined enough nerves and tendons too, so even after the wounds healed he couldn't do much with it. He never did feel sorry for hisself though. Certainly helped when a settlement from the band saw manufacturer started coming in the mail. Everybody called this Wooten's Check. Day the first installment arrived he toted it right down at The Fencepost Cafe and let folks pass the check around. They oohed and ahhed, and asked him what on earth he aimed to do with his newfound wealth.

First he bought Tammy a proper wedding ring. The original had been a knockoff from Gene's Pawn & Gun. Then he bought hisself a fishing boat, which he promptly sank one night when he ran into a sunken treetop poking up from underneath the surface of De Soto Lake. Ray Posey, who was along for the ride, like to drowned. He also bought a nice radio that could pick up baseball games. One day Tammy asked why he didn't just go watch the sport played in person. "Thataway you could see it," she said. The idea seemed so outrageous that he didn't even know what to say back. So he said nothing, which always drove Tammy crazy—and not in the good way.

He bought Tammy an aboveground swimming pool and paid someone to build a deck around it. She was still off from work, taking care of him while his hand healed. She spent all her free time on that deck, worshipping the sun. When time came for her to return to the water department, Wooten begged her not to go. But she loved her job. The only woman who kept a desk in the county building and wasn't a secretary or a typist. Pitiful as that pickup truck looked too, it gave Tammy Treeborne Ragsdale some freedom and a notion of possibility in a life that all sudden seemed set—and her not yet thirty years old.

After half an hour the line of mourners yet stretched beyond the pole barn. Lee Malone was still singing, pennies inside his guitar shifting every upstrum. Janie bent over to check on Crusoe. Her momma'd warned her about taking the dirt boy out from underneath the chair before the crowd cleared. She thought about doing it anyhow. She was imagining the shocked looks she'd cause when she felt a vibration in the air and looked up. It appeared as if the trees surrounding the pasture had come to life, leaves removing themselves from branches and taking flight. Nobody had time to take cover. The grasshoppers were on them. Tangled up in hair, down inside socks and shoes, mashed between tits, down earholes and up shirtsleeves. Everybody started flogging anybody within reach and the tent came down. Janie grabbed Crusoe and crawled out. Some folks were trying to fold back the canvas, which only confused those trapped underneath. She saw Buckshot snatching grasshoppers midflight. Janie ran for shelter, whupping the big yellow bugs where they clung to her dress and her skin and her hair. She tripped over the fresh dirt covering her grandmomma's body. Getting up, she nearly bumped right into Lee Malone, who just stood there strumming, covered head-to-toe in bugs as if he was made of honey.

After the swarm passed Janie found her parents together beneath a poplar tree. Her daddy was scratching where the grasshoppers had crawled on him and her momma sat in his lap. Ren motioned for Janie to sit too. "I love my girls," he said, and smooched her forehead. He patted Crusoe twice. Nita leaned over and smooched Ren on the mouth. Janie turned from this. She saw her aunt Tammy plucking grasshoppers out of her uncle Wooten's beard and pinching them in two with her long painted nails. And right there was Jon D. Crews, watching waxwings and swallows and chickadees tear apart left-behind bugs. Janie, Crusoe in her arms, dodged the birds as she ran thataway. Lyle and Van Crews there too, Van talking to Luther Treeborne and Ricky Birdsong about the Conquistadors.

"They don't stand no better chance than a slug in a salt mine," Van was saying. "Shit, it don't take much brain to hand the damn ball to that Snell boy."

"Hey Sister," Luther said. He'd untucked his Hawaiian shirt to give his gut some breathing room. The fabric stuck to his skin.

"What's that you got?" Van said. "Looks like a nigger dummy I used to have. You boys remember? Scared these two plumb to death, I mean."

"When's this one here going out for football?" Luther asked, nodding toward Jon D.

The men waited for the boy to answer.

"Want to go play?" Janie said.

"Can I?" Jon D. asked.

"Go on," Van said. "Me and Luth need to get us something to eat before it's all gone. You hungry Ricky?"

"I got to go mow Miss Strickland before it rains," Ricky said.

"Well son, that's the Good Lord's business if it does," Van said. He slapped Luther on the shoulder and told Lyle to wait for him in the truck.

Janie wanted to show Jon D. what her uncle Wooten had done to the woods, but the boy wasn't interested. Instead he took off his shoes and headed toward Dismal Creek.

Janie set Crusoe in the cradle of some hemlock roots then she and Jon D. hunted salamanders in slow green pools bottomed with flat black rocks. They handled the grinning creatures careful as crystal then let them go wiggling off again. Buckshot had followed them down to the creek. The dog chomped at bubbles floating on the surface of the water. Before long Jon D. got bored. He climbed a boulder then swung from a dangling vine. Buckshot barked and leaped at the boy's bare feet. Janie tried the vine next. Jon D. caught her on the backswing. She pulled down an elephant ear and folded it into a cup—way MawMaw May'd shown her. This made her want to cry. But she wouldn't. Not now. She fought the urge as she and Jon D. shared creekwater out of the rubbery green leaf.

"Reckon what happens once you die?"

"Heaven," Jon D. said. "Or hell one."

"MawMaw May never did go to church."

"Neither do we," Jon D. said.

"I seen her body out in the woods."

"Lie."

"Did too," Janie said. "Swear."

"Show me where at."

She led him to the holler but couldn't find the exact spot. Whispered to Crusoe for help. It did no good. Jon D. tried getting Buckshot on the scent. Maybe there was blood on the leaves, he said. But the fool dog kept getting distracted by squirrels. There were so many. Buckshot would take off running with his head held up till he crashed into a tree or a rock.

They gave up hunting for the spot where Maybelle's body was found and climbed up the holler toward the junk garden. Jon D. loved fooling

around there nearly as much as Janie herself did. He was always asking
about Hugh, but kindly shy over it. Not all the grasshoppers had flown
off. Still the clearing seemed quieter, less alive.

Jon D. dug through some assemblies till he found one that showed
bassfish with the legs of men walking up from out of a river and into
a church. "How come you reckon Granddaddy Hugh didn't sell this
stuff?"

"I don't know," Janie said.

"Van says he could of sold all of it at one point in time."

"He did some I think."

"Reckon what happened to the money then?"

"I don't know," Janie said.

"Van says one of these is what killed her."

"That ain't true."

"Told me and Lyle that it smushed her plumb to death."

"Shut up," Janie said. "Your daddy don't know anything he's talking
about."

Jon D. shrugged and went back to lifting aside assemblies.

They poked around the junk garden while the sky turned into a
mashed peach, the sun a bloody pit falling down down down. Buckshot
bedded on some clover and fitfully napped. Janie could hear vehicles
pulling up the long gravel driveway toward the road as the last mourners departed The Seven.

"What if he buried it?" Jon D. said. "Like De Soto did."

Janie wasn't in the mood. She didn't even care about showing Jon D.
what her uncle Wooten'd done anymore. "Let's go get something to eat,"
she said.

They had to pass through the new clear-cut to get to the house though.
"Timber's good money," Jon D. told her, repeating something he'd once
heard his daddy say. Janie ignored this comment and walked on ahead of
him. At the house she and Jon D. fixed a plate of cold fried chicken and
six deviled eggs. They toted the food outside and climbed up on top of
Hugh's studio. Buckshot sat below and barked for scraps.

"If I couldn't eat but one thing ever again it'd be fried chicken,"

Jon D. said, wrapping crispy skin around half a deviled egg and pop-ping it into his mouth.

Later, Wooten and Lyle walked past. Wooten had the chain saw in his good hand. When they got to the clear-cut he showed Lyle how to prime it, yank the cord so the motor rattled as if it was held together by coat hangers, then caught life. Janie and Jon D. watched Lyle lay into a tree. The top swayed. He pulled out the saw then kicked. The tree creaked, tilted, came back upright. Wooten said something and pointed.

"I wish it'd fall on them both," Janie said.

"Don't you wish something like that," Jon D. said.

She couldn't help it, she did—and worse. Wooten took the chain saw from Lyle and made another cut. They both kicked this time, and the tree came falling down. If somebody saw inside her head, Janie thought, they'd lock her up till the end of time.

Signs to Show the Way

1958

They came in broad daylight. Emboldened or ignorant, desperate, it did not matter which. Her momma was at the library. Janie let them in when they knocked. She'd been in her bedroom, lost in a map of the Elberta River Valley. A topographic map colored shades of green and brown and blue, with black lines like fingerprints spreading out from the valley's higher places to its bottomlands. The inevitability she'd felt when her grandmomma died, when her aunt and uncle began logging timber and building a new house on The Seven, had not lessened with this awful thing they'd done. If anything it now seemed heavier.

Lyle Crews didn't appear surprised that Janie had no money. He gave her five minutes to pack her things. She already had a list:

clean clothes
extra bloomers (two pair)
maw m vegetables (beans peas cream corn)
quilt x1
map of elberta county
peaches
one of daddys knifes

In back of the pickup were the rattlesnakes Lyle and Goodnight had caught. Janie put her bag next to the humming crates then climbed into the cab. She sat in the middle, straddling the shifter, with Crusoe on her lap. The rattlers droned louder as Lyle sped down the road. She didn't ask where they were going. They passed through town, crossing the Elberta River, and took 22 headed south.

Lyle turned left at a sign that said WELCOME TO THE N. W. BARFIELD NATIONAL FOREST—LAND OF MANY USES! Houses were fewer out here and just as likely abandoned. Janie knew some of the national forest roads from riding around with her daddy. Soon she was confused though. The choked woods and kudzu fields all the same. There were no signs. Lyle turned and turned and turned, as if trying to get lost. They ate the peaches Janie'd brought and placed the pits on the sun-spackled dashboard. She imagined burying these pits wherever they eventually stopped, a part of Elberta growing in some strange new place.

Eventually Lyle pulled into a horseshoe-shaped parking area and backed the pickup into the edge of the woods. Janie looked at a mildew-covered map tacked to a bulletin board showing nearby trails. They followed one out to some old Authority ruins and set up camp among what remained of a stone foundation resembling filed-down teeth. Janie wondered had her granddaddy set foot in this place. She knew he'd helped build the De Soto Dam but didn't know what else he'd done for The Authority. She could ask Crusoe, but knew the dirt boy wouldn't answer in the company of others.

She sat down and shucked off her boots. It was blamed-hot, but Lyle was building a fire. He blew to help the flame catch then added more wood to the teepee. Janie moved back from the fire. Goodnight sat next to her. She'd stripped down to her bloomers and brassiere. When Janie glanced at the older girl's body a little nut of jealousy inside her cracked open.

"Let's eat," Lyle said. He grabbed Janie's bag and fished out a jar of green beans, then uncapped it and set it in the edge of the fire.

Maybelle kept a full pantry all winter into spring. After Hugh died Lee Malone bolted more shelves onto the wall to hold her canned harvest. Janie remembered her grandmomma lifting her up to pick jars of vegetables off those pantry shelves. Inside the jars the vegetables resembled something dead. Maybelle loved eating and was herself a wonderful cook. She taught Janie how to bring whatever was in a jar back to life. You couldn't treat a vegetable just any old way and expect it to taste good. On the stovetop, in the oven, more salt, fresh herbs, how much butter, what heat and for how long, hog jowl or bacon to season and taste. MawMaw May knew all the secrets, Janie thought.

Pearl onions spun upward as the jar warmed. Janie pulled it out of the fire when bubbles started running up the inside of the glass. She wedged the jar into the loamy ground between the three of them. They used her daddy's pocketknife to spear the beans and onions. The beans held their crunch and sweetness as if they'd just been picked off the vine. When they were finished, Lyle chucked the jar into the bushes. Janie thought she'd retrieve it later. Goodnight cleared the ground of twigs and rocks then spread out a ratty quilt. She and Lyle were soon asleep, leaving Janie and Crusoe to watch the fire, and daylight, burn out.

The couple woke at dusk. Janie hadn't slept. Lyle stripped to his drawers and stepped off into a flooded sinkhole. Black water swoll up onto the bank as his head dipped below the surface. Goodnight rolled down her bloomers and pissed on the ashes and white-hot coals. Smoke curled up between her sprawled legs. Back at the truck, Lyle checked for signs that anybody had been snooping. The ground appeared clear. Whoever came this deep into The N. W. Barfield National Forest, Janie thought, meant to keep to hisself.

They got in the cab, and Goodnight turned on the radio. Pedro Hannah was talking about Tammy being missing. Nothing new to report, but he was confident that Elberta's hardworking law-enforcement officials and volunteers would find Tammy safe soon.

Janie herself hoped to never be found. As Lyle headed south again, dark descending onto the forest, the girl figured they were headed first to meet whoever wanted to buy the rattlesnakes. They could be in Bankhead by morning if Lyle drove straight. But still he wasn't, Janie noticed. They stopped again when the sun returned and camped near a noisy stream. This became their routine—drive all night, sleep all day. Each time they were ready to get back on the road, Lyle fed the rattle-snakes from a container of white mice, some of which had died in the heat. Seemed like he was trying to get up the nerve to do something that Janie figured had to do with her. She'd forgotten the drops Doc Barfield prescribed for her injury. Mucus gathered in the corner of the eye if she went too long without lifting the patch and rubbing. There wasn't much pain though.

By the third day, after camping next to a waterfall that moved like a horse's tail, the truck was running low on gas. Janie watched the orange needle drop and drop, wondering if she should say something before they ran out. Rounding a blind curve, they saw a service station. A sign said GAS/ICE/MINNOWS & CRICKETS. Lyle pulled in and sat there with the engine running, tapping his thumb against the steering wheel.

"What's the matter baby?" Goodnight asked. "Is this it? Is he here?"

Lyle let out a long breath through his nose. "Y'all get gas," he said, then opened the door and headed around the corner of the cinder-block building, where the bathrooms were located.

Goodnight grabbed a length of garden hose from behind the seat. From the bed she took a canister and a funnel. She chose a vehicle that couldn't be seen from inside the service station then stuck the hose in the tank and began sucking. Janie kept lookout. The gas came in gur-gling spurts, splashing Goodnight. The canister was nearly full when a family pulled up next to them. Goodnight looked up from siphoning, smiled, then went back to work with lewd determination, causing the driver to back out.

After they'd poured the gas into the truck, Goodnight and Janie got in the cab and waited for Lyle. Goodnight rolled down the passenger window and dangled her foot. She eyed what looked like a few coal miners going into the service station. They eyed her back, and she bounced her bare foot at them.

"Where we going to?" Janie asked.

"We're going to Florida," Goodnight said.

"Ain't you worried they'll come after you?"

"Ain't you, Little Miss Questions?"

Those first days after the kidnapping it would of been a relief to get caught. Janie had prayed to God for it. Fool. Held a little Bible given to her one day at school, clenched shut her eyes and muttered toward the ceiling. Would of been the same kind of relief she now felt being taken by Lyle and Goodnight. Blame could be laid elsewhere so long as whatever happened was, in the girl's mind anyhow, outside her control. This was the story Janie Treeborne told herself. She'd begun to see herself as an actor, a character, and in this portrayal of herself she liked the notion of running off to Florida with two older kids.

"I been to Florida before," she said.

One day her grandmomma'd woken her up and told her to get dressed. The car was already packed. They drove to the county line then pulled off at Chief Coosa's Overlook. A familiar pickup truck was parked at the pullover.

"Got room for one more?" Lee Malone said, holding an overnight bag in his right hand.

"Sister, get in back."

"Where's Buckshot at?" she asked.

"He ain't coming this time," Lee said.

They rode a good stretch without talking. Even Janie the girl could feel a tension. She leaned into the wind, let it dance her hair and tickle her neck. Maybelle slowed down coming into Bankhead and pointed out a restaurant called The Bird's Nest, which set just up and across the road from Big Connie Ward's used-car lot. Janie leaned forward to listen and look as her grandmomma pointed out other places from her childhood. Lee dangled his arm out the window and slapped the door in time with whatever came on the radio. Beyond Bankhead they hit a stretch of road where nine armadillos lay split open like somebody had fixed them thataway.

"They ball up," Lee said, making a fist. He glanced at Janie in the rearview mirror. "Carry leprosy too."

"Lie," Maybelle said.

"What's leprosy?" Janie asked.

"Like in the Bible," Lee said. "Boils and blood and puss." He turned toward Maybelle and said, "I do not."

"Lie again," she said.

Lee kindly scoffed. After a moment he reached over and not-so-slyly pinched her arm. She slapped his thigh and it made a raw sound. Swerved, gravel sprayed the underside of the vehicle. Lee grabbed the steering wheel and she grabbed his hand. They held like that for a little while then both let go.

"Let's see if we can't make it in one piece."

"Aw, foot," Maybelle said, a grin sneaking onto her face.

Hours later they turned onto what Maybelle called the Gulf road. Janie couldn't see the salt water for tall dunes covered with silver grass. But she could sure enough smell it. Smelled like when you didn't wash between your legs for a few days. She waved at seagulls waddling in groups alongside the one-lane road. Sand swirled in front of the vehicle like ill-formed ghosts. When Janie finally caught sight of the open beach and the navy-blue Gulf of Mexico stretching out toward the horizon, it was unlike anything she could imagine. Seemed like the edge of the world. Here shadows came and went too quickly to know if they had been there all. Everything was the present, everything forever moving on.

"Can we stop?" she asked.

"Not here Sister," Maybelle said.

They drove the rest of the day, eventually turning away from the Gulf. Janie pouted where she sat in the hot backseat. They stopped only to piss on the side of the road. Maybelle had packed a cooler with coke-cola and baloney sandwiches, and Lee'd brought a basket of Elberta peaches. Janie ate half of one then chucked the rest out the window when nobody was looking. The broken peach bounced off the road into some weeds.

It was dusk and they'd crossed into Florida time they came to a little brick motel with a fishpond out front. Maybelle stopped the vehicle but left the engine running.

"We ought to just keep on," Lee said, ducking below the dashboard. "I ain't tired yet. Let me drive for a spell."

"This is far enough," Maybelle said. She got out and walked into the motel's office while Lee hunkered down farther in the front seat.

Janie could see an old man and woman standing behind the front desk. Her grandmomma was pointing at the vehicle as if to prove it was there. She waved and Janie waved back—but not Lee Malone. The old man took down a set of keys and handed them to Maybelle. Then he and the old woman followed outside and watched as Maybelle took a bag, and Janie, out the backseat. The girl didn't understand why Lee wasn't getting out too. She tried to say something, but her grandmomma shushed her.

"You go," Lee whispered to the girl, winking that it was alright.

He snuck into the motel room after the old man and woman had gone to bed and turned out their light. Maybelle seemed to relax some then. She went into the bathroom and washed herself. Janie had never imagined a trip to Florida could wind up so boring. This motel didn't even have a swimming pool out back.

"Tell me a story," she said to Lee.

He said, "You know where we're going to, don't you?"

"Nuh uh."

"Why, to the Fountain of Youth, Sister!"

He went on to tell how before Hernando de Soto arrived another Spaniard had landed farther south in Florida and discovered a freshwater spring that if you drank from its water you'd live forever and ever.

"And we're going there?"

"That's right," Lee said. "Who knows, maybe even take a sip ourselves."

"But how'll we find it?"

"There's signs to show the way," Lee said.

Janie fell asleep between her grandmomma and Lee Malone that night, and she dreamed about eternal life. A peach that could never be eaten down to its wrinkled pit, a walk through The Seven that never ended. She sank down into the Fountain of Youth till she became a bald baby, a salamander, a pink tadpole with purple scab eyes. Then, sometime before dawn, she woke alone on the hard motel mattress. She could hear them talking, but it took a moment to spot her grandmomma and Lee in a slat of blue light.

"Go in the bathroom and shut the door," Maybelle said.

Janie did as she was told. She pinched herself to wake up. After a few minutes she pressed her ear to the door. Heard nothing. She climbed up onto the toilet and looked out a small window facing the swampy woods out back. Something moved among the branches and brush. Looks like, Janie thought, some big-old birds. She cracked the window and whistled. The birds stopped moving. She'd never seen birds so big— not even cranes. Maybe Florida birds were different, she thought. They started moving again. When the first one stepped out of the woods, Janie saw it was no more bird than she herself. She slung open the bathroom door and hollered, "They's some men out back!"

Maybelle was holding the door to the room partway open. The woman who owned the motel stood just outside. Lee was crouched below the window with a rolled-up phone book in his hand. They all three looked at Janie standing there in her nightshirt.

"You old bitch," Maybelle said, snatching the motel owner by the neck and pulling her into the room.

Lee dropped the phone book and scooped up Janie. He pushed past the women and ran across the parking lot. Janie saw the old man standing by their vehicle with a ballbat in his hands. Lee pressed the girl's face into his shoulder and said, "Don't look." She felt him slam into the man, heard him grunt. She was thrown into the backseat. Her elbow hurt from the landing. She saw her grandmomma running toward the vehicle then. Maybelle jumped behind the wheel and cranked the engine. Janie watched Lee Malone land a fist upside the old man's head two times, then kick him where he lay in the gravel. The other men were coming around the side of the motel. They toted lumber and chains and, looked like, a few guns. Maybelle hit the gas just as Lee jumped in back next to Janie, the door hanging open like a tongue as Maybelle swerved out onto the road and sped away from several wayward gunshots.

They drove through farmland not so different-looking from Elberta, except for being flatter than a pancake. Lee was bleeding on his face.

He wouldn't let Maybelle see how deep was the cut. Oak trees with big tumorous roots crowded the road. The only water in sight held a spoiled orange tint. Not a single sign pointed toward the Fountain of Youth. For a while Janie kept determined watch. Then the girl gave up. Fishing boats set catawampus in sandy yards where dogs were chained to iron bars hammed into the ground. For the next two nights they parked at tin-roofed rest areas and slept in the car—Maybelle and Janie did anyhow. Lee sat up all night on the hood keeping lookout.

It was night again when they got back to Elberta. Janie woke to blue lights, the car easing off into a ditch. Sheriff Guthrie peered into the back window, then trained his flashlight on Lee Malone in the passenger seat.

"You was speeding."

"We come a long way Sheriff," Lee said.

"Who you got back there?"

Maybelle turned around in the driver's seat. Something passed over her face and she frowned. "I, I don't know."

"Belle," Lee said, touching her arm.

She moved away from his touch. "Who are you?"

Something was wrong, something was happening. Janie didn't understand.

The sheriff laughed as if Maybelle was pulling his leg. He patted the door two times and said, "Slow down now, hear."

Janie stayed at The Seven for a few days after they returned from their trip. The way Maybelle acted frightened the girl. She had no interest in telling stories, in walking the woods. Janie wanted to go home to her parents, but she didn't want to hurt her grandmomma's feelings by asking. Finally the morning came when Maybelle carried her home. As Janie got out of the car, her grandmomma grabbed her by the wrist. "We swam in that Gulf," she whispered. She was shaking. "Tanned our legs, hear me now Sister? Ate boiled shrimp and taters with corn still on the cob. Hunted ghost crabs at night then woke up early for ice cream breakfast. Just you and me Sister. Hear now, just you and me."

Janie never had told this story. She didn't know how come she'd decided Goodnight would be the first to receive it. She felt a pang of betrayal, but also lightness. She lifted the patch and rubbed the mucus out of the corner of her blind eye.

Before Goodnight could react to anything Janie had said, Lyle came hurrying around the corner of the building. He got in the truck, put it in reverse and started backing out.

"Wait," Goodnight said, "the snakes."

Lyle peeled out onto the road. Goodnight kept asking what happened, what did the man say, what about the snakes, but Lyle would not respond. Even Janie realized he wasn't going to no matter how many times Goodnight asked. Several miles down the road Goodnight seemed to realize this too and she hushed.

Rather than drive that night, they made camp in a field behind an Indian mound. Janie'd been taught by her grandmomma how to pick out real Indian mounds from natural knobs. Used to there were mounds on The Seven, Maybelle told her, till somebody dug them up. An owl watched from a hickory tree while Lyle built a small fire. They ate another jar of vegetables—butter beans this time. Janie sat across from Goodnight, her face aged in the flickering light.

"Let me see him." Goodnight gestured at Crusoe. Janie passed him around the fire. "Look here Lyle, what if we have us one of these."

He ignored her yet. Something had happened in that service station bathroom.

When Lyle was ready to sleep he climbed into the truck instead of onto the pallet next to Goodnight. The rattlesnakes stirred and thumped. Goodnight got down on the quilt. Without turning over she said to Janie, "You can lay down here if you want to." Janie did. With her back to Goodnight, she hugged Crusoe till she fell asleep.

Lyle woke them up in the middle of the night. After several days it still felt disorienting for Janie to get up in such darkness. She stretched then went off to change into a clean pair of bloomers. The old ones she balled up and stuck in her bag.

Time they got to Bankhead it was daylight. Lyle aimed to get some decent food. He parked outside The Bird's Nest restaurant. "Need me a damn cheeseburger," he said, taking money out of his britchespocket and handing it to Janie. "And fries too."

Janie opened the door and got out with Crusoe.

"Not with that goddamn thing," Lyle said.

Goodnight held out her arms. Janie reluctantly handed over the dirt boy then went inside the restaurant.

The walls were pink-and-honey-colored cedar. On them hung miners' helmets and lamps, black-and-white pictures of grim men sparkling with Earth's flammable innards. The floor was scuffed green tile, some squares missing like a drunkard's teeth. A frizzy-haired and painted waitress shuffled up and asked Janie what she wanted to order.

"Cheeseburger and fries to-go."

"We don't do that for breakfast," the waitress said. "Got biscuits. Eggs and grits. What else . . . hash browns."

"Okay," Janie said. "Biscuit."

"Sausage?"

"And egg."

"Be just a few minutes," the waitress said.

Four men wearing faded ballcaps sat at a table near the back of the room and watched Janie over the tops of coffee cups. The men could of been statues but for their blinking eyes and the occasional phlegmy cough. She could feel the waitress watching too as she adjusted the patch covering her eye and smoothed the money Lyle'd given her on the tabletop. She glanced out the window to make sure they hadn't ditched her.

"You want something to drink while you wait?" the waitress asked.

"Coke-cola," Janie said. The sounds and smells of grilling meat and fried things made her mouth water. She wished she'd ordered food for herself too.

When the waitress set a bottle on the table, Janie jumped. "You alright?"

"Uh-huh."

She drank half the coke-cola in one gulp and checked at the wall clock. Next to it was a corkboard covered with announcements and ads and, right in the middle of them all, a poster of her aunt Tammy's face with the word MISSING written above it. Janie reached for the bottle and knocked it over. "Shit," she said. "Shit, sorry. I'm sorry."

The waitress went for a rag to clean up the spill. A bell chimed and the cook hollered. The waitress returned from the kitchen with a greasy sack. As she handed over the order she said to Janie, "I'm here just about every day."

Back at the truck Janie gave the sack to Goodnight. Lyle gestured for change while Goodnight unwrapped the biscuit and held it out to him. He took a bite and said, "This ain't cheeseburger."

"It's breakfast," Janie said.

He griped as if the time of day was somehow Janie's fault as he backed out of the parking lot then turned around, heading farther into town instead of back into the national forest. Big Connie Ward's used-car lot was coming up on the left-hand side of the road. Out front was one of his famous Peach Days displays. He would borrow animals from Ray's Taxidermy and re-create elaborate scenes culled from Elberta's history. Bankhead did not have a history like its neighbor to the north. For this particular display Big Connie had set up a life-size De Soto figure to wave folks into the lot. As the pickup truck approached, De Soto moved. Walked. Janie wondered if she was imagining this. But no. De Soto now stood in the middle of the road, wildly waving for them to stop. Instead Lyle sped up.

"Fuck," Goodnight said. "You're going to fucking hit him!"

At the last moment Lyle swerved, narrowly missing not De Soto but Big Connie Ward hisself.

"Did he recognize us?" Goodnight asked, turning in the seat to look back.

"Shut up," Lyle said. "Just shut the hell up."

He turned off the main road soon as possible, without a clue as to where he was headed. Kept turning, turning, driving deeper into the hills. They followed an old logging road to its inevitable end. Lyle hid the truck in a clear-cut then got out and disappeared hisself. Goodnight started building a fire, knowing not what else to do.

"They're liable to see smoke," Janie said.

"Fuck do you know?"

"I know stuff."

Goodnight couldn't get the fire to catch. She screeched, gave up, pulled her knees to her chest. "Like what?"

"Stuff."

"Who about?"

"Nobody."

Goodnight chucked a green pinecone at the girl. "Well why'd you bring it up for then?"

The yolky sun hung directly overhead time Lyle returned from wherever he'd been. Goodnight wrapped him in their ratty quilt and whispered in his ear. Janie toted Crusoe to the shade, smashed flat some ironweed and rabbit grass, then bedded down. Her eye'd begun to hurt. She clutched it shut and tried to sleep.

They stayed in this clear-cut through the day and the coming night, when Janie abandoned the weeds and fixed herself a nest in the cab of the pickup truck. She laid Crusoe in the floorboard. The keys dangled from the ignition switch. She flicked them when she could not sleep. The truck was a stick. She wondered could she drive it away.

Sleep ran shallow when it came. Somewhere among it Janie heard a voice singing, *Very deeply stained within, sinking to rise no more* . . . When she sat up she saw Lyle leaning against the truck. His eyes closed. Janie touched the soft patch hiding her injury and listened to him for a while. When she slid open the back windowglass Lyle hushed.

"How come you keep your eyes shut?"

He walked around and climbed into the cab. Janie worried she'd said the wrong thing. "Just can't keep them held open," he told her. "Don't know how come."

"Try."

She was surprised when he did. Three words escaped from Lyle's mouth before his eyes pinched shut again. "See," he said.

They sat in silence but for night sounds. The fire'd extinguished itself. Goodnight lay asleep next to the ashes. Janie couldn't stand silence anymore. She'd run off, or been carried off, and still couldn't escape the

guilt and the horror of what she'd done to her aunt, because it lived in
every quiet moment, or stillness, of which there now seemed to be an
infinite number.

"What happened back yonder at that service station?"

Lyle shifted in the seat. "You got to swear not to tell."

The man who said he'd buy the rattlesnakes had instructed Lyle to
walk into the bathroom at this service station, go in the last stall and sit
down on the commode. There'd be a hole in the wall, he said. Lyle was
to put his lips to it and whistle so the snake man'd know it was him.
This didn't seem right, but Lyle did as he'd been told. Sat, pursed his
lips into the cool interior darkness of the cinder block wall and whistled.
For a moment nothing happened. Then something warm and fleshy
touched his lips. He jerked back and wiped his mouth. Nothing else happened, so he put his lips back to the hole and whistled again. This time
the fleshy thing pushed past his lips and bumped his teeth. He jerked
back. Something wasn't right. He heard laughing on the other side of
the wall and asked who was there. Slowly, the red head of a pecker peeked
out of the hole.

Janie could feel the anger and shame coming off Lyle like heat. She
interrupted, said, "That don't mean you're—"

"I know I ain't."

"I know," she said. "I know." Then, after a minute: "Try looking at
me when you sing."

He turned in the seat so he faced Janie then began singing, *I was
sinking deep in sin . . .* She tried to tell him with her one good eye that he
could keep his open. *Far from the peaceful shore . . .* He was singing a
hymn, a song for God, but, the more he sang, the more it felt like he
meant these words for her. Janie folded her legs underneath her rear end
and leaned back against the passenger door, watching his eyelids twitch
like moth wings. Don't, she almost said out loud. She pulled the eye
patch up onto her forehead. Lyle did not flinch. She felt something down
between her legs. It was hard to sit still anymore. She hugged Crusoe on
her lap, which only made the feeling stronger. Terribly wonderful. She
thought she might shriek. The fear over doing so only made the feeling

better. Lyle was singing louder, louder . . . Janie grabbed one of the peach pits off the dash and quickly stuck it inside her bloomers. She wiggled so the pit slid down to the right place, knowing Lyle'd seen. She rocked back and forth against its hardness till she didn't know anything other than that she wanted Lyle Crews to quit, wanted to quit herself, and wanted to never quit anything all at the same time. She was so far gone she didn't even notice Goodnight approach the truck with a big stick.

The driver's-side door swung open and there was a sickening whump when Goodnight hit Lyle in the head. He doubled over in the seat and she set her sight on Janie. "Go on!" Goodnight hollered. Janie fell out of the passenger door with Crusoe. Goodnight was beating the pickup with the stick now. Janie ran. She just ran. Didn't even realize she'd left her bag behind till she made it back to Bankhead. Morning then. The eye patch had slipped off her head at some point too. She fished the peach pit out of her bloomers and threw it away.

She snuck behind The Bird's Nest and watched the cook smoking cigarettes. He was fat and had curly brown hair shaped like a toadstool on his head. Janie was hungry. Starved. She hid Crusoe in some brush then walked around front and went inside. She'd just stepped through the door when somebody said her full name.

"Have a seat," Big Connie Ward said. He wore a white collared shirt and a blue-and-brown-striped tie slung over his shoulder so it didn't dip onto his plate. "Honey, get this young lady a plate of eggs and a hot biscuit," he said to a waitress, a different one from the other day. "She looks a little peaked if you asked me."

Janie sat down and the waitress poured coffee. Big Connie slid over the sugar and cream. "What you doing all the way down here Sister?" he asked. "You ain't running around with that Crews boy and his nigger gal are you?"

"Nuh uh," Janie said.

"That's good. I'd hate to know you put in with a couple truck thieves."

The waitress soon brought a plate of scrambled eggs and one steaming biscuit. Janie didn't want to eat in front of Big Connie Ward, but she couldn't help herself. She opened the biscuit and heaped on butter and peach jelly.

"That eye's looking alright."

Janie said nothing, which was what Big Connie wanted her to do.

"Shame about your aunt," he went on. "You know I was thinking, wouldn't it be something if they was somebody—and now I'm just spit-balling here, if you'll bear with me for just a minute—but wouldn't it be something else if somebody who knew what happened to your poor-old aunt Tammy could come forward and speak up?"

Janie sipped her coffee. Too hot, it scalded her tongue. She wolfed down half the biscuit then wiped the other half across the greasy plate.

"Somebody who could just put a end to all this mess," Big Connie said, leaning onto the table with his elbows. "You know my boy Pud, don't you? Hell, sure you do. I was talking to Pud just the other day about this very same thing. Seems like whoever come forward would be a hero, don't it?" Big Connie waited to see if the girl would say anything. When she did not, he continued talking. "Every bit as stubborn as the rest of them ain't you? You understand what'll happen if she ain't found before long don't you?"

"Yeah," Janie said.

"I don't believe you truly do." Big Connie splayed his hands out on the table, a gold class ring with an orange stone anchored in the center banded his first finger. Looked like he'd got his nails a manicure. "I don't believe you do," he said. "But I know this, you're going to tell me where Lyle Crews and that gal are at right now. Start there. Then you can go home or not. That's up to you to decide. But for now you're sure enough going to tell."

He Was, You Know, Thataway

1929

The door to Hernando's Hideaway stood wide open and Ruben waited behind the bar, among half-full glass bottles time-dulled and chipped. Hugh placed Crusoe on the pine slab and the bartender regarded the dirt boy with no more interest than he might the sunrise.

"What'll have you stranger?"

"Anything," Hugh said.

The first drink went down rough. He ordered another. This one easier, the others following it too. Hugh knew he was good-drunk when all sudden he came awake prone against the floor. The Hideaway emptied. He hollered and got no answer except for his own voice. Sawdust covered the left side of his face. A tender lump the size of a quail's egg on his head. Crusoe was sitting upright beside him. Ruben had nailed a note to the bar asking Hugh to latch the door when he left.

Fog lifted off the river in sheets as he walked its bank, picking through resurrection fern and bleached driftwood gone hard as rock. Here and there broken bottleglass shined blue and green and brown-that-favored-black in the milky moonlight. Hugh fished out pieces worth keeping and tried to forget what he'd done. What he yet had to do.

Instead he thought about his art. The only thing he truly remembered about his first assemblie was the deep-down urge to make it. He turned this memory over and over in his mind, same as the river-smoothed glass in his hand, as he cut toward a drooping wire fence. He hurried across a field full of purple thistle and goldenrod growing up to his waist and taller. Time had passed, summer ending, and still he could hear stone smashing bone, feel the force of impact in his hand. Haunted, he'd gradually quit gathering assemblies. Maybelle was asking what was the matter. What was the matter? He'd had to lay into Velston again after doing in the birthmarked man. The foreman's leg kept twitching while Hugh reburied the corpses, then the two fresh bodies. About fitting. No, Hugh thought, fitting would of been dragging Velston and the birthmarked man into the river with stones tied around their waists. But they might not stay sunk. Might come back up. He still wasn't sure whether he'd leave them in the cemetery or carry them over at The Seven with the rest he'd hauled there and buried in a clearing.

He left the overgrown field, sticking to a pinebrake instead of risking trouble on the road. He sensed the stink of death upon hisself and worried Maybelle could too. Hugh felt their time together was marred by his great secret. If he could just finish this undertaking, he thought, then they could start fresh. Beyond the trees a spermy cloudtail passed across the moon's bruised face. Wild dogs yelped in the not-so-distance. For a moment he got turned around and lost. He asked the dirt boy if he knew where they were and got no answer in return. Eventually he righted hisself and found the path to Freedom Hills.

Partway down the path a long kingsnake slithered out from the groundcover and crossed his boots. Kingsnakes, Caz always said, were good signs—like an owl screeching twice. Once foretold death, three times a marriage, four trouble, five a journey, six the arrival of guests. But twice was a good sign. Hugh tried remembering how many times the owl in the split oak had screeched the morning Loudermilk showed up on The Seven. Once, twice. All Hugh could remember now was the screech the birthmarked man had let out as he brought the stone against his head.

He found Lee Malone out back of his house, sitting with the guitar he called Rosette propped on his lap and a jar of corn liquor on the ground between his bare feet.

"Get a seat," Lee said, "you son of a bitch."

He sat on a bucket, Crusoe on his knee. Lee slid over the jar and he took a swallow. They were silent. Both men comfortable with this condition. They preferred each other's company to anybody's, from the time they were boys who spent their days catching harmless snakes, swimming butt-naked in copper-colored creeks, racing the valley's dirt paths till their toenails chipped and bled. Even drew blood one summer and mixed it. Hugh'd never thought twice about how befriending Lee might look to folks in town. Treebornes were apart. Folks in town paid little mind to them. Lee was his brother. Always said they'd do anything for each other. Now he was about to ask Lee to prove this long-ago promise still truth.

"I need help," he said.

"And folks in hell need a cool drink of water don't they?" Lee strummed a big open chord. "How's that my problem buddyroll? I'll tell you my problem. Them damn fools at Roger's chucking coins. You believe that? Like them niggers got enough to be chucking in the first place. Acting like it's the funniest damn thing they ever seen to chuck money at a man while he plays guitar for them." Lee plucked a few sorry notes then said, "You know, folks liable to think you crazy toting that thing around."

Hugh ignored this appraisal. "Will you help me or not?"

Lee took another drink. "Depends," he said. "Saw your picture in the paper. Yankee what's-his-name about to make you famous, huh."

"I never said that mess they wrote." Truth, Hugh didn't know about the newspaper story till Maybelle mentioned it the night they met. Days later a digger named Nawgahyde smacked him upside the head with a copy of the *Times,* and Hugh saw a likeness of hisself drawn above a couple-paragraphs credited to Seth A. Loudermilk. The diggers had been teasing him ever since. "Didn't even know he was doing it."

"Well he did," Lee said. Then, changing subject: "It's a pretty little-old feller. Still don't look right though, grown man toting a mud doll all over creation."

He kept on about Crusoe, a variation on the conversation repeated every time he saw the dirt boy. Sometimes Hugh wondered was Lee pulling his leg. After several minutes he wound back around to fussing about the folks at Roger's Lounge—a floating bar on the Elberta River where Lee sometimes still performed.

"How come you don't just sing some other way if you don't like them teasing you?"

"We can only do how we're made to buddyroll."

"Sounds like some horseshit to me."

"Nobody asked you if it did artist. Now what you needing from poor old me this time of the goddamn night?"

Hugh straightened up and started telling. Lee set down Rosette. Her strings wommed and he hushed them with his calloused fingers. "Come again?" he said more than once. And Hugh did. Still, Lee wondered had he heard right. Killed two Authority men and was unearthing a cemetery before it flooded.

"And ain't nobody noticed them men missing yet?"

"They did," Hugh said, "but we ain't skipped a lick of work for it. Even the bosses ain't nothing but parts and pieces down yonder."

"And you still working for them?"

"That ain't the point."

"Seems like the point to me."

"You ain't listening."

"Oh I am," Lee said. "Heard you clear as a church bell on Sunday morning."

They walked to The Seven and hitched Byron to the wagon. Hugh put two shovels, a pick, and a roll of burlap in the bed while Lee climbed up on the seat with Crusoe. They set off with the moon yet high and the mule miffed at being called to work. Its coat the ragged gray of cold fire-ash, and had been from the time Hugh bought him.

Other side of town they picked up an old logging road. The air in the woods hung close and still. Only owls stirred among blue-black treetops. None screeched. The road petered out and saplings thumped the wagon's underside. Byron stopped frequently to munch weeds and briar, to blow airy farts. An owl swooped low and spooked the fool creature. Byron would go no farther till Hugh beat him on the flank with a balled fist.

The brush threaded in and out of itself, making impassable stretches. They doubled back twice. They could hear the river up ahead, but could not see it running. Lee sang, *Went and bought myself a new car, filled that sucker up with gas . . .* and Byron brayed along like an ill-mannered drunk. Every little bit the mule would drop a pile of steaming shit and haw loudly as he continued onward through the dense woods. *Brand-new engine in perfect condition,* Lee sang, *and a woman just about as fast—*

"Will both of you just shut the hell up," Hugh said.

Neither man nor mule would.

When they came out of the woods into the cemetery clearing, Lee hopped down and kissed the ground like a sailor back home from sea. "Any these your kin?"

"We ain't all us whites kin."

Lee laughed. "Then how come you to care what happens to them?"

"Here," Hugh said, pitching Lee a shovel. "Dig."

They lit a few pine knots and stuck them in the soft ground. When they opened the plain pine coffins they found the corpses buried with keepsakes: a piece of hard candy, pins, pages torn from the Bible, playing cards, a dried lock of hair with ribbon yet tied around it. Come dawn Hugh and Lee had four corpses wrapped in burlap and loaded in the wagonbed. Hugh insisted they rebury the coffins with as much care as if nothing had been removed. Not for fear of being caught—no one would flinch at the sight of a looted cemetery where soon would be a-hundred-plus feet of water—but for the rightness of the gesture.

The sky was beginning to blush pink and red like a lover's neck. Soon, Hugh knew, the loggers would be tromping nearby. Starlings cut overtop the cemetery clearing.

"What you aim to do with them two?" Lee asked, nodding toward where Hugh had buried Velston and the birthmarked man.

"Worry about that last."

"Crazy as a goddamn duck," Lee said, pitching a final load of dirt then tamping it down. "Let the lake take them buddyroll."

"If I'm crazy then reckon what it says you're out here with me?"

Before leaving Hugh pressed wax paper to the headmarkers and scratched back and forth with an oil pencil till names and dates appeared. He folded the paper and stuck it in his shirtpocket. They departed ahead of full light, reaching the path down into Freedom Hills time the first batch of tamales at Dyar's was ready to be served.

"Be by after dark," Hugh said.

"Dark tonight?"

"Yeah dark tonight."

"Shit fire."

"You got somewhere else to be?"

Lee waved as he walked off. He stopped just a little way down the steep path and hollered back, "Do what you supposed to now artist."

Back at The Seven Hugh unhitched Byron and let the mule roam while he buried the four corpses in a clearing out behind the pasture. In the kitchen he ate a stale chunk of cornbread then went down at the springhouse and drank buttermilk from a clay jug while he sat for a spell with Crusoe. Fuck Lee Malone, he thought, staring at a dozen assemblies he'd gathered since Loudermilk left. He had been doing what he was supposed to do—and more. Fuck, and this was supposed to feel good? It didn't, he didn't. Fuck Velston and the birthmarked man's dead asses too, he thought. Ought to just let the lake take them. Hugh got up and checked the cooling machine he'd for some reason built. Sometimes it ran so cold it spat snow. Back at the house he locked the headmarker etchings in a box, along with a land deed, some old coins of no real value, and the stones his daddy had swallowed on the day he died.

Caz's dying was drawn out, but, looking back on that time, it began on a day when Hugh the boy woke to a cold and driving rain. The house felt empty in a way it hadn't before. Hugh tried shaking this feeling as he fried eggs, heated biscuits, smeared on the biscuits an extra gob of peach jelly, and ate alone. Rain pecked the roof as if trying to tell the boy something he already knew. It'd been years since Caz stayed out all night. A common occurrence for a time. Hugh could look back on those days and be grateful because if not for his daddy being the way he was then he wouldn't of met Lee Malone. After he'd finished eating that morning Hugh fed the chickens, fixed a breakfast plate for Caz and set it on the woodstove, then left for Prince's Cannery, where he worked so long at peeling peaches that moon-shaped scars would forever mark his fingers and thumbs.

The rain yet drizzled that night, the plate on the stove where Hugh'd left it. He sat on the porch and fiddled with an assemblie. His daddy had let go of berating him over the things he made. Hugh was too distracted to work though. He built a fire and stoked it so warmth spread throughout the two-room house. His momma's quilting rack hung from the ceiling, holding a piece she'd began before taking off with a traveling riflemaker from Wyoming. Hugh could not remember his momma, but he'd learned from Caz to despise her and the riflemaker, who wore a buffalo-fur coat. Caz burnt all the quilts she'd made. Father and son nearly froze to death that first winter without covers. Hugh didn't remember this either, but he did too. Memory, he'd learned, could be inherited. He was staring up at the quilting rack, wading memory, when his daddy stumbled inside covered with bloodred mud.

"I been out hunting gold," Caz announced. "And, son, I have seen a big-old wall holding back a mountain of water and one day that mountain's bound to crumble upon us."

"What you mean Daddy?"

"The Lord said, 'Behold, that which I built I'll break down, and that which I planted will one day yank up by the roots, even all this land.'"

The next day Caz began digging on The Seven. Before long you couldn't walk anywhere without coming across a hole. Some were chest deep to a man, others divots.

The idea to dig for gold was not new, but it had not taken hold of Caz in a number of years. Hugh believed the notion originated with Granny, Caz's first wife, who died one winter while ice draped the valley end to end. Granny, an Elberta Indian, spoke of the valley's unmarked graves from her people's war with the Spanish. De Soto's caravan had passed through on the way to what would become Arkansas, where his men chucked his lifeless body into the Mississippi River—the biggest unmarked grave in the country—and it hung up on sandbars, passed through petrified forests, and spun over silty gravelbeds where fish long as children floated unblinking, all the way out to the Gulf of Mexico. De Soto was liable to be circling the world yet. After Granny died Caz married Irina Wade, Hugh's momma, a little woman with wet black eyes like a deer, who went into unexpected fits that some folks credited to God, or the Devil one. She hit Caz, he claimed, with a fire-poker once, and his ear looked like cabbage till the day he died. Irina wasn't but fifteen time they wed under a brush arbor, nineteen time she gave birth to a live son named Jesse Absalom, and twenty-one time she fled Elberta with the traveling riflemaker. Some years Caz coaxed a living from a cotton patch. He fed his son what he could kill and grow on these seven hundred acres, which came to him through a grant for something to do with Granny and her people, though Caz told it was due to his service in the war. Truth, nearest Casabianca Treeborne came to the fighting was squatting in a poke salad patch while a ragged bunch of homeward soldiers stumbled past.

One day Caz dug too near the house and the foundation collapsed. The floor split, and the woodstove dropped and cracked on one side. To have the house raised and reset, Hugh traded the wagon his uncle Frank the cripple had once used to hunt foxes. Caz never knew this cost. Likely by then he no longer remembered he'd once had a brother named Frank, who lived the final fifteen years of his life useless from the waist down because a forgotten bullet worked its way up his spine and rendered him so.

After his memory, Caz's words went. That winter it snowed in Elberta for the first time in thirty-three years. Caz continued his hunt for De Soto's gold. Hugh worried he'd one day find his daddy froze to death. He imagined pouring boiling water on Caz's purple body so it'd come loose from the stubborn ground. For days and days the snow lay up in trees, shimmering like spilled sugar, then a rain fell and formed a layer of crunchy blue ice. The fishpond froze solid. Caz looked less a man and more like something that would scurry from underneath a bluff into daylight, only to retreat before it could be definitively seen.

That spring Caz went missing. After searching for days Hugh found him at what Caz said Granny always told him was an Elberta Indian mound. Caz'd dug out a good chunk of the mound time Hugh got there. A shovel lay near where he was yanking on a yellow root. Hugh tried getting his daddy to rest in some shade. Caz pushed his son away and began forcing stones into his own mouth. He gagged, choked. The skin around his lips tore. He spat out one stone and furiously rubbed it, then forced another past his bleeding gums.

After this Hugh chained his daddy to the busted kitchen floorboards. Caz pried loose the nails and escaped. Hugh brought him back and chained him to an oak tree. For months he fed Caz corn mush and raw eggs, gave him buckets of water to drink and rinse hisself if he saw fit. Caz did neither. Hugh once tried praying. *Good Lord in Heaven*, he began. It was no use. He didn't believe. Yet the old man sat underneath the oak tree and spoke in many different tongues. Howled and spat if his son came near. Caz was missing half his teeth. Gums so infected he could not fully close his mouth. One day Hugh came outside and found the chain broken, Caz gone. He searched all over The Seven. He knew what he would find, but did not know when or where. Then one afternoon he came upon bits of teeth down by Dismal Creek. A little farther downstream he saw several bloody stones. In a slow pool floated his daddy's naked white body. When Hugh dragged Caz out, he could feel more stones underneath the skin at his stomach.

Four nights in a row Hugh Treeborne and Lee Malone dug till dawn and came away from the cemetery with eleven more corpses. They'd discovered a group of unmarked graves as well. The soil seemed damper— the Elberta River inching nearer. Hugh worried he hadn't buried Velston and the birthmarked man deep enough. He could of chucked a stick over the stone wall to where the logging crew had reached.

"Ain't making it," he said.

"Hell we ain't," said Lee.

Hugh squatted down, gripping the shovel for balance. "It's my fault."

Lee wiped his forehead. "Ain't your fault somebody decided to plant these graves right here buddyroll. You just took on the burden, Lord knows how come."

"Won't never move them all in time."

"Give up then," Lee said. "Just like with that damn yankee wanting them whatever-you-call-thems. And what you done since? Where you at artist? Out here in the dark of night digging up a bunch of dead bodies, like a goddamn fool."

"Fuck you."

"Nuh uh," Lee said, dropping the shovel and raising his hands. "Fuck you buddyroll. Fuck all this." He started walking off.

Hugh hollered, "Go on big-talker. Just go on then!"

Lee held up a middle finger as he disappeared into the woods.

After Hugh had returned to The Seven and buried the corpses in the clearing he sat with Crusoe in the old chicken coop he called his studio. Caz always kept chickens. Named them after folks in the Bible. It was Hugh the boy's job to feed the chickens dried corn kernels and whatever bugs and worms Caz pulled off plants in the garden. Hugh hated those chickens, always pecking his toes or else flogging his head. Shit all over—and stunk too. Sometimes Caz would wring one's neck. He got a kick out of saying something like, Son, let's fry up old Jeremiah tonight. After Hugh found his daddy's body floating in Dismal Creek and had buried it in the cemetery at Elberta Second Baptist, he went home and wrung the neck of every last chicken in the damn coop. Plucked them bald, lopped off their heads and yellow feet, gutted them then carried the warm carcasses to Lee, who set up a deep iron vat out behind his house and filled it with oil. Lee broke down the chickens, soaked the parts in buttermilk while a fire heated the oil, then he dredged the parts in flour and dropped them in the vat. The oil overflowed and a party broke out. Lee played on his guitar Rosette whatever songs folks wanted to hear. Hugh woke up the next morning—head feeling whacked by a board—with a skinny black woman against his side. He didn't know her name. This was how an old chicken coop became his studio. This was the kind of story, he thought, Loudermilk wanted to hear.

Weeks later, summer extinguished, the diggers were still hounding Hugh about the article in the paper. One man named Rabbit said he thought Hugh would of done got rich and took off to New York City by now. It was Philadelphia where Loudermilk came from, but same difference—million miles from Elberta, Alabama. Underneath the men's teasing was an honest wish for Hugh to make good though. He no longer believed it possible—if he ever truly had. But this he kept secret from the men. Why poison the wells of others? He'd been the one who threw open the henhouse door and waved the fox inside.

When the men weren't teasing Hugh and each other they speculated about what might of happened to Velston and the birthmarked man. Drowning seemed most likely. That didn't make for good bullshitting though. Some claimed Velston'd simply become the statue of De Soto once again. Hugh kept his mouth shut on this matter too.

Working without Lee, he'd fallen behind reburying the corpses and instead dragged them underneath the house. He placed them far in back in case a dog caught scent. Despite their age and state of decomposition the corpses gave off an odor. He dragged the cooling machine under there and ran it, hoping to blow out the stench. He needed time. Maybelle could tell something wasn't right. As milder weather painted the trees, which began dropping their leaves, she asked more often why he'd stopped gathering assemblies and, recently, how come he didn't invite her to sleep inside the house.

After work one evening he fished around in boxes till he came across a pamphlet called *Wild Alabama*. Used to, they'd hand them out free in town. It'd been umpteen years since he'd seen the face on front of this water-damaged copy: oiled mustache and bird-beak nose, hollowed-out cheekbones and flat eyes. Hiram Transtern was a short man and prone

to chewing dogwood twigs as an affectation he believed endeared him
to Elbertans. Looked more poet than explorer—serious and sad. Transtern
had led expeditions into the Egyptian desert, Pacific islands where men
ate each other and worshipped monkey heads, then one day he walked
right into the Elberta County Courthouse and asked for a set of maps
nobody knew existed. Word of his arrival soon spread. Oodles of folks
claimed they saw Transtern cross the river and begin his journey. Longer ago the story, the more folks who were there for it. Some even
claimed Transtern let them see the forgotten maps that showed exactly
where Chief Coosa had been buried with all his treasure. Whoever, if
anybody, did watch Hiram Transtern float across the Elberta River then
walk into that great stretch of wilderness later to be named after a sena-
tor who held dear his peaches, those folks were the last to ever see the
man—living or dead.

Then, twenty-some years later, his son Hiram Transtern Jr. came to
Elberta with a hot-air balloon. This time the town got it right and held
an official ceremony to see off the famous explorer. Hugh remembered
bits and pieces of the day: the balloon's bright orange cloth, the burner's
blue flame, a four-piece veterans' band playing loud and out of tune,
fried dough sprinkled with sugar. Transtern Jr. waved and waved till he'd
floated beyond the tree-lined horizon. Then the band quit. Everybody
milled around, not knowing quite what to do.

Unlike his daddy, Transtern Jr. did return—though with nothing to
show for his weeks spent in the wilderness but for a few mild injuries
and a wooly beard, and minus one beautiful hot-air balloon. But he'd
returned, and Elberta, Alabama, embraced the Transterns' failure more
than it ever would of dared to their success.

When Maybelle arrived at The Seven later that night, the Transterns
and that balloon were still on Hugh's mind. He showed her the pamphlet.

"And nobody ever found it?" she asked.

"No," he said. He could sometimes forget Maybelle wasn't from
Elberta. She seemed to fit so well. "But any time they uncovered a arti-

fact or a grave the whole town would just seize up," he said. "I mean, for weeks. Sometimes it'd be months."

The words that'd come from his mouth stunned him. Hugh knew what he had to do. But Maybelle was staying tonight. He'd asked her to stay. He wanted to do the things they did when they lay down together, more often before he fell behind with the corpses. A night spent with Maybelle would be a sacrifice though, one less night he had to finish what he'd started before the river swept into the cemetery and he no longer could.

He let the cooling machine run for a while before taking her hand and leading her inside the house. It was loud. Of course she asked what on earth the noise was. He told her he had a surprise, then pulled the mattress near where cool air seeped up between floorboard cracks. Better to confront it, he thought. They got down on the mattress and kissed. Stinks, she said, her skin turning to gooseflesh as Hugh undressed her. He told her an animal must of got up under the house and died. The smell wasn't bad as he'd feared and it did feel good for such cool air to blow on their naked bodies—even in the fall.

After they made love Hugh waited till he thought she was asleep then snuck outside. He crawled under the house, cobwebs catching on his face. The brittle bones made awful cracks he feared she would hear even over the sound of the machine. He chose hands and ribs because they snapped easier. The ancient perfume made him slightly drunk. He laughed, then stopped hisself and listened for her stirring above.

He carried the bones to the studio and put them in a tote sack. Grabbed a shovel. He whispered for Byron the mule, who'd wandered out of his stall. Hugh thought he heard the creature around back of the house. Retching. Sometimes Byron would munch milkweed and foxglove, other plants and roots, that made him sick.

Instead of finding the mule Hugh came upon Maybelle there in the dark. He smelled something sour. She gasped when she saw him and asked what was he doing prowling around thisaway. He told her he couldn't sleep.

"What's that sack?"

"Junk," he said, using the word she sometimes used for things he gathered. But he'd stalled answering. Maybelle said she didn't believe him and took the sack. "Wait," he said. "Don't." Too late; she'd emptied the bones.

"Oh my Lord! Are these, are they human?"

Hugh could no longer lie. He told her all of it, from the beginning. He could see Maybelle trying to hide her horror; her face like a watermelon dropped on brick. She kept asking who they were, who were they.

"I don't know," he said.

"What do you mean don't know?"

"I mean I don't know who they are May."

She looked down at her bare feet. "You ain't some kind of pervert are you?"

"Jesus, no," he said.

"Well what are you doing with a bunch of bones Hugh?"

"Listen," he began, "I under—"

"Just tell the truth, damn you!"

Hugh knew what he said next would bind or break them, same as he knew walking into a river would get a man sopping wet. When he'd finished explaining his reasoning and the plan he now had, he could not tell which outcome had occurred. Maybelle seemed rightly disturbed by all this. But she did not leave. She got dressed and climbed onto the wagonseat next to him. Her reckoning wasn't complete, but it began as they set out across town on the wagon, the sack of bones and a shovel stowed in back.

They waited in the brush for the night guards with their torches and blades to settle in with a late meal and a deck of playing cards. As he dug, Hugh disturbed the ground as little as possible. It had to look authentic, he said. With Maybelle's help, he arranged the bones in the bottom of a hole no more than a few feet deep. He sprinkled in some arrowheads and broken pottery from his collection, then filled the false grave and smoothed over the dirt. Maybelle swept away their footprints with a green pine branch.

On the way back she said she wasn't feeling well and asked if he'd drop her off at the apartment she still rented in town. Hugh feared this would be the last he saw of her. Worry sank into his gut as he returned home to change into his Authority uniform, then doubled back to the worksite. Tormented him till he squatted in the woods with a sick stomach as blue light broke overtop the receding treeline and spilled onto the muddy riverbank like a burst yolk. He wiped with leaves then pulled up his britches and watched the first workers arrive. Mist swept low as men slid down into the channel and began cutting into the earth. Hugh took his place among them. It wasn't a couple hours into the shift till a digger hollered, "It's a goddamn skeleton!"

The new foreman—a man named Alan—told them to take a break. They ate lunch early, balled up the greasy butcher's paper from their sandwiches and chucked it at each other. Alan was waiting on a radio callback from headquarters. Another lunch hour passed. Still getting paid—least they hoped this was truth.

They started a game of tackle on the riverbank. Some men stripped naked and swam, the river cold and calm. Hugh Treeborne had climbed up the rise where folks sometimes picnicked and watched the scene from above. What luck, the men all agreed, daylight inching toward dusk. An Indian grave right here. What goddamn luck, they all said, over and over, getting paid to just fool around.

This is How She Survived

1958

For a while Janie was able to track the days. Eight since she left Elberta, six since she left Lyle and Goodnight, five since her run-in with Big Connie Ward. Then one morning she woke up and had lost count. She wasted a whole day trying to remember. Crusoe no help. The dirt boy seemed to be withdrawing into hisself, like a piece of paper folded till it could not be folded anymore. Janie nearly wanted to beat him to pieces against a tree trunk. She spent two more days like this before she understood that she had no choice but to start counting from when she could last remember. "Three," she said. "Three three three," she repeated to herself as they walked deeper into The N. W. Barfield National Forest.

She cussed herself for leaving behind her bag. No clothes, no food, no map. She tried to draw one in her head. Maybe on The Seven she could of; not here. She ate what she could find: handfuls of blackberries, unripe muscadines that popped out of their hard skin like snotty pimples. She plucked honeysuckle flowers, removed the innards and sucked sweet sticky drops of nectar while annoyed bees bounced off Crusoe's face. Gradually, a crusty yellow disc grew over her blind eye. She scratched off the crust and rinsed in the river. Each morning it came back. Her eye itself throbbed day and night. After one long day of walking that involved crossing many streams and creeks, her boots rubbed dime-size blisters on her heels and pinky toes. She stripped barefooted and let Crusoe smear hisself onto the sores. She tore her dress and wrapped pieces around her feet. They camped in Authority ruins, an abandoned pilot house, clearings doused in canted light. Crusoe built fires, and they watched bugs drift down toward the flames till they got too close and burnt up. Morning came and they walked again, crossing abandoned strip pits grown over with pine trees and tall grass, clear-cuts dusted with a fine layer of gray ash and sparkling coalgrit, leaving behind all signs of man, walking wide creekbeds that looked like busted-up roads, returning to the Elberta River and following as it wound through The N. W. Barfield National Forest.

In spite of the pain it was hard not to notice the wonder and beauty of being among such wilderness. Her grandmomma had driven this notion into Janie so hard and true it never would come out. Stretches of the forest were how the girl imagined the innards of churches and castles she'd read about in books from the library where her momma worked. Quiet, enormous. Moss ran across the ground like carpet. The animals here were not easily spooked. Herds of deer with wet black noses, a gray fox toting a robin in its sharp pointy teeth, owls roosting in knotholes and split stumps, groundbirds searching for seed and materials with which to craft nests. Janie and Crusoe could get right up on them. Hours, maybe, passing while they just watched. The pace slowed so much you'd be hard-pressed to call what Janie was doing running off.

One day they stopped at a forgotten picnic area along the Elberta River. Janie crawled underneath a concrete-slab table and passed out. She woke later to blue-black clouds piled overtop the valley, and settling into its bunches and folds. The clouds burst open, and Janie and Crusoe quickly gathered wood before it was all soaked. The day grew dimmer as the rain fell steady as time itself. Hillsides were washing out, the river white and rising.

Just before dark Crusoe wandered out and returned with a handful of mushrooms. He set them near the fire. The mushrooms sweated and shriveled. Janie ate them all, the skin so tender it popped when she bit down. She laid down on the concrete while Crusoe went back into the rainstorm. He returned with a fistful of herbs and made a poultice he warmed in the fire. The rain had slickened the dirt boy smooth as a laid egg. Teeth gaped out from his holey jaw. Janie thanked him, held the poultice to her eye and soon fell asleep.

Same time, along this same river, Tammy Treeborne Ragsdale was struggling to loosen her hands from a rope that bound her arms to a chair she hadn't stood up from in she didn't know how long. Whoever'd brought her here had quit coming days ago. She'd messed herself twice. Sores covered the backs of her hairy thighs and filthy rear end. She was so starved she would of eaten the rocks on the floor if she could just reach them. Her plan had been to secret a rock next time she was let up to piss and use it as a weapon against her captors. But that time was yet to come—and might never now.

She was being held in a cave, she thought, or way back underneath a big bluff. She could not see for a T-shirt tied around her face, but she could feel cold blowing out from somewhere deep underground, smell mold and taste its bitterness when she hollered for help, which she did now less and less. She could hear crickets and rats, sometimes feel them crawl across her bare feet. When the rain started falling, water pooled on the floor. It soon covered the tops of her feet. Tammy did not sleep unless exhaustion took over. Sleep she fought because she knew it kin to Death.

Ricky Birdsong had taken her. This much she knew. But he wasn't the one who'd been coming to let her up from the chair and feed her. It was one of the others who'd been wearing masks the day they took her. One time, when she'd been let up to piss, Tammy tried to push up the T-shirt they always kept wrapped around her face. All she could make out in the darkness was rock that looked like it was bleeding. Another time she was able to glimpse the outline of someone beyond a light shining on her as she took a shit. This person was big, had a beard. Could it be? She let slip, Woot! The light was cut. Whoever it was dragged her back to the chair and here she'd sat since. She might of kept sitting however long it took to die had the rain not started falling, running underground, pooling up where she was being held till it'd covered her feet, reached her ankles, now partway up her prickly shins.

Just like her momma, Tammy'd never learned to swim. Not a soul knew this—not even Woot. How many hours had she spent next to water, tanning her legs? Nobody questioned her staying dry. You couldn't look pretty in a filthy river or the lake. Tammy reclined on the shore or, later, on the pool deck with sunglasses on her face and a magazine or book she never read by her side. She always felt a little jealous of her brothers and, back in school, the boys in her class, watching them jump off bluffs and splash around in De Soto Lake, of Wooten floating on his back in their aboveground pool. There were summer days Tammy'd get so hot she nearly threw herself in without thinking. At least the pool was shallow enough she sometimes could get the courage to wade in up to her waist. She'd cup water in her hand and splash it onto the back of her neck. Somebody would of taught her to swim had she just asked. Probably poked a little fun at first, but they would of taught her. Now here she was maybe about to drown because of stubborn pride—the Treeborne curse.

Outside the rain fell harder. Sounded how Tammy imagined being trapped in bottom of a kitchen sink would. She took in a great-big breath then bent her wrists farther backward than she knew her body able, folding her fingers all over each other as she pulled and bucked against the rope. The chair nearly tumped over. Drown for sure, you damn fool, she thought. But now the rope had slack. She breathed in, prepared to try again. This time the knot slackened enough that Tammy could slide out her left hand. For the moment it felt unattached to her arm. She thought of Wooten. She opened and closed her rubbed-raw fist till the blood flowed back into it, then she pulled the T-shirt down around her neck and witnessed a whole other darkness.

She didn't dare stand right away. When she did she stumbled to a wall and braced herself till her eyes adjusted better. She squatted down and drank rainwater till her stomach ached. She was hungry enough to eat a rat or a bug—if she could get her hand on one. She stood up, fearing how deep the water might get, then walked several steps before realizing she had no idea which way to go. Panicked, she looked to see if she could still make out the chair. There, just barely. One more step and she might of been lost. Unbound yet still trapped. She sloshed back through the water and sat down again.

Back downriver, Janie woke up and vomited. She'd dreamed of Pedro Hannah's voice being played in reverse, of a possum trapped in a dresser drawer. In her head she could still hear the creature scratching to be let out. Her throat felt like she'd swallowed coals from the fire barely burning at her feet. The mushrooms, she thought. She crawled out from under the table and rinsed where vomit had dripped down her chin.

The river'd risen overnight. She drank from it and felt hungry, then splashed back to the picnic table. Crusoe turned his head where he sat. Looked like not much more than a melted candle. Janie went hunting clay. Her stomach fussed and she thought of her daddy, who always carried the *Elberta Times-Journal* into the bathroom. She missed him. It hurt no less knowing that, especially now, she could not go back home. Crusoe tried forming the words to thank her. For what? Letting him get thisaway? Everything you touch, she thought, falls apart. Everything you touch. Even anger, feeling the emotion resign itself to her like a wart.

Days passed without her moving out from under the picnic table. The concrete dug into her hip. She tossed and turned. Crusoe kept a fire burning and a fresh poultice on her eye, which she couldn't open anymore. The dampness kept the blisters on her feet from healing. Every so often Crusoe stumbled off and returned with something for Janie to eat. Black walnuts, a sliver of minty bark to chew, more mushrooms bruised blue, honeysuckle flowers muddied by his hands. Janie wouldn't touch the stuff, which piled up next to her like the offering it was. Hunger passed. The girl was on the verge of something new and dangerous.

One morning she was ready for that next step. She gathered the strength to walk down at the river—the distance shortened by days of ceaseless rain. Crusoe was in no shape to stop her from it, though he tried. She pushed the dirt boy away and picked a spot to enter the surging whitewater. It was ice-cold. She stepped back as doubt coursed up her rear end into her skull. Had it not, she wouldn't of noticed the catfish there.

The catfish was this big to the girl's leg and had long ropy whiskers attached to its flat head. Janie watched its ugly mouth open and close as if it sang a silent song. "We got to catch him," she said, surprising herself and forgetting what she'd come to the river to do.

If only she had her bag, her daddy's pocketknife. She imagined stabbing the fish in its gill plate and lifting it from the water. The engorged river had covered most of the bigger rocks along the bank. Eventually she found one the right size though. The catfish still hadn't moved. Crusoe was watching it. Janie told the dirt boy to grab one end of the rock. She grabbed the other. They raised it high then let go. The rock shot sideways when it hit the water and stirred up so much silt they had to wait to see whether they'd hit the catfish.

When the water cleared, there the fish floated yet. Crusoe said, "Grab the tail."

"What if it fins me?"

"Get in front."

Janie waded in downstream. The current sucked at her legs. She'd been finned before, but this fish's fins were as wide as her hand was across. She looked down to see where she was stepping. Careful, if she fell the current would carry her off. Another version of herself was trapped in the water she waded. Crusty eyeball, chapped lips, hair greasy as duckfeathers. When she could of touched the catfish's back Janie held up a hand and counted down from three, then she fell astraddle the monster and held tight.

The catfish shook. Janie hollered for Crusoe to grab him, grab him. The dirt boy did and they dragged the fish onto the bank. Dead leaves stuck to its skin, a slimy belly blushed pink and pearl-white. The fish was still shaking and shaking. Janie was afraid it might flop back into the river. It seemed important to keep ahold of this thing. The way the fish had been floating right there by the bank, like it was trying to come onto land. Evolution, she thought, hurrying to find another rock to use. She waited for a clean opening then brought the rock down on the fish's head. It made a dull sick sound against bone. Blood trickled from a split. The fish's mouth looked stuck now. Janie bent over, and the fish came alive again.

"Hit him!" Crusoe hollered.

But Janie couldn't stand to. "No," she said. "Help me."

They cleared out twigs and leaves from the innards of a trough near the picnic table, then lifted the catfish in there. Just enough space to swish its tail. The water turned rosy-pink as the catfish surfaced and tried to feed on raindrops dimpling the water. Janie tried to touch it, but the fish retreated from her hand.

That night she ate more mushrooms blackened bitter by the fire. Flames small enough to fit in her hand. Wind yanked sheets off the river, spraying Janie and Crusoe where they hunkered underneath the picnic table. Another day or two, Janie figured, and the water will rise above this spot. Before the catfish she would of been alright waiting for this to happen. But the mud dweller had reminded the girl that there were things worth caring for and other chances to do right. She heard the catfish croaking and got up to check on it. The wound on the fish's head was already crusting over, like Janie's eye. She picked algae off a rock, rolled it into a ball and dropped it into the trough. The catfish ate. She rolled another algae ball and dropped it. The fish was, Janie decided, like her, a girl.

Come morning they rigged up a sled with green vines and rubbery treebranches, and rolled the catfish out of the trough and onto it. Janie tied a vine across the fish's broad back. Crusoe walked behind the sled in case the fish slipped loose. Janie saddled the lead vine over her shoulder and pulled, digging bare toes into the soggy ground for leverage.

They headed away from the rising river. Seemed like most of the day was spent making that first hillside out of the bottomland. They finally reached a clear-cut where rain pounded through what few skinny treebranches remained. The cut was vast and ugly. Every so often they stopped and lowered the catfish into a mudhole, splashed orange water into her bright-red gills. A beard of dirt formed on her jaw and she looked wild-eyed from lack of oxygen. Janie worried the catfish would die before they got wherever they were going.

✣

The sky stayed clouded over and it wept. Janie couldn't tell time of day. They were crossing another sorry bottomland now. Had walked what seemed like miles when a sandy bluffline appeared to the left. Trees clung to its washed-out ledges till, soon, the yellow stone could no longer be seen for dense foliage. They were in what amounted to a holler. At their feet a clear stream bubbled up from patchy moss and sand.

They rolled the catfish into an ankle-deep pool. She let out a pained bleat. The stream too shallow to cover the fish's head. Janie splashed her gills then looked up. The bluffline went on and on, rising higher, far as she could see. She glanced down at her own bloody and muddy feet. They needed a dry place to rest. But a place near water too. She scanned the bluffs for shelter. There, within a stand of pines, something glimmered.

Crusoe waited with the fish while Janie climbed the bluffline. Halfway up she found it—a vehicle wedged among the trees. The bumper missing, the tires long rotted. Janie touched the warped hood and ran her fingers through rust spread all down the fender. She popped the trunk then looked all around, as if somebody might be tricking her.

She fetched Crusoe and the fish, then pulled stuffing out of the mildewed seats and clogged the holes in the trunk with it. The rain slowly did its job then. Once there was enough water, Janie and Crusoe heaved the catfish up into her homemade tank. It was coming on dark. Crusoe splashed rainwater off the hood and built a fire. The vehicle faced out across the holler. Janie climbed inside and fixed a bed on the front seat. The windshield reminded the girl of a movie-theater screen, which reminded her of her aunt Tammy. She listened to the catfish, still thinking about her aunt, till she fell asleep.

Upriver in the cave, Tammy had not moved from the chair. She wondered how much work Wooten had done in her absence. Maybe she'd been gone long enough that the house was framed, electricity and plumbing done, rooms drywalled. Wooten Ragsdale was a hard worker if he was nothing else. She'd give him that. Sure, he didn't go to a regular job—he didn't need to with his check—but he worked hard at everything he did. Tammy knew better than to think that Wooten would go on working with her missing though. It'd be a wonder if he could even get up out of bed. How did he find out, what did he do when he did? She hoped Ren was taking care of him. But Ren had plenty to deal with on his own. Thinking about her big brother got her thinking about their momma, and she wondered how Maybelle would act if she was the one trapped down here. It was Maybelle who Tammy blamed for her own failure to get to Hollywood. Daddy couldn't help how he was—*provincial*, Tammy thought, was the word—but Momma, she'd left home and still wound up in Elberta—Shithole, Alabama, USA. Gave up on her dreams. Tammy gazed toward where she imagined the ceiling. Her mind cast moving images into the darkness. Scenes from movies she'd watched—a rancher's widow leaning against a fence, a tuxedoed man ordering a cocktail, an attractive couple just about to kiss. The camera always cut away just before the kiss. Tammy wouldn't be like her momma. Damn the dead, she thought. Come morning a glint of light would fall down into this hole and she'd find a way out.

At daylight Janie got out of the vehicle and pissed. The sun had cracked the clouds. She shook Crusoe to life, and they climbed to the tiptop of the bluffline. She sighted back toward where she thought Elberta was hidden among the treetops then tracked toward Bankhead. She could make out a gap in the quilted forest. Coal mines. They hadn't gone far at all.

They climbed back down and checked that the catfish was alive. Janie fed her crickets, pinching off the legs so the fish would have an easy time. Then she found a suitable pocket of clay and dug up several loads. She set Crusoe on her lap and worked him over some. Fixing the dirt boy would take time. She slathered on a thick layer of clay then put him in the sun and sprawled out beside him. The sun felt nice, even as a lonesome buzzard circled overhead. This seemed like a place they could stay for a while. Just needed food.

Later that day they snuck into town and hid behind The Bird's Nest. The cook sat on a milk crate smoking a cigarette. Janie could hear a radio playing in the kitchen. When the cook went into a storage shed, she took off through the back door. A tray of warm biscuits was on the counter. She grabbed as many as she could tote. The radio was tuned to The Peach. Janie waited, listened, but Pedro Hannah said nothing about her aunt, or anything that would let the girl know how many days she'd been gone. The screendoor creaked. Janie took off through the kitchen and out the front of the restaurant. It wasn't till she'd grabbed Crusoe that she thought maybe some of the diners, or a waitress even, had seen her flee.

Over the next several days Janie swapped up the times she went down to the restaurant to steal food. Fried chicken, meat loaf, fried okra, fistfuls of every cooked pea imaginable. She gave some of this food to the catfish. While she was in town she also studied Big Connie Ward's used-car lot. The roadside display now gone. She saw no sign of Lyle or Goodnight there. For a spell she considered writing a letter and mailing it to Jon D. Crews. But what if somebody got ahold of the letter and read it? Worse, what if Jon D. didn't care?

The weather kept dry and hot. As the ground hardened, slabs of earth broke loose from the bluffline and crashed down the wooded holler. Night after night Crusoe burnt fires on the hood. Janie leaned back and watched embers shoot up past the pinetops, flaming out among a hundred-million stars carelessly assembled from one end of the horizon to the other, and listened to the earth breaking apart all around where they camped.

Down the bluffline she discovered a coal seam. She knocked several chunks loose for the fire. Slowly, she rewound Crusoe's innards with green vines and with springs yanked out of the vehicle's seats. Each day she lathered on a fresh layer of clay. Before long the dirt boy was looking a sight better. The clay was sandy so he sparkled now. Janie's feet scabbed over too, and her eye became damp again and dripped gloopy tears down the side of her nose. She picked at the scabs and imagined using them to tell time, like the rings inside a treetrunk.

She was crouched behind The Bird's Nest one morning eating a stale biscuit when she decided to snoop around Big Connie Ward's place instead of watching from afar. She waited for a break in a line of dusty pickups bound for the coal mines then darted across the road.

In back the garage door was rolled partway open. Janie got down and crawled underneath then pulled Crusoe through behind her. The garage was cool and smelled musty. She wanted to linger there. Smell reminded her of her daddy's pickup truck. But the garage also made her think of whatever dark place her aunt had been left, the girl feared, to die. She hurried down a hallway toward the showroom, where a silver convertible rotated on a mirrored platform, and was surprised to find Big Connie's secretary already at work. Janie'd spied on this woman before. Looked like she wasn't long out of school, though Janie didn't recognize her from Elberta. Maybe went to Bankhead High. The secretary wore a tight skirt that showed off her wide rear end. Janie ducked into a bathroom and waited for the secretary to start fixing coffee. Then she left Crusoe in a stall and snuck into the showroom to see if she could find a copy of the *Elberta Times-Journal*.

She looked on every tabletop and desk. Not a newspaper to be found. The secretary was banging around in the breakroom, talking to herself. Janie didn't have long. She opened several drawers. Nothing. *Thinks he can motherfucking up and get rid of me for somebody else*—the secretary was saying. *We'll just see about that shit.* Janie made another pass through the showroom. Along the wall stood a dry aquarium bathed in warm orange light. The tank was filled with, at first glance, nothing but dead leaves and dirt and a flat rock. Odd, Janie thought. Then something moved and she saw a black chevron pattern among the leaves. She stepped back as if the glass did not separate her from the rattler coiled in the corner of the tank, its head as big as her clenched fist.

When the breakroom door swung open Janie crouched behind a desk. The secretary turned into the bathroom and, a moment later, shrieked bloody murder. After the woman ran out the front door, Janie retrieved Crusoe from the stall. Heading out, she bumped into a trash can and it spilled. Along with the rotten black fruit peels and wet coffee grounds and boogery tissues were several copies of the *Times-Journal*. Janie grabbed as many copies as she could tote then hustled out through the garage before she could be seen.

She spread the damp newspapers on the hood of the vehicle. The already dry ones she began to read. The first was printed before Peach Days. July 7, the banner said. Not far down the stack she came to an article about her aunt Tammy missing. She read every word then read each again. The letters mocked her like a child's tongue.

She went through every newspaper in the stack, then through the damp ones. A thunderhead peeked over the treeline. After a certain date there were stories about Janie missing too, but she came across not a single word about her aunt Tammy being found yet. Maybe there were copies she didn't have. The thunderhead rumbled, flashed lightning, and fat raindrops fell from the blue-black mass. Janie had to know what else had been written. She got up to head back down into Bankhead. Crusoe begged her to wait till the storm passed, but she would not.

From inside the cave Tammy could tell it was raining again. The water on the floor would rise. She stood and felt her way into the darkness. When the water got deeper she turned and walked another direction. The flow pulled at her as it drained off into a deeper unknown. When her feet found dry rock she shouted for joy. She got down on hands and knees and felt all around the spot to make sure she wouldn't fall. She was shivering cold. She tucked her legs up against her chest and sat there trying to warm up. The rain kept falling, but the water did not reach her here. She had for the moment found higher ground.

When the illumination Tammy'd been waiting for arrived it did not dawn with a rising sun, as she'd imagined, but leaped down into the darkness behind a clap of thunder so loud the rock she leaned against shook. The chair she'd been sitting in was now smoking and glowing blue from the lightning strike that'd snaked its way underground, and the water itself was on fire too. Tammy backed away from the heat.

Behind her she sensed a drop-off and heard water pouring off into a deeper part of the cave. For a time she imagined going with it, her body calcifying with the wet pale stone waiting to violently catch her at some dark bottom. Slowly, the fire on top of the water died out. A ball of flame climbed the wall and burnt on the ceiling. Tammy walked over to the glowing blue chair and gazed upward. Later, she remembered being surprised the water was cool after being on fire. She could see a tunnel of fire overhead now. She stared as if it might allow her passage to somewhere else. Her eyes watered and it became difficult to keep them open. By the time she realized hounds were baying up above, the fire had all but burnt out. Then she heard voices on high shouting her name. A smoldering bush fell from the ceiling. Tammy dodged it, wondering if the voices calling for her were real. Remembering a story from the Bible about a burning bush. She wasn't sure what to believe anymore—not even when a man who said he was Orville Knight dropped down next to her on a rope.

If Janie had known her aunt had been found she might not of gone back into Bankhead that day and walked right through the front door of The Bird's Nest with Crusoe in her arms. Every last table was full with the lunch crowd. Mostly miners. They stopped eating and watched the girl grab a newspaper off the rack. A few loose pages fluttered onto the floor. Janie bent to pick them up. She'd been biting her nails. Her heart went like a hummingbird's wings. Finally she gave up, leaving the fallen pages, and turned to leave.

Doing so, she glanced at the cash register. Behind it stood another waitress, behind her the corkboard. Where Tammy's face had been now hung a drawing of Janie's own face and the word MISSING written above it.

A hand reached out and touched her.

Somebody said, "It's the one."

Somebody else got up from a table and moved toward her.

Janie ran outside and into the road. The driver of a coal truck swerved to miss her. The truck flipped and smashed into the railing surrounding Big Connie Ward's used-car lot. Chunks of coal scattered across the pavement. Janie'd dropped Crusoe. He'd broken apart. She picked up as much of him as she could—some coal mixed in—and used her dress like a basket. Everybody had come outside the restaurant to witness the commotion caused by the strange missing girl and the dirt doll they'd heard she toted. They called out for her to wait as she made for the woods.

Back at the bluff Janie plastered newspapers up on the windows of the rusted-out vehicle she now called home. She tried keeping order, the newest hung last. This was, the banner said, the twenty-eighth day of August, 1958.

Nearly a month her missing.

Here's What Didn't Make the Paper

1958

🐦

Ricky Birdsong was in his garden when the patrol car pulled up. The garden was sorry with late-summer vegetables: purple Indian tomatoes, fat string beans, trucker corn. Ricky liked stripping off his shoes and going barefoot, crooked toes digging down into the cool turned dirt. His hip didn't hurt near as much thataway. He heard the engine rattle off, the doors open then slam shut. He wasn't stupid; he knew they'd come. He knew what he'd done was wrong; knew the moment Lyle Crews asked him to do it. So why? Jesus said it was because Ricky wanted to feel useful again. Jesus was always digging deep for reasons. All Ricky Birdsong could think about the moment the law showed up was whether Lee Malone would pick the vegetables before they turned. He wished he could just know. Ricky considered asking Jesus, but he was busy making toadfrog houses at the end of the row.

When Sheriff Guthrie and Deputy Polk appeared at the side of the house, Ricky took off into the woods. He splashed down a nameless creek, stubbing his toes and bruising his feetbottoms. He hurdled dead logs like it was nothing at all and scrambled over algae-slickened ledges pouring clear cold water. On a good day Ricky could still move. All Birdsong men were athletes, folks said, because of Elberta Indian blood.

His run ended at an old gristmill far down the nameless creek.

Ricky'd stopped because he forgot for a second why he was running, then remembered and holed up in what was left of the mill. Doing so, he stirred loose a swarm of red wasps. By Doc Barfield's count later that morning, Ricky was stung sixty-seventy-something times before the sheriff and the deputy pulled him out and dunked him in a pool below the spillway. Wasps lit them up too, and Ricky liked to drown them all. When they got back to the house Deputy Polk put Ricky in the patrol car while the sheriff began hunting the property for evidence.

Aaron Guthrie didn't know exactly what he was looking for. A body, a confession? Sheriff of Elberta County was an elected position and Aaron's beginning qualification for the job was being able to chuck a football and have it land in the outstretched arms of whichever Conquistador was streaking wide-open toward the end zone. Over the years he'd learned some things about police work though. He noticed the busted bathroom door in Ricky Birdsong's house, the flood mark on the hallway wall. The sink, he also noticed, looked backed up. He found a wrench in a closet then got down on his bad knees and opened up the pipe. Nasty water flushed out on him. He held his hand underneath to catch whatever else might come with it.

"I'll be shit," he said, when a peach pit landed in his outstretched palm.

Deputy Polk was watching from the doorway. "That from a peach?"

"Afraid so," the sheriff said.

"Want me to bring him in?"

"I'll talk to him," the sheriff said. "Let's get Ricky taken care of first."

On the way to Doc Barfield's the sheriff licked wads of tobacco and stuck them on the worst wasp stings. "My pawpaw used to do this," he said, pressing a wad onto the deputy's fevered skin. "Us kids would poke a hornet's nest and expect nothing to happen. Bunch of little fools, didn't know better." Doc Barfield gave all three men shots for the swelling. Ricky's eyes drooped shut and he slept during the drive to the county jail.

Wooten Ragsdale and Ren Treeborne were waiting out front.

"Don't fool with me now Woot," the sheriff said. He could tell the men were drunk—looked like they'd been at it for a while.

"We just want to see him," Wooten said.

Deputy Polk began helping Ricky Birdsong out of the patrol car. Wooten charged and hocked a wad of spit that landed in Ricky's hair. The sheriff shoved Wooten, but he hardly budged. Ren grabbed his brother-in-law before he could swing at the law and dragged him toward his idling pickup truck.

"Get the hell off me!" Wooten hollered. He got in the cab and beat the door panel with his bad hand till the plastic cracked. "Son of a bitch took my wife!"

Time a paperman showed up, Ricky was locked in a cell. He'd sprawled out on the floor, cheek pressed against the cold concrete. The sheriff told the paperman all he could tell, crediting the arrest to anything but truth. Did it matter? After what Big Connie Ward told him he knew, the sheriff thought he had, in fact, suspected Ricky Birdsong all along. Made sense. Crime often came from affairs of the heart. The sheriff did tell the paperman about the peach pit he'd found at Ricky's house—but off the record. Aaron Guthrie had held the position of Elberta County sheriff for thirty-something years because he knew what to tell, what not to, and when. No charges filed at this time. And no, they hadn't found the missing girl with her aunt.

After the altercation at the jail Ren and Wooten bought another bottle of whiskey from Delmar Rodriguez and drove around the county till dark. They wound up parked underneath the water tower. There wasn't any chain-link fence keeping folks out—or at least discouraging them—so Ren and Wooten walked right up and climbed the steel ladder. The water tower was painted blue, not yet made to favor a gigantic peach. Blue as a bird's egg, Ren thought, looking up at ELBERTA spelled in big block letters.

The men sat on a metal-grating platform however-many-feet above the ground with their backs against the hollow tank. From there you could see Lee Malone's house. Ren wondered if Lee knew they'd arrested Ricky yet. It was awful, but the thought occurred to him that maybe Ricky being arrested for kidnapping Tammy would distract folks from suspecting Lee had anything to do with Maybelle's death. Ren knew Lee didn't, knew he couldn't . . . He'd read the letters and the songs Lee wrote to his momma when he cleaned out the cottage she rented in town. Words so pretty and true he'd cried. But Ren Treeborne also knew that when it came to questions like the ones surrounding Lee Malone and his momma's relationship what one man knew mattered no more than a flea on an elephant.

"Look there," Wooten said, gesturing toward town.

Ren passed the bottle. "That's all of it."

Wooten tipped the bottle to be sure. He handed it back to Ren, who staggered to his feet and chucked the bottle far as he could then unzipped his blue jeans and started pissing.

"They ought to of played you at quarterback."

"Too big and slow," Ren said, shaking hisself dry.

"Shake it more than twice you're playing with yourself," Wooten said, and laughed till he violently hiccupped. "Them was the days really. Boys in my class looked up to y'all seniors. Not a care in this fucking goddamn world did we?"

"We got old."

"Shit," Wooten said. He craned his head to look up the water tower's tank. "I wanted a kid, you know."

Ren sat down by his brother-in-law. "I know."

"They'll find Sister."

"I hope so," Ren said.

The men went silent. Then Wooten said, "I'll kill him."

"Don't do that."

"I will," Wooten said. "I'll kill Ricky Birdsong's fool ass myself. And if he laid a hand on Sister I'll kill him twice."

After a while Wooten passed out and slumped against Ren. When he stirred in fitful rest his bad hand flopped onto Ren's lap. Ren picked it up to move it. Skin cool and soft as silk. He never had seen so much blood coming out of such a big body as he did the day Wooten's hand got ruined. Tammy had threatened to kill Doc Barfield if he didn't save his life. They were all of them at the hospital: Daddy, Momma, Luth, Tam, Nita. How pitiful, Ren thought, looking back, something so awful needed to get them together. He could still remember how Wooten looked white as toilet paper as he lay in bed with somebody else's blood pumping into his body. Up on the water tower, Ren petted Wooten's bad hand. He turned it over and touched the scars to his cheek. Then he kissed it. His brother-in-law did not stir. The regrown underskin was smooth as face cream. They told that when the band saw caught bone it pulled Wooten farther into the machine. The blade ran up his wrist as if he was cake. Had the motor not overheated and thrown the breakers Wooten might of lost his entire arm. Ren tried imagining what it must of felt like being yanked into a machine—the force, the shock, that brief and pure instant when Wooten realized what'd happened, but nothing yet hurt. Like being held inside God's mouth. Then the flood of pain. Ren laughed and kissed his brother-in-law's hand again. It wasn't kissing like he kissed Nita, or any other woman. He kissed Wooten's bad hand everwhichaway he could think to kiss it, and doing so thrilled him to the bone, till all sudden Wooten snapped awake and jerked the beautiful thing away from Ren.

"You was asleep."

Wooten hiccupped. The bad hand nestled in the good one like a caught bird. "We ought to get home," he said. "Tammy needs me."

Ren let the pickup roll downhill. He'd forgotten to switch on the headlights, so he missed the turn and ran through a cattle fence. They stopped and tore loose barbed wire and a busted post from the undercarriage. The tires looked alright. They got back onto the two-track and at its end turned onto the road. Up ahead was Lee Malone's place.

"Pull in yonder."

Ren did then asked, "What for?"

Wooten fell out of the truck and weaved across the yard like the ball player he'd once been, stumbling in holes Buckshot had dug sniffing out armadillos and moles. He disappeared around the house. Lee's vehicle wasn't there. All the lights were off. Ren sat half-in-half-out of the cab, wondering what to do. He hissed Wooten's name. Then he heard glass breaking and saw Wooten sprinting around the house. He jumped in the cab and slapped the dashboard, saying, "Hurry, gogogogo!"

Ren reversed out then shot down the road, fishtailing a little till the tires caught. He checked the rearview mirror and shifted into a lower gear. "Woot, you didn't hurt nothing back there did you?"

"Not no more than that nigger's hurt," Wooten said.

They cut through the square, crossed Water Avenue, thundered across De Soto Bridge. Reflective tape sparkled on construction barrels, like jewels on the riverbed. When they reached the trailer it dawned on both men then that Tammy was staying at The Seven with Nita—not out here where she'd been kidnapped from. Doc Barfield and the sheriff's idea. It was late. Wooten got out and went inside to sleep the remainder of the night.

Before going to the dam Ren drove past Lee Malone's house again. He slowed down. The old man's truck still wasn't there. He drove on, hoping he was the only one paying mind to Lee's whereabouts that night.

Earlier, Lee Malone had driven over at Ricky Birdsong's place. He knew better than to come here. He parked where nobody could see his truck from the road and took a hammer out from underneath the seat then whistled for Buckshot to follow.

The front door was unlocked. Lee found a flimsy butterknife in a kitchen drawer. Out back he leaned into the deep freezer and began knocking loose bloody ice and stiff clothes yet frozen to the bottom. He chucked it all in a sorry creek out back. Buckshot tried fishing out a piece of fabric and Lee called him off. They walked back through the garden. Lee resisted picking vegetables that needed picking, worried somebody would notice, though he doubted the sheriff or the deputy were that attentive.

He checked the boy's bedroom to see if there was anything else that needed hiding or disposing of. On a shelf were all Ricky's football trophies and plaques. Lee picked up one: HIGH SCHOOL FOOTBALL PLAYER OF THE YEAR, 1948. Ran for nearly three thousand yards. They put Ricky's picture in the Birmingham paper. Debra Birdsong never could stand the sight of Lee Malone, but he got ahold of a copy of that newspaper anyhow and, with Maybelle's help, delivered it to the Birdsongs'

house. Debra had Ricky carry her down at The Fencepost the next morning so she could show it off to all the big-talkers and bullshitters and
used-to-bes.

He peeked in the bathroom where Ricky had tried drowning hisself
a month ago now. On the floor he saw a wrench and a length of pipe
removed from under the sink. His brain did that awkward churning
of memory till it recalled the peach pit Ricky had swallowed and he'd
fished out of the boy's throat. The sheriff had surely found it there in
the drain, which meant he'd surely want to talk to Lee Malone.

He sat down on the couch. When he'd heard they'd arrested Ricky
Birdsong he'd thought about going down at the jail and springing the
boy loose. But say he did, then what? Take off? Where to? The whole
South would be after a nigger and a retard on the run. Don't give them
reason, he heard his momma momma saying. Mr. Prince had chosen Lee
Malone to own and operate The Peach Pit based on probability. A long
shot maybe, but a man like Mr. Prince did not get rich by making bad
bets. When Lee was younger he liked to think that Mr. Prince saw a
singular greatness beaming from within him. This wasn't right, he realized, the older he became. Mr. Prince had seen a black boy given op-
portunity by something common as death, by white folks who raised
him strict in religion. He hadn't chosen someone in Freedom Hills to
take over The Peach Pit. He'd chosen someone already come out from
the Hills. Foot. Even a rich man, Lee Malone now thought, could wind
up wrong.

As he sat there on Ricky Birdsong's couch Lee replayed the previous
day's events in his mind. It was such heavy rain and everybody was bitter
about wandering around in a storm, doubtful that Tammy would ever
be found—alive or dead. Big Connie Ward was leading the search party.
He spotted the smoke rising up from the ground. The men dug out
dead leaves, brush and fallen branches, a deer carcass time-stripped and
furred with moss and tender shoots of grass from the entrance to the
cave. The hounds went wild when they got Tammy's scent. The lightning strike had run down right into the cave where Tammy was being
kept. Lightning could do mysterious things. Lee knew folks who'd been

struck and not a mark left on them, others whose backs looked like a privet branch. They could hear Tammy down there. Wooten had to be held from flinging hisself into the hole. Deputy Polk offered to go down first. Instead Big Connie Ward rigged a rope around Orville Knight's skinny waist and lowered him. Orville hollered when he laid eyes on Tammy, hollered again when she flew into him. Wooten knocked a few men upside the head with his bad hand trying to get to her. They cussed, wished he'd go on headfirst and break his fool neck. How many days had they spent traipsing after his wife? Now they'd found her. Tammy might of been Maybelle's daughter, but she'd deafened Lee Malone. Tried to blow his head off. She hated him. Lee wasn't going to do the song and dance, act a noble nigger. Ren didn't care, Luther neither, if Lee and Maybelle were together after Hugh died. It was all Tammy. Maybelle had abided her daughter's hatred as a mother would. Lee couldn't blame Maybelle, but he didn't have to like it—especially not now. But, foot, he'd been out there hunting for Tammy like the rest of them, even when enough days passed that he and others felt like they'd be better off just hunting for Sister.

When they raised Tammy up from that cave she didn't know her husband standing in front of her. Maybe wasn't, some of the men thought, so happy to see him. She was bone-thin. She screeched when Wooten held her close and cried into her tangled mess of hair. She was trying to say something: "Ur, gur, bur, bir, birrr, bird, bird, bird . . ."

That's all it took.

"We ought to lop off his pecker and feed it to the damn dogs," Big Connie Ward said.

All the men agreed. They were making plans to hunt down Ricky Birdsong that moment and do just what Big Connie Ward had suggested—or worse, if they could imagine it in the meantime—when Lee Malone spoke.

"Hold on," he said, "let the—"

"Be just like a nigger to be involved with one of the most godawful crimes against a innocent woman Elberta County's ever seen!" Big Connie bellered.

"Con," Ren said. He was clearly upset that Janie hadn't been found with Tammy. He cleared his throat. "Wait just a minute and—"

It was too late for talk though. And Big Connie Ward was right, Lee Malone now thought, sitting on Ricky Birdsong's couch. If the boy did this, Lee was somehow involved. All of them were, whether they'd admit to it or not.

When he felt hisself falling asleep Lee got up and drove home. Buckshot ran inside the house first. Lee heard the dog whimper and fumbled for the lightswitch. Buckshot hobbled out of the kitchen, sat down and licked his bloody paws. Lee followed the bloodtracks to a scattering of broken windowglass and a rock this big in the sink. He bandaged Buckshot's paws then fed him a bowl of milk and white bread. The dog tore the bandages loose while Lee swept up the broken glass then wiped the floor with water and bleach.

They sat together on the backporch—man and dog—and listened to a recording Lee'd made thirty-some years ago. He'd listened more times than he cared admitting to since Ren dropped it off. Lee'd told Ren there was no rush in cleaning out Maybelle's things from the cottage. He'd rent to no one else. The boy wouldn't listen though. Seemed to embarrass him, going through his momma's belongings, finding this recording and no telling what else. Time, Lee would of hoped Ren didn't see the love letters, the little ditties he wrote for Maybelle Treeborne. But Lee Malone was long past such foolish pursuits as saving face.

He scratched his dog's neckfolds and tried remembering the last time they'd been together there. The Seven would have been a safer place. Meeting in town was asking for trouble. Perhaps that was part of the fun. Some days Lee and Maybelle lay in bed till lunch, touching and bucking the way he'd imagined when they first met and denied the great truth between them. The murk and the memories were smeared on Lee's mind like grease. His newly deaf ear was ringing. He adjusted the metal box in his pocket. Doc Barfield said this would eventually stop. He'd get used to the change. Foot. The man he'd become, Lee Malone thought, would be unrecognizable to the boy cut into the black disc he now removed from the record player and slipped into a paper sleeve.

Lee could perfectly remember the room where he'd recorded: cement floor, strips of carpet nailed up on brick walls that once echoed factory sounds, a single microphone in front of a folding chair facing the wall. He could yet remember the smokestacks other side a tall chain-link fence across the frozen street where a green and white taxi left him standing ankle-deep in snow, holding Rosette and nothing else. Never seen so much snow in his life. Wisconsin colder than a well-digger's asshole. The snot in his nose turned rock-hard the moment he stepped out of that taxi. Place looked just like the man he'd met in Florida told him it'd look. Lee hadn't believed the stranger. He always needed to see things for hisself. When he sat down on the folding chair Lee figured to play the same music that got him noticed on the circuit. Same music his daddy the piano man banged out at their house in Freedom Hills. There were old-timers still on the circuit who claimed they remembered Ray Malone. Lee was able to channel their memories through his own, out of his throat, his fingers, into something beyond time. On the circuit he forsook the music he'd learned from Momma Pat and Mr. Robin and the other True Believers. Too harsh, no rhythm. He was black, goddamn it, and he'd play the music of his people because he was fucking good at it, which was how come a stranger bought him a train ticket to Wisconsin so he could record. But when he opened his mouth to sing into that lonesome microphone, when the white man with black cups over his ears said, "Rolling," what came out of Lee Malone's mouth was some mashed-up version of his daddy, yes, but also the hillbilly spiritual singer that Momma Pat and Mr. Robin raised him up to be. He belonged not wholly to one tradition, or to one people; he was his own damn man, motherfucker, and neither did he represent everybody, or just a single part—he was many parts, all those pieces unknown and unheard from each other till that moment, everything all at once, and he owed it to hisself, to the music with a capital *M*, to sound thataway.

They didn't ask him to record a second song. Gave him the disc that afternoon. On one side his newly recorded song, on the other some forgotten singer from before the first great war. They'd written on a sticker: BLUE HANDS MALONE. By then Lee had long stopped noticing the way the dye at the textile mill colored his skin. That day in Wisconsin he would of scrubbed in a bucket of lye had one been handy though. He hated hisself for this, for letting a bunch of white men make him notice the stain. For letting a name they'd put on him bother him so deeply. On his way back out onto the frozen street Lee passed a man holding a guitar made out of a bright-red-and-gold cigar box and what looked like a mop handle. The man who'd sat at the recording console shook this other guitar player's hand and repeated something he'd said to Lee Malone upon their meeting. The guitar player smiled, bashfully bowed his head, then headed back to make, as the white man called it, magic.

On the train back south Lee imagined his voice sizzling out from radio antennas anchored all over the country. Magic. He couldn't help it. He pictured the radio tower atop the Prince Building in downtown Elberta. Must of been a hundred feet tall with a red blinking light on top. He saw this antenna and others stretching high high high up into the sky, his voice winding out from them, tailing off like a cloud caught on the rockiest mountain peak.

The snow began melting as the train clanked south, fields emerging full-green, rivers and creeks turning lazy brown-gold once again. Magic. Lee Malone wasn't a complete fool. A black man becoming famous for playing guitar was likely as a blizzard hitting Elberta in August. He didn't care how many records folks were buying in New York and Chicago. But when Maybelle Treeborne had told him he could do it, he should do it, forget the fact she was saying this so he would leave town, to keep them away from each other, when Maybelle told Lee to cash in that train ticket and go make a recording, then he'd believed in hisself some powerful way he never had believed before in his life.

The power of women—magic.

The train rolled on.

He sat upright and watched the country pass from the window of a crowded car, feeling he was returning to his own inevitable doom. Proof recorded on the black disc hidden underneath Rosette where she lay in her velvet-lined case. All the songs he knew, all the songs he'd written, and this the one he'd chosen to record. Love was confusion. Love was magic. Here Lee Malone was headed right back to its source. Lie and say it's not for her, he thought to hisself. Lie lie lie, you fool, but it won't make the difference you hope.

When the train stopped at a depot somewhere in Tennessee, Lee got off to wet his face under a faucet. The platform was crowded with folks in suits and colored dresses. He imagined disappearing among them. Could make Memphis and play guitar on Beale Street. Find an island in the Mississippi and build a log house, sit by a fire each night and grow old and fat, let his toenails lengthen till they curled underneath his feet.

The train began pulling off.

Lee had to run and jump to catch on.

Now that she was home Tammy Treeborne Ragsdale felt an urgency to run and jump to catch on to something too. At present she snuck past her sister-in-law, who was sprawled out asleep in a recliner chair. Mouth open, arm folded up underneath her big body—Tammy couldn't believe the weight Nita had put on these last six-seven months. Did nobody else see? The house was hot and dark, and Tammy was glad to step outside. Geronimo picked up her thin shadow, the cat yawning and flicking its fluffy tail. Tammy wore nothing but a gray T-shirt and a new pair of bloomers. Goldenrod and ironweed itched her bare legs as she headed into the pasture. She paused and looked back to see if Nita had woken up, noticed her missing from the bed where, just a few months ago, they'd laid out Maybelle's body.

Tammy had not been home a day yet and already she was fed up with the way folks treated her. Like something that might shatter—the sugar eggs her and her brothers were gifted when money was good, or the ceramic figurines Wooten gave her on holidays and birthdays for some reason. Like handling one of them, she thought. Even Doc Barfield—and wasn't it in his doctor's code not to—acted as if he'd never touched a warm body in his life. Kept rubbing his hands together, way you do sitting by a nice fire, and they were still cold as ice down there between her legs. Tammy wanted to holler, Go on feel me! I ain't gonna break! If anything, she thought, stepping into the clearing where they were building a house, this whole ordeal had forged her hard as Birmingham steel.

She walked out onto the concrete slab. Wooten, or someone, had raised one wall. She'd hoped things would be further along. This the rub between them—her always expecting more than him capable of delivering. Was it her fault? She did not love him anymore. Yet it was Wooten on her mind down yonder, in darkness so pitch it made her whole body hurt. Made her feel like something forever on the tip of her tongue that could not be said.

Tammy touched a nail that wasn't flush with a two-by-four. Off in the distance Geronimo prowled Hugh's assemblies for snakes. She'd told Wooten when he asked to just move all that junk, she didn't care. And one day he had. She hadn't realized he'd move it thataway, bulldoze it like garbage. There was no use crying though, no use regretting. After all, her daddy'd toted it out here and left it. Tammy never knew why, never asked.

She found a hammer and spun the instrument in her hand. It felt light. She raised and swung. The nail jumped. She swung again, the nailhead already flush, and yet again. Again again again, pounding a dimple into the stud. Sawdust sprinkled onto her freshly washed hair. She found another unflush nail and beat it down till the wood cracked. This was Wooten's problem—not a lick of attention to detail. Exactly how come he'd allowed hisself to be snatched into a band saw and half-ruined. She felt bad for thinking this, but the hammering felt so good it allowed her to ignore the guilt. Felt nearly as good as pulling a pistol on Lee Malone during the Peach Days parade. Everybody there had witnessed it. She'd fired three times. So how come she was free? How come she'd stood so close to him yet missed? Tammy didn't want to think too much about it. She just knew it'd felt good. Nita'd told her some folks suspected Lee had been involved with the kidnapping. This was wrong. But folks needed to feel like they were doing right. Tammy too. The gun, the house, this. There were no more unflush nails so she simply whacked the wood wherever she saw fit.

The racket woke up Nita, who tried to drape a quilt around Tammy and take away the hammer. "Come on," she said. "Woot'll be here before long. You don't want him seeing you thisaway do you?"

"Nita I ain't gonna break."

"You been through a lot honey."

"Everybody has."

"Come on back up at the house with me."

Tammy found a bottle of whiskey in the bedroom closet and set it on the kitchen table next to plans for their new house. Nita grabbed two coffee cups and Tammy filled each one to the brim so the liquor spilled when they raised the cups to drink.

"Daddy still kept it hid even after we left."

"I sure do miss him," Nita said.

"He couldn't remember where he put the stuff once he got bad sick. I'd have to sneak a bottle somewhere he could find it hisself. Proud as the day run long."

"He was a good man."

They drank. Geronimo came scratching at the door. Tammy let the cat inside. He purred and slapped at her toes.

"I couldn't quit wondering what Momma'd do."

Nita smiled, unsure what to say.

"Drove me plumb crazy," Tammy went on. She took a deep long drink. "Down there just wondering how she, of all people, would act in my situation."

"We're all our mommas."

"I hope you don't believe that."

Nita laughed. She hunted a snack in the kitchen. The cabinets were empty, but she found in the fridge a slice of German chocolate cake left over from Maybelle's funeral. She unwrapped it and sniffed then took a spoon out of a drawer.

"You ever been in that kind of dark Nita?"

"What was it like?" she asked, sitting back down. "Or you ain't got to tell."

"They had on masks," Tammy said. "All of them except Ricky."

"Reckon what for?"

Tammy shook her head. "It was a skeleton and a devil and a gorilla." The women drank in silence till the coffee cups were empty, then

Tammy refilled them. She watched Nita lick stale chocolate frosting off the spoon and the plate. Made her feel nauseated. She asked, "How you and Ren doing?"

"He's still moved out of the house."

"Treebornes are a mule-headed bunch."

They were silent again. Geronimo jumped up onto the table and plopped down between the two women. The cat raised his hind leg like a cheerleader and began licking his tiny pink butthole.

"I already kindly feel like it didn't even happen," Tammy said.

Nita grabbed her sister-in-law's bruised hand. She opened her mouth like words were going to come out. None did.

"You got fat Nita."

"I know," she said. "I know I have."

"You got to take more care of yourself."

"I know it Tammy."

"Start tomorrow. Or now. I reckon it's already today, ain't it?"

They finished the whiskey then crawled in Maybelle's old bed. The mattress springs fussed. Nita snuggled up against Tammy's bony back. Geronimo joined them there, loudly purring and washing between his legs.

Tammy resented Wooten for being absent tonight. Resented herself too for wanting him there. If Wooten and Ren weren't in jail, she thought, they were laid up somewhere drunk. Nita being so big did feel good though. Wooten's size had always been one thing Tammy liked— the way he filled up a space. It was certain. Truth, Tammy never would of had the guts to go to Hollywood, California. She'd heard that's what folks thought she'd done when she first went missing though. Tickled her to death in a way. Maybe one day a Treeborne would do something so adventurous, she thought. Never one of hers though. It was clear she and Wooten never would have a child. But there was Sister. Maybe she—

Tammy stopped, bolted upright and shook her sister-in-law awake. "Nita," she said, "Nita, where on earth is Sister at?"

Stories We Tell

TODAY

❧

"Me and Aunt Tammy was more alike than I cared admitting for a long long time," Janie Treeborne said. She drummed her slippers on the floor and assessed the young man. "Now you don't understand something like that in one swooft moment. It's the piling on of moment after moment strung out across all damn-blasted time that leads to what you call true understanding, which don't always amount to how you wished it'd be.

"See, I wanted to be my grandmomma," she went on, "because Maw-Maw May didn't live long enough for me to outgrow her. Aunt Tammy did, and she died right yonder in that bedroom. Times I still hear her back there fooling around with that movie camera. She ruined a good many reels before I got the mind to carry them over at The Seven for preserving. Something'd happened by then, understand. Me and Aunt Tammy become closer than kin. Me and her, we wound up each other's best friend."

Janie ambled into the kitchen where the microphone couldn't pick up her mutterings. She returned to the living room with two ripe Elberta peaches balanced on a small plate. She pulled a knife out of the pocket of her gown then sliced the peaches in half, exposing wrinkled brown pits set inside bloody hearts.

"Foot if I'll know the difference where I wind up," she said, wiping the knife on her gown. "MawMaw May's folks, the Chamblisses, they're all buried down Bankhead area. I ain't been to Decoration in years though. Your daddy used to go with me. Treebornes are scattered out. Time, I got interested in tracking us all down. Putting us on maps. That's all them boxes you see right yonder there. Go through them before you leave, if you want to.

"Daddy used to give me a map every birthday and Christmas—sometimes just because. Aunt Tammy and me, we hunted maps at flea markets all over this area. I collected maps my whole life and see where I am—never gone a goddamn place! Filled up a whole room with maps till Aunt Tammy needed to move in. This old schoolteacher of mine—Miss Miller was her name—she once give me a passel of maps her sister found when the county swapped courthouses. Most of them just fell apart soon as we took them out the cardboard tubes. Hugo, I remember, he was still a puppy back then. Just big enough to fit a pullet egg in his mouth. Cutest dog you ever have seen. They call his color salt-and-pepper, and he had this smudge of white on his head like spilled coffee creamer. Dog would trot right onto them maps and make hisself a bed if you didn't watch out! I hung the oldest ones up at the fruit stand. Beautiful beautiful hand-drawn things, I mean, signed by a S. N. J. We never did figure out who that artist was. Them maps though, I made sure to keep."

Janie popped out the first peach pit with her thumb. It spun across the dirty linoleum and the young man went to pick it up.

"Leave it," she said, biting into the fruit's flesh. She popped out the other pit and it spun across the floor too. She passed the plate to the young man. "I reckon I just enjoy wanting and loss. If you don't too it's because you ain't felt them true enough. What do they call that? A addiction don't they? Now I might go on and tell you them walks in the woods are my clearest memories of MawMaw May. I might tell you anything! Truth, they ain't. It's the losing her. Wanting her back. Same with my folks. Same with Elberta. Same with my poor Hugo beast. Now I loved that dog, buddy. He'd take my pullet eggs if I didn't watch out! I'd find them busted or buried here and there in the yard. Only dog I ever did let sleep in bed with me. He was a great-big leggy creature and used to chase flies whenever they got inside the house. He got old. That's all. He got old and he died.

"But going back to memories—

"I been sitting here on mine how many years? Waiting, I reckon, same way folks wait over the sick. Waiting for somebody to slip on in and take them away. Well guess what? I been waiting for somebody that's done here. No, it ain't you. I been waiting on myself and didn't know it. You see, it ain't memory that ever goes, but us being able to peel it back."

His Masterpiece

1929–1930

Hugh opened the cooling machine and reached inside to check some part. The machine shuddered and exhaled cold chemical air.

"I still kindly smell them," Maybelle said. The weather had turned cold. Too cold to run this machine, she thought. She felt nauseated too—as she often did lately.

"Just your mind," Hugh told her. He banged on something with a wrench. "Hold on a minute. Damn thing still ain't doing right."

He fooled with the machine's innards a while longer. Just when he was ready to quit, the engine backfired and, a moment later, snow blasted out of the chute. There, he said, as flakes swirled throughout the house. The snow melted when it touched their hair, their clothes, their skin. Dampened the floorboards and the papered walls and the mattress. Maybelle stuck out her tongue to catch some, and Hugh took ahold her hand and slipped a gold ring onto her finger. The ring was tight but it fit. He leaned in and kissed her, and they collapsed and made love twice. After, they toted a jug of muscadine wine to the backporch.

"I ever tell you you're uglier in person than in the paper," she said.

He kissed her temple. She loved that joke. "Never claimed to be a looker."

"Or a artist."

"Some things claim you."

She played with the cowlicks on back of his head. "When you reckon that yankee's coming back?"

It'd been four-five months since Loudermilk left with a backseat full of assemblies. Hugh said he didn't reckon the yankee would return.

"But what if he does?" Maybelle went on. "Now that you're done with that other mess maybe you can start back gathe—"

Hugh interrupted. "What if he does May."

Planting the bones at the worksite bought enough time to finish exhuming the cemetery and decide what to do with Velston and the birthmarked man. Still mad at Lee, Hugh'd consulted Maybelle about what to do. She told him she wasn't having anything to do with the decision. Which wasn't quite truth. They were together. She was with child, though she still had not revealed this to him. She was putting on weight; he'd figure it out soon. Her presence on The Seven maybe not an affirmation of the thing Hugh Treeborne had done, but a kind of forgiveness for the inextricable nature that'd driven him to it. In the end Hugh left the Authority men in their borrowed graves and let the water cover them.

After the first of the month, time payday came, Hugh and Maybelle hitched the mule to the wagon and rode into town. She wore one of his heavy coats during the long cold trip. They waited at a counter behind which stood a judge named Aderholt. The judge said a few words, asked a couple questions. Hugh and Maybelle said yes they did. The judge stamped a certificate and the couple kissed. They bought roast beef sandwiches and carried them down at the river. Hugh wished he could tell Lee he was married. He'd passed by The Hills a few times since the night Lee walked out on him. Never was home. Fool could hold a grudge too, Hugh thought as they ate.

Later, as they loaded Maybelle's belongings into the wagon, Beachy the butcher came out to say goodbye. He gave them a country ham. That night Maybelle sliced into it, the interior sparkling ruby red and marbled white with delicious fat. The ham smelled nutty and sweet. She could eat no more than a slice before feeling sick.

Though Hugh'd moved the corpses out from underneath the house, he hadn't reburied all of them yet. He delayed too long and the ground froze. He'd have to wait for spring. Meanwhile, he had no excuse for not gathering assemblies. At least none Maybelle allowed him. He loved her, so he did not tell what he'd learned Loudermilk had done. He braved the biting cold, and hauled assemblies out of The Seven's many crooks and hollers. Pieces he hadn't seen since his daddy was alive. He stacked them in the clearing behind the pasture where he'd put the now frozen corpses. An unintended monument.

That winter Hugh considered quitting The Authority. His mind changed one chill night when he pushed into Maybelle from behind, wrapped his arms around her, and felt something move inside her stomach. He didn't remark upon it as they made love or afterward, lying there finger-threaded and bare. The sense of pride and fear he felt rendered his tongue useless. Then, come morning, it seemed too late to mention. The knowledge too obvious to speak. He did not blame her for keeping this from him. After all, he was keeping a secret of his own. He began doing things to signal that he knew about the child and accepted their future though. Framed a crib, cleared extra land to garden that year, carved small horses and owls for the child to play with. From a cedar chest he took the last surviving quilt his momma'd made before she ran off with the riflemaker and he placed it with the wash for Maybelle to find.

The counter at the post office hid her growing belly all winter. Not from Dee Sargent though. Early on she'd placed a hand on Maybelle and asked how long. Dee herself was childless and thought it for the better considering Tucker's propensity for going on historic drunks. Maybelle's secret was safe with Dee, but she did not linger in town those days for fear of someone else noticing her condition. She'd have to tell her superiors at the post office sooner or later. They'd bring in another postmaster. Likely a man. She wouldn't get her job back after the child came.

The Seven's isolation, which'd fascinated Maybelle at first, would become her. She had to tell, but not yet.

By March the weather had warmed to the point where folks in town debated how many cool nights the peach orchards were getting, which would determine the length of this year's harvest. For days unbearable humidity blanketed the valley. Like being slapped in the face with a wet sponge. It would of been miserable enough had Maybelle not been pregnant and forced to walk the miles between work and home.

One day it got so she could no longer tolerate the weather in town. She closed the post office early and left. The wool dress she wore kept slipping up her hips as she walked. Her body no longer felt like it belonged to her, the baby had taken on such size within her. Tall oaks shivered along the path leading to The Seven. The postal service had given her only two dresses. An ordeal apparently. Both now fit snug. She sweated, thinking she would of gladly worn button-up shirts and loose britches like men—or, on a day like this, nothing at all.

Hugh was nowhere to be found when she got home. It was Saturday, she remembered, his day off. She felt too exhausted to search for him. She hollered his name a few times then sat on the porch and watched lightning flash in the bellies of black clouds bulging over the treeline. The sky beyond them sickly green. The world gone quiet; air soupier than it'd been all spring. Hot hard raindrops began pecking at the ground. Maybelle stepped down into the yard and called for Hugh again. Only the blood that beat in her ears replied.

She busied herself fixing supper, using the last of some vegetables they'd put up before winter killed the crops. She was looking forward to gardening this summer. She'd sketched on an envelope where she wanted things planted. Fixing supper always reminded Maybelle of her mother, who was not a good cook at all. She tried not to think about Alice when possible. On the verge of becoming a mother herself, Maybelle could imagine how it felt not knowing where your daughter was or if she was even alive. Sometimes she told herself she'd travel down at Bankhead after the child was born. A lie she believed no more than up was down.

Near dark she caught sight of Byron crossing the pasture. The mule cocked its ears as she approached. The rain had stopped and some great unseen pressure filled its void. She asked the mule where was Hugh. Byron clacked his teeth then continued into the woods.

She took hold of the mule's tail, walking to the side so she could not be kicked. Bursts of lightning showed a worn path before her. The clearing was the last place she expected Hugh to be, despite the ground thawing. But a flash of lightning revealed him wielding a shovel, surrounded by assemblies and corpses. Maybelle waited for another charge. When it came she saw the dirt boy Crusoe upright and staggering on his own two legs. No, she thought. She felt the child pressing against her bladder. She begged it to quit. The next round of lightning strobed for such duration it might of signaled the universe's last act. The mule hawed and Hugh spotted them. A peculiar look came over him and he began wildly gesturing at her, then he scooped Crusoe and ran thataway.

He grabbed her. She'd never seen him so frantic. He was saying something, but she couldn't hear what. She tried to tell him that she thought she'd lost him. Her words also consumed by a yet unseen clamor. Something that sounded like kadunk. She spoke again and her words were lost. Hugh's mouth was moving, but she could not hear him. Kadunk kadunk kadunk. To their left a tree jumped into the sky. Kadunkkadunkkadunkkadunk. Another tree, then another and another, hundred-year hardwoods, all around, lifted up out of the ground. Hugh dragged her away. She smelled on him dirt and sweat and death, and the air hummed. Above them swirled the brownest thing ever imagined, swaying, brown tentacles grabbing all they could. A cow flew past. Lumber, kartsy rock. They were in the woods, which were no longer woods, running toward the fishpond. She couldn't hear anything but kadunkkadunkkadunkkadunk. Treetops snapped and rolled past like paperballs. An assemblie nearly took their heads. Kadunkkadunkkadunkkadunk. Something wet trickled down the side of her face and neck. Hugh had picked up a sheet of tin, and they were still running. Stumbling. He fell in a depression and pulled her down.

He held the tin overtop them as it rattled and bent. He mouthed something. She hollered back. The tin slowly curled, slicing into his palms. She could see everything that should of been rooted now airborne. Trees, pieces of houses, the things he made, art, water, dirt, bodies, floating among a terrible terrible brown cloud.

The tin wrenched loose.

Hugh rolled on top of her and dug his fingers in the ground. She felt the child kick and only then did she remember that she was carrying it. The selfishness of survival caused her to sob. She tried to remind Hugh about the child. He was hurting her. It was too loud. He was saying, Shut your eyes and it'll be gone before you know it. Just shut your eyes May. But she would not. She saw Crusoe take flight. A shovel fell from the brown mass and jabbed upright not two inches from her. The handle wobbled. She could not look away. A sandstone slab bigger than a tractor flipped across the pasture. She could not look away.

She didn't feel Hugh being lifted. It happened all at once—like a bad burn. Something whipped her throat. Her dress was torn from her body. Hugh was no longer there, she realized, seeing shards of glass stuck in her belly.

Then everything ended. Her ears were whistling. The shards of glass moved up and down, up and down, updownup, with each pained breath. Just like Hugh'd said, it was over, it was gone—and him too.

It rained twelve days straight after the storm sheared the valley, water gushing down hillsides laid bare and pooling up in low-lying spots. The Elberta River topped its banks, covered the docks, seeped into town. Homes slipped off foundations and floated into woods. Piss ants abandoned wet earth, climbing any tree they could find and stripping bare the leafy tops. Owls, birds of all kinds, snakes both poisonous and not, rabbits, forgot their differences and hid together underneath any dry bluff they could find. Some dared under the hoods of vehicles, inside attics crowded with forgotten things, and waited there while catfish floated through yards like unloosed ships. The people of Elberta, Alabama, thought the rain would never quit. But on the thirteenth day it did and floodwaters slowly began their retreat, carrying off debris and wreckage, creating mountains of mud. What cotton grew rotted and other crops washed away along with the rich black topsoil, leaving patches of clay resembling open wounds.

The dirt boy couldn't see a thing. He climbed out of a hole and ripped off what was left of his clothes. Roots ran clear through his body and anchored him to the ground. He yanked loose then angled his head and fished moss out from his earholes. He took a step, feet heavy as cinder blocks. He cracked what stubby toes weren't missing, then walked without aim, knowing no more than a stone, while a reluctant sun split blue-black clouds piled up overhead like burial mounds.

The sun would not move, even as the bunched-up clouds evaporated and gave space. Memories yet escaped the dirt boy. He felt as if he was walking in a time misplaced as he waded floodwaters topped with rusty orange needles that slopped against his waist. He stumbled and the current pulled him under. Drifted till he caught hold of a tree and dragged hisself to shallower water. On he walked, loosening up as he did. Now if he could just remember. Flying, lifted, flung. A vague notion he'd been named—but by who and for what?

He held out his arms for feelers and tried making sounds with what was left of his jaw. Wild animals called out in reply as he followed a rain-fattened creek that jumped belowground then seeped back up as if the earth wept. He couldn't remember the names of these animals. He ran from what he did not know, descending into a close-walled holler where water rose past his chest. He gripped the slick rock walls with nubby hands. His foot slipped and he was again at the water's terrible mercy, drifting no telling how far before he stopped.

He crawled up onto a ledge and back into a crevice and lay there for a time among some bones. A steady knocking came from deeper within the rock, taunting him. He couldn't remember anything except flying.

How long was he gone and how far had he flown? Without memory he was only dirt—eroded bits and pieces of hills that once were mountains rising from a vast ocean. A wanderer. But wanderers come from someplace, so the dirt boy must of too. Though, till he figured out where, he was but a searcher; lost.

He came out of the holler into a hardwood grove. The sun warmed the trees, so branches creaked and popped like a ship at sea. He gazed upward. This did not fix his eyes. He walked on, pictures and words coming to him broken and half-formed. He tried them on the stub that was his tongue. They sounded painful as it felt to form them. He crossed a creek where see-through fish darted here and there in chalky blue water. On the other bank the woods were in sweet-smelling bloom, he noticed. Also something sharp and metallic, something favoring rot. With his next breath of this odor came a rush of names: yellow honeysuckle, blue flags, wisteria vine, tin, camellia blooms, bodies, Indian braids and purple hollyhock, wild laurel, Death. And another memory: before being lifted, before flying, a man on his back holding a piece of tin. A woman there too. The tin whistled, slowly peeling. They were hiding from something. Up high, the dirt boy had spotted the tin turning flips. But not the man, not the woman, then the world had sucked into itself and all became black.

Top of a hill the dirt boy sat on a log and wandered fingers to his eyes. He picked till a toadstool cap came loose from one eye then the other. Now he could make out a town snuggled inside a riverbend, which hooked off into a great-big forest that stretched toward the yet-gloomy horizon. Memory came easier with sight. He knew the town's name, the river that'd lent it, and he recognized its flooded square: a statue of a Spanish conquistador, a cafe and several shops, beyond them, painted houses with fenced-in yards and fruit trees, a peach orchard, mansions up on the riverbank among towering oaks yet reaching limbs across a soupy red road. Elberta, De Soto, The Fencepost, people, human folks. This rush of knowing jolted the dirt boy so much he lost his balance and nearly fell.

He sprawled out on a flat rock. Buzzards appeared circling overhead, thinking the dirt boy something dead. The big bald birds rode an up-draft like screws being loosened from a hard board. An inky flock gathered above the hill and shat and shed greasy feathers long as the dirt boy's legs. He collected a few feathers and stuck them in his knotty head and squawked. Two buzzards landed and unrolled tongues from their beaks. The dirt boy could of disappeared wrapped up in their wings. They waddled toward him. He ran. The buzzards did not hunt him but lifted back up into the sky, coasting toward something easier to collect.

He crossed hill upon hill, daylight giving way to dark. He came upon uprooted trees, climbed over their great-big trunks and picked his way through their twisted tops. He saw at eye-level bird nests and beehives. No eggs, no honey. Holes where the trees had stood now filled with rainwater. In them floated playing cards, a sack, more peaches, a dead cat, what looked like an arm, household objects, a calf with its skin ripped clean off, red socks, a coffee cup. Some treeroots reached taller than the roof of a house would and held stones big enough to crush a wagon. He stopped at a rain-filled cavity electrified with minnows. The fish surged together, maybe trying to tell him something, but what he did not know.

He took a flooded path around a sanded-down bluff toward a row of cigar-shaped houses the color of cooked liver. A pack of wild dogs wandered out of a field where black-eyed Susans sprouted like yellow plates. All down the path folks sat on porches and in yards. They whistled and prayed as the dirt boy passed. Some chucked handfuls of dried beans at him, or came down and tried knotting ribbons on his arms and legs.

It was dark time he reached the end of the path. There stood a house with the door cracked open. The dirt boy saw the woman from his broken memory inside this house, sucking on a honeycomb as if it was a hammered thumb. He saw too a man with blue arms not far off from his own color. When the dirt boy entered the room the woman sensed his presence and picked him up.

"Where'd you find this at?"

The blue-armed man came over and petted the dirt boy on the head. He pulled out the feathers and put them on a shelf. "Out in the woods," he said. "You can carry it back to him."

The woman held the dirt boy on her lap. "You really ain't coming? I know y'all argued, but he got flung off and kindly beat up." She did not mention the injuries she'd suffered. "He can't cut this tree off the house by hisself. And he won't let me try."

"But he'll send you over here in this condition," the blue-armed man said.

The woman instinctively touched her stomach.

The blue-armed man picked up a guitar. He plucked a string that rattled and buzzed. He plucked another and another, driving out a rhythm, and sang, *State lines ain't good for much, except for keeping you and me out of touch.* He sang till he ran out of words then he just hummed and plucked a simple melody, which shifted like the floodwaters outside the door. The final note, when played, took much longer to fade out than it should of.

"Well," he said, propping the instrument against a wall, "I reckon we ought to head on if we're going to."

He told the woman to go ahead. Wasn't safe for them together. He knew a boat, faster than walking around the flood. She listened close to his directions then picked up the dirt boy and headed thataway.

This was not the place the dirt boy hunted. He waited till they were well out from dry land before diving off the boat. Looking up, he saw the woman's face beyond the rippling surface as he sank and sank all way to the silty bottom, where a catfish big enough to swallow him stirred up from the mud and leaves. Rusted hooks dangled from the fish's thick scarred lips and its wide pale face and its bloodred gills. The fish acknowledged the dirt boy with a timeless stare then brushed past, long whiskers wrapping around him like a blessing, and was gone.

He swam to the bank and walked on. It was daylight time the dirt boy came to a familiar spring in familiar woods. All sudden he remembered this water and his strange birth from its bank. Startling awake to the man from his memory's big tan face. The way the horror of existence rolled and rolled and rolled as he held the man's hand that day, walking together across a shaggy pasture, past a barn standing with no walls, down to a fishpond beyond it, to a tangle of honeysuckle big as a parked vehicle. There were blackbirds among this vine. Slick-feathered, red-winged creatures fluttering like wind-whipped cloth.

The man tossed seed onto the ground, and a few birds lit down and pecked it. He strewed more and more, coaxing the birds closer. The dirt boy could see his own reflection in one's unblinking eye. A dark dark boy with eyes blue and deep, and hair—the dirt boy had hair, he realized, touching it then—soft and black, growing in sweeping cowlicks all over a head that seemed too big for his body.

The man shot out his hand and grabbed this blackbird. It cried out dik-dik-dik and ruffled up the feathers around its neck. He told the dirt boy to stand still as he pressed the struggling bird up against his throat.

Water began pooling up in the dirt boy's mouth. He could feel the bird's itty-bitty heart. It quit crying out and an itch started in his throat. Water leeched out of his cheeks. The itch became painful as it fell down into the dirt boy's chest, spread throughout his jaws and threatened to pry apart his head.

Then the man opened his fist and the blackbird burst out like a wad of shot. It landed back among the vine. The other birds moved away. The pain vanished as the dirt boy wrenched open his mouth and struck his tongue to life.

"Who am I?"

The man did not answer. He motioned at the blackbirds and said, "Shoo." They took to the sky in a murmuration, folding and spinning into themselves, as if he'd somehow stitched them together. Before long they'd left sight of the clearing, except for the lonesome one, which remained, working its beak up and down like a pump handle, stretching so hard the dirt boy wondered if its bones would tear through feather and flesh.

Back at the spring the dirt boy pushed aside fallen branches. He caught sight of his ruined reflection and splashed it gone. The image returned. Eternity squeezed itself into what remained of his busted head. He felt his consciousness expanding like the elaborate fungal threads buried in the loamy forest floor. The man who made him believed everything was created from all the same parts, not a thing in this world in and of itself. The dirt boy splashed gone the clods dangling from his knotted vine and wound wire innards. Though the image returned to the water's surface, he was, he knew now, something more than what could be seen.

The storm had slung Hugh sixty-some feet by Maybelle's count. When she found him his clothes were missing, as was one boot. With some effort he was able to cling to the mule, who was unharmed and unimpressed by the storm. Maybelle led them to the house. An oak tree had fallen through the roof. She tied a tarp between it and the wall, and this is where the Treebornes waited out the days of intense rain that followed.

Both Maybelle and the unborn child, as far as she could tell, were fine. Her cuts would heal before long. Meantime, she cooked root vegetable stocks. She scrambled quail eggs with hog brains, fed Hugh fresh honeycomb mixed with candied nuts, a raw egg dropped in buttermilk. She cleared limbs off the springhouse and emptied its reserves—blackberries, smoky jars of persimmons, pickled beans and onions and green tomatoes, peach butter and molasses. She cooked for herself as much for him, her appetite like a motor that leaks oil. She wanted dessert. Pound cake with chopped pecans, and top milk poured over it. These cravings seemed as much a living part of her as the child she carried in her stomach.

Once the rain stopped she went into town to check on the post office. A window had been broken, but otherwise the building looked fine. Though the mail would not run for weeks, folks were waiting outside the door. They had stories to tell. A relative asleep in bed with clean bloomers tucked under her pillow was lifted across the road and not a hair on her head harmed—the bloomers where she placed them before going to sleep. A hickory behind Elberta Second Baptist fell and formed the shape of a cross. A whole deck of cards stuck in the side of a barn as if thrown there by a magician. Goliath, the crane, had toppled onto the dam. Dee and Tucker Sargent found their fighting roosters huddled in a culvert, pecking each other's eyes out.

When she got home that evening she found Hugh standing on his own weight. Bruises on his body the color of rotting bananas. "You lost your mind," she said. "Here, sit back down."

He ignored her and pushed through the fallen tree's branches to the trunk. He thumped it like you might a cantaloupe to check its ripeness and said, "I need you to go get Lee Malone for me."

After she left, Hugh sat on the porch and fretted over sending Maybelle across the valley alone. No other choice to his mind though. His experience in the storm had given inspiration for a new assemblie. He needed a frame, and the oak tree seemed divined.

After what Loudermilk had done, Hugh thought he'd never make another assemblie. It wasn't just the gamble he'd lost, the money that never was, but how the yankee, by taking credit, had become him. Hugh'd let this happen. Not again.

Maybelle and Lee showed up later that night. Hugh kissed her and asked was she alright. Even touched her round belly, which was as near as he'd come to outwardly acknowledging the child. It was plain to anybody who looked that she was in the family way. He hugged Lee's neck too. The men laughed to keep from crying, everything bad between them now gone.

Come dawn Lee began cutting the tree off the house while Hugh supervised from an overturned pail. Took half the day. Lee loaded as much wood as he could fit into Hugh's wagon. Woodrow would be glad for the fuel to smoke his hogs. The rest of the tree's trunk he piled next to Hugh's studio. "Hope you ain't expecting me to strip and plane it for you too," he said.

Hugh told him he would handle that and did.

As his body healed, Hugh worked the oak tree down and used the timber to build a large frame. He constructed a pulley system in the studio so he could raise and lower this new assemblie. He cut mesh wire and attached it all over, then began shaping this wire by hand and with the taps of a tiny wooden mallet. He had in mind to create an entire history. Onto the wire he slathered clay. When it dried he added another layer, then another. Each movement of his hands, minute though they were, called to mind the shifting of the earth. Maybelle could do nothing but watch—afraid if she spoke it would break the spell.

❧

No one asked Lee Malone to track down and bury the corpses on The Seven. One evening he just showed up with a shovel and began work. At dark Maybelle carried him a cheese sandwich. He thanked her then ate it on the walk home.

As far as Maybelle could tell, Hugh had not noticed Lee's presence or the work he'd done for them. He rarely left the studio. She'd heard The Authority was beginning to rehire men, but Hugh'd shown no interest in going back. She could not coax him inside the house no matter how late the night wore. She worried the child would come while she was alone and Hugh would not be able to hear her across the yard. Meantime the new assemblie grew and it grew. He'd flipped the frame so he could lie on his back and work on it from below. Maybelle worried the pulley might give and the assemblie crush him.

One night she found Hugh plucking the feathers of broke-necked birds, which in the days following the storm were as common as pokeweed. She was restless from the continuing spring humidity and heat, and from carrying a living thing inside her.

After a long silence she tried convincing Hugh to come inside the house. She wanted to make love with the cooling machine blowing on them. She yearned for Hugh to put down his art and be with her, his wife.

But he would not.

After she left, Hugh continued plucking dead songbirds. Tiny bodies cold and rigid in his hand. He realized Maybelle wanted him. But this history of Elberta meant more than either of their desires. He took a knife and gutted the birds in turn then pinned up their hollow carcasses on the wall. He would use feathers to represent the waters running all throughout this land. Inside the house he heard Maybelle trying to start the cooling machine. She hollered out of frustration and kicked the thing so it rang out.

When he was through Hugh walked down at the spring to rinse. Being alone on The Seven rarely unnerved him, but this night he felt the immensity of these woods and their blue-black darkness. He remembered how his daddy would disappear into them as if entering another universe. Having reached the moon-sheened water, Hugh saw why he felt the way he did. There was the dirt boy. Hugh asked him where he'd been at but the dirt boy did not reply. Hugh scooped a handful of clay then stopped hisself. He would fix up Crusoe tomorrow, he decided. Tonight he needed rest.

Maybelle was faking sleep when he got down next to her. "Look what I found," he whispered, setting Crusoe on the floor. "Thought he'd been lost for good."

Maybelle rolled over to see, her roundly shape visible underneath the quilt. "I wonder would we be better off if he had."

Bring Her Back to Elberta

1958

Janie cut her hair with scissors stolen from The Bird's Nest. The blades were dull and pulled so much she cried. She cut her hair all way down to the scalp while Crusoe sat watching locks pile up around her scabbed feet. She'd put the dirt boy back together in a crude way. Seams showed, his head dented like overhandled fruit. She buried the hair to hide her scent. Someone would be coming, now that they'd recognized her at the restaurant.

She had enough food to last four-five days. They could be out of the county by then. Which was the next one over—Poarch? What lay between Bankhead and the Gulf was uncertain. Janie opened the trunk. The catfish slashed tea-colored water. She touched the fish's underside, something hard beneath the skin. Maybe babies, she thought. The fish turned a shoveled head into Janie's hand, like a dog, and gazed up with eyes fogged gray. Janie imagined honey-colored eggs squirted out of the fish's underside. Whenever her daddy caught a pregnant fish he spooned out these eggs and spread them on a saltine cracker. Janie wouldn't eat this catfish's eggs though. No, she'd hatch them—and those fish would lay eggs, which would hatch and grow in the safe harbor Janie aimed to build them. Somewhere. Generation upon generation upon untouched generation, swimming in one wet world.

"Can't carry it forever," Crusoe said. He'd climbed up onto the bumper of the vehicle and was peering down into the trunk.

Janie cried off and on the rest of that afternoon, knowing the dirt boy was right. She ate a butter biscuit and a bruised peach—ate it skin and all. She pinched the legs off several crickets and dropped them into the trunk. The crickets sank to the rusted bottom. The catfish would not feed. Animals always know what's coming, Janie thought.

Before they left, Crusoe built a fire with green branches to draw the searchers thataway. Janie helped pile on more and more branches till the pyre rose twice as tall as herself. They burnt the last of the coal chunks too—firesmoke turning black from white.

It was good-dark time they crossed the road outside Bankhead and came down through a pinebrake to Big Connie Ward's used-car lot. Bats swooped in and out of foggy yellow light shining down on the vehicles. A line of pickups barreled past, miners headed for the owl shift. Janie tapped Crusoe when the road was clear. They jumped the railing then hustled behind the building. She listened at the garage door while he caught up.

All the keys hung in an unlocked cabinet next to the secretary's desk, which, Janie noticed, was emptied and cleaned off. The keys were tagged with a plastic peach, written on it the make and model. Janie looked out the window and found a pickup truck like the one her daddy drove. She grabbed the key. Rain began falling as she helped Crusoe up onto the bench seat. She had to sit on the edge to see overtop the dashboard. This a surprise. She needed to remind herself she'd only been gone a month. Felt like years.

The chain strung across the entrance snapped off the posts when Janie drove into it and got caught underneath the truck. It sparked a ways down the road then spun off into the ditch. She was still bad with a clutch. When she shifted, the truck heaved, stalled, and Crusoe fell into the floorboard. Raindrops streaked the windshield like lead. Janie felt for the wiper switch and tried to restart the engine. *First, second, third, fourth,* she heard her daddy saying, like a song, as she wiggled the shifter to try again. Crusoe climbed back up and stood with his hands against the dashboard. The radio switched on. Janie couldn't make sense of what Pedro Hannah was saying. . . . *ninety-nine cent for two or pick one* . . . Now they were rolling. Janie heard her daddy say *Alright* whenever it came time to shift. They picked up speed and she shifted to third then cranked down the window and hollered. She felt a lightness she had not felt in months. They were headed south. No telling how fast. Too fast to see the owl swoop down from out of darkness till it'd caved in the windshield.

She swerved and plowed through a barbed-wire fence, losing grip of the wheel as the truck sped across a pasture. Lightning stretched fingers across the sky. Janie mashed the gas instead of the brake and the truck shot forward. Crusoe fell again. The truck hit a deep dip and she fell off the seat too. She was looking up at the dead owl, its heart-shaped head poking through busted glass, as the truck began to slow. Her elbows and hands stung. When the truck stopped she opened the door and tumbled out. She got tangled in barbed wire. Headlights appeared at a bend in the road, slowed down at the busted fenceline. Janie struggled loose as the lights turned toward her. The Peach was still playing: *For those of us who ain't heard yet, Tammy Ragsdale has been rescued and brought back home safe.*

It was raining hard time Janie and Crusoe got back to the vehicle on the bluff. The fire they'd built had blackened the hood and windshield. Crusoe used the fat and clumsy fingers Janie'd rolled for him to pick glass out of her elbows and hands. Her head hurt so bad. He set the pieces of glass on the dashboard and they sparkled whenever lightning stabbed down from the sky. The rain fell harder. One piece of glass he pulled out kept coming and coming and coming . . . Janie hit him. It was a piece of the rearview mirror. She wiped away her blood and looked at herself. What she saw reflected she would not of believed had she not been holding the mirror piece in her own two hands.

Crusoe kept her awake with stories. He was grown all over with tiny yellow mushrooms, like warts. Janie idly picked them off and thumped them in the floorboard. He told how it felt when De Soto walked on him with heavy wood-soled boots, how the warm Elberta Indian blood

settled down into him and remained wet for years, how all things forgotten or buried were slowly working their way up, even things the girl
did not yet know existed, how Elberta peaches felt when they pushed
out from branches budded white, little dangling green orbs that slowly
took different shape and color, the plucking of each ripe one like a gong
going off inside the dirt boy's head, which, as he talked, grew bigger and
bigger and bigger, as if Crusoe contained all the secrets the girl felt were
forever just out of her reach.

It was sometime before dawn when Crusoe became quiet. The rain
had mostly stopped. Janie heard treeroots tearing loose. She climbed up
on the seat and looked out. She could feel the ground giving way, yet it
didn't seem real—not even as the rusted-out vehicle gained speed sliding down the bluffline. The newspapers came loose and blew away. One
wrapped around Crusoe's head. Trees and rocks flashed past outside
the windows. The vehicle skipped a ledge and they were airborne then.
When the vehicle landed Janie bit her tongue, got slung against the steering wheel and knocked out.

When she next opened her eyes she saw God. No, De Soto. She'd
died, maybe. No, no—De Soto'd come down off his pedestal and crossed
the river for her. He'd come to bring her back to Elberta. She groped for
Crusoe in the darkness. De Soto was saying something, speaking, she
thought, Spanish. Awake, Janie somehow understood, got to keep you
awake. She tried and she tried, but it was hard to remain conscious. She
was being toted. She felt Crusoe on her lap and held on tight to what
remained of him. De Soto shook her whenever her eyes fell shut. Maybe,
she thought, dying won't be sleeping forever and ever. Maybe it's being
awake.

She came to on a cot and vomited onto a carpeted floor. Wiped her
mouth and rolled back over, facing a white wall. A door opened.

"Looks like she threw up Daddy."

Janie knew this voice. Pud Ward. Big Connie poked his head into the room. Janie tried to sit up, but a lurking coldness kept her from it. She had on a big-old Conquistadors T-shirt. She panicked—where was Crusoe?

Pud pointed. "It's right yonder." He toted the dirt boy to the cot. Crusoe's head had come off his body.

"Must of been some ride you had," Big Connie said. He was wearing his De Soto outfit. It was muddy from the night before.

Janie ignored him, whispering to Crusoe.

"Reckon she's knocked stupid?" Pud asked.

"Just needs time," Big Connie said. "Clean up that mess on the carpet then get her washed. Not too much, hear. We'll swap outfits before y'all head out. I'll go ahead and dial Aaron though, tell him to head down thisaway."

Pud cleaned up the vomit then led Janie to the bathroom. He stood just inside the door and said, "Go on, I ain't watching."

She turned on the faucet. The sight of water jumping out surprised her. She could see Pud in the mirror, his face blushed red. On her face, a black bruise. She put her hands in the water and it ran red-brown down the drain. She splashed her face. It burnt. She rubbed, gasped. Drank. Bruises on her arms and legs the color of ink and honeycomb. She caught a whiff of herself and remembered she didn't have bloomers on. Quickly, she splashed water down between her legs. She was leaning over to wet her head when Pud stopped her.

"Daddy says you can't look too clean when they first see you."

They waited in Big Connie's office. For what, Janie didn't know. Every flat surface was filled with Conquistadors stuff. Trophies, half-deflated footballs painted with scores, pictures and faded newspapers in black frames. She could tell Pud was trying to come up with something to say. He walked over to a bookcase. "Ain't this here one of your granddaddy's doohickies?" The assemblie was made of pebbles and sticks, bent fruit jar rings, and twisted cloth that'd been painted then scorched till it looked like a storm swirling overtop a painted flat Elberta. Down

underneath town lay buried bones and peach pits, some half-sprouted
and others growing full-on trees that reached up through the layers of
earth toward a light in some far-off beyond. "They used to be scattered
all down thisaway," Pud said, holding the assemblie out for her to see.
"Daddy found this one in a creek yonder. I know what you think, but
he ain't all bad."

Janie kept quiet. She poked a bruise to see if it'd hurt.

Pud put the assemblie back on the shelf. Before long Big Connie
opened the door. He was shirtless, curly black hair covering his pale chest.
"Here," he said, and pitched his muddy outfit to Pud. "Go put it on."

Big Connie waited out front for the sheriff while Pud, dressed like
De Soto, and Janie headed into the woods behind the used-car lot. She
toted a piece of Crusoe under each arm. The sun was fighting its way
up a steeped sky. They walked toward the southern end of Bankhead.
After a while Pud stopped and said, "I got to carry you now." Janie let
him pick her up. "Sorry," he told her, stepping out of the woods, "but it's
for looks." He checked the road both ways then headed up the ditch
back toward town.

When they got there the sheriff's patrol car was parked by the entrance to the used-car lot. Janie saw Aaron Guthrie and Deputy Polk
standing with Big Connie Ward. All three drinking coffee out of little
white cups. The pickup Janie had wrecked was parked next to the
smashed railing she'd also caused. Folks were standing outside The Bird's
Nest, pretending to smoke cigarettes and not watch what was happening
across the road.

Pud set Janie down.

"Thank you son," the sheriff said, shaking the fat boy's hand.

"Yep," Pud said. "I—"

"What a mess," Big Connie said. He was now wearing Pud's clean
checkered shirt and blue jeans. "Aaron, the poor thing was too scared to
get in my vehicle when Pud found her, so the boy offered to tote her all
way back here by hisself."

The sheriff waved toward the showroom. The door opened, and out stepped Ren and Nita Treeborne. Janie like to have dropped Crusoe when she saw them. She threw herself into her daddy's arms and buried her face in his shoulder while her momma stroked her sheared head. Her mind swimmed with the familiar smell of his cologne, cigarettes, riversand. There was his pickup truck. They could leave. She could go home.

Instead he let go and said, "You got to go with Sheriff Guthrie, Sister."

Janie grabbed ahold of him again and he pried loose her fingers one by one. No, she said. She wasn't going anywhere with them. No. She wanted to go home. Her daddy had her by the wrists, dragging her toward the patrol car.

The sheriff opened the back door. "Come on and ride with us."

"What about him?" Janie hollered, pointing at Big Connie Ward. "Ask what he did!"

Ren forced the girl into the vehicle, then the sheriff closed the door. Ren wanted to smash the window with his fist and pull his daughter out. He'd never doubted that she was alive, but he hadn't considered how broken she might be.

"Poor thing's gone wild," Big Connie said.

"Looks just like a animal," Nita said. She turned and walked off, and Big Connie followed with a packet of tissues.

Deputy Polk locked Janie Treeborne in a cell at the head of a long hallway. The girl could hear other prisoners cough and snore, shuffle back and forth across their little private patch of concrete. She wondered who they were, why they were here. She wondered the same thing about herself. Big Connie and Pud had lied about finding her. What else might they of told?

The day wore itself out into night. Nobody came for her. Janie didn't fool with sleep. Deputy Polk had let her keep Crusoe. Nothing she could do for him here though. Minutes mounted to hours. She wondered how long she'd be held. She imagined all the things Big Connie Ward had done to Lyle and Goodnight when he'd found them. Janie assumed he had, even though she'd lied to him about their whereabouts that day he cornered her at The Bird's Nest. Truth of what he'd do would be much more horrible, she'd decided time a slant of daylight fell into the cell, than anything she could imagine.

Shortly after dawn, Sheriff Guthrie led her over at his office. There was a cot made up against the wall. He asked her to sit down while they waited for Doc Barfield.

The sheriff left the room while Doc examined the girl. He found seven fat gray ticks on her body. He dabbed many scrapes and cuts with peroxide-soaked cotton balls. She sucked through her teeth, trying to be tough. He checked bruises, felt for breaks. None. He cleaned and bandaged her scabby feet. He shined a light into her eye, said she was lucky. He cleaned the blind one, dousing it with saline, and gave her a new patch to wear. She put it on and fixed what little hair she had over the strap in back. Doc asked her to lie down and put up her feet. After he'd checked down there, they were through.

Meantime, the sheriff had gone over at Woodrow's and brought back some ribs and a copy of the *Times-Journal*, which he kept facedown on the desk. "I never had somebody this young," he said. He picked up a rib then slid the go-plate toward the girl. "Once I maybe had to keep a little nigger boy from over in The Hills for a spell. Couldn't of been no younger than you are though. How old are you Sister?"

"Thirteen." She picked up a rib and sauce dripped on her leg. The sheriff passed her a napkin. Janie wiped the sauce then gnawed on the end of the rib where the cartilage was. "Where's my daddy and momma at?"

"We can call them later if you want to," the sheriff said, licking his greasy knuckles. "I'm sorry to put you in that cell all night. Polk's fixed up this bed here though. You'll be safe till all this gets sorted out."

They ate all the ribs then took turns sopping up the leftover sauce with white bread.

"Whatever on God's good earth would make poor Ricky Birdsong do something like this is a damn mystery to me," the sheriff said when he was through.

Janie could of told him, could of yet spoke the truth. Instead she grabbed another piece of bread, dredged it through sauce, then shoved it in her mouth.

The Last Last Conquistador

1958

Pud Ward got hisself a new haircut and toted a green plastic comb everywhere he went so he could keep each strand put in perfect place. Not many folks in Elberta got the chance to begin again. Pud wasn't going to mess this up. Even the Birmingham newspaper sent somebody to talk to him and take his picture standing next to the statue of Hernando de Soto. The *Times-Journal* printed a similar picture on the front page, alongside a story detailing the fat boy's rescue of the missing girl Janie Treeborne.

Pedro Hannah, of course, invited Pud on the radio. The whole town listened as Pud dedicated a song to his momma. Made the sheriff cry. Janie wanted to tell the fool to shut up. Pud's momma had died during childbirth so he'd never even known her. Why cry? Pedro thanked Pud from the bottom of the whole entire town's heart for what he'd done. "It's plumb heroic," he said. A few days later Big Connie Ward had a new Hernando de Soto outfit made for his son. They both dressed up for a big party at the used-car lot, where a cream-colored sedan was raffled off. The winner, who nobody had heard of, was absent so the car remained parked. "A goddamn fix," Deputy Polk said, tearing up his ticket and dropping it in an old coffee cup on the sheriff's desk. At school they had to put Pud in a classroom by hisself. All the other kids just couldn't hear the story enough times: Tell it again Pud, tell how you found her.

This feting culminated with Pud Ward joining the Elberta County High School Conquistadors football team. He wore 67 just like his daddy. Big as he was and being a senior, Pud was meant to intimidate the other team, which he mostly did from the sideline, sipping water from paper cones and keeping his tight black britches from riding too far up his asscrack. The Conquistadors would experience a down year, Jon De Soto Crews the only bright spot. Despite this Pud Ward never threatened to enter the game till its waning minutes, the outcome long decided. Big Connie Ward would take to his feet, shaking a glass jug filled with acorns, and holler, It's The Last Last Conquistador! This embarrassed Pud Ward so much he often forgot the playcall, which caused his teammates to hate him more, though not a one of them was fool enough to say so out loud.

Pud began visiting Janie the day after she was taken to the Elberta County Jail. The sheriff didn't mind. He was hisself unsure how to act toward the girl and seemed to genuinely like Pud, not just put on because of who his daddy was.

"It's broke ain't he?" Pud said, pointing at Crusoe.

"I'll fix him once I go home."

Pud took a bite of an oatmeal creme pie he'd got from the vending machine. "I reckon you still don't know what all happened."

Janie didn't say anything.

If you shut up, she knew, folks will talk.

Pud said he'd gone to take care of Tammy in the cave after Janie, Lyle and Goodnight left town. Let her up to pee, fed her peaches or baloney sandwiches, stuff like that. He was afraid she'd recognize him so he wore his daddy's De Soto outfit as a disguise. When he realized that Tammy would now live or die because of him he panicked and quit going to her. Tried to just burn the cave from his memory. The search party was out every day looking for her. Looking for Janie by then too. Folks figured the disappearances were connected. Nights Pud would get in his pickup truck and push the vehicle to its limit then let go of the wheel.

But he didn't mean it. The boy always grabbed back ahold of the wheel when the pickup veered off course.

He confessed to his daddy, expecting Big Connie would fly into him. Once he'd hit the boy so hard Pud messed hisself. But Big Connie did not hit him this time. Instead he laughed. He laughed louder than Pud had ever heard him do.

"Daddy, you okay?" Pud asked.

"Shit and shineola," Big Connie said, wiping a tear off his face. "Kidnapped by her own damn family." When Big Connie sobered up he told Pud to draw a map to the cave. The boy did. "But first," Big Connie said, "we got to tie up some loose ends."

This happened after Janie'd lied to Big Connie about Lyle and Goodnight's whereabouts. He'd been asking around Bankhead ever since. One morning a hunter said he'd seen the vehicle in question out beyond the coal mines. Big Connie turned Troop loose there. He could hear the drumming of the rattlesnakes before he saw the truck. Troop had Lyle pinned up against a cutbank, barking and lunging at the boy's calves. Lyle was swinging a limb at the hound and hollering, Get, go on now dog! Big Connie didn't see the girl Goodnight till she'd chucked a rattlesnake at him though. He kicked out of reflex and the snake flew toward Troop. The snake struck, and the hound yelped and limped off. Big Connie Ward drew his pistol then and threatened to blow Lyle and Goodnight to smithereens if they moved. Time he found Troop, a knot big as a softball had swelled up on the hound's front left hip. Big Connie lanced the poison then used a rope to tie off circulation above the blackening wound.

"You best pray this dog don't die on me," Big Connie said to Lyle and Goodnight, who rode in back of the truck, on the way into town. "Pray hard."

Troop wouldn't die—not from this snakebite. After that became clear Big Connie Ward had to figure out what to do with the pair. He could, he knew, do anything he pleased. The boy nothing but a river rat, the girl half his blood. Pud was just getting around to telling what his daddy had decided to do with them when the sheriff knocked on the door.

"Well, I just come by to see how you was," Pud said, standing up to leave.

"Nobody asked you to," Janie told him.

There were places to put kids like her—so why ain't they? She'd stolen property, conspired to kidnap, kidnapped her aunt. No one seemed to acknowledge this though. They were keeping her in jail as if she was in danger; not the danger herself.

She dreamed of Ricky Birdsong those nights. She never had seen him play football, but in her dreams Ricky flew down the grassy field at a gallop. Leg did not limp, eyelid did not droop. Took off his helmet and peaches spill out. The fruit rots quicker than a leaf burns, pits swallowed by the hungry earth. A tree sprouts up just as quick and encases Ricky Birdsong in the heart of its trunk. Everybody rushes down off the bleachers then to pick a peach from this miracle tree. Pick the branches bare, and eat the fruit skin and all. Then somebody takes an ax and swings it into the trunk. Thunk. Again, swing. Thunk, thunk. Pieces fly. Thunkthunkthunkthunk—that's when Janie'd wake up.

The day Pud Ward came with schoolwork for her, Janie knew she'd be let out soon. He'd also brought schoolwork of his own. He sat in the sheriff's chair reading a novel about a string of churches being burnt down and a little baptized boy befriending the town misfit. After a while Janie asked what happened to Lyle and Goodnight.

Pud closed the book on his finger and said, "Daddy took care of them."

"What'd he do?"

Pud promised to show her soon as she got out. "But you got to be careful."

"How come you to care?"

"Because I like you."

The sheriff was catching on to Pud's crush too. Later that same evening he mentioned to Janie how Pud Ward sure was a good boy. "I'm

glad to see him out for football," the sheriff said. "Spells trouble for a
town when your biggest boys don't go out for football no more." The
sheriff got up and opened the window. Lit a cigarette and halfheartedly
blew smoke outside. He patted his heart then loosed his belt buckle and
sat down again. "What Ricky Birdsong done to you and your aunt was
wrong."

"It was us," Janie said.

The sheriff inhaled, shook his head. "Listen," he said to her, "you ain't
got to protect nobody Sister. You hear?"

✦

Janie was let go on a Saturday. She knew this because her daddy picked
her up on his day off—unless that had changed too.

"What ought we do Sister?"

"Go fishing," she said.

First they stopped at The Fencepost and bought two greasy cheese-
burgers fixed with mustard and pickles and onions, and a sack of fries.
Then they drove over at the Quik-Stop and bought a dozen raw chicken
livers. They ate the burgers and fries during the drive out at De Soto
Lake. The radio on and the windows down, grit swirling up from the
floorboard. Pedro Hannah was going on about the Conquistadors.
Night before, Jon D. Crews had outscored Painted Bluff High School
by hisself in the team's first win of the season.

Ren parked near the water and left the switch on so they could listen to the radio while they fished. Janie reached into the cold gelatinous
blood and hooked a liver onto her line. Ren did the same. Neither said
a word about this being the exact spot they were fishing when the call
came that Maybelle had died. The lake had dropped several feet since
then, exposing pink and red and orange bands in the sandrock. Janie
flicked the pole and her line sailed out across the lake. The liver plunked,
a red-and-white bobber marking the spot.

"Your aunt and uncle sure are ready to see you," Ren said. "Tam's done got herself a movie camera, been recording everything." He kept on talking about his sister's new hobby for a moment. "Uncle Luth," he said, "he's still sleeping down at the veterans' hall for now. Can't wait for you to see our new camper though Sister."

"What new camper?"

"Mine and yours," he said. "Got it parked right uphill from the fishpond, and you and—"

"What about our house?"

"Oh, we don't need that big-old place. Just me and you."

"What about Momma?"

Ren began reeling in his line. "Think I lost my bait," he said. He grabbed the line and checked. "Nope, still there."

"What about Momma?"

"Listen, this don't mean me and your momma don't love you." He cast his line. "Sometimes . . . Your momma just needed to, she needed to rest. To go away for a little bit. It don't mean she don't love us Sister."

Lie, he thought. It did too. At least it meant Nita did not love him. He would move on. Already had in some respects. Tammy, his momma's will, the land. Christ he was mad for a minute. But he moved on. The money did not matter. Ren made a decent living with The Authority. Piece of paper with his name on it surely did not matter. He'd seen that belief shattered many times over. So why was he hurt, why angry, when he found out his momma had left all of The Seven to Tammy? Jealousy, pride. Something else. Like finding out you did not belong, you were not who you thought. This jarred Ren to the center of his being, to what churchfolks called the soul. He loved Tammy. The fear and panic and worry felt those days her missing caused him to lose eleven pounds. Then Sister too. When they realized the girl was missing Ren felt helpless in a way he did not know a grown man could feel. Tammy, he knew, was being no more vindictive than was her nature, lording this mess with the land over him and Luth only because it made her feel proud. We're all born with particulars. He would love Tammy however she was. His sibling duty. He'd go on doing it no matter what.

With their daddy and momma gone, with Luth, well, with Nita now living in Tennessee, Tammy and Ren had each other. And Sister. Thank Lord, he thought, we still got Sister.

He vowed to never lay blame on his daughter, but Janie's disappearance had severed the last rotten fabric of Ren and Nita's marriage. For years Nita and Ren had picked and pulled at the frays rather than do the careful work of threading a needle. The town had reacted to Janie missing by hosting prayer vigils in front of the school, on the football field, in the square where De Soto stood. Ren and Nita were paralyzed those days. The sheriff didn't want him part of the search anyhow, which felt like an accusation of his failure as a father. An accusation Nita herself was quick to point out. Ren quit going down at The Fencepost because of how folks acted when he showed up. He could only sit at the house watching Nita eat pound cake after pound cake, ice cream, peanut brittle, and seethe to hisself as they awaited word of their daughter's whereabouts.

One of the last times Ren went to The Fencepost he nearly smashed a jar half-filled with peach jelly upside Frank Tolbert's head. Frank sat at the next booth over, reading the *Times-Journal*, which had a story about Janie on the front page every day her missing. Frank had closed the paper and, in Ren's opinion, chuckled at the wrong time.

"Just say it, you fucking coward!" Ren hollered, grabbing the jar as he stood up from the booth.

Frank leaned back and raised his hands. He looked around the dining room, eyes saying, Y'all see this, right?

Orville Knight escorted Ren out onto the sidewalk before anything else could happen. "Walk it off," he said.

Ren jabbed his hands into his pockets and stalked down the street to Gene's Pawn & Gun. No idea why he went there. The shop was empty, except for Cookie Simpson. She smiled from behind the register. Can I help you? Ren knew right away that Cookie could help, and she did several times those weeks Janie was missing—on a desk in the back room where Gene Kilgore played solitaire and counted money on the rare day he bothered coming in to work. Nita had found out about Cookie before she left town for her cousin Bennie's cabin in the Smokies the day after Janie was found. She said she couldn't love Ren knowing he'd been stuck up inside of another woman. He almost felt noble giving her a good reason to leave.

The camper he bought was silver—and Janie hated it from the start. You had to tiptoe or else the whole thing rocked. No foundation. Geronimo buried his leavings in the underneath space, despite Janie running the cat off time and again. She wondered how her daddy could do this? Sometimes she'd stare at him stooped over inside their new tiny home and think to herself, I wish you'd just die. It was ugly, she knew, but that's the way the girl felt.

First chance she got Janie went over at The Peach Pit to see Jon D. Crews. His motorcycle wasn't where he usually parked it. From across the orchardfield Buckshot spotted Janie and ran thataway. She was as glad to see the dog as anybody since she'd been back. She lay down in the grass and let him flop on her chest and lick her forehead. She asked Buckshot where Jon D. was, and the fool dog sat up, cocked his head, then took off to show her.

Jon D. Crews looked like he'd been stretched between two tractors. His skin darker, arms thicker from football workouts. He'd let his hair grow long for a boy. If not for the freckles thrown across his face, Janie might of wondered was it truly him.

"I'm back," she said. "Come by to see you."

"All your hair's gone."

"Cut it."

"Looks weird," Jon D. said.

"Where's your motorcycle at?"

"Daddy sold it."

"How come?"

"We saw you in the paper," Jon D. said. "I saved them. Don't know when I'll have time to give them to you though. I'm on the Conquistadors now."

"Pud told me."

"Can you see yet?"

"Doc says I won't never be able to."

Jon D. squatted down and scratched Buckshot on the hip. The dog kicked and unrolled his tongue. "Well, I'm supposed to be working."

"Where's Lee at?"

"Over at Poarch County visiting Ricky Birdsong."

"Want to go down at The Washout when you're through?"

"I got football," Jon D. said.

"Who cares?"

"I do," he said. "Janie, you can't just come back here like nothing ever happened. I ain't even sure I want to be your friend no more."

Janie tried to put Jon D.'s words out of mind by helping her daddy clear brush from around the fishpond. Ren aimed to drain the pond then restock it with bass. He dug through the earthen dam, and they watched years of sludgy brown pondwater running off into a holler. September had proved a hot and dry month. What water remained in the pond soon evaporated. Prowling its muddy bottom Janie found oodles of dope bottles, fishing lures hung up on petrified stumps and limbs. She kept some of these, cleaned them up and set them next to the two halves of Crusoe on the windowsill above where she slept.

Otherwise she spent her time spying on her aunt Tammy, who seemed only to be able to stand viewing life through the lens of her new camera. They'd exchanged barely a word since Janie'd come home. The camera made little ten-twelve-second movies. Set the lens then crank a silver key to start the motor, pull the key and the camera made a sound kin to spinning bicycle spokes as film ran off its spool. The spool itself no larger than a good-size biscuit. Wooten had surprised Tammy with a playback machine. Sometimes Janie watched her aunt watching her movies projected up onto a wall inside the partially fin- ished house. After Tammy was found, Orville Knight and others had spent long days on The Seven helping Wooten get the house in moving- in shape.

One day at school Pud Ward slipped Janie a note asking if she'd come to the ball game that Friday. She wrote back, *Show me and I will.*

The next day they got in his pickup truck—Crusoe on the seat between them—and drove south beyond the Elberta River. It was early morning, a cloudy fall day that made shadows jittery and fleeting. She didn't ask where they were going, and Pud didn't offer to tell. She'd prepared herself for whatever she might see.

In Bankhead Pud pulled into his daddy's used-car lot and killed the engine. He got out and Janie followed, leaving Crusoe in the cab. A glare made it difficult to see inside the showroom. When a cloud shifted, absolving the windowglass of its opacity, there stood Goodnight wearing a damn skirt and blouse. Look at her, Janie thought. Goodnight disappeared in back then returned with a pot of fresh coffee for when the salesmen arrived. Mornings devoted to drinking hot sludge and jawing about what was in the paper.

"See," Pud said. "Told you Daddy took care of it."

Goodnight noticed them standing outside and unlocked the door. "Hey lovebirds."

"Ah," Pud said.

"What y'all doing down thisaway?"

"Ricky Birdsong got arrested," Janie said.

"Uh-huh," Goodnight said, smiling. "Why don't y'all come in."

She poured coffee. Pud asked how she liked working at the car lot. "He's been good to me," Goodnight said. "I shouldn't complain."

They talked a while longer. The conversation sounded to Janie's ear like one meant to come off as mature. Pud and Goodnight were acting as if far longer than one month and two weeks had passed. Summer had ended—and what with it? Janie didn't understand how they could leave the past alone. She heard the last-surviving snake dry-rattle in the glass tank. Her inclination was to pick at the past till it scarred.

Pud eventually excused hisself to the bathroom, leaving the girls alone. Janie figured this her chance to get some truth.

"Here," Goodnight said, digging through her purse, "I got something for you." She checked to see if Pud was still in the bathroom. "Make sure he puts this on." Goodnight shoved a square of gold foil into Janie's hand. The girl felt a squishy rubber ring inside the package. "Don't let him do it unless he does, hear?"

After visiting with Goodnight, Pud and Janie walked across the road to The Bird's Nest. The restaurant was empty. They sat down and ordered pancakes and runny eggs. Pud broke his yolks and swirled them with the syrup. They drank more coffee. Janie still had so many questions. Like, was Goodnight brainwashed? Slowly, coal miners arrived from the owl shift. Their skin and the green longsleeved shirts they wore sparkled black with grit. Several of the miners acknowledged Pud Ward as they came back from washing their hands and faces. Before long every table was full.

She and Pud were waiting, but Janie wasn't sure what for till Lyle Crews walked through the door. She knew it was him, but couldn't believe his face, sooty except for white circles around red-lined eyes, nor the gut pushing against his shirt. Can't be, she thought. Lyle looked much older—a fate worse than others Janie'd imagined befalling him.

"Looks like you seen a ghost babygirl," he said, pulling out the chair next to Pud and patting the fat boy's back. He took a wad of tobacco from his mouth, wrapped it in a napkin and wiped his hand on his britches. "How's Bubba doing?"

"Might make All-State," Pud said of Jon D. "Team's a piece of shit though."

"You still playing?"

Pud said he was. Lyle ordered black coffee and white toast smeared with peach jelly. When it came he ate as if somebody might take the plate before he finished.

"Y'all see Goodnight?"

"For just a minute," Pud said.

"Heard they sent Ricky over at Poarch County."

Lyle continued talking. He said Ricky Birdsong was always doomed. Might be true, Janie thought, but we didn't help. She remembered how Ricky looked the day they kidnapped her aunt. Eager, like he was fixing to join a game. They'd used him just like everybody else had, moved on. Eventually Lyle slid a couple coins onto the table and stood up.

"Well I need to sleep," he said. "Got me on this owl shift. It was good seeing y'all though. Tell Bubba I wish I could get time off to come watch him play."

"It ain't right," Janie said.

"What ain't babygirl?"

"You know it ought to be us," she said.

Lyle came around the table and put a hand on her shoulder. "You might as well get that idea out of your little head," he said. Then, staring across the table at Pud Ward: "Everybody got what they deserved, ain't that right?"

She Could of Done Worse

1958

🐦

It would be a wet winter, Tammy could tell. She hated admitting it, but, like her momma, she was sensitive to the weather. The rain started in October. Some days nothing but a pissy-old drizzle, others it looked like strings dangling from a ripped seam. The aboveground pool they'd moved onto The Seven overflowed, the fishpond spilled its banks. Tammy figured most of the fish Ren'd stocked had swam away, some maybe making it down the holler to Dismal Creek. The ground between her and Wooten's new house, which they'd somehow finished enough to move in, and the camper she'd convinced her brother to park out by their momma and daddy's gravesite flooded knee-deep in places. Ren was busy as Hernando de Soto Lake rose against the dam's backside. One day Tammy waded out to the camper to check on Sister and the girl wasn't inside. She found her sitting with the dirt boy at Hugh and Maybelle's gravesite.

"You'll catch a cold," Tammy said.

Janie looked up, tucked wet black hair behind her ears then turned back toward the weeping headmarker.

"I don't want nothing but the year I died on mine," Tammy said, kneeling next to the girl.

"What for?"

"So nobody won't know how old I was." Tammy cackled. The girl did not.

"How old are you?"

"Old, Sister," Tammy said. "Now come on and get out of this rain."

They sat in rocking chairs on the front porch of the new house and stared out across the flooded property. Tammy pointed and said, "Lake Treeborne." Sister did not laugh at this joke either. She was turning into a solemn young woman—not unlike how Tammy herself used to be. And look at her now. The life Tammy lived a horrid betrayal of the one she'd wanted. What about palm trees, the Pacific Ocean? Traded Hollywood for a house and a husband who now spent all his time building a workshop where he aimed to repair boat motors and small engines. At least business'll be good, she thought. If this rain keeps up, folks'll need boats to get around.

"Men are fools Sister," she said.

The girl didn't respond. She sipped coffee and pushed off the porchboards with her rubber wading boots. Her legs needed shaving, but Tammy refrained from saying so. The girl had become sensitive about her looks. Her hair was growing back unevenly, but nothing could be done except wait and let it.

"You'll learn one of these days."

The girl made a sound to let her aunt know she hadn't gone deaf and dumb. Much of Janie's communication was limited to this. Took her a month being back to speak more than a word or two to Tammy. The girl was lonesome, spending all her time fooling with putting that dirt doll back together. Inside Janie, Tammy just knew, things that needed saying were boiling so badly. A runaway, her momma gone. Now first love. That's right, a runaway. Tammy knew. It was a lot for anybody, let alone thirteen-going-on-fourteen.

"That Pud Ward's a big boy," she said. "So is Woot. I reckon we just like them thataway don't we Sister?"

Janie could not hide her surprise this time. She buried her face in the coffee cup she held with two hands.

Tammy grinned, pleased at getting the reaction. "You ain't got to be embarrassed with me," she said.

"I ain't."

Foot, Tammy thought. But she let the girl be.

Janie got up when she heard the pickup truck coming down the road. Pud Ward stopped by Hugh and Maybelle's house so he wouldn't get stuck. Tammy and Wooten had missed their chance to plant grass around their new house. Next spring, she thought, waving at the fat boy. He honked back as Janie splashed toward the truck, leaving her aunt and the dirt boy behind a curtain of rain spilling off the eaves.

Tammy leaned over and examined the dirt boy. Her daddy had given it a name but she couldn't remember what at this moment. Sister was doing a decent job putting the thing back together, she thought. Looked much better than the one the girl had tied up on the porch back when Tammy and Wooten still lived in the trailer other side of the river. That thing, Tammy thought, getting tickled at herself even now, looked like a hot dog wiener dropped in dirt. But this one, Crusoe, that was the name given to him, Crusoe had an uncanny quality. "Looks like it's just me and you son," she said.

She'd watched her niece work on the dirt boy, using Hugh's tools: a scraper, a little hand shovel, a blunt hatchet, pliers and cutters. Tammy knew this behavior worried her brother, though Ren never admitted so. He feared how she'd turn out with no momma. Tammy tried easing his concerns, telling him that Pud, the Ward boy, would soon bring Sister out of her morbid obsessions. This seemed to give Ren little comfort though. He blamed hisself for what'd happened to Janie. But Tammy knew it wasn't her brother's fault. Tammy knew the truth. Janie was a girl, she was growing up, testing herself. Better now before the world started on her. It would soon, Tammy knew.

She also knew how love could change you in a lick. It had been love with Wooten Ragsdale. Love so pure Tammy worried her only recourse, her only way of tolerating this kind of love, might of been to turn a pistol on herself one day. Not no more though, she thought, hunting the keys to the county-owned pickup truck she yet drove. More than two

months since her return home and she still hadn't gone back to checking water meters. Nobody had asked about the truck yet. Tammy hadn't
told anybody so, but she wasn't ever going back to that job. When she
found the keys she hollered off the porch to let Wooten know she was
leaving, then she got in the truck and drove across town to the old
Elberta Rampatorium.

She'd spent hours in the courthouse basement figuring out who
owned the land the Rampatorium was built upon. Turned out The Authority did. Mitchell Dodd, her boss at the water department, got word
Tammy was at the courthouse one day and came by to say hello. Tammy
was friendly with Mitchell, who she'd always liked, and deflected his
awkward attempts at finding out how come she was browsing land
deeds and when she'd be back to work at the water department. "Everybody sure does miss you," Mitchell said. Tammy told him she sure did
miss them too. Mitchell was nosy; word would spread.

Tammy'd sent a letter to The Authority offering what she thought
was a fair price for the land and the structures still standing on it. She
expected a quick reply then a deal done. After all, the Ramp was just
sitting there going to pot. A drive-in theater would be a boon for the
town. If she couldn't go to Hollywood then she'd bring it to Elberta.

She parked near the concession stand then toted a catalog of available movie reels up at the projection room and sat there flipping pages.
Rain leaked through the mossy roof, washed crooked gullies down the
slumping terraces. Tammy would need to flatten those out some so cars
could easily park. She'd need a load of gravel to spread around the lot.
She'd need to install speaker posts. Folks would listen to The Peach
before the movie started, Pedro Hannah's voice coming out of each
individual speaker becoming a multitude in effect, then tune to a fre-
quency that played the movie's sound. She'd need so much, she thought,
looking out the tiny square window framing what remained of an enormous screen. The projector Wooten had bought for her home movies
was not powerful enough to work at such distance. She was trying to
track down a used one that would by calling the classified desk at newspapers across the state.

Wooten had bought her the camera too. This was his way: buy in place of what he could not say. Tammy had been recording anything that looked interesting to her eye. When the rain was at its worst this month one of her daddy's assemblies turned up in the fishpond. She recorded Ren wading out to retrieve it. His yellow poncho with The Authority's *A* in bright blue on back and the lit cigarette dangling between his lips hissing in the rain would make for a gorgeous picture, she thought, though the footage would be black-and-white. Squint and you might mistake Ren for a star hisself.

He'd toted the assemblie to Tammy and Wooten's new house and set it on the kitchen table. Looked like Chief Coosa trying to hold on to his soul as it escaped from his body. The soul itself a fistful of lacquered goldenrod. Geronimo jumped up and sniffed the assemblie. Rain beat down on the tin roof, sounding like corn popping on a stovetop. It was Ren who brought up the storm their folks had survived.

"Feels like I somehow lived through it too," he said, "even though I wouldn't of been born yet. You ever get them kind of memories Tam? Somebody else's."

Tammy knew what he meant. "Not really," she said.

Didn't matter; Ren went on talking about the long-ago storm. The dam had been ruined, folks died. Downtown somehow untouched by the wind but for a toy wagon wrapped around De Soto's head and the scores of broke-necked birds scattered in the flooded streets. Tammy knew the stories. Nobody thought she listened, but she always had.

"Looked like a ship had sailed right through the dam," Ren said, doing one hand thisaway and finishing a beer with the other. "Momma and Daddy lived through a lot."

For a long pause the siblings considered the history of their family, its future yet being spun out from the present. Then Tammy let boil up from her guts something she'd wanted to ask ever since their momma died.

"You don't reckon she did it to herself do you?"

Ren shot Tammy a look then went to get another beer. Sister was leaning over the table, examining the newfound assemblie. "Not right now Tam," he said.

Janie looked up. "I know there's people that do it to themselves."

"Well your grandmomma didn't," he said.

"You don't know that."

"Damn if I do!" Ren said, slamming his fist against the table so hard the assemblie jumped.

Tammy sharply remembered how it was when you felt one certain way but folks still saw you in the same old light. Not a thing you could do, especially if you were a girl. This very feeling was what opened up the split between her and her momma. Tammy'd loved those walks in the woods too. Things changed. Sister would find out, if she hadn't already.

Back in school Tammy'd stand behind the marching band building smoking cigarettes while her classmates ate lunch. Mad as a sore-tailed hen, gut growling with hunger, and just puffing puffing puffing away. Elberta could constipate the soul. But movies . . . The marching band building set up above the football field. While she smoked Tammy would see Ricky Birdsong running hills, slapping the flagpole then skipping back down to the bottom where he'd turn and start up the grassy slope again. Tammy knew he saw her too—and she liked this reciprocated watching. At least he had ambition to leave Elberta, Alabama. Tammy's momma had told her about all the letters colleges were sending so the boy would come play ball for them. Ricky Birdsong was going to get his pick, looked like, of where he wound up.

Tammy didn't hate Ricky for what he'd done. Wooten on the other hand wanted to kill him. She convinced her husband otherwise by letting him climb between her legs and slip inside till he didn't want to kill anything anymore. Nita thought Tammy was protecting Ricky Birdsong. She'd read in a magazine that victims often will. That wasn't it though. And now Nita was gone, the bitch. Living in her honeymoon cabin like a sad old fat-ass. Tammy couldn't blame her, though she still did. Tammy and Nita'd swapped a few letters, which Tammy did not tell her brother about. More letters, more secrets. Knowing, Tammy figured, would only make Ren worse off than he already was—horrible, screwing what's-her-name who worked down at Gene Kilgore's pawnshop. Sometimes ignorance truly was bliss.

Ricky Birdsong had not acted alone. Tammy knew Sister was involved. It didn't need saying. What good would it do? One close look at how the girl'd acted around Tammy since coming back home would of proved it. But the town had decided Ricky Birdsong was guilty. Tammy felt safe in knowing that nobody else had put together two and two to make four. She'd go to her grave with what Janie'd done.

Despite what Ren or anybody else thought, Tammy Treeborne Ragsdale had a sense of blood and what it meant. The girl, Tammy knew, was being torn apart. By herself, by her grandmomma's death, by a boy. Such loss made for unbelievable recording though. First time Tammy turned the camera on her niece the look that came across the girl's round and plain face reminded her of a story her momma used to tell on herself. Maybelle was seven-eight when one summer a traveling preacher came to Bankhead. He had with him a camera, the first Maybelle had ever seen. One night after dinner the preacher showed her how to use it. Then the next day she snuck the camera out to show her friends. Turned it on each one of them and said, "Now hold still." Most of the dirty-faced Bankhead kids smiled like imbeciles. But one boy started crying when Maybelle aimed at him. "Hold still," she demanded. But the boy wouldn't stop crying and shaking. Finally she asked what was the matter. "I don't want to die," the boy said. "Please don't shoot me Belle," he whimpered, mistaking the camera for a gun.

It could work thataway, Tammy thought. Killing the future for the posterity of a moment that'd soon become past. She could of done as bad or worse than Sister when she was that age. Maybe had, seeing where she'd wound up. Married a safe man to make a safe life, knowing better, hating herself for it, and now she was preparing to blow it all to smithereens. God, it would be good. Wooten could keep on living on The Seven, in the new house they'd built if he wanted to, but they would not go on being married.

Tammy knew Wooten would quit giving her money if she dropped his name, which is how come she wanted to get the drive-in near opening shape before she told him she wanted a divorce. That word. So much work yet to do. The screen listed right and was pocked with shotgun holes and black mold and covered in poison ivy. The concession stand had been plundered and left exposed to the weather for years. Tammy had not one good lead on a suitable projector or an opening night movie picked out yet. Still, she hoped for a summer debut. She would not blame Wooten for how he reacted to all this change. The whole town might blame her though. Say she must not of been able to tolerate his bad hand. Foot, that pitiful-old hand never bothered Tammy. In fact she used to like when the scars first healed up and Wooten would rub between her legs till she screamed. It'll be fine, she thought. Let them talk.

When Tammy got home Sister was sitting on the porch. The girl had reattached the dirt boy's crushed head to his body using baling wire and green creeper vines. She was smearing on a fresh layer of marbled purple clay.

"Why don't we bake him in my oven?" Tammy said. She led her niece into the kitchen and took out a large roasting pan. They placed Crusoe down in it then Janie positioned the dirt boy's short arms across his chest, like a funeral pose. They let the oven warm up, then slid him inside and shut the door. "Let's go out and shoot while we wait," Tammy said.

The earth made embarrassing sucking sounds each time they stepped. In spots they sank to their knees. Tammy loaded the pistol with six bullets. Aimed and squeezed. There was a loud pop then a ting when the bullet hit the lid of an old washing machine. Geronimo darted away from the noise and scampered up a tree.

"I don't do this for protection," Tammy said.

"Okay."

"Women just ought to have fun Sister. Here, you try."

Janie held the pistol out in front of her body with both hands. She aimed at the trees above her granddaddy's art then fired. The bullet thunked into wood.

"Janie, Janie Treeborne," Tammy sang, "Queen of the Wild Frontier!"

The girl picked up both empty casings. They were warm to the touch. She closed them in her fist and shook as they cooled.

"I see it coming out in you," Tammy said.

"See what?"

"You run off. It wasn't nothing to do with this kidnapping mess." The girl didn't say anything, so Tammy went on: "I don't aim to make you upset. I run off once myself."

"Where to?"

"Oh, down at the beach. The Gulf seemed about far as you could get back then. I'd wanted to go to Hollywood. Hell-bent on leaving Elberta, I mean."

"What'd you do?"

"Worked at a restaurant, taking orders and cleaning up dishes. After work I'd just walk the beach up and down, up and down, long as I pleased. Waves coming in, pretty seashells by the gobs. Used to collect them. Bet you didn't know that did you? One day, I remember, there was just hundreds of dead jellyfish the brightest purple and blue you ever saw. Looked like hand pies to me, way they was shaped. Sister, it was lonely as could be down yonder and I loved every damn-blasted minute of it."

"How come you to be back in Elberta if you liked it so much?"

Tammy raised her eyebrows and laughed. "I asked myself that same question a hundred times. Got married. Divorced."

"Before Uncle Woot?"

"Yeah."

"When I left I missed it."

"Some ways I did too," Tammy said. "Hey, you want to hear something else?"

"Yeah."

"Promise not to tell."

"I won't."

"I'm buying me that old Rampatorium. Remember it? Where they used to show outdoor movies. Aim to turn it into a drive-in movie theater."

"What's a drive-in movie theater mean?"

"Folks'll bring their cars, pull up and watch movies from the front seat. Tune in on the radio for sound. Might even run the Grand out of business!" Tammy cackled. "You know I could use some help fixing up the place if you got the mind to."

"Alright," Janie said.

The rain quit and the floodwaters began draining. All of Elberta sang. Flopping fish turned up in yards, in the downtown streets. The paper printed pictures of these oddities and others. A ski boat stuck up in a tree near the high school that kids dared each other to climb up in and sit. Furniture washed into ditches exactly like it'd been arranged inside homes. Folks had to be careful starting their vehicles, in case a cat had crawled up under the hood. The Fencepost hosted a fish fry with all the fish folks found, and served fries and coleslaw and hush puppies with a slice of raw onion and lemon on the side. De Soto's square was trampled and muddy after this event. The floodwaters washed away much of Wooten's workshop, his tools and lumber as well. Tammy helped find and catch what could be so. Meantime she and Janie'd cleaned out the Rampatorium's concession stand and repainted the walls. Tammy had talked to Orville Knight about flattening the terraces and spreading a truckload of gravel. She was just waiting on a letter from The Authority saying they'd agreed to sell the place to her.

❧

One day in November the sun broke through a winter sky so beautiful and warm that Tammy couldn't resist putting on her bathing suit and tanning her legs. She carried a chair up onto the pool deck. She was reclined there when Pud Ward showed up.

"Oh, sorry," the boy said when he saw her.

"Sister!" Tammy hollered. "Your date's here."

Pud Ward handed Tammy a stack of mail. "Seen it'd run when I drove up," he said. "How you been doing Mrs. Ragsdale?"

Tammy leaned forward in her chair so her breasts pressed against her bathing suit. "Call me Tammy," she said, trying to make the fat boy uncomfortable. She adjusted her bathing suit strap. "Pud Ward, you best treat her right."

"Yes ma'am," he said.

Tammy knew what the boy was after, she thought, watching them drive away in his pickup truck. Football season was nearly over. The Conquistadors had no chance at the playoffs. Tammy knew what Pud Ward was after, but she couldn't yet tell whether Sister had or aimed to give it to him. The girl was wearing his class ring. She had to fold a piece of paper around the band and wear it on her thumb so it'd fit. Tammy didn't need to imagine her niece up at the water tower with this boy. She'd been that girl, scooched over to the middle of a sticky vinyl truckseat, fishtailing up the washed-out hill. The sky pinpricked, radio turned up, hot nervous breaths fogging windowglass. A star falling, screaming down toward the earth. Engine cut off, but the switch left on to play The Peach. What romance. A flash of lightning back west, lonely and left behind as those nights Tammy spent parked underneath the water tower herself. How about tonight, come on, just let him feel some. Pull him out from the zipperhole of his blue jeans and he'd lay both hands on the dashboard like he was ready to talk to God. When we going to screw, huh, when? Just beat harder, beat faster, beat till he hushes and wilts and forgets whatever you want him to.

Tammy thumbed through the mail Pud had brought. Finally, a letter from The Authority. She took off her sunglasses and ripped the envelope.

They'd rejected her offer to buy the Elberta Rampatorium.

That night when Janie got home dried tear tracks shimmered like a slug had crawled down the girl's cheeks. Tammy was drunk on her daddy's whiskey. The letter from The Authority had destroyed her, but she managed to ask the girl if she was alright.

"Yeah," Janie said.

"Let's go shoot."

"I don't like that."

"Well what the hell do you like Sister?"

Janie picked up Crusoe and led Tammy into the woods past Hugh and Maybelle's gravesite. Tammy marveled at the girl's sure-footedness, which she'd also once possessed. Enough moonlight seeped into the woods that each individual tree could be distinguished. Tammy tried seeing the woods how the girl must, how her momma did, to do what she'd done. The trees were tall, sure, old, pretty. They were still only trees to Tammy.

Janie led them down at Dismal Creek then up a gurgling branch to a spring. Tammy sat down on an overturned boat while the girl eased the dirt boy into the water.

"You'll ruin it."

The dirt boy sank then bobbed back up and floated in a manner that, in the dark, resembled swimming. The moon unfurled a tongue of yolky light. The dirt boy passed through to the far side of the spring, where Janie waited to pull him out.

"Your grandmomma used to tell us this was the Fountain of Youth," Tammy said. "That De Soto discovered it."

"That ain't true."

"Is that right?"

"Fountain of Youth's down in Florida," Janie told her aunt. "And De Soto wasn't hunting nothing but gold up here."

Tammy wasn't used to inspiration seeding itself in her. They were halfway up the hill before she realized it had happened. The movie she needed to show opening night at the Elberta Deluxe Drive-In Theater would be about Hernando de Soto! There wasn't a movie about the conquistador though, least as far as she knew. And now she didn't even have any land to open a drive-in on and show such a movie if it did exist. Well, she thought, seed sprouting into leafy glory, I'll just make the movie my own damn self.

The clearing was still in deep mud on the backside of the house. Tammy offered to tote Crusoe, but Janie would not let her. Stubborn, just like her grandmomma. They trudged on, splattering red dots up the backs of their legs with each step. Wooten was in his workshop, a radio blaring out into the night. All sudden Tammy stopped. Inspiration wasn't through with her yet. She looked all around the wide flat clearing. If she could not buy the old Rampatorium then she'd build her drive-in theater right here.

Tammy taught herself how to direct from a book she found at the Elberta County Public Library. For some reason Mrs. Elliott—the sole librarian since Nita left town—wouldn't allow her to check out this book. So Tammy stole it.

Janie would sometimes flip through its pages. There were camera diagrams, lighting charts, and, on the first page, a list of tips for aspiring moviemakers:

-Creating comes from memory
-Know your frame
-There is no process
-Failure does not matter
-One idea does not make a movie
-Dream
-Story, story, story

Tammy would crow these sayings while filming. She'd decided not to appear on camera herself. Figured she'd be able to use her family for every part. But, after the initial few days of filming, it became clear she'd need other actors. She asked Pedro Hannah to say something about it on the radio. Day after he did, thirty-something folks showed up on The Seven. They became both cast and crew. Small sets were built in the woods, the pasture, the clearing, which was also being excavated to make way for the drive-in screen and parking rows. Everyone dressed how they imagined the Spanish and Elberta Indians would of dressed, and they spoke lines in heavy accents, also imagined, though Tammy had no way to record sound. The first couple weeks of shooting focused on the Elberta Indians. Folks who had nothing to do with the movie showed up with sandwiches and cold beer, and tried to puzzle out what the actors were doing and how come. One day somebody from the *Times-Journal* took pictures, which ran on the second-to-last page, above the classifieds.

Wooten had not lost his mind over the drive-in theater plan. But Tammy hadn't yet told him she wanted a divorce. Winter remained mild. If this weather held she could keep filming into December. Wooten and Ren had framed a screen and begun planting speakerposts into the ground. Tammy swore that she'd tell Wooten about the divorce soon as they finished building her concession stand. The projection room would go on top. Wooten would have to finish that too. Tammy still aimed to learn how to run the projector herself. She wouldn't need him. She'd finally got a lead on one to buy in a town near the Mississippi border.

One day she was watching Wooten and Ren lay the concession stand's foundation when both men stood up straight and puzzled over something on the ground. Tammy got up from her rocker and went to see what they'd messed up this time.

When she got there, Ren was holding a bone. Too big for a deer, not quite that of a cow. "What's it from?" she asked.

"I ain't got the slightest," he said.

Wooten kicked at the dirt where they'd been working. "Look here," he said. "Another one."

Janie'd joined them too. The girl got down and began digging with her hands. Before long she'd uncovered the smooth curved portion of what looked like a human skull.

Till Death Do They Part

1930

Maybelle gave birth in the summer. They named the child Renton, called him Ren for short. To her surpise, Sampley covered for Maybelle at the post office till she could return. Meantime money dwindled. The Authority was still taking on men to help clean up the damage done by the storm till construction resumed. Hugh refused to wait in line for a job. He'd planted those bones to stop this so-called progress, but nature, after all, had steered Elberta back on its intended course. He stayed gone for nights at a time, searching out objects for his history. He had to put more ceiling beams up to bear its weight. He'd been stopped by the law after crawling through Woodrow's barbecue pits, picking out just the right charcoal pieces. Covered in soot, toting still-warm coals in the basket of his shirttail. Maybelle worried they might not let him go next time, might haul him off to the asylum in Poarch County. I need you here with me sometimes, she told him, for what little good it did. Not off chasing whatever it is in your head.

The garden they'd planted bloomed lush and wild. Okra this tall, three kinds of purple tomatoes dangling on vines, white corn, bulbous yellow squash, pickling cukes, watermelon and cantaloupe and so on. Once Maybele recovered from giving birth, the crops were again hers to tend. She laid Ren on a quilt in some shade while she hoed and picked.

Doted on her fat little baby boy, his arms like the sausages hanging in Beachy's butcher shop. She would pinch those arms till they turned pink and he cried, then she'd laugh and kiss him till he stopped.

Sometimes Lee Malone came by with fresh peaches. Maybelle sliced them and they ate. Usually Hugh could not be bothered to join. Summer rainshowers were replaced by fall and its long-shadowed light. Maybelle fixed cobblers with the peaches Lee brought her then. They talked less about Hugh and the possibility of Loudermilk's return, and more about themselves. She told of her childhood in Bankhead, leaving on a whim to become an actress, failing, being sent to Elberta by the postal service. He told her about his momma momma dying, the white folks that raised him, meeting Hugh for the first time, about Caz, about traveling the circuit and working at the textile mill, and now working for Mr. Prince. One day Lee showed up with blood on his shirt. Told her it was nothing and reached into the crib for Ren. She saw the pain on his face though as he lifted the child. She kept asking what'd happened till Lee raised his shirt and pulled back a bandage. The knife wound looked like a small mouth. The skin around it was discolored. Maybelle sat him down and stitched the wound with fishing line. Lee laughed and joked while she worked, and Maybelle tried not to blush when she held his hip to crank the sutures.

In many ways these were her best days. They'd take aimless walks across The Seven, Lee toting Ren and sometimes singing to the child. His voice killed Maybelle each time she heard it—same as it had the first. She drank up the place like a sot does wine, yet felt homesick each day, which she could not reckon with nor explain. A rhythm never found again.

These days passed, like all days do, and Maybelle returned to work. Sampley acted miffed about her being around again. This September, six months after the storm. A funny thing started happening. Alyson Tillis came in with one of Hugh's assemblies. Said it'd appeared out behind her barn. That word—*appeared*—troubled Maybelle. It implied a lack of control. She thanked Alyson and put the assemblie in the sorting room. Odd, she thought, how the woman recognized what she'd found. Maybelle didn't mention the incident to Hugh, thinking it sheer coincidence. But, by the day, more folks brought in assemblies that'd been blown across the valley during the storm. Each encounter was matter-of-fact. Here, they seemed to say, this belongs to you.

She let the assemblies pile up till Sampley began fussing. She could not carry them to The Seven by herself. Asking Hugh, she felt, was not possible.

One afternoon she walked over at The Peach Pit and waited for Lee Malone to come down the orchard. She wanted to show him something. He met her back at the post office and she snuck him into the sorting room. It wasn't much bigger than a mop closet and smelled strongly of paper and ink. They had to whisper. Every so often someone would unlock a P.O. box and take out a bundle of mail from the other side of the wall.

"They done all the work for him," Lee said.

"Reckon we should tell?"

"No, not yet."

Lee offered to haul the assemblies onto The Seven. But Maybelle got worried. What would Hugh think if he found out she'd gone to Lee? She told Lee no and, rather than sneaking Hugh's wagon, asked Dee if she could borrow theirs. Tucker refused, but Dee defied him—and paid with her jaw. The women did the work themselves, adding to the assemblies that still sat atop the mass grave.

Maybelle did not see Lee Malone for some time after this. She feared she'd offended him. Sometimes she would dream alternate versions of her and Lee in that sorting room. These dreams hung over her head for an entire day, sometimes longer. She worried Hugh could read her thoughts. She still hadn't told him the truth about the night he sent her to Freedom Hills to ask Lee to come help cut the tree off the house—and she never would.

What stuck out in her memory of that night was how empty The Hills were when she got there. The only person she could find was a Chinese man who ran a general store. He was lighting blue and red and yellow paper lanterns strung up on a dogwood tree. She asked the man if he knew Lee Malone and he answered in, she guessed, Chinese. Gestured with his hands. After a while the man quit and walked away. Maybelle realized he meant for her to follow. He went a stretch down the lane and pointed at the woods. At first she saw nothing but trees. The man pointed again and ushered her on. She had to cross a ditch before she could make out the barge on the river. She nearly tripped over some kids playing on the bank, who stopped and stared as she walked onboard across a wobbly plank.

What Maybelle saw on the barge reminded her of the tent services presided over by her father in Bankhead and towns like it to the south and west. She pushed through a crowd dancing to music like nothing she'd ever heard. Her father knew all the best guitar players, he said, and enlisted them to play folks down at the altar where he would save their souls. Music always had been her favorite part of church. After the tent cleared out her father and the other men would bust out bottles of booze, and play and sing sometimes till dawn. Jim Chambliss wasn't very good. Even Maybelle the girl could tell, watching from the darkness where the women cleaned dishes and nursed babies to sleep. He did not drink. Said he was drunk enough on God. This music on the barge sounded near to her father's church music, but different. She couldn't decide exactly how. She pushed toward the source, thinking only to find out.

Then she saw him. Though they'd never met she recognized Lee Malone from things Hugh had told her. Arms blue from the elbows down, it looked like his hands were threaded to the guitar by invisible wire. He lifted a boot then stomped the makeshift stage. Time itself became meaningless. The barge bobbed with the crowd and with the river's movements. Maybelle understood then why everybody was here. Words less important than how they sounded. She watched two men pulling giant catfish out of the river. They sliced open the fish's bellies and dropped steaming handfuls of guts over the side. They dusted the fish whole in cornmeal then plopped them in a big pot of bubbling grease, pulling the fish out after just a few minutes and tearing off crusty chunks of flesh that they folded inside bread and passed to waiting hands.

Maybelle took one herself. Somebody pulled her to dance. Hot grease
burnt her tongue and her lips as she ate and spun. Her partner smelled
like mint. Another somebody poured liquor into her mouth. She spat
and spilled on her dress. Folks laughed, folks cried. Maybelle looked
up at the sky and was reminded how life and death stood but a hair's
width from each other, and oftentimes bumped. Could again any moment, the music called to everyone on the barge. She tried to keep her
eyes on Lee, but her vision began to blur.

She came to sprawled among cattails. The kids who'd witnessed her
arrival now touching her hair. When she sat up they screamed and ran
away. She vomited on herself then crawled to the river and stuck her head
in the water. She came up gasping, and there he was, Lee Malone, walking off the barge with that guitar in hand.

"Hugh sent me," she said.

Lee stopped. "I wondered if the fool hadn't died."

"He needs your help."

"I bet he does," Lee said. "And who are you? Some of his kin?"

"I'm his wife," she said.

This memory sustained Maybelle throughout the fall. Ren was a
fussy baby and the history consumed Hugh's waking hours, so she dealt
with the child herself. She felt lonesome in a way singular to marriage
and motherhood.

Then one day Lee stopped by the post office again and told her he'd
heard from a man named Dyar that a yankee had showed up in Poarch
County. He wondered was this their man Loudermilk. If so, there was
scant time to gather up assemblies before he arrived in town. Without
hesitating, Maybelle offered to help.

They met in the clearing after she put Ren to sleep. Hugh in his studio with the enormous assemblie hanging over him. Maybelle knew so
little about art, even after spending time witnessing her husband make
his. She tried to go by her gut-feeling. Ones that struck her like a fist.
As they worked, Lee Malone sang, his voice in harmony with crickets
and the odd bird of the woods calling out from the darkness. This went

on for nights. They stored the assemblies they picked in the spring-house. Sometimes Lee would take off his shirt and jump in the water before going home. Maybelle felt ashamed watching him swim and wished she knew how so she could join him. Ashamed each time a feeling she both fought and welcomed came crawling back there in the dark as they rifled through all her husband had created.

She and Lee had been at it for several nights with no new word about the yankee sighting. Maybelle often asked herself why she was out there. Not for Hugh, she knew. He never would care what happened to his art. A few days before she'd asked what he would do if Loudermilk showed up again. The storm, she thought, might of changed his mind. Hugh told her it wouldn't matter, he would ask the yankee to leave then keep doing what he'd always done. No, Maybelle was not doing this for Hugh Treeborne. This was for her. Might as well admit. She stopped what she was doing and confessed her feelings to Lee Malone, as if it'd make a difference. She was married—just one of many reasons why they could not be together.

Lee sat down on a crate made to look like a bird's cage, whatever had been the bird missing from its perch. He did not let on whether he was surprised by Maybelle saying she had feelings for him. He was not; he felt thataway too. But he did not say this. He measured his response to her not against the moment they were in, but through an understanding of time. Now was not right; later maybe.

"I was thinking to go up at Wisconsin," he said.

"To live?"

"No, hell no. There once was this man I met told me I could come up yonder and record my music. Been thinking to take him up on it."

"Well you ought to then," she said, turning her back to him. "Who knows what could happen if you were to wait."

She was glad Lee was leaving town, Maybelle told herself as she lay down alone that night. You're married, you fool. Pledged to love till death do you part. She thought back to the days when her body knew she was with child but her mind had not accepted it. Woke up sick and hurried away from the house so Hugh would not hear. How come? Now this, another secret. Maybelle was learning that marriage, like everything else, was full of them.

As winter blew into the valley Maybelle let bitterness and anger foul her innards. Even the baby put her on edge, though he could not help his coughing fits. One day she lashed out at Hugh while he lay underneath the assemblie, accusing him of being no better than a bump on a log, among other more vulgar insinuations.

"Lee's right about you," she said. She regretted speaking his name, as if those three letters might reveal how she felt.

If Hugh noticed the redness on his wife's face he did not mention it. He said he had something to show her and he crawled out from under the massive assemblie. He raised it to the rafters, hand over hand, and secured it, tugging the corners to be sure the assemblie would not fall. From a shelf Hugh took down a metal box and opened the lid. The headmarker etchings inside. They were beautiful, Maybelle thought, unfolding each one. Names and birth and death dates adorned with drawings and, in some cases, poetry or scripture. But these weren't what Hugh wanted to show her. He handed her a page torn from a newspaper:

A new gallery showing by renowned Philadelphia artist Seth A. Loudermilk, who has traveled the world studying naïve art and interviewing those who create it. Loudermilk's newest work was inspired by a series of dreams he had while camping next to a river in darkest Alabama. He calls these pieces "assemblies" and says—

"That snake took your art and—"
"And I let him," Hugh said.
"We ought to write a letter." Maybelle felt tears coming. "We'll write this paper and tell them that yankee lied!"
"Won't do a lick of good," Hugh said.

He was right, though she tried to convince him otherwise. Why had he told her the truth if he refused to do anything about it? How much did this feeling have to do with her own restlessness? She considered using the child as motivation. But she feared what might happen if this failed. What burden she might place on Ren's head by doing so. Life would be difficult enough, it seemed, without that guilt for both of them to bear.

Just before the new year Lee Malone showed up with a black disc in a yellow paper sleeve. Maybelle had no means by which to play the thing and felt like she was being made a fool with the gift and his unannounced return. Lee wouldn't reveal how the song he'd recorded went, which angered her further. After supper, down by the pond, their breaths visible in the air, Maybelle asked him to sing it—feelings for him crawling back. You'll hear it one day, he told her. This faith was heartbreaking in a way she could not name.

Not long after his return Lee was promoted to orchard manager at The Peach Pit. He'd come to The Seven to share the good news. Folks in town didn't seem to realize he'd been promoted yet. Lee worried what would occur when they figured it out. Said Mr. Prince didn't understand what it was like for him to be in this position. Maybelle was only half-listening to Lee though, sitting near the woodstove and bouncing Ren on her lap.

Lee changed the subject, asking whether there'd been word from the yankee yet. Maybelle told him about the newspaper article, what Loudermilk had done. An easy enough decision. In this moment she wanted to hurt them, Lee and Hugh both.

"Well," Lee said, "it wasn't for us to do."

"You're just scared," she told him.

She was right, Lee Malone was scared. He betrayed his friend every day he woke and his mind rushed right toward Maybelle. To betray Hugh in yet another way by—by what, by getting Loudermilk to confess? By getting Hugh some kind of credit? Foot, Hugh knew what Loudermilk had done. Sometimes knowing was enough. Lee understood how Maybelle interpreted his reaction as plain fear though. But he knew hisself and Hugh Treeborne knew that so long as they assemblied, so long as they sang, so long as they loved and so long as they lost, the pit of why they did so would remain hard and unchanged.

He was reminded of an old drummer named T-Model who he'd known on the chitlin' circuit. Sitting by the stove, he told Maybelle how T-Model kept a piece of paper taped onto his snare drum. On this paper he'd written a list:

eat
sleep
look
comb your head
do nothing

They sat in blooming silence. The baby Ren cooed and blubbered and clenched his fists. Maybelle patted him. After a while Hugh came down from the studio. Filthy from head to toe. The man worked as if at the end waited peace. It did not. Only more work to be done, Maybelle knew. She would forgive him this or not. But right now the baby was crying and her breasts ached and she just wanted her husband to touch her.

Hugh placed a hand on her shoulder. "I love my family."

His touch left a stain. She couldn't quit staring at it.

"They love you too," Lee said.

In the middle of the night, Maybelle woke to the sound of Ren coughing. She toted the baby outside so he wouldn't wake up his father. The sky showed all it held. She pulled back her coat and rolled down her dress, but Ren couldn't quit coughing long enough to latch on. She toted him down at the spring and splashed cold water onto his face and chest. Took the baby's breath. She sat down on the leafy bank and gazed toward the years ahead. They appeared sloped. She saw herself flying downhill like a greased melon given a good hard kick. Trees cycled green

to brown to fire yellow and red, to bare, again and again and again and
again. Her skin did like a candle left in the sun. She heard a clicking, a
clicking, clicking, then it stopped. She saw beyond these woods surrounding her the Elberta River running as time itself. Eternity, seemed
like, would threaten to consume Maybelle Chambliss Treeborne every
remaining minute of her life, like the unsatisfiable monster she knew it
to be. She saw her marriage to Hugh, which already seemed far-gone,
his early death to cancer, and she glimpsed what she and Lee Malone
would settle for long after the kids were grown and Hugh'd been buried in the pasture up the hill from where at present she sat.

She was almost back to the house when she caught sight of a shadow
slinking past the studio. Someone toting an assemblie. She did not cry
out nor give chase to this form. Somewhere down the lane, she knew, a
big black vehicle was hidden in the brush. The way stretched on. Many
more Elbertas to pilfer and plunder. Night long yet. The vehicle humming its futuristic hymn as it slid through darknesses unknown.

The Hole in Lee Malone's Guitar

1958

A song never hurt nobody, Lee Malone kept telling the sheriff. He could put in a word with the warden if he just would. Lee swore not to play anything that'd rile up the prisoners. Didn't they deserve a little bit of pleasure, same as the rest of us? It took several trips visiting Ricky Birdsong in Poarch County before he convinced Aaron Guthrie of this. One day the sheriff arrived to pick him up and said, "Go get that guitar then."

Lee fed Buckshot all the raw bacon in the refrigerator, crying and kneading the dog's skinfolds as he ate. He kissed the dog's wet black snout then set him running free out back of the house—same as he did each time he left to visit Ricky Birdsong. The dog stopped at the edge of the property though. His person wasn't coming; he'd go no farther. Lee hollered and waved his arms. Buckshot tucked tail and shivered. The sheriff was honking. Each time he left to visit Ricky, Lee had to break off a branch and whip the dog till he disappeared into the pasture. Doing so like to killed him. But Lee had to, in case he did not return, which was a possibility he had no choice but to accept.

He thought about the dog all way to the Poarch County Correctional Facility. The joy he felt watching Buckshot run, things he'd learned from him. A dog the only creature capable of unconditional love. He couldn't let the sheriff see him cry, but he couldn't stop the memories: Buckshot toting a rotten deer leg through the woods, chasing a red rubber ball into De Soto Lake, over and over, asleep in bed and whimpering at dog dreams.

"Everything alright?"

"Yeah," Lee said.

The prison appeared at the end of the long straight gravel road. Looked like it'd been built to hold expensive paintings and marble statues. The soapy granite front faced a big enclosed yard surrounded by cement walls topped with gleaming sharp wire. Cornfields grew on three sides, the stalks dried yellow, this being late November. A guard holding a shotgun waved the sheriff through a sliding gate. He parked the vehicle near an administrative building then let Lee Malone out of the back.

Lee kept his eyes trained low going down the hallway. No sudden movement, nothing open to interpretation. He held Rosette's case with both hands. There were more gates and more doors studded with locks big as Bibles between the prison entrance and the room where Ricky Birdsong and another fifty-some white prisoners sat on folding chairs. There would be no black prisoners invited to this special performance. Somewhere down another hallway set the Yeller Mother. Fried brains quick as The Fencepost's skillet did eggs. Lee knew he could wind up taking his seat on her yet. The sheriff was hanging Maybelle's death over him. After six months, the investigation yet ongoing. He'd asked Lee about the peach pits found in Tammy and Wooten's mailbox, and at Ricky Birdsong's house. But the sheriff did not appear to believe Lee would be so stupid as to leave behind a clue like that. And these visits to see Ricky. One wrong move here all it took for someone like Lee Malone to never leave.

The warden and a couple guards were waiting. The sheriff shook their hands while Lee set down the guitar case, unlatched it and touched Rosette.

"Now who's this nigger you brought?" the warden asked.

"Lee Malone," the sheriff said. "One of our most upstanding citizens. Grew up playing music in a True Believers church. Tends a orchard. Lee's a real model to others of his race."

"What's that stuck in his ear?" the warden asked.

"Lee had a little, uh, accident back in summer. Ain't that right Lee?"

Lee looked up and tried to meekly smile. He began tuning the instrument, which he hadn't played since the day they buried Maybelle Treeborne. Part of Lee thought he'd never play this guitar again, some kind of penitent tribute to her. But, he thought, listening to each string stretch as he tuned, the boy needed it. Maybelle would understand.

"Well I hope the thing'll play with a big-old hole punched in it," the warden said, pointing a grubby finger at Rosette.

Lee strummed to show off the instrument's sound.

The guitar didn't have a hole the day he found it. When he was younger Lee sometimes slept at a fishing shack on the river to escape the heat in Freedom Hills. One morning not long after the storm ravaged Elberta, Lee watched a pale face emerge in the swirling yellow water outside the shack. No telling how long bodies would keep turning up in the valley, especially now with the storm-flood receded. Only after Lee'd waded in and dragged this one out did he realize a guitar was gripped in the dead man's hands. The instrument looked to be made of rosewood and a flat pick was wedged between the strings, which groaned and bled water when Lee pulled the pick loose. Turtles had been at the dead man's face and curled ears. His skin looked like toilet paper that'd fallen into a commode. A tarnished ring dug into his stiff third finger. Lee felt inside the pocket sewn over where a heart had once beaten then propped the guitar against the porch. This time Lee needed help. Getting off The Seven, he thought, would be good for Hugh Treeborne.

Time they got back with the wagon the dead man was stinking something awful. Piss ants and mulch beetles crawled across the body.

"How long you reckon him in the water for?"

"No telling," Lee said. "Pretty young though."

"Well, I sure don't know him from Adam."

Lee swatted a blue-black fly at the corner of the dead man's mouth. The fly lit then landed right back where it'd been.

"How come you not just let him float on past buddyroll?"

"How come you ain't just let them others sink?"

Hugh sat down on the porchsteps and touched the dead man's guitar.

"He was holding on to it," Lee said.

"I'll be shit." Hugh picked up the instrument and strummed. "Play us something."

"Nah."

"Come on and play," Hugh said, offering the guitar.

Lee ran his thumb down the strings and began twisting the tuning pegs. He remembered his daddy showing him where his fingers went to chord the piano. His daddy could play all kinds of music, even what folks called hillbilly. White music. Played it like a bad joke. His daddy was high-yeller, Lee's momma momma called it, and sorry as a yard dog. But he sure could sing. Oh, she'd say, he sure could sing. Before Lee's daddy sang he'd always say, Now this here never has been written down by nobody. Older than your momma too. And Lee's momma momma would guffaw and slap and smile. Lee never knew where beyond his daddy these songs came from. As he got older he realized their origin didn't much matter so long as the songs rolled on toward the future—just like they'd been doing for ages on end.

"Get on with it," Hugh said.

"Give me one blessed minute and I will."

Myra on the other hand couldn't tolerate music. She said Lee's singing was no-count. Drove her crazy—and not the way Lee so wished. He tried pushing Myra from his mind as he strummed the dead man's guitar, hunting a rhythm and some words. Sometimes when he was drunk he'd make up filthy songs and sing them to Myra just to get a rise. He hummed, trying again to forget his ex-wife. Even Hugh didn't know about Myra Lytle. She'd left Lee in what felt like another life—truth not six years ago this day. Lee pressed down the strings with his left hand, his right sweeping down, up, up, down. He hummed and hummed and he mumbled till far-flung parts of hisself began coming together. This feeling beat any dope or booze he'd ever tried. Forget Myra Lytle. Forget Maybelle Treeborne too. It was a wonder Lee hadn't been sleeping at the fishing shack the other week when she came to find

him in Freedom Hills. Hugh'd been badly injured in the storm, but Lee
still didn't think it right to send Maybelle there alone. Not for her or for
Lee, who could of been killed by any number of folks had they known
a white woman sat by his woodstove all that long-ago night.

He shut his eyes and he sang:

My billfold it is empty and
somebody stole my best comb.
I lay around this house just trying to figure out
why you left me here all alone.

"Goddamn it buddyroll," Hugh said when Lee was through.

Lee was holding the guitar by its neck and bottom, vibrations
running all throughout the instrument. He tilted the guitar forward,
sloshing water out of the sound hole. When he tilted the instrument
farther out jumped a fish. Lee and Hugh got to laughing so hard they
cried slow tears. They sat down on the porch and shared a bottle of peach
whiskey.

"You ain't toting that dummy," Lee said.

"Not today."

"Reckon that yankee'll ever show back up?"

"Might," Hugh said. "Might not."

"A mite's what grows on a chicken's ass."

Hugh did not laugh. Lee wondered did he get the joke. Then, all sudden, Hugh reached out and clasped Lee's hands in his. "When the
storm got me I seen it all from above," he whispered as if sharing a secret. "How it's all laid out down here."

How it's all laid out. Lee knew how it was all laid out. So did this
warden, who was big and fat and wore a cream-colored bow tie around
his big fat neck. He wanted Lee searched for contraband before joining
the prisoners. The guards approached. One reminded Lee of the police-
man who came hunting him after he showed his grubby little-boy's
dick to Annie-Fay Wilhite—a white girl at the True Believers church
who always smelled like cinnamon sticks and fresh-cut grass—because

she threatened to have her daddy string him up and lop it off and feed it to the dogs if he didn't whip that sucker out from his britches and show her right now. Annie-Fay's daddy one of the men who terrorized the blacks leaving Elberta back into what became Freedom Hills. "Ew," Annie-Fay said when she saw Lee the boy's pecker, "looks like a burnt dill pickle." Lee's new parents more likely the only thing that kept him alive after this incident, though not from a vicious beating with a cane swung by Annie-Fay's daddy.

The sheriff tried easing the warden's concerns. "Lee ain't toting a thing but that guitar and the prettiest voice you ever heard. Come on now C.R., let's enjoy the show."

The warden was convinced and the guards backed off. Lee picked up Rosette. Pennies he kept inside her body shifted. "Now you sure that thing'll play?" the warden asked.

"Yes sir," Lee said as he slipped the leather strap behind his neck and fixed it on his shoulder. His hearing aid whined. He reached in his pocket and adjusted a knob on the little tin box.

A buzzer buzzed and the door to the cafeteria opened. The prisoners all sat up straight as posts when the warden entered. They looked generally bored, Lee thought. He spotted Ricky Birdsong up front and center. The boy had shed weight since last Lee'd seen him. His lip was split and a yellow bruise shaded his left cheek like bad makeup. Overall seemed like Ricky was doing alright in prison though. He made and sold a version of his daddy's brittle with sugar packets that other prisoners and guards secretted him, using an aluminum can and balled-up newspapers as a burner. Not like Lee could of helped the boy had he not been doing well. Aaron Guthrie pulling strings was the only reason Lee Malone had been allowed to visit the white prison block at all. The privilege could at any moment be revoked.

"Now there'll be some entertainment today," the warden bellered from the back of the room. "So listen up!"

Lee stepped on a fruit crate that would be his stage and tested a chord. Didn't sound right. Another. Still not it. He picked a hillbilly melody. During the drive over Sheriff Guthrie had warned against playing nigger music. Lee's mind wouldn't focus on where his fingers landed. He kept remembering how, the day he found the guitar he came to call Rosette, him and Hugh'd finished that bottle of whiskey then watched a roof drift past them. Underneath, maybe, an entire house filled with furniture and keepsakes and drowned bodies. Who could know? The whiskey gone, Hugh pitched the empty bottle into the river. It bobbed, the water mending itself, then floated off too.

"You ought to keep that," Hugh said that day, nodding toward the dead man's guitar. "Ain't like he needs it no more."

"I don't want to own something like this."

Lee already had a guitar bought off Manuel Dyar, whose daddy was a Mexican that hopped a train, and whose momma was a black woman born in the Mississippi pineflats where Manuel's daddy broke his leg when he jumped off. Nobody remembered how the couple wound up in Elberta, Alabama, but they did remember the Dyars pushing a tamale cart up and down the streets while baby Manuel rode underneath the warming compartment with a fist stuck in his mouth. When he wasn't sucking fist Manuel Dyar was singing. He learned to play guitar. All his days Manuel Dyar was small and misshapen except for two long hands and ten slender fingers. But only folks in The Hills knew Manuel Dyar for his music. The rest of the valley knew him for a garfish he caught in the Elberta River. Ten foot long—still a record—and Manuel broke his wrist fighting the sucker over an eight-hour stretch. Manuel kept the garfish on show in his living room. For a nickel anybody could go in and look. You could touch its papery flesh for a penny, but for no longer than five seconds at a time. Manuel counted Mississippi though so you got your money's worth. Then one day Manuel Dyar electrocuted his-self to death plugging in his new candy-red guitar. Whole house burnt down to ashes—garfish included.

Rosette soon took the place of the guitar Lee'd bought off Manuel Dyar. She fretted without effort and sounded bright and clear. One night the summer after Lee Malone found her he performed at Roger's Lounge. He needed to be at The Peach Pit early the next morning. Didn't want to disappoint Mr. Prince. Time he finished playing a streak of red light marked the horizon though. He walked toward it, toting a jar of beer in one hand and Rosette in the other. The peach harvest had recently peaked and he thought he'd bring a basket to Maybelle after work. They'd been spending more time together. The ever-present child and at least some remaining good sense kept Lee, for the time, from pushing friendship beyond its bounds. He cut across a useless field, grass hip-high and damp, thinking of Maybelle, and was about halfway to the treeline when a boy snuck up silent and forced him on the ground.

The boy pressed his forearm against Lee's throat and bore down hard. He was as black as if he'd been cut from night. Lee gurgled, his vision splotching, and reached for the space just above the boy's shaved head.

"Give me money," the boy said, showing a knife meant for filleting fish.

"I ain't got none."

"Lie one more time and I'll cut open your nigger neck."

Lee got loose enough to land a fist upside the boy's hard head. He fell and Lee reached for the dropped knife. A rush of pain. The boy thumbing Lee's eyeballs. Lee swung wildly, hitting him a few more times. They rolled like reunited lovers across the field. Lee tasted blood and he felt the boy's heat all around. Pinned down again. Lee felt an unbearable itch at his side, saw a burst of light, then was all sudden let free.

The boy had Rosette, shaking her. The worn-smooth pennies dropped inside her body jangled. The boy chuckled. He had but four teeth in his head. Toting pennies was something Lee's daddy always did. The boy set Rosette's bottom against the ground and held her slender neck in his hand. He stomped. It took but once. As the boy began picking pennies from the grass, Lee felt a powerful burning at his side. His shirt was wet.

"Bleed nigger," the boy said, then shook the change in his fist and burst into feathers that formed the shape of an owl. He flew off, leaving Lee shivering where he lay.

After a time dandelion fuzz blew onto his face and he fought, fearing it owl feathers marking the boy's return. Was this It? he wondered. Everybody's heaven is his own making, Momma Pat used to say. And hell too, Mr. Robin would finish. Lee heard hollow voices begin singing. The voices were his momma momma's and his daddy's. His strong and clear as wound-tight metal, hers high and soft as an angel's ought to be. He harmonized with them. After a while a dog wandered up and licked the sticky hole in Lee's side. He talked to the dog till it grew bored and padded off. The voices seemed to depart with this creature. Lee hollered for them to come back, please, but they would not. He dragged hissself over to Rosette and reached inside what was left of her body. The space empty, silent.

At the prison he transitioned the hillbilly melody into a song about passing mile-marker signs and city-limit lines, searching for peace he'd never known. He'd come up with this one on the train back from Wisconsin. A few brave prisoners tapped their slippers on the concrete floor. Lee watched the guards taking note. The warden gnawed on a cigar where he stood cross-armed next to Aaron Guthrie. Waiting for Lee to slip up, waiting for a reason, though none was needed. Lee knew old men who, in their youth, had gone to prison and been leased out to coal companies. He knew about the dogs and the hoses and the ropes used in cities like Birmingham and Montgomery. He knew that one more black body gone missing in the backwoods of Poarch County would not require explanation.

When he finished the song, a prisoner hollered, "Nigger!" The guards just smirked. Lee looked down at Ricky Birdsong and wondered if the boy had any notion why he'd been sent to this place. He would of swapped spots with the boy if he could. Now what would Mr. Prince think of that? Time, Lee thought he'd leave The Peach Pit and the rest of his property to Ricky Birdsong. Fool. There was no stopping fate. You either gave yourself up to it willingly or were consumed by its immanence. Lee strummed a few major chords and said, "Thank you for having me today." A younger him might of dropped into a tremendous blues then, the way he did most nights at Roger's. Instead he tried remembering what song he was singing the night he lay bleeding in that field. He tried remembering two days later when Maybelle stitched shut the wound he did not want her to see. The plaid dress she wore, so pretty it hurt to look. At present he picked out an introduction to "The Great Speckled Bird." He beat the guitar with the heel of his palm as he picked, tilting Rosette so he could see inside the busted hole, as if doing so might reveal a way in which all this could of been prevented. All what? Life, hurt? This was Maybelle's favorite hymn. A song of adoration and praise. Lee Malone was about as religious as a stump, but he loved this song—as he did her.

Some folks never would understand that. Tammy, he thought, chief among them. Lee'd run into her just the other day at the old Rampatorium. He often took Buckshot there and let the dog run around the useless lot till he wore hisself out. Tammy like to scared Lee to death when she hollered at him from the projection room. He knew hisself a fool to climb those stairs. Alone with the woman he had, for a moment, been suspected of kidnapping—the very same woman who like to have killed him last summer.

Tammy sat with a catalog open on her lap. Looked like she may of been crying. "I tried to buy it," she said.

"Buy what?"

She gestured. "This."

Lee looked around the room. "Oh. You always loved movies, ain't you?"

She cry-laughed and said, "Yeah."

Buckshot was barking outside. Lee whistled and the dog bounded up the rotten stairs. He nudged Tammy and she petted his head.

"The Authority don't like to sell," Lee said.

"I made them a fair price."

"It ain't always about the money."

She cry-laughed again. "You sound just like Ren."

"How's he doing? I ain't seem him lately."

"He's good," Tammy said. "You know Nita left."

"I heard that," Lee said.

"This is as much as me and you ever said to each other."

Lee smiled. "Yeah, I reckon so."

Buckshot fell out on his back and Tammy rubbed the dog's belly with the toe of her shoe. "Spoiled rotten," she said.

"Lord yes."

"Momma loved him."

Lee agreed.

"Whew." Tammy stood up and folded the catalog under her arm. She wiped her tears with her thumb. "Well, enjoy the rest of your walk."

As Lee sang "The Great Speckled Bird," his mind jumped between this encounter with Tammy and the period after the storm when the barge would dip so low that Roger had to kick folks off or sink. Those exiled to shore built fires and cooked rabbits and squirrels over open flames. Fights broke out, babies were made. Stories got told about the old Indian woman whose name nobody remembered that'd warned of a wind that would gouge this valley so bad its soul'd seep out and blow away. Kids played in sand among the cattails while the grown-ups talked and stared at the sky, waiting for the end to appear. One night Woodrow went and halved a steel drum and smoked chickens to feed the masses. Bamboo poles were cut for catching turtles that the kids then turned on their shells and counted how long it took the creatures to flip over. Lee sang the blues for them. He'd heard and could play it all. Hard-driving songs you could dance a woman to, slower tear-your-heart-out-and-stomp-it-flat songs that let you sit there feeling good and low-down sorry for yourself since nobody else would. Railroad, hillbilly, church of course. The songs Lee Malone sang belonged neither to him nor to anybody else. Melodies and words shifted, music a living thing thrumming unseen throughout the air. Best you could hope for was to grab ahold for a while and hang on.

He stared directly at Ricky Birdsong as he sang the song's final words, . . . *on the wings of that Great Speckled Bird.* The boy's bruised face revealed nothing. What did Lee want, what did he expect from this? A song would not save Ricky Birdsong no more than one'd saved Lee hisself. That didn't mean it wasn't worth singing.

After the performance Lee put Rosette in back of the sheriff's patrol car then climbed in next to her. They drove out through the prison gates and down a long straight road.

"That was a nice thing you did," the sheriff said.

Lee caught his eyes in the rearview mirror.

"Figured I'd let you know we dropped the investigation of Mrs. Treeborne's death," the sheriff said. "Deemed a accident."

As they drove across Poarch County, Lee Malone thought about how the world had not ended after the storm, and how it hadn't ended either when Maybelle died. We're all of us barreling on in fits and starts toward some inevitable conclusion though. Seems the trick, he thought to hisself, the world going past outside the car window, is being alright with that.

Stories We Tell

TODAY

Time sometimes folded together like the front end of a vehicle driven head-on into an oak tree. How long since the young man last visited? Janie tried to hammer the time passed flat while searching his peculiar face for a clue.

"Buckshot went missing," she said.

"Excuse me Miss Treeborne?"

"Don't you Miss Treeborne me." She hushed as if she'd say no more. Of course Janie Treeborne could no more be silent than a flower could become a rifle. "That was the last time Lee visited poor-old Ricky in jail though. Some of the used-to-bes set up a trap down below the ballfield and it did not a lick of good. Peach pickers were always claiming dog sightings. One Sunday afternoon Watson ran into Buckshot in a field up yonder above the old cannery. Not only did the devil escape, but he took four of them pretty little-old birds Watson had blasted out the air! Ain't your daddy told you any of this?"

"No ma'am."

"Well," Janie said. If she didn't know better she'd wonder if the young man sitting before her was a Treeborne at all. "My daddy, he figured Buckshot was traipsing wherever him and Lee used to hunt. So they went to walking The Seven. Searched all over it, I mean. When's last time you been out yonder?"

"I never have Miss Treeborne."

"Lie," she said. "Why would you lie to your old grandmomma this-away?"

The young man frowned. He started to say something. Instead he shifted in the wicker chair and cleared his throat. "Can you show me where they saw him?"

"Saw who?"

"The dog."

"I don't like to be out after dark," she said.

"No. On one of those."

Took Janie half an hour to find the map she wanted folded among newspapers that seemed to the young man of no consequence. He cleared the kitchen table of dirty dishes and laundry, trying not to balk at the old woman's considerable white bloomers lying among a pile of nap-worn dresses and gowns. They pinned down the map with a glass ashtray and pieces of sandstone. Janie put a kettle on the stove then scooped coffee grounds into a press. Took her another moment to situate herself, then her finger raced across the paper. She stopped on The Seven and traced its borders two-three times. She wrote with a pen *The Seven*. She marked places Buckshot was seen with a small cross. Then, with a little prompting, she began writing the names of other places not marked on the map: *Birdsong houseplace, The Washout, Livingstown, Prince's Peach Cannery, Dismal Creek.*

"Daddy did the best he could," she said, putting down the pen. "But I was mad, buddy. Sometimes still am. Piece of paper just didn't mean squat to him, I reckon. And look here, he was right. Piece of paper don't mean squat, does it?"

She leaned back and gazed at the map as if she could take the entire valley into her mouth, like some great-beaked bird, and carry it away from where it set.

"My buddy Thomas Dale took me up in his airplane once," she said.

"Thomas Dale had him one of them little-old Mexican dogs. Awful things, shaking and yapping all the time. That's ugly in me, but oh well. Anyhow, he brung it with us. Took off from a pasture out yonder at the lake. That dog was just carrying on, I mean. When we got up there it felt like we hit a pocket of nothing. The dog hushed. My innards come plumb up my throat. You could see clear down to Bankhead. Thomas Dale, he tipped the wing and I thought I was fixing to spill out! It was, well, it was just beautiful, you know. That was my fifty-sixth birthday. Lord."

"Miss Treeborne, can you point out the dam for me?"

"Dam?"

The kettle whistled. Janie poured boiling water onto the grounds then replaced the lid on the press. The young man took two green cups from a cabinet next to the fridge. Janie thought she used to keep a special cup for him. This cup had on it the Conquistadors' logo—a glowering bearded man wearing gold armor and wielding a spear—and the young man, when he was still a boy, still her grandson, he would drink cold chocolate milk from this cup while flicking his earlobe and turning sleepy-eyed in her arms. He'd nap and she'd whisper, The Good Lord's got a plan for you son. The untroubled innocence of youth enough to cause Janie Treeborne to utter such foolish words against her better self.

"I ain't got cream," she said.

"That's fine."

"Used to you liked cream in yours."

The young man smiled. "That's right," he said. "I did."

"They called it a security problem."

"Called what one?"

"You know they threw MawMaw May a retirement party down at The Fencepost, don't you? Fixed her a yellow cake with chocolate icing. She ate the thing with her hands, like a baby. I didn't think too much of that at the time. 'Retire, foot,' she said—just laughed and laughed and laughed while Daddy and them posed next to her for a picture they run in the paper.

"She held on to them keys though. Folks would find letters stuck up in the crooks of trees, scattered down underneath the bridge, set out on rocks by the dam, placed in De Soto's very outstretched hand. Most folks knew who done it and just give the letters back to the mail carrier when he came around on his route. I reckon they realized what was going on with her. How could I? But the postal service found out and all hell like to broke loose. Started talking felonies and foolishness like that. They called it a security problem. Foot."

In the Eye of the Looker

1958

Janie hadn't seen Pud Ward since before the bones were found on The Seven. She figured he'd read the story in the paper: UNKNOWN REMAINS DISCOVERED ON LOCAL FAMILY'S PROPERTY, EXCAVATION ONGOING. Football season was over, and all the big-talkers and bullshitters and the used-to-bes gathered in daily mourning at The Fencepost, which kept them, for the moment, from moving on to the subject of the Treebornes and those bones, and the archaeologist who'd arrived to excavate them.

Sherrill Robinson had a wide face and kept her straight brown hair tied behind her neck. She'd gone to college in Tuscaloosa, dug up pyramids and opened the tombs of Egyptian kings for a while after graduation, then came back home to teach. She missed fieldwork though and was thrilled to return to it on The Seven.

The end of football and the discovery of the bones also brought Jon D. Crews back into Janie's life. He was struck more than anybody by the find. "Walked right over them no telling how many times," he said, again and again. Jon D. helped keep watch on crowds that gathered as the excavation took place, patrolling the property on his motorcycle, which he'd bought back with cash the Conquistadors Club had given him for making All-State. Janie and Jon D. both battered Sherrill with questions while she worked. The first bone was part of a leg, Sherrill told them. Janie had been right about the skull, which likely belonged to, Sherrill figured, a young man at the time of his death. She judged these bones, and the many others she uncovered in the clearing over the coming weeks, to date back into the 1800s, before Alabama became recognized as a state.

"What was it here before then?" Jon D. asked.

"Just a place," Sherrill said.

Over time she showed the kids how to clean bones with picks and soft silken brushes. Janie, Sherrill pointed out, had a natural steady hand. Tammy hovered and recorded Sherrill's work. It would, she said, be perfect for her De Soto movie. The camera ran off some gawkers who didn't want to be caught on film. But Wooten, Tammy complained, kept ruining shots as he stomped around, fussing about when he was going to be able to finish building the concession stand, projection room, and movie screen. He didn't see how a bunch of bones should keep them from continuing their work on the drive-in. The archaeologist, he told Tammy when they laid in bed at night, was up to something no good.

Sherrill liked walking The Seven, Janie noticed. She trailed the archaeologist at a distance till one day Sherrill invited her along. They came across an assemblie half-buried in the groundcover. Sherrill was taken with this strange object. Janie decided the archaeologist could be trusted and led her to Hugh's studio. When Sherrill saw the incomplete history hanging from the rafters she wanted to know everything about Hugh Treeborne's art.

They laid beneath the assemblie and Janie struggled to tell. It'd been so long since she heard the stories herself. Foot, she thought, MawMaw May ain't been dead but six months. Seemed like longer though. Sherrill Robinson was a forgiving listener. Allowed the girl to start and restart as often as needed. The stories Janie began telling underneath the assemblie stretched out across long days on hands and knees, holding a brush and a pick. Sometimes Jon D. would add to a story he remembered. As Janie's telling loosened up she felt unbound by memory and free to interpret the history her own way. A delightful discovery. Often a day of excavation ended with coffee on the porch. Sometimes Tammy joined them, pretending not to eavesdrop on what the archaeologist said.

Turned out Sherrill already knew a good amount about Elberta, Alabama. "Hiram Transtern wasn't a true scientist," she said one day. "Nothing but a sideshow man. That's how he started out. His family had bought this collection of artifacts from all over the world, and Transtern's sorry ass paraded it across the country, giving what he called lectures. The man didn't know a thing about science or the art of excavation!"

Janie'd never heard such blasphemy; it excited the girl. "What about De Soto?"

"Murderer," Sherrill said.

Tammy interjected: "He ain't done it."

Sherrill shrugged and smiled at Janie, who was grinning ear-to-ear.

Days when there wasn't much to do at the dig site, Janie and Jon D. would ride his motorcycle down at The Washout. He ran the sandy hills to keep in football-shape. Janie's daddy had surprised her with a new fishing pole and a tacklebox of her own containing a starter collection of lures, sinkers and hooks. It was too cold for much to bite. She liked the routine though, liked watching the lake drop and drop by her daddy's hand. She prowled the widening shoreline for treasures and imagined her daddy turning a knob, mashing some button—Janie had no idea how the dam truly worked—and two big-old gates slowly swinging open, water spewing out like when you pinch the tip of a garden hose. Sometimes she could leave her body at The Washout and float off downriver, chasing bend after bend, past places she'd waded and some where she'd never set foot, out of Elberta County, beyond Bankhead, on and on through places with no name she could speak, the river branching out into deltaland where dolphins broke the silver surface with their smooth blue backs, crooking and craning through root and through rot to a bay, to the Gulf of Mexico, to the whole world waiting.

One afternoon in December Janie and Jon D. pulled into the pine-brake overlooking The Washout and heard voices below the bluffs. Plenty of kids came here, but rarely in winter. They moved close to the

ledge. Next to a fire sat Pud Ward with June Renee Bishop—Miss
Elberta Peach 1958. The couple had a quilt over their laps and some
beer next to them. The fat boy said something and June Renee laughed
like a looneybird.

"Let's just go somewhere else," Jon D. said.

"No, I don't care."

"Lie," he said. "Come on."

But Janie refused. As she watched Pud and June Renee begin fooling around, she thought back to a night in his truck, parked at the
water tower. He'd cracked the windows and cut the engine. Janie'd
schooched close. She knew what she was supposed to do when Pud took
his pecker out. Already stiff. She opened the condom Goodnight had
given her and rolled it down over his purple head. She beat and she beat
then Pud all sudden stopped her. Yanked off the condom and threw it
out the window. Janie could tell she hadn't done something right. Exactly what, the girl still did not know, but it sure looked like June Renee
Bishop knew better.

Jon D. nudged Janie, bringing her out of the past. He held a rock
the size of a rabbit's head. He raised his eyebrows then reared back and
let loose. The rock fell short but skipped right upside Pud Ward's cheek.
The fat boy hollered and gripped where he'd been hit. June Renee tried to
calm him down and see what was the matter. Jon D. yelled, "To hell
with you!" and they ran back to the motorcycle. He peeled out, tires
fouling the air. He was right. Janie did care. Made her so mad she could
hardly stand the thought of herself.

They rode down at Livingstown. Van Crews draped burlap over a
dope shipment when they walked inside his shop building. He gave Janie
a limp carrot to feed a llama. The creature snatched it and chewed with
big blunt teeth then whistled for another. "That's all," Janie told it,
brushing the llama's coarse filthy hair with her fingers. Smelled worse
than a herd of billy goats, she thought. Tits swoll and fever red. Van had
given up making llama products since Big Connie Ward allowed him
back among his graces, though he would work without pay till he made
up for the missing dope shipment from last summer.

"Hear they let Ricky out," Van said. "Ought to of left him in there to die. I reckon your uncle can handle him if he dares come back around though."

Janie'd already heard this news from her daddy. But it hadn't occurred to her that Ricky Birdsong would ever go anywhere else.

"When we leaving?" Jon D. asked.

"Come good dark," Van said.

Janie and Jon D. hung around the rice paddy while the last red sunlight fell at a harsh angle across the bottomland.

"How come you to help your daddy sell dope?"

"Because," Jon D. said. "Who else will?"

A flock of ducks dive-bombed the fields then paddled across the steely water, snapping black bugs off the surface. Stray cats came calling. Janie pulled a green bottle out of the mud and chucked it at the mangy creatures. She looked at Pud Ward's class ring, which she still wore on her thumb. She pulled the ring off and chucked it in the water too.

Tammy wanted to film De Soto and his caravan arriving in Elberta before taking a holiday break. Janie had been cast as the Elberta Indian princess De Soto falls in love with. She should of known who her aunt would ask to play the conquistador hisself.

Pud Ward showed up wearing his letterman's jacket over his De Soto outfit—and Big Connie dressed the same too, just in case he was needed to step in. They were filming down at Dismal Creek. Janie could hardly stand looking at Pud Ward—let alone having him on The Seven. He toted a Japanese sword a veteran had brought back from the war then pawned to Gene Kilgore for dope money. Tammy gave direction then started the camera. Pud lumbered down the creekbank and stepped into the icy-cold water, trying not to flinch as it filled his boots, gazing up at the treetops as if they might yank him skyward.

"Now what is it I do here?" he asked.

"You're amazed," Tammy said from behind the camera. "Be amazed!"

"Oh yeah, that's right." He swung the sword back and forth a few times then stopped. "Hold on. Let me try it just one more time."

Janie wasn't allowed her eye patch. She wore a thigh-length dress made from cowhide. Freezing her ass off. She studied the pages her aunt had written:

DE SOTO sees ELBERTA PRINCESS picking blackberries in woods. She's bent over. Looks prettier than a deer. DE SOTO calls out. They talk best they can without no common language. He lays a kiss on her head. ELBERTA PRINCESS squeezes them blackberries so they pop in her fist. DE SOTO wants her to leave valley, come with him. ELBERTA PRINCESS kisses DE SOTO and scratches his filthy-old beard. Both cry. END SCENE.

There were no blackberries this time of year, so Tammy gave her niece a handful of winterberries instead. "Alright," she said, "we need some romance in this thing Sister." She backed off and began circling. "Go!"

Janie tried hard not to look at the camera as she feigned berry picking among dried weedstalks. She could feel Pud approaching. She hated him. Hated herself. Feelings were hard to keep separate. Love, hate, all of them.

"Hey there!" he hollered.

She stood up and, without meaning to, crushed the berries in her hand. Pud tried to lean in and kiss her anyway. She shoved him, staining his tunic.

"Cut. Cut!" Tammy said.

Pud was smiling. "Ain't this something else? A real-live movie in Elberta."

"She never would go with him," Janie said.

"Who?"

"The princess. She wouldn't go with him no matter what."

They reset the scene. Janie held another fistful of berries. This time Pud kissed her. Pop went the berries. Tammy pushed in on the girl's face. "Cry," she said. "Cry now."

But Janie would not.

"Cut!" Tammy hollered. "Take a break."

Janie cocooned herself in a mule blanket. Pud came over and sat next to her. "You don't know what she'd do," he said.

"That's the point of acting," Janie told him, tears now welling up behind her eyeballs. "You can make it up however you want."

The week before Christmas the Treebornes gathered for a breakfast Maybelle would of cooked in years past. Biscuits with chocolate gravy, bacon, scrambled eggs. Geronimo was perched on the far end of the counter, yowling for something to eat.

While the biscuits baked Wooten took a trip down at The Fencepost. He returned with a copy of the *Elberta Times-Journal*.

"Lordy be," Ren said, holding the paper away from hisself like the words might rub off on him if he didn't. "Come here and see this Tam."

"Done it to hisself," Wooten said.

"What is it? I'm fixing a plate for Sherrill before she's got to—" Tammy scanned the story. "Couldn't live with hisself could he?"

Tammy abandoned breakfast, and the Treebornes loaded up and drove down at The Fencepost. Place was jam-packed. A booth near the register emptied and they sat.

This time around Janie felt some comfort in the rituals of death. She was, she thought, growing into herself. Everyone at The Fencepost had eternally full cups of coffee to hold while they talked. Lucy the waitress was red-faced and sweating as she made her way back and forth across the dining room, delivering plates of butter biscuits on the house. Time itself moved like syrup across an empty plate while Elberta, Alabama, mourned Ricky Birdsong in a tiny restaurant near the river. It was told his brain had shrunk small enough to fit in the palm of your hand. "Small enough it'd fit right here," Millard Andrews said for anybody who'd listen, poking the hand that'd handled Ricky's broken body. Janie's uncle Luther even walked over from the veterans' hall and joined in. Eyes not so glassy, he ate hash browns covered in ketchup, and six slices of buttered toast. Sherrill was the only one missing, Janie felt.

"I'm going by the old Rampatorium," Tammy said, getting up from the booth.

"The Authority don't like folks messing around out there," Ren warned.

"To hell with The Authority," she told him.

By now Janie knew a lie when she heard one. She told her daddy she was going to see Jon D. at The Peach Pit, then followed her aunt.

Janie and Jon D. had spied on Sherrill Robinson a few times, so the girl knew which room at the Elberta Motor Lodge the archaeologist was staying at. Room thirty-four. She watched her aunt stop, look every which way, then knock. The door opened. Tammy checked again to see if anyone was watching then stepped inside.

That evening Janie was sitting on the porch with Crusoe when Tammy got home. Striped moths big as hummingbirds clumsily orbited the light. Janie asked where she'd been.

"Thinking about what to do."

"Was Sherrill helping you?"

Tammy looked sideways at the girl and half-grinned. "She has some."

"Well, what you going to do?"

Tammy sighed. "I feel sorry," she said. "Over Ricky. That's Momma in me I reckon."

The girl recognized regret same as she did a lie. She'd had none in her life till this last year. Regret, she'd learned, felt much worse than committing the act which birthed it.

"It wasn't even his idea," she said.

Tammy didn't respond. She retrieved her camera, cranked the key then pulled. The reel spun. She pushed toward Janie. The girl stared at a backward reflection of herself—the eye patch, hair just now grown long enough to touch the bottom of her ears—and, deep within the lens, a flickering point of light. The reel clicked, clicked, clicked, then stopped.

This Didn't Make the Paper Either

1958

The water tower looked like it touched the bottom of the gray winter sky. The tank was painted blue and shaped like a hamburger bun. Ricky Birdsong knew he was walking toward the water tower, his feet were moving underneath him, but the tower seemed to draw no closer. A vehicle blew past and the driver honked. Ricky looked to see if he knew this person. Behind him he could no longer see the house where he'd grown up, where his momma used to make funeral flowers while she wore a housecoat that looked similar to the one Jesus, who was walking next to Ricky now, sometimes wore. Ricky buttoned up his letterman's jacket. He didn't fill it way he used to back in school. Jesus wanted to know if he was cold. Ricky told him no and walked a little faster—afraid The Savior might try to change his mind.

They said something was off in his brain. All that football, all them hits. To Ricky Birdsong it wasn't thataway at all though. Seemed to him like something was off with them from the moment he stepped down from that big silver bus coming back east from Mississippi. It was still August, like the day he'd left, and the ECHS marching band beat a swinging rhythm while the cheerleaders high-kicked and showed teeth. The world looked to Ricky Birdsong just the way it always looked. He didn't believe the doctors at the university when they said he couldn't play football anymore, which meant he couldn't be a student there either unless he paid. Paid with what? Look at me, he thought, standing naked in front of a hospital mirror. He asked the doctors what he was supposed to do.

"Go home son," they said.

"Millwork maybe," his former coach told him.

Ricky did go home—and now look. Home had eaten at him. But the Ricky Birdsong inside this body was yet the same Ricky Birdsong who once scored five times in a half against Poarch County, the same Ricky Birdsong who head coaches from eight southern universities came to Elberta, Alabama, all on the same Friday night, to watch him play ball. Him, goddamn it, the same Ricky who helped his momma arrange funeral flowers for Decoration Day, a line of wagons and wheelbarrows down the side of the road, folks standing around the yard and jawing, eating peanut brittle, while he hunted out their orders. If nobody could see past a drooping eyelid, past the way he sometimes talked, or hobbled when his hip hurt, if nobody could see the brain they imagined dark as the valley before the De Soto Dam, the brain those university doctors said had been sloshed up against the inside of his skull one too many times—they had pictures, see here—the brain that to Ricky Birdsong was firing so much it was all he could stand most days just being alive, if they couldn't see him and understand him, then he'd just have to fucking show them hisself.

Downtown was all done up with Christmas lights and decorations. Love's Hair, Best Southern Meats, the post office, Gene's Pawn & Gun, The Fencepost Cafe. Fake snow and ceramic figurines displayed behind windows frosted with glitter and paint. Jesus was not impressed. He'd seen it all before, year in and out. A bitter cold snap had settled into the valley and the streets were vacant. Ricky passed underneath a tinsel-strung banner hanging across the square where Hernando de Soto stood eternal watch. Somebody had placed a red and white Santa hat on the conquistador's mighty head. Ricky never much believed the stories about De Soto coming down from his pedestal to roam—not even when he was a kid who ought to of believed in such magic. Back in school some boys in his class attempted to steal the statue one night. Drunk as skunks, they didn't realize how damn heavy the statue was till they'd torn the bumpers off two pickup trucks. The sheriff found the boys passed out in the grass the next morning. He woke them and carried them over at The Fencepost for coffee and butter biscuits, their foolishness punishment enough.

Ricky Birdsong walked into the same little cafe and sat on a stool facing out the window. Orville Knight and a few other big-talkers—all wearing insulated coveralls in varying shades of blue or brown—hunkered in a booth near the kitchen. A radio behind the cracked counter played The Peach. Orville holding court yet one more time about going down into that cave and finding Tammy Treeborne Ragsdale. Previously Orville was most well known for a low-speed crash in which he shit on hisself, but otherwise escaped injury. He'd paused for a moment when Ricky walked through the door, then kept on telling. The men were eating peach cobbler with knobs of melting vanilla ice cream on top.

"Must of been a good hundred-foot drop," Orville said. He took a bite of cobbler and, chewing, called out, "Lucy honey, freshen everybody's cup."

The waitress did, then she brought a cup and the coffeepot to Ricky Birdsong and poured. "You want anything to eat?"

"I don't believe so," Ricky said. "Thank you though."

Lucy smiled. She was a senior with pretty bangs and legs that moved like scissors when she crossed the dining room.

Ricky took a sip of coffee. Jesus was waiting for him on the sidewalk. The few folks who passed by did not realize it was Him standing there. Why would they? Jesus looked no different from the bullshitters sitting in the booth. The coffee warmed Ricky's innards as he drank and his mind hummed like a throttled lawnmower. Most days the present was all he could comprehend. It'd always been thisaway though. Problem being Ricky lived among folks wrapped up so completely in the past. His own, their own, pasts of others, them who came before and after, all us, he thought. Living was hard on Ricky Birdsong before the injury. He wanted so much to explain this sensation to someone. Once he'd tried with Lee Malone. They'd walked up at the ruins of the old peach cannery. Buckshot the dog was sniffing underneath a broke-down fruit truck—likely on a rabbit or a fox. "All you can do in life," Lee said after Ricky finished talking, "is keep open your eyes and be satisfied with yourself."

Times, the past did wash up over the present and Ricky Birdsong sank down into it way you do De Soto Lake on a hot hot day. This began happening while he sipped coffee at The Fencepost Cafe. All around him a people's particular past hung on the walls in pictures and jerseys and clipped newspaper articles stuck inside frames. Ricky saw hisself racing down the ballfield, everybody on the bleachers rising to holler, Fly, Ricky, Fly! Tormented him now whenever somebody uttered those three words, which they often did. In the photo, burning headlights shine toward the field to fight the coming darkness. The marching band sways, playing "Fight On, You Conquistadors!" Burnt popcorn and hot dogs, the saltiness of girls on Ricky's fingers. The night at the lake when he had two at once, or one right after the other. Don't you forget me when you're gone off to college Ricky Birdsong, says Inelle Davies, taking his hand and shoving it in her warm soft crotch. Stepping off that big silver bus, he'd looked for her among the crowd gathered to greet his return. Forgot him herself. Sometimes Ricky Birdsong slipped into a place where an entire day passes thisaway, not realizing till he comes to on the floor, or wherever he's fallen, a knot on his head, blood crusted around his sore nose, the tinny taste of a bit tongue. But not today. Ricky drank coffee and he tried to win this one off, tried to stay in the present where he had something yet to prove.

He'd been out of prison a few weeks now. Coffee there was weak and watery, but prison wasn't so bad as folks said. Most things in life weren't, he'd come to believe. Maybe that was the secret to surviving? Prison was forever the present moment. Inside those walls waited no future but the day that dawned outside and whatever past a man possessed did him not a lick of good. Before he was let out Ricky had started making brittle similar to what his daddy used to make when he was still alive. Hollowed out an aluminum can and stuffed it with day-old newspapers or toilet paper and set it on fire. Other prisoners gave him sugar packets, he gave them brittle. His brittle didn't have nuts like his daddy's did till some guards caught wind of his venture. They gave him even more sugar packets and a few cups of pecans from a tree beyond the cornfields. Everybody at prison started calling Ricky Birdsong The Candy Man.

Lucy came over again to refill his cup, catching Ricky looking at a picture of hisself on the wall. "That you up yonder?"

"So they say."

Lucy smiled again. The big-talkers in back bursted into laughter over something. She sat down on the stool next to him. "Must be something having your picture up on a wall."

"I reckon so."

"Mine won't never be."

Up close the girl smelled like pear and unsmoked cigarettes. Reminded Ricky of Tammy Treeborne when they were in school. He panicked at this memory, as if Lucy might see through his skull like the doctors did with the big clanging machine they slid him into for an hour at a time. Tammy. He'd known what the Crews boy was asking him to do wasn't right. So why do it? Ricky still needed to answer this question for hisself. He was sick and tired of all the reasons Jesus gave him. Forgiveness, Jesus said. Forgiveness.

"Listen," Lucy said, "I don't want to be the one to do this, but Elmo needs you to leave soon as you can finish that cup alright. It's on us."

Ricky looked over his shoulder at Elmo Rogers, the dark-haired cook, standing in the kitchen window with a cigarette dangling from his purpled lips. He nodded then Elmo nodded back and cracked an egg onto the flattop.

"I heard you used to be some ball player," Lucy said. "My boyfriend's on the Conquistadors now. Eighty-eight, Pruitt."

"Fight on," Ricky said. He took one last sip of coffee, left a nickel by the cup, then walked out the door and continued on across town with Jesus.

The girl was right—Ricky Birdsong was the most decorated athlete in Elberta County High School history. Birdsongs had always been pure-dee athletes, the men and the women both. Caught the most rabbits when the fields were burnt after harvest. Birdsongs had strong calves and sturdy ankles that made for easy cutting and lunging in tilled dirt. This rabbit hunt the valley's oldest sport, tracing back to the Elberta Indians. After the hunt ended greasy meat was roasted over fires then cooked in its own gravy with dumplings big as a man's clenched fist. Ricky's folks, Ronnie and Debra, they used to light out on runs together just for the fun of it—long before it was fashionable to do such a thing. Debra even ran while she was pregnant with Ricky. Some folks blamed what happened to the boy on this habit. He had, they claimed, a medical predisposition. Folks thought the Birdsongs were loony anyhow. Work on your feet all day then go running? Ronnie was some football player too, and young Ricky shared his daddy's build and his speed and his predilection for hurling hisself into lesser, slower boys. Headhunter, they called Ronnie Birdsong, who first noticed a smidge of hisself in his only son the day the boy tackled an eighty-pound nanny goat that had wandered into the yard and started chewing on his momma's funeral flower arrangements. Tackled the goat so hard it stood stupid for the rest of its own days, drool dangling from a puckered lower lip.

If the rabbit hunt was the valley's oldest sport then football was its favorite. Ricky Birdsong joined the ECHS varsity squad the year he turned ten. Didn't look ten though, a mustache kindly like the fuzz on a peach strapped his upper lip. He was the valley's secret till Roger Manasco wrote a story in the *Times* that got picked up by several out-of-town papers. Then the whole state knew—before long, beyond its borders. Coaches rolled into the valley in big black vehicles. Tall men, every one, with gravelly voices. They visited for hours while Debra Birdsong sat making funeral flowers. Ronnie fixed a dark and bubbling stew, brittle that made your teeth ache for dessert. Flowers piled up around the coaches as they made desperate pitches for Ricky to play ball at their college one day. Before leaving they told Debra Birdsong where their families held Decoration, making it up if they lacked this tradition of gathering in a cemetery the third Sunday in May to picnic and remember the dead.

From the top of the hill where the water tower stood Ricky Birdsong could make out Lee Malone's house, other side of a pasture that sometimes held a herd of rusty red cows. Lee'd visited him in prison just about every week. Time, Ricky thought Lee was going to break him out, especially the day he came with his guitar. Ricky kept imagining the old man reaching into the hole busted in the instrument's side and whipping out a gun, shooting their way out like in the movies that used to play at the old Rampatorium. Ricky walked underneath the water tower. Scattered all over the ground were busted beer bottles, condoms, candy bar wrappers, mashed cigarettes. Sometimes you might find a watch here, a class ring, loose change, a broken pair of sunglasses. Often somebody's bunched-drawers or a soiled sock slung out the window of a vehicle before it took off downhill to meet curfew. Ricky Birdsong hisself had come here many nights back in school. Sometimes with Freeda Hooper, a girl from Livingstown who let Ricky call her his girlfriend for a spell. Him twelve, her sixteen. Freeda liked spreading wide her legs and holding Ricky's face down between them. He didn't do anything, just kept his head still while Freeda rolled her hips and sighed like she was bored. Ricky was caught in this position at the pasture's edge one night and carried off by the Conquistadors, who whistled and whipped him with wet towels, then tied him to a weight-lifting rack for three hours and forced him to drink a bottle of booze on the fifty-yard line as the sun appeared like a bloody eye opening on an ashen face.

The ladder going up the water tower was cold to the touch. Ricky began climbing. Each time he grabbed a rung blue-green paint chipped off and stuck to his palm. Jesus had already zipped up top. It started sprinkling rain. The higher Ricky climbed, the stronger the wind blew. He slipped, caught hisself then snaked an arm through the ladder from the backside. He'd never had the guts to ask Tammy Treeborne up here, though he'd always watched for her. She never dated much back in school. By junior year the not-secret of Ricky wanting her became like a sick animal lying out in the open. He couldn't put it down. He was terrified of heights. A fear which would of spelled doom for any other boy in the valley, climbing the water tower a rite of passage, like swimming butt-naked across De Soto Lake and back, or sneaking into Hernando's Hideaway to watch Holly the Oyster Girl pop out of her shell and dance topless with a papier-mâché pearl big as a basketball in her hands. Ricky always hated when the Conquistadors would get drunk and fool around at Chief Coosa's Overlook, wrestling, chucking rocks off the bluff and waiting to hear them clatter down into the abyss. He never even liked standing on the top row of the ballfield bleachers and looking off the backside.

At the top of the water tower Ricky gripped the railing. His knees buckled as he forced hisself to look out. Tire marks mashed into the pasture mazed in and out of one another in loops and curls, some leading astray then doubling back toward the two-track road. Ricky could see all of downtown, past it big houses spaced along the Elberta's eroding bank among now-bare oaks and poplars reaching into the winter sky hung low. Ricky reached too, as if he could grab the sky and break off a piece. The sky went on oblivious to him and spat more cold rain. Jesus laughed and leaned against the tank. He reminded Ricky what the sheriff'd said the day he brought him home from prison: Leave son. But Birdsongs of some incarnation had been living in this valley since before De Soto. If the line were to end it wouldn't be because it'd taken root some other place. It'd be because this valley, in all its beautiful brutality, swallowed up the end of that line like a snake caught ahold of its winding tail.

Sometimes back in school Ricky would see Lee Malone standing on his screened-in back porch looking up at the water tower. Ricky liked knowing Lee was down yonder watching. Nobody credited Lee, but he was the one who came up with Fly, Ricky, Fly! He was maybe Ricky's biggest fan. His friend. Kindly a daddy too time Ronnie Birdsong drowned in De Soto Lake the year before Ricky graduated from ECHS. Lee loved the game of football, though he never had the chance to play it. After Ricky came home from Mississippi, Lee made sure the bullshitters and big-talkers and used-to-bes who gathered for butter biscuits and coffee at The Fencepost quit all their teasing once it'd gone on long enough. Alright now, he'd say—and that was it. Usually they listened to

Lee Malone, though Ricky couldn't figure out how come, since Lee was a nigger. All he knew was that Lee had been good to him. Ren Treeborne too, Jesus reminded the boy. Another Conquistador. And Ren's brother Luther, who'd once told Ricky he ought to join up with the service. It's kindly like being on a ball team, he'd claimed. Ricky and Luther had played together one season before Luther graduated and enlisted hisself. Ricky had seen Luther climb the water tower too, doped up and shirtless, wildly holding a crushed beer can in one hand. He followed Luther's advice. But soon as the service saw his hospital records they turned him down. Not even The Authority would take him now. Ren said they couldn't have an ex-con working at the dam. It was a security issue. He promised to help Ricky get more yards to mow though. Winter, he reminded the boy, wasn't long in Elberta.

Ricky Birdsong and Jesus watched the light snuffed out of the sky. It grew cold up top the water tower. Ricky tasted metal when an owl hooted four long times. He willed a light to come on inside Lee's house. If it would, Ricky told Jesus, then he'd climb down the ladder. But a light would not come on. A lone vehicle passed along the road and up into the deep-dark hills west of downtown. Ricky crawled to the edge of the grating and peered down. The ladder rungs were slicked over with a fine layer of ice.

He walked laps around the tank. His hip began hurting and he felt other joints cementing together too. He did jumping jacks till the grating shook as if it'd come loose. He stopped then. Jesus pointed out a line of welded-over holes going up the tank. Fly, Ricky, Fly. An out-of-focus moon appeared from behind a weeping cloudmass. Ricky put his ear up against the tank. Sounded like the ocean was on the other side. Now the Gulf Coast was one place he'd considered going to when he got out of prison. Ren even said he'd drive him there and help him get set up if that's what he really wanted to do. Truth, it wasn't. In the end nowhere else would be Elberta, Alabama. Even Ricky Birdsong knew that.

He grabbed the poorly welded-over holes with his fingertips. They cut as he pulled hisself up. The tank flattened out the higher he climbed. He inched along like a slug. Jesus up there waiting. At the very tip-top was a flat spot just big enough for Ricky's tennis shoes to fit. The wind pushed back his thinning hair, which danced atop his great-big skull like weeds in a river's current. Ricky Birdsong whooped, held out his arms for balance. Jesus applauded. Had the water tower been shaped like a peach, way the town would reimagine it a decade later to attract more tourists, Ricky Birdsong never would of been able to climb to its top. Maybe he would of sat there on the grating till morning, till the sun melted the ice off the ladder rungs, then climbed back down. But this was only a water tower, this was only the present, and Ricky Birdsong did stand high up yonder, whooping, arms held out as if he was ready to take flight, and he would stand nowhere else on this earth again.

Blood's All You Got Left

1959

Excavation was a lot of squatting, a lot of being down on your hands and knees in dirt. For Christmas Sherrill Robinson had given Janie her own set of picks and brushes. Every little piece of bone they uncovered on The Seven had to be marked and tagged and organized. Janie loved the detail in this work. She began thinking maybe she'd become an archaeologist when she grew up. Some of the bones had already been sent to a lab in Tuscaloosa. Janie and Jon D. had all kinds of stories for what the results might tell. Neither believed the bones were, like Sherrill claimed, only about 150 years old.

When spring neared, and with it, Conquistadors practice, Jon D. couldn't come over as much. Selfishly, Janie'd hoped he wouldn't play football this season, though she enjoyed spending time alone with Sherrill. Sherrill was the kind of adult that made you forget her age. She'd told Janie she could ask her anything, so the girl often did.

"You ever seen a real dead person, or just bones?"

"Once I saw somebody drown in Florida," Sherrill said. "I remember they dragged him up on the beach, and his belly was poking out something awful and his face had turned this light light purple grape color."

"What was you doing there?"

"Work," she said. "Had a dig near Ocala."

"De Soto?"

"No Sister. There's more to study than Hernando de Soto. That's the problem with somewhere like this getting so fixated. It narrows down your perspective. And don't you repeat this, but your aunt isn't helping with this movie of hers."

The other day Tammy'd hired Jon D. Crews and fourteen other Conquistadors to play parts in De Soto's caravan. Janie bloodied the boys with old paint from a can in her granddaddy's studio before they battled Elberta Indians—played by Livingstown boys—out in the pasture where Janie and her daddy still lived in the camper. Pud Ward relished being the Spanish leader. The scene soon went from pretend to real violence. Tammy kept filming, and afterward nobody said a word about what had conspired.

More often Tammy wanted to capture nature. Janie led her aunt on walks across The Seven. Sometimes Sherrill joined, holding Tammy's hand when she thought the girl wasn't looking. But Janie saw. One night, when her uncle Wooten was out drinking, the girl saw Sherrill sneak from the couch, where she'd started sometimes sleeping, into Tammy's bedroom. There wasn't much to witness on these walks; the land still dormant. One time the women came across four gun-frightened deer in a bottomland though. Another time Tammy used an entire reel on icy-green rapids at Dismal Creek. Janie thought The Seven fascinating as anybody, but she wondered who else on earth would ever watch this.

Wooten had finished the concession stand and was working on the top-floor projection room. The screen had been framed, but the big square panels Tammy'd bought still needed to be painted then fitted. There was time yet. Meanwhile she needed to finish the movie.

One afternoon she filmed at The Peach Pit. Lee Malone permitted Raul and Pee-Po to forgo their work and watch. Even joined them, flipping over a plastic bucket and taking a seat. Lee couldn't make much sense of what was happening in this scene. Janie was acting in it though. Dressed like an Elberta Indian, looked like. The girl appeared uncertain

as her aunt circled with a camera. Lee admired Tammy for figuring out
the next phase of her life. He still hadn't figured out how he'd live
his own.

During a break, he went to say hello to Janie. She sat in the grass,
scratching Buckshot, who'd finally returned home of his own volition,
on the rump. Sometimes it startled Lee how much the girl resembled
her grandmomma, even with that dark hair Janie had. The resemblance
was not limited to her looks, but how the girl moved about the world.

"How you doing Sister?"

"Good."

"Having fun?"

"Not really," she said. "Wish I was on The Seven with Sherrill."

Took Lee a moment to put this name to a face. "Oh," he said.

"I'm going to be an archaeologist too one day."

"Well I'm sure you'll make a fine one," Lee said. "And if it don't work
out then you can just run this place for me."

When filming ended for the day Pud Ward offered Janie a ride home.
She was tired, and feeling sorry for no reason, and she wanted to go with
him, so she said yes. He cut through town then turned off the road and
headed up through the pasture toward the water tower. Janie said nothing, leaning against the passenger-side door. She felt sickly excited when,
at the top of the hill, Pud stopped and shut off the engine. Yellow police
tape was still strung up around the tower's base from Ricky's fall.

"Creepy up here now ain't it?"

"Will June Renee not wonder where you are?"

"Ah," Pud said. "Janie, I'm sorry."

She waited a moment to answer then said, "I still ain't screwing you."

Pud laughed, and they were able to talk more freely. Reminded Janie
of when he visited her at the sheriff's office. She'd missed him. She said
it: "I missed you." Pud said he missed her too. "I lost your class ring,"
she confessed. He told her it didn't matter, he'd get a new one. All at
once Janie Treeborne imagined a life: Big Pud Ward running his daddy's
used-car lots while she raised a chubby baby that had her looks and his
good nature. The speed with which the girl's mind conjured this image

felt disorienting and thrilling. She ached with wanting from her toe-nails to her scalp. Wanting Pud to touch her, hold her, do something.

"I ought to get you home," he said.

❧

In March a reporter from the *Times-Journal* stopped by The Seven ask-ing when Tammy aimed to show her Hernando de Soto movie. The whole town, the reporter said, wanted to know. "End of the month," she told him.

Janie didn't see how this would happen. The drive-in screen and pro-jection room were still half-finished. But Tammy had found a projector in a flyspeck town near the Mississippi border. That next weekend Janie loaded up and rode with her aunt to pick it up. A chubby man wearing wire-rimmed glasses rolled the projector out on a cart, and helped load and secure it in back of the county-owned pickup truck Tammy still drove. The man looked sad to see the projector go. "Nobody watches movies anymore," he said. Tammy cranked the engine and they made the town square, where a limestone Confederate veteran stood among grass bordered by begonias, then headed back toward Elberta.

Janie watched her aunt driving. No radio, just silence. The girl no longer saw a woman cruel and destructive. When had this happened? She saw in her aunt the ability to start over, become anew, and she felt profound admiration every bit as surprising as the first time her body bled itself. Hatred, she realized, was in truth a sick kind of love.

❧

On a windy day, all the miniature orange flags Sherrill had planted to mark the dig site snapping and popping, Janie removed the last bone, tagged it, and put it in a plastic container that resembled a tacklebox. They celebrated with a meal at The Fencepost. Sherrill was waiting on word of her next assignment. It hadn't occurred to Janie that there would be another one. She kept this embarrassment to herself though. The uncertainty of where Sherrill would go was driving Tammy to drink nightly jugs of muscadine wine from the Quik-Stop. The empties she toted out back and shot to pieces.

"I'm worried about your aunt," Sherrill told the girl.

"She was acting thisaway before you got here too."

"With that gun?"

Janie said yeah. "Shooting at Granddaddy Hugh's stuff."

"That's a shame," Sherrill said. "An archaeologist can't help but wishing she was there when things were still new. That's how I feel about that stuff your grandfather made. To see it when he was making it, you know?"

"I'll show you something when we get home," Janie said.

Back at The Seven she led Sherrill down at the spring. They opened the springhouse and flipped over the boat, where the best surviving collection of her granddaddy's assemblies remained.

"Where did these come from?" Sherrill asked.

"Crusoe did it."

Sherrill appeared confused by the girl's answer. She squatted down and examined an assemblie done on windowglass. "I have a friend who knows more about folk objects than I do," she said. "I'll get in touch with him before I leave."

Tammy somehow managed to assemble fifteen minutes on film. Ren stitched together dozens of white sheets and hung them across the drive-in screen's frame. No time to fit the panels before the date Tammy'd promised the paper. Janie and her uncle Luther took up money. Two hundred folks had come to The Seven for the world premiere of *The Last Conquistador*.

Before the movie started Janie climbed up to the hastily finished projection room. It was stifling. Her aunt was there, waiting for the sun to set so she could begin the movie. Meantime Janie took a rag and wiped beads of moisture off the projector's lens. She shooed Geronimo away, glanced out the window and said, "Won't you just look down yonder at all them heads." Some folks sat inside their vehicles, others were on quilts spread below the makeshift screen. Tammy got up and peered out the window herself. She turned to the girl and blinked, as if a curtain on some great secret had been pulled back. Carefully, she removed the reel from its canister, hung it on the projector then flicked a switch.

The reel started spinning. The film slapped slapped slapped slapped. Tammy'd forgotten to thread the film through the sprockets and gates. Janie reached to stop it and her fingers got wrenched. She stuck them in her mouth. Her aunt, for some reason, did not seem bothered by this. Instead rifling through her purse. Tammy took a pack of cigarettes and shook one loose. She struck a match and the film burst into flames, which seemed to enjoy themselves as they burnt green and blue and yellow-white.

Janie yanked the plug out of the wall. The reel slowly stopped spinning. She grabbed a broom and beat the film till the flames died down.

Folks milled around the clearing, waiting to see if the movie might yet play. When they realized it would not, they folded their quilts and packed their belongings. Some wanted their ticket money returned. Most were too embarrassed to ask though, instead silently joining the procession of vehicles headed back into town.

✦

The next week a letter arrived in Elberta telling Sherrill she was being sent to Wyoming. *Must leave directly as possible*, it said.

Janie knew Tammy wouldn't be able to watch Sherrill Robinson leave, so the girl stood in the yard and said goodbye for her aunt.

"I guess she's mad at me," Sherrill said.

"Yeah."

Sherrill laughed and wrapped her arms around the girl. "You're a strange one Janie Treeborne. Oh, nearly forgot. I heard back from my friend and he wants to come take a look at your grandfather's, what are they, assemblies. Make sure your aunt doesn't run him off, okay. This needs preserving."

After Sherrill left, Janie went to check on her aunt. She found her in the bedroom watching films. Tammy'd positioned herself in front of the projector, so the images moved across her backside and were distorted time they reached the wall. Janie had to touch her to get her attention. She asked Tammy to go riding. Something about being in a moving vehicle always helped the girl feel better. It might, she thought, help her aunt in this case too.

The N. W. Barfield National Forest was greening and filling out its understory. April in Elberta could go either way; sunny and warm or cloudy and cool. Tammy stopped at a gas station outside Bankhead, and bought a bottle of muscadine wine and two egg salad sandwiches while Janie waited in the truck with Crusoe. They drove on into town. The Bird's Nest was packed for early lunch. Janie noticed a young couple toting a baby around the used-car lot. She'd been wrong in some ways about Big Connie Ward. Another to add to her growing list. Folks were neither good nor bad—her aunt included. Janie hoped someone would say the same for her. She reached into Tammy's purse and pulled out a tube of lipstick. Put some on herself then took a map out of the glove box and gave directions.

It took an hour of wandering to find the holler. They came in from above and walked down the landslide to the wreckage. Eight months later and some of the newspapers were still stuck on the windows. Janie tried peeling them off but they tore. She looked inside the trunk. The water had leaked out, or evaporated one, and scavengers had carried off all of the catfish but for its spine. Nestled in that bleached curve were things the fish had swallowed: a set of car keys, a broken knifeblade, a babydoll's plastic foot, caps from countless coke-cola bottles thumped into the Elberta River by bored fishermen.

Tammy paid these strange objects no mind. She climbed up on the smashed hood and opened the wine bottle. Janie set Crusoe in the trunk and joined her there. Tammy handed the bottle to the girl, and she drank. The wine sweet. Tammy smiled. They ate the egg salad sandwiches while daylight ran out into the trees and was capped by a dusk swarmed with the season's first papery moths. When it was empty Tammy pitched the bottle into the woods.

"About time," she said.

Janie returned to the trunk and folded Crusoe's arms across his chest. Her aunt had already started walking out of the holler. Janie shut the lid, but it popped back open. Was she doing right? Crusoe offered no sign. She tried shutting the trunk again. Open it popped. Her aunt hollered for her to come on before they lost all light. Janie looked at the dirt boy one last time and she let the trunk be, leaving it open for someone else to discover.

Stories We Tell

TODAY

❧

"Down at The Fencepost they dump out the last sip in every damn coffee cup."

"How come?" the young man asked.

Janie Treeborne shrugged and pitched wet grounds from her own cup off the side of the front porch. "Superstition, I reckon."

Beyond the orchardfield a black dog trotted along the shoulder of the road. Janie held up a hand and squinted, trying to make out whether she recognized this particular creature. Yips and howls in the woods. The dog perked its ears then cut up the field and trotted figure eights among peach trees so long-suffering the branches splayed out wider than they grew tall. Down near the bottom of the slope, where the roadside stand now stood empty, a few stubborn trees hung heavy with the valley's last ripe fruit.

"I got to talking didn't I?"

"That's alright," the young man said.

"I reckon we run out of time."

The young man said, "I think we got enough."

"Time's all they could talk about in them meetings The Authority had," Janie said, ambling inside. "Pedro and me went to every last one, buddy. Jon D., he come to a few at first. Then he decided the writing was up on the wall. Time to move on, he said. They said. Time to rethink the ways we live. I reckon there's something wrong with what the dam does to the river downstream from here. Silt, I don't know. Time it'll get worse and worse, they say. All that time though and not a single goddamn minute to stop and listen at us.

"I should of carried you around places. Go down at the radio station and visit Pedro if you can. I'm sure he'd love to see you for a minute. When you go carry some of this lunchmeat so them dogs that's been running around don't bother you." Janie opened a cooler and fished out a graying slab of sliced ham and handed it to the young man. "You can't miss the Prince Building. Pedro aims to remain up yonder when the water comes. Says it'll hold. I reckon we'll see. Just make sure and tell him Janie Treeborne sent you. He believes I'll meet him there when the time comes. Then what?"

The young man had no answer. He did have one more question though: "Can I see the film Miss Treeborne?"

Janie turned on a small battery-powered radio and jiggled a warped antenna until Pedro Hannah's voice emerged from static:

Gladys Livingston
Richard Bolivar
Bebo Keller
Rita Wadsworth
Paul and Mary Ellen English
Janie Treeborne
And me, your host, Pedro Hannah

She settled into her recliner chair while the young man recorded the radio DJ's recitation. A blade of late sunlight cut the living room in half. Light, dark. When Pedro reached the end of the list he started reading the names over again.

Janie could leave.

But she won't.

She'll feel the explosion, the dam breaking apart, feel it down inside her chest. Still she will wait. Wait for the dark water to roll through her orchard, to bubble up between the floorboards, slip underneath the door, break loose the hinges, debris riding the frothing surge as it washes over her slippers, furniture floating, peaches, her legs rising toward the ceiling, maps and pictures turned to paste, her lungs now choked—

Janie Treeborne could yet leave.

But she will not.

"Just don't tell Pedro no different, hear," she said then reached into a box and pulled out a round canister.

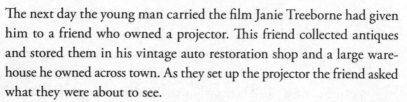

The next day the young man carried the film Janie Treeborne had given him to a friend who owned a projector. This friend collected antiques and stored them in his vintage auto restoration shop and a large warehouse he owned across town. As they set up the projector the friend asked what they were about to see.

"History," the young man replied.

Whoever'd spliced the fire-damaged film, the jumps were jarring. Wasn't quite the eight minutes Janie said existed when *The Last Conquistador* was shown almost three decades after the initial botched attempt. The young man had newspaper articles that confirmed some things, but, over the course of their conversations, he'd often wondered how much of what the old woman said was true in the generally accepted sense of the word. Only person who could confirm the stories she told was Jon De Soto Crews. When the young man called earlier in the summer, Jon D. had said he didn't want anything to do with the media though. The young man wasn't sure whether Janie Treeborne knew he was not her kin, whether she remembered she was an only child who'd never married, if the young man was just another story she told herself for comfort against the truth that the Treeborne line had ended with her aging, ended long before The Authority ever decided to wipe Elberta, Alabama, off the map. But truth, the young man now believed, wasn't for the author to reveal. Time would.

In this case, the young man realized as he watched the images thrown up onto a wall, time already had. The only scenes that survived the fire back in 1959 were the ones Tammy Treeborne had filmed absent of actors. A creek flowing between knotty cedars, a deer eating wildflowers among a deep pinebrake, two finches fighting in a dusty yard, the face of a bluff cast in lapping shadow, hardwoods curving upward to impossible heights. The final shot was from Chief Coosa's Overlook. Treetops to the horizon, not a person anywhere. The land all that remained to be seen.

Elberta Dawn

1958

❧

The day of her death Maybelle Treeborne woke up at her cottage in town and put on a pair of ratty canvas tennis shoes so she could walk to The Seven. Years ago the night had begun working deep down into her bones. She'd felt it there, razor-sharp as the spurs on Tucker and Dee Sargent's roosters, lingering when she woke this dim blue morning and set foot on the bedroom floor. The first moments of each day were devoted to rattling the night loose from her body, chiding and cussing the devil it was, tormenting her thisaway when she longed for peace. At least she still slept. Plenty folks her age couldn't. After putting on her shoes she let Geronimo outside then considered fixing a pot of coffee. She'd given up on breakfast. Used to love it. There was only her now to eat it, unless Lee stayed over, which he hardly ever did. She didn't blame him. Takes a special kind of person to wake among such ghosts and memories. She decided the coffee could wait and began walking.

Walking was something she meant to never give up. After Hugh died the first thing she did—before even telling their kids he was gone—was strike off on a walk. She didn't give a rip if people thought that in poor taste. She could no longer remember where she'd walked to that day—how many years ago? Found Hugh in a chair on the porch. Geronimo purring, brushing back and forth against Hugh's paint-splattered

britches. Them big beautiful brown-gold eyes open yet without life. Two
rough hands resting on his lap as if—forever the artist—he'd posed
hisself thataway in death. The thought yet made Maybelle cackle. The
disease so slow, yet death so quick. After she found him she'd struck out
to the spring, she now thought. That's right, that's exactly what she'd done.
Never had learned to swim, but she rolled up her britches that day and
waded in till they got wet then stood there till she was ready to tell
everybody that Jesse Absalom Treeborne was dead.

When Maybelle got to The Seven she fixed some coffee. She kept
enough makings around despite nobody having lived in the house for
years. While the coffee made, Maybelle walked out to her husband's
headmarker and squatted down in front of it. Geronimo had followed
her there, as the cat would often do. He flashed his tongue across the
bulging pink mass where an eye had been taken when he was a kitten.
Looked like a wad of chewing gum stuck on his face. Summer was
coming on humid as a dog's mouth, the sky rapidly brightening and
warming the stone as Maybelle touched her husband's name, the year
he was born, the year he died. Summer was her favorite weather though.
She liked sweating because it meant you were doing something. She
touched her own name carved there next to Hugh's, separated by a Bible verse. She didn't know what had got into her and made her put the
verse there. She wasn't religious thataway. But here was some proof:

MINE HERITAGE IS UNTO ME AS A SPECKLED BIRD, THE BIRDS
ROUND ABOUT ARE AGAINST HER; COME YE, ASSEMBLE ALL THE
BEASTS OF THE FIELD, COME TO DEVOUR.

She touched the blank space beneath her name as if her fingers might
bring out from the stone's grain something that should not be known.

A rifleshot pealed out from the woods.

Maybelle stood up and listened as the shot faded. Figured it belonged
to Lee Malone. The Seven was flat lousy with wild game, even this time
of year. Lee used hunting The Seven as a reason to see her more often.
They needed these reasons for safety, for the laws written to keep them

apart, sometimes for sake of their own guilty minds. Falling in together after Hugh's death was natural to Maybelle. That didn't mean the memory of Hugh never troubled her or Lee. It surely troubled Tammy. The betrayal Tammy manifested in her mother's love for Lee Malone cut even deeper for her than the color of his skin. Maybelle cooked the animals Lee killed and cleaned, and they ate together at the kitchen table, or out on the front porch when the weather was good. They took special pleasure in eating, no longer worrying what food did to their bodies. A slow satisfaction known only to those who outlive the vanity of youth.

Time, when she was young, Maybelle had been vain enough to want to be in movies herself. She never even had seen a movie when she left Bankhead though, following an advertisement in the paper about an open audition in Birmingham for a war epic. Packed two canvas suitcases and toted them four miles to the depot because her daddy refused to carry her in the buggy. Her momma traipsed after her for a good stretch of the way, hollering and crying, cursing the day Maybelle Chambliss was born. Standing on the yet-hot sidewalk in the middle of downtown Birmingham later that next night, every star and planet she'd known masked by city lights and factory smoke, her momma's words ringing in her ears, Maybelle cried considering all the things her folks' narrowness caused them to miss. She vowed to never be narrow herself as she bedded down on a park bench. Next morning in a department store washroom she splashed water under her arms and down between her legs then changed into a clean dress. She hid her suitcases in the bus station then headed toward the movie palace.

A line of folks waiting to audition stretched down the block and around the corner. Maybelle took her place with them. More and more folks kept arriving. A hot dog vendor pushed his cart up and down the curb, hollering, "Ask for them, we got them!" Maybelle was sweating through her dress. Not a lick of shade till an awning just outside the golden doors. The man in line ahead of her wore what looked like an authentic Confederate soldier's uniform. Maybelle watched him eat three hot dogs without so much as blinking his yellowed eyes. Later that afternoon the line cut off two places behind her. Those who'd stood all day in the heat and were now denied entry tried pushing into the lobby anyhow. Police officers astraddle chestnut horses arrived, swinging wooden paddles till the crowd dispersed.

Maybelle looked up green marble columns running toward a high gold ceiling. The movie palace cool as an icebox, its lobby upholstered wall-to-wall with blood-purple carpet. A man wearing a dark suit led her into the auditorium where rows upon rows of empty seats faced a stage. Two more suited men and a woman smoking a cigarette sat at a folding table down front. They asked Maybelle her name then told her to climb up onstage. Yet another dour man came out of the wings and handed her a sheet of typewritten paper. One of the men raised his hand so she'd begin. Maybelle glanced at the page and cleared her throat.

After she finished reading she was led backstage to a dressing room. It had no ceiling, and she could see outlines of ropes and cables up yonder in the darkness. A vase of pink camellias stood on the table next to a sweating water pitcher. Maybelle poured a glass and nervously drank. After a while the man who'd motioned her offstage and the woman with the cigarette entered the dressing room. Up close they were both pale-skinned. Voices sounded like leaky tires. The woman was skinny as a beanpole and the man had an oily mustache which he couldn't quit worrying with his fingertips.

"You were wonderful," he said. "And you never acted before?"

"No," Maybelle told him, "I ain't."

The woman guffawed. "Ain't." She poured a glass of water then took a medicine dropper from between her breasts. She squeezed a few drops of a caramel-colored liquid into the glass then stirred with her finger and sipped.

The man sat down on the love seat and patted for Maybelle to join him. He told her again how wonderful she'd been. At this point Maybelle couldn't even remember the words she'd read for them. The man said he just adored the shape of Maybelle's face. He made his hands into a square and framed her blond head. Wasn't it something else her being so tall, he said, and not the least bit awkward over it? You didn't see that very often. The woman giggled and rolled her eyes. She drank and did her worst pretending she wasn't in the room, especially when the man, scratching his mustache, asked Maybelle to take off her dress.

"Keep on your undergarments for now if you wish," he said. "We need a better glimpse at your figure though. Can you give us that?"

Men in Bankhead had never made bones over what they thought about Maybelle Chambliss and her looks. Bankhead wasn't the kind of place where a man, especially a coal miner, would feign purity—even over a preacher's daughter. She'd had boyfriends, gone what they used to call courting, which often amounted to sitting on the weedy river-bank while a farmer or a miner, or the son of one, worked up guts enough to kiss her on the mouth then try for more. The desires of men, of man, were one thing her folks' religion did not seem to cover. Her folks acted like no such desire existed in the world. But Maybelle knew better. She heard her daddy late at night, saw desire's toll writ on her momma in blue bite marks and yellow-green bruises, in two hollowed-out eyes sinking deeper and deeper into a prematurely wrinkled face framed by broombristle gray hair.

"Somebody else will if you won't," the man said.

Maybelle grabbed the glass of water off the table and slammed it up-side his head. She felt the glass break, cut her hand. The woman hol-lered and ran out of the dressing room. The man was folded over and pawing his bleeding face. Maybelle took off too, finding her way through the bowels of the movie palace and out a back exit into the day's last blinding light falling slant between the cavernous downtown buildings.

Now, on The Seven, a much softer light filtered through the tree-branches and gathered on the surface of the spring. Maybelle splashed away the old woman she saw there. She sat down on a flipped-over boat her boys Ren and Luth had abandoned years ago. The hull made a noise like a drum, bending under her weight. She pinched her stomach and said, "Hey you fat hog you." Laughed out loud then took off her tennis shoes and dipped her feet in the cool water. She hollered for Crusoe. She'd been having trouble seeing the dirt boy. She tried hiding this, especially from Sister. A grandmomma had to be magic. A mother perfect. She had not been, she thought, enough of either. Though it was never that simple. She could have told Tammy about her experience in Birmingham. She could tell her yet. Lately Maybelle sensed in her daughter a great uhappiness that only terrible acts might relieve.

After wading, Maybelle put on her tennis shoes and walked uphill. Geronimo appeared in the woods. "Come here you old devil," she said to him. The cat flicked his tail and raced on ahead. Another rifleshot cracked the stillness. Maybelle moved like something was after her, so fast she like to of tripped over the cooling machine when she came to it.

She brushed off fallen leaves then pulled till roots attached to the underside of the machine snapped loose. Most of the red paint had rusted or flaked off in the thirty-however-many-years since Hugh Treeborne toted the machine out here and left it. Time came back to Maybelle so she could feel the cool air blowing on their naked bodies and smell the sweet decay of the corpses Hugh'd moved out of the path of the water. She tumped the machine over on its side. Far too heavy to tote. Geronimo brushed against her leg. She looked uphill. Pasture couldn't be more than a hundred yards off. Maybe, she thought, I'll get the machine there then Lee can help with his truck. She'd use the bluffline as her guide.

She rocked the machine forward on its corner, strained and pushed. Wom. She sat down and rested. The cat walked across her lap. Two more rifleshots came close together. A shadow moved among the underbrush. "Boy?" Maybelle said. "That you?" All three kids were pestering her about her eyes. They'd even taken away the keys to the vehicle she bought from Big Connie Ward after she retired from the post office. Retired, foot. Eyes, foot. To hell with any of it! Hugh was the same way over doctors and only relented to visit one when he coughed up blood. If you could see Hugh's innards, Doc Barfield had said, it would look like his lungs and stomach had grown wings upon wings just waiting to open up and fly. What a thing to say! Maybelle thought. She pushed the machine again. Her footing slipped and the machine rocked backward. She caught her balance and it. She wasn't going to let it be lost. Not this one, not this time. She moved the machine another foot or so. Sounded like water was still in the tank. She tried to figure out how to drain it, thinking to make the machine lighter, but could not.

She braced the machine with her back as sunlight broke the understory, casting the woods white as Spanish gold. The cotton dress she wore stuck to her thighs and sweat rolled down her ankles into her tennis shoes. She kicked them off then got up and pushed again. The machine moved but a hair. The woods stretched on and on, up up up, like they ended in heaven. Heaven, foot, she thought. She looked around and couldn't make out the bluffline anymore. Where could it of just gone? The cat too. Both vanished. A jaybird shot past. Maybelle fanned the back of her dress then rocked the machine forward. Wom. The jay shot past the other direction, a beautiful blue streak. On she pushed. More woods, all woods. She braced against the machine and tried catching her breath. The groundcover began slipping out from under her. The machine shifted, smashing her toes. Where am I? This never happened. Not to her. Not to me here.

Lie.

Lie lie lie you awful old woman.

All you ever do.

Maybelle heaved herself into the machine again and, doing so, lost her balance and fell. The machine rolled backward and pinned her against the ground.

She could feel the metal cutting into her stomach. A shard of sky showed through the treetops, like an entryway to somewhere she would not name. She tried to push the machine off, but it wouldn't budge. Well foot, she thought. The treebranches swayed, teasing her onward from where she'd fallen. She smiled as eternity revealed itself in all its terrible certainty. She hoped Hugh'd seen it coming too. How to end is always a concern. She coughed and nearly did not catch her breath. A rifleshot broke the air once more. Lee Malone. Lee Lee Lee . . . He was near to her. So many squirrels were running through the treebranches it sounded like a wave turning over. Green acorns fell, drumming the machine, stinging her forehead and arms, rustling through the groundcover. A dog barked. Maybelle cackled, coughed. The dog barked again, farther away this time, chasing them squirrels, I reckon. Maybelle could not feel her legs or feet anymore. After all these years here she lay.

Acknowledgments

There is in fact an Elberta, Alabama, but the setting of this book is a town and a landscape of my own creation.

I owe much to the work of many writers who came before me, among them: Rick Bragg, Larry Brown, Gladys Chambless, William Faulkner, William Gay, Barry Hannah, Zora Neale Hurston, Edward P. Jones, Rodney Jones, Harper Lee, Gabriel García Márquez, Carson McCullers, Lewis Nordan, Flannery O'Connor, Charles Portis, Jessica Sampley, Brad Watson and Katherine Tucker Windham.

I'd like to thank all the folks at Picador who had a hand in bringing this book into the world. Especially Elizabeth Bruce, who so deftly inhabited the voices in these pages and, in her editing, strengthened my vision in ways that both startled and thrilled me.

Thank you to Amelia Atlas at ICM for advocating for this book to exist on its own terms. I couldn't have asked for a better agent beside me throughout the publication process.

Thank you to every teacher who encouraged me to write. Especially Marcia Adkins at Bevill State Community College, Rick Bragg and Bill Keller at The University of Alabama, Teressa Andrews at Meek High School, and Elizabeth Miller at Farmstead Elementary School, who, after I'd sped through my first-grade classwork, would sit me down at a table and charge me with making up stories for her.

The University of Wyoming's Creative Writing MFA program gave me a vocabulary and a framework for grappling with the work writers must do. Most importantly, the program allowed me the luxury of time to write in one of the most gorgeous places on this earth. Moving to Laramie was the best decision I ever made; I wouldn't be the man or the writer I am today without those years spent on the high prairie. Thank you to all UW folks who read my work and let me read theirs. Especially Tim Raymond, who graciously read a draft of this book and encouraged me during a time when I needed it.

I'd also like to thank The Jentel Artist Residency Program in Banner, Wyoming, for its support and the time to work on an early draft of this book with beautiful views of the Bighorn Mountains.

Thank you to Jason Burge for being a Southern lifeline out West. Those weekends spent cooking, watching college football, hunting, drinking, and listening to you talk about books had a profound impact on my work and will continue to for as long as I write.

Dan Freije for countless hours of unmatched conversation. Your loyal friendship has been a balm during the ups and downs of writing this book.

Alyson Hagy for friendship, challenging me to always consider why I write, advising me to get a dog, and treating me like a peer when I could claim but a handful of unfinished stories to my name.

Brad Watson for being a friend, a mentor, and an exacting writer. Every writer needs a place to claw and scratch his way toward, even though he'll never get there. Brad, your work is that place for me. Thank you for your unflagging support.

Joy Williams for tough feedback, the books you have introduced me to, and for so thoroughly appreciating my karaoke performance in Portland, Oregon, that one summer.

To all my Wyoming friends—Go Pokes!

Thank you to Lee Bains III for reading more drafts of this book than anybody else. Lee, you continue to show me what it means to be an artist and a man. Your music keeps me going, and I'm thankful every day that we stumbled our way into each other's lives.

Nathan Barfield for believing in me when there was not a lick of credible evidence to support doing so. Thank you, Nate, for teaching me what it's like to have a brother.

Blaine Duncan for being a true friend and encouraging my work early on. I'll always hold dear our time spent in Tuscaloosa.

Philip Williams for friendship that truly feels free from judgment and filled with love. Thank you for every last one of those days at Lewis-Smith Lake.

To all my Alabama friends, especially Bo Hicks, Kelly Duncan, Meghan Holmes, Matt Patton, D.J. Saldana, Jenny Sanders, Aaron Suttles and T.D. Wood—Roll Tide!

I am blessed to have grown up in a big family. Thank you to all my kin. Especially Jimmie Nell, Naint, Aunt Bill and Aunt Jo. Love y'all.

Thank you to Ark, Galina and Mark Zhorov for the warmth and love and the food and drinks you've shared, which has made it much easier for me to live far from home.

Margaret Louise Johnson for showing me how to age with humor and honesty. Your appreciation for classic country music and Southern cooking helped me figure out who I am. Thank you, Granny, for the stories you told me these last several years.

Jessica Sampley for giving me a copy of Larry Brown's *Dirty Work* when I turned fourteen. I have been changed ever since. Jec, you expanded my worldview in innumerable ways. I'll never be able to repay you, but I can and do thank you for it.

Celia Sampley for all you've passed down through our family. Because of you I love nature and Elvis Presley and storytelling and laughing and animals and gospel music and talking to folks. This book wouldn't exist without all your words, MawMaw, and all those miles we tromped together through forest and field.

Savannah Johnson for being my best friend and a sibling I can aspire to be like. I don't know what I'd do without you on this earth, Sister.

Debra and Ronnie Johnson for modeling hard work and humility.

Thank y'all, Mom and Dad, for the privilege to write books. I'm sure it's been scary watching your oldest child pursue something as uncertain as this career. Y'all never let on though. That trust and belief has been an invaluable gift for me—one of too many to count.

Hugo for the unconditional love only a dog can give. Hugo, you deserve a cowriter credit for all those hours spent at my feet, and all those long walks you took me on that cleared my mind and renewed my spirit for the work ahead.

Irina Zhorov for believing me when I said I was going to publish a novel. More so, thank you for challenging me to try new things, to think differently about what I read and write and say and believe. For taking me places I never imagined setting foot. For never letting me off easy. For enduring love and unyielding support. Without you, Irina, this book could not have been written.

Last, I want to acknowledge the land I am sprung from, all the folks who inhabited it in the past, and those who will inherit it in the future. May this book amplify the voices of that place and its people for as long as stories are told.

About the Author

CALEB JOHNSON is a writer who grew up in the rural community of Arley, Alabama. He graduated from the University of Alabama in Tuscaloosa and earned an MFA from the University of Wyoming. Johnson has worked as a small-town newspaper reporter, an early morning janitor, and a whole-animal butcher, among many other jobs. Currently, he lives with his partner, Irina, and their dog, Hugo, in Philadelphia, where he teaches while working on his next novel.